SPACE ELDRITCH II
The Haunted Stars

Edited by Nathan Shumate

Published by
Cold Fusion Media
http://www.coldfusionmedia.us

COLD FUSION
MEDIA

SPACE ELDRITCH II: The Haunted Stars

Cover illustration by Carter Reid

Cold Fusion Media
http://www.coldfusionmedia.us

TABLE OF CONTENTS

A DARKLIGHT CALL'D ON THE LONG LAST NIGHT OF THE SOUL

MICHAELBRENT COLLINGS

Gerrold Mason turned over, and for a moment he thought he had seen red hair. Red hair with subtle threads of black and brown running through it, like a dark rainbow that portended not the sun breaking through the clouds, but the clouds' triumph over all that was bright.

It was an omen. He should have recognized it for what it was.

Then the red hair disappeared. Just like it always did. Though now he saw a flash of lighter red, this shade stitched through with bright threads of blonde, as if a confused painter had seen father and mother and remained unsure which parent's hair color should rule.

Then he was alone. Alone in the dark, in the deep black inkwell of a wormhole and hearing a single voice, over and over: "Do you love me?"

The voice changed, becoming deeper, smoother. The voice of Gerrold's lone shipmate.

"How are you feeling today?"

Trixie. Her voice had exactly the qualities determined to be most soothing to those who needed assistance of a—what was it the Company basketmen called it?—"mental and spiritual nature."

Gerrold hated it. Hated the voice, hated *her*. But it wasn't like he had a choice. Trixie had come with the trip. At first he had been thrilled with the upgrade, until he realized she wasn't just there to help him, but to keep an eye on him. To make sure he didn't implode.

He was lucky he still had a job, he supposed. The Company didn't like publicity.

"How are you feeling today?"

He looked over at her. She had light hair—probably because of some long-running research study that showed headcases were less likely to snap in the presence of a blonde—and was fairly attractive without being sexual. The perfect companion on a long trip: calming, helpful.

Bitch.

"Are we there?" said Gerrold, though he knew they had to be, or at least that they had to be close. Trixie wouldn't have started yammering if they weren't.

"We're on approach."

"How long?"

"Three hours, give or take." She smiled in exactly the right way to show she was just an *aw shucks* kinda gal, and not the typical stick-up-my-butt shrink he *could* have been saddled with. Like Gerrold should note she gave an approximate time value rather than exact information and appreciate that fact.

Trixie blinked, and her image flickered for the barest fraction of a second. Even with long periods in hypersleep, the trip had been long enough that Gerrold had grown to recognize the flicker as a signal that she was changing tacks with him. Evidently she had realized he was not interested in talking about his feelings—

(*shades of red and brown shades of red and blond and Do you love me?*)—

and had shifted protocols: trying to get him to open up another way.

"Would you like me to open up a com-link to Shane?" she asked.

That took Gerrold aback. She'd never offered that. For a second he almost smiled, almost looked at the floating holo by his bed as a person rather than a collection of photons. Then he realized she must have just downloaded new protocols while he slept.

Humans dream—computers uplink and run systems checks, he thought. *She's not a friend, just Trixie 2.1. Just some Company software keeping watch over Company hardware.*

"What time is it? Where Shane is?"

"It's..." (again that minute flash as her image responded to the query) "...5:40 a.m. in Middleton."

Gerrold shook his head. "Let him sleep."

He ached to put the call through. He wanted to see Shane. He hadn't seen the boy for months, not in the flesh, and the last com-link had gone... badly. But he didn't want to wake the kid up. He was still dealing with things. Still processing the loss.

"When are they coming back?" That was Shane's favorite question. "When are Mommy and Dalia coming back?" And no matter how many times, no matter how many different *ways* Gerrold tried to explain it—ways that all boiled down to *never*—Shane never seemed to understand.

"What about God?" he would ask. And Gerrold had no answer. Because while it was easy to talk about God when you were in church and surrounded by happy people and nothing bad was happening, it was a lot harder to believe when you had just been told why there would be no possibility of an open-casket funeral for your wife or daughter.

(*"Do you love me?"*)

Even worse was the fact that Shane didn't understand why Gerrold hadn't come home. Even though *that* reason was even simpler: poverty.

Iago once said, "Poor and content is rich, and rich enough." Which to Gerrold was proof either that Shakespeare was an ass, or that Iago had no children. Because while poverty could be bearable, poverty with *children* could not.

So when the Company called not ten minutes after the news, Gerrold said yes. Even though it meant he wouldn't be coming Earthside. Even though he knew it was just a way of keeping him—and, by extension, the Company —out of the public eye.

Even though it meant not seeing Shane. Not holding, not touching him.

Because they were paying him double wages, and hazard pay. And if he didn't come back at all, they'd triple *those* rates, and all of it would go into a trust for Shane.

When Gerrold was young and single, just a blaster doing micro-jumps to Sol-based shops that needed some kind of attention, he wouldn't have worried about poverty. He could sleep in his spacer, or just on the couch of a friend. Even when he was a bit older, money didn't matter so much to him.

But when Dalia came... it all changed. He held her in his arms, and felt the most intense love blossoming within him. Even what he felt for his wife wasn't the same, because what he held in his arms depended on him, truly and utterly. And with that understanding came the realization that below the love that now throbbed like bright life-blood through his mind and heart, there was something else. Something darker.

Fear.

He could lose her. He could lose her in an instant.

He was no longer alone, he was no longer young, and doing high-risk jumps to asteroid mines was no longer an option.

So he signed with the Company. And he became a FixIt. A man who would go anywhere, do anything. He was a Company Man, through and through. Which meant he surrendered his soul, surrendered his joy.

But he found a steady paycheck. He took care of his children. And whatever joy he lost in his life was made up for by their smiles, and by their embraces when he made planetfall in between jobs.

Being a Company Man was solid. It was secure. And it was safe. Which was important for a man who needed to take care of his children.

It was safe. No one would touch a Company Man. No one would dare touch *anything* the Company had a part in.

At least, until TF-653.

"How close now?"

"Barring movement, we should be there in less than an hour."

Gerrold flicked a quick glance at Trixie. That wasn't her name, of course. But neither was "Patricia," which she kept trying to get him to call her. So he would call her Trixie because that was a good name for a prostitute and as far as he was concerned that was all she was: just a thing, bought and sold and doing a job without any real feeling. If he had to anthropomorphize her, he'd do it on his own terms. And he actually fancied it irritated her, though that was about as possible as her stepping out of the holo and planting a big wet kiss on his cheek.

Still, sometimes he did think he caught emotions flitting across her face. Irritation, annoyance. Or, as now, fear.

"Has there been any?" he asked. "Movement?"

She shook her head. Sometimes Gerrold missed the more hands-on interface of his spacer, but having Trixie do everything for him was damn handy from time to time.

"No," she said.

"Hail the base," he said.

"I've been doing so continuously since we left the wormhole," said Trixie. "No response."

"Put it on ship speaker," said Gerrold.

Trixie flickered, then pursed her lips. Just the *right* exasperation. "Wouldn't your time be better spent preparing for the—"

"This *is* preparing, Trixie," said Gerrold. "Put it on. Cease hailing, though. I just want to hear the frequency."

She nodded. A moment later a light static came on the speakers. Hissing, like the sound Gerrold might make if he had burnt his fingers. Or perhaps the sound he might make if more seriously injured but dared not make a noise: the sound of restrained, contained agony traveling across the void of space, from the base on TF-653 to Gerrold's ship. The sound of pain in the dark.

("Do you love me?")

Gerrold shook his head. "Shut it off," he said, surprised at how disquieted he felt. Then he almost screamed, "Wait!"

Trixie hadn't moved. She didn't need to in order to carry out his orders. But the static stayed on, so he had stopped her in time.

"What is it?" she asked.

"Shh!" was his only answer. He listened, his brow furrowed deeply. Then he added, "Amplify."

The static hiss increased, the sibilation pulsating through Gerrold's quarters, throbbing through his mind and body until it was hard to tell where the sound ended and his own heartbeat began.

Low sounds emerged. "Amplify," he said again, more shouting it this time in order to be heard.

The sound grew, no longer pulsing but arcing around him like lightning captured in this tight space and now raining destruction all around in its attempt to escape. And below the lightning was something else. Something new.

Something terrifying.

***

The sound Gerrold heard was powerful. Powerful and horrific. More horrific than the officers on the com-link, telling him they hadn't recovered all of Amy's body, that Dalia's own form was shattered beyond recognition. More powerful than the explosion that had taken their lives. And yet...

And yet so very small.

So very short.

Just a few words, silt in the deadly undertow of the static. Four words.

"Do you love me?"

Gerrold heard the words, though they sounded nothing like they had the last time he heard them, when the rain was pounding down on her and Dalia was waiting in the car and he wondered if his life was coming to an end.

"Do you love me?"

They were Amy's words, it was even her *inflection*, for God's sake, so soft and pitiful, so hopeful and hopeless at once.

But the voice wasn't hers. It was the voice of a demon. A monster, something that had chewed up the souls of the damned and vomited them forth and kept only the bones to gargle with.

"Do you love me?"

Gerrold felt strange. The floor spun below him. The static disappeared, replaced by rain falling on a long-distant wife and child. The room disappeared, fallen into a well darker than any wormhole, blacker than any hypersleep he had ever known.

Do you love me?

Gerrold woke, and couldn't be sure where he was, or what was happening.

He saw a flash of red hair, streaked with brown. Another flash of red, this one highlighted by blonde.

Then a face leaned into his field of vision. "Gerrold, are you all right?"

"What?" For a moment Gerrold couldn't place the face. Then he realized it was Trixie. Realized where he was.

Realized what had happened.

He bolted upright on the bed that was the only real piece of furniture in his quarters. The ship he rode in was enormous, larger than the terraforming base he was going to check out. But that was only because it carried every piece of equipment necessary to do any repair, fix any problem. He was a Company FixIt, and FixIts *always* came prepared.

"Did you hear that, Trixie?" he shouted.

"Hear what?" She looked concerned.

"The *voice*, dammit."

Trixie straightened up. She flickered, then frowned. "Gerrold, I've been monitoring the frequency non-stop. There have been no vocal contacts whatever."

"I—" Gerrold thought about arguing, then shut himself down. What would be the point? What did he hope to accomplish? He wasn't going to change a piece of software's mind—there was no mind to change. The best he could hope to accomplish would be to convince Trixie he'd lost his *own* mind, thus forfeiting his job and his benefits.

Gerrold couldn't afford that. *Shane* couldn't afford that. Not with all that it cost to keep him in the best hospitals. Company hospitals, of course—they knew they had Gerrold coming and going, damn them.

He stood and attempted to look like nothing untoward had ever happened in this room. "Where are we?"

"Geosynchronous orbit over the TF base," answered Trixie. Flicker. "You sure you don't need to talk?"

Yeah, like that'll ever happen.

"No," said Gerrold as smoothly as he could. "Let's just get down there."

Gerrold suited up for a solo drop, just him and his suit in the airlock.

He never went down with any major equipment, at least on the first trip. Doing so just labeled him as a FixIt and, since FixIts had the complete authority to do whatever was necessary to resolve low productivity at Company facilities—up to and including servicing mechanical issues, replacing personnel, or assassinating administrators—he found his presence caused extreme... *nervousness.* Better to get the lay of the land in as low-profile a manner as possible.

So it was just him and the dropsuit and the sound of the last transmission Company HQ had received from TF-653 before everything went dark.

"Go ahead and play it," said Gerrold.

"You sure?" asked Trixie. "It might be better to come back inside where it's comfortable before—"

"Just play it, Trixie."

A moment's pause, then:

"We're moving!" screamed the voice, a panicked shriek that Company computers had identified as that of Mikael Arturovic, one of the mechanics at TF-653. "Everyone's dead and they're all waiting for me to die, waiting for me to die and join them. Waiting." A long pause, then. "We're *moving! Save me! Save me, they're here! The dead! THE DEAD ARE—"*

Then nothing.

The Company send various missives, but there were no further responses. Stranger, a scan revealed that Arturovic had been right in one of his blathering statements: he *had* moved.

Terraforming occurred through the use of huge bases that gradually shifted a hostile planet's environment to within human tolerances. It took anywhere from one to twenty years and cost hundreds of trillions of dollars. The bases themselves were massive constructs, usually built into the sides of volcanoes or other ready sources of geothermal energy—or right *over* them, the bases were so enormous.

But the long-distance scan revealed that Base 653, originally located at Company coordinates 25.1.71.3 on TF-653, had—*completely impossibly*—moved to coordinates 37/2350.1.115/81111.3. The base—larger than many cities—had apparently *shifted* over a thousand miles in the space of minutes.

And stranger still, all systems of the terraforming base appeared to be functioning. Scanners, internal and external life support systems, even the tie-ins that linked to the geothermal power supplies. Everything was alive and, to the best of the Company's reckoning, fully functioning.

The only thing that *wasn't* working, it seemed, was the crew at the base.

Accordingly, a FixIt ticket was issued. But for the first time, no FixIt wanted the job.

No FixIt but Gerrold.

Gerrold put his helmet on. Locked it. Trixie appeared and looked at the fittings, though he knew that was (like everything about her) a programmed response meant to give the subject (him) a feeling of care and security. She had already scanned him a thousand times before the holo ever showed up.

"Looks good," she said.

Gerrold nodded. He gave a thumbs-up to show he was ready.

A moment later, the floor dropped out from under him.

He plummeted toward the planet below, guided by a series of thrusters and magnetic impulses that he didn't even pretend to understand. But they got him down time after time, and that was enough.

The planet hung below him, and he realized with a start that this was the first time he was seeing it. Most of the time when he went to punch a ticket, he had some prior knowledge of the planet he was dealing with. There were close to a thousand terraforming planets on the outer edge, but only a few hundred colony worlds with people already on them, and Gerrold was at least passingly familiar with all of them.

TF-653, though, was a mystery.

It was gray. No blue, no red, no yellow. No bright primary or even secondary colors at all. Just a teeming, shifting swirl of gray on dark gray on light gray.

How boring, he thought. Must be a drag looking out the window.

Then, even as he thought that, it all changed. The grays seemed to catch fire, tinged with yellows and reds and oranges at the edges, and then exploding in a glorious mixture of every color imaginable. It was so bright that Gerrold had to shield his eyes, even though the dropsuit's visor darkened automatically to accommodate the flash. But even with the darkened visor and his own arm covering his face, he suddenly found himself plummeting down through swarms of fiery wasps that exploded into darkness all around him: the remainder of the flash burnt onto his retina.

When the last traces of the burn had passed and he was able to see clearly again, he gasped. TF-653—(is *that* TF-653, *or did someone replace it somehow?*)—was still below him, but it looked completely different. It was now almost earth-like, with white clouds and blue seas apparent, even browns and greens below.

"What the hell? Trixie, what just happened?"

Trixie's voice piped into the com-piece in his ear. "We don't know."

"We don't know?" Gerrold was incredulous. "How can the Company try to terraform someplace when they don't even understand its basic climato-logical patterns?"

Trixie was silent for a long time. Long enough, in fact, that Gerrold started to wonder if he'd somehow fried her circuits. Then she spoke again, and her voice was subtly different. A bit lower, a bit more strident. Trixie 2.2? Gerrold wondered.

"You're not cleared to know the details of TF-653, Mason."

Gerrold felt his jaw clenching. "Listen, I don't know who I'm talking to but it sure as hell isn't my companion. So either talk to me in your normal voice or get off the line." Silence again. Gerrold hated when the Company tried to co-opt Trixie's voice, like they could speak through her and he wouldn't know the difference, wouldn't be able to tell the difference be-tween a Company Manager and Trixie; between a cold, soulless *thing*... and his computerized companion.

A moment later the com-link clicked again and a new voice came into his ear. Probably the person he'd just spoken to, though he had no way of knowing. It was a gravelly bass voice, the voice of someone who enjoyed too many cigars, too much cognac, too much power.

The voice of a Company Manager.

"Just get in there and find out what happened, Mason."

"Bullshit."

"Do you know who you're—"

"No, and I don't care. I'm currently falling at over twelve thousand kilo-meters per hour into a possibly hostile environment that no one briefed me about before departure, so unless you're in a dropsuit right behind me I couldn't care less who you are, only whether or not you're going to be help-ful."

Another silence. Gerrold was through atmo now. It really did feel like Earth, or at least a planet well into terraforming. Light clouds, blue sky. The dropsuit took care of adjustments for him and he knew it would put him down on the hoverpad that was the highest point of the base. He had de-bated walking in from ground level, but he didn't know what ground condi-tions were. Besides, he reasoned, he might as well go down as up. He could always leave on ground level if need be.

The com-link clicked again. Same voice. "Mason, we can't tell you much, because we don't know much. Pretty much what you do."

There was a pregnant pause. Gerrold decided to help it along. "Except...?"

"Except the way we found TF-653."

"Which was?"

"A Company ship found a planet which at first appeared to have almost perfect characteristics for terraforming. But upon later approach it was shown to have to have two different atmospheric realities."

"I think I just saw that."

The Manager continued speaking as if Gerrold were a non-being. Which, to Management, he supposed he was. "So the atmo changes periodically from very close to Earth-norm to extremely hostile."

"Extremely?"

"It's basically vaporized battery acid mixed with atom-weld drippings."

Gerrold felt a tightening of his gut that had nothing to do with the drop. "You said this happens periodically? What does that mean?"

"It means it happens irregularly. We haven't figured out a pattern. It appears to be random: clean, clear air one moment, then sudden shifts to toxic grease. It could be thirty hours one way, or only five minutes. But it shifts without warning and it takes only seconds."

"How is that possible?"

"We don't know. But we figured we'd put a terraforming base there. Fill it with scientists for observation purposes and at best we'd get a new planet to sell. If the terraformers can't figure out how to deal with the situation, then at worst we end up with some interesting information."

Interesting information. Gerrold had been with the company long enough to know that "interesting" was code for "profitable."

"What kind of interesting information?"

The Manager sighed. "Just get down there and find out what happened."

"With the people?"

"With everything."

"How do you recommend I go about that?"

"You're a FixIt. Do your job."

Then the com-link clicked and Gerrold was on his own.

He stood on the hoverpad for a moment, just waiting. Waiting and hoping, though he knew in his gut there was no way anyone was coming out of the door in the steel-colored wall nearby.

The sky was blue. But the area around him bore clear evidence of Management's statements: the plastine surfaces all around, surfaces that could have born direct missile strikes with little more than scorching, were pocked and charred. Some places appeared to have been patched with jury-rigged chunks of plastine, and Gerrold felt his pulse speed up at that. Plastine was extraordinarily hard stuff to work with—even with the full resources of his FixIt ship, it would have been difficult. So the fact that the people on the terraforming base had managed it was a clear demonstration of their unusual competence. Not just your average wrench-jockeys, not the folks who typically worked a terraforming base. Management had sent a special group here.

What could have caused them to stop transmission? he wondered. What could have kept the base intact, but stilled their voices?

There was no buckling, he realized at the same moment. No evidence of structural changes. So whatever had moved the base had done it with perfect care, with infinite caution.

"Trixie?" he said.

"Yes, Gerrold?" she said, and he was surprised at how relieved he was to hear Trixie's "real" voice—not the voice of a Trixie being controlled by faraway men in dark suits with nothing but profit and expansion on their minds.

"Can you scan the base for me?"

"I've already done so. Repeatedly."

"Humor me. Do it again."

She was silent a moment, then: "Nothing."

"No life forms whatever?"

"None."

"Any chance they're taking refuge somewhere nearby?"

"Theoretically possible, though hardly in keeping with what was indicated in their final transmission."

Gerrold sighed.

"And I'd get inside," she added.

"Why?" he asked, then knew the answer even as Trixie responded.

"Atmospheric shift. My files don't contain any information on it, but it might be wisest to be inside when it happens."

"Noted," said Gerrold.

He walked to the door, investigating it only briefly for evidence of damage or violence that was sentient in genesis. He had once worked a ticket that involved a Company building going offline due to terrorist attack. There had been blood, the particular splayed scorch-marks of grenade strikes, shrapnel.

This door looked fine—or as fine as the rest of the outer hull of the base appeared. No burning other than that clearly caused by the hostile atmosphere, no blood or buckling to indicate attempts at forced entry. Though he supposed that any blood would have been dissolved in the atmosphere if it was half as bad as Management said.

He waved his hand and the door opened to the chip set into the back of his wrist, the chip that identified him as a FixIt to all Company property and personnel and opened all but the most secure doors and files and programs to him.

He stepped inside the base.

He expected to enter a corridor. Instead he walked into a small, featureless room that he recognized as an airlock, even as he was surprised to find it. But of course it would be here. This base was essentially a space station set on *terra firma*, wasn't it? A small piece of Earth that would slowly grow across the face of the planet like a virulent fungus until the planet's natural self disappeared and was overtaken by the version of it inflicted by the Company.

A klaxon wailed, and another, smaller door opened. A pleasant voice, reminiscent of Trixie, said, "It is now safe to enter the base. Welcome, and have a nice day."

Gerrold stepped through the inner door. He kept his suit on, kept his helmet sealed. He could see on his heads up display that the interior base environment was at Earth norms, but until he had found the base personnel and/or determined what had happened to them he would keep himself locked into the safety of his dropsuit.

There was power, obviously, otherwise the door wouldn't have slid open for him. But the second he moved through and the door whispered shut behind him, he felt like he was in another world. A darker one.

The corridor he stood in was illuminated only by emergency lighting that cast a pale glow into the space. "Lights," he said.

Nothing happened. There was a manual switch a few feet away, and he walked to it. Flicked the switch. Still nothing.

"Trixie?"

"I'm... eading you... rouble getting..." Trixie's voice cut in and out for a few seconds, then cut off completely. At the same time, there was a tremendous rushing sound that reminded Gerrold of waves pummeling at a rocky beach. Nothing calming about it, it was the sound of stark reality being pounded to dissolution.

The atmo change is happening. Must be fouling up the com-link.

On the heels of that thought, the lights in the corridor all but died, as though they had been drawing what power they had from the blue skies outside, and when those blue skies turned a dull, acidic gray, they lost their will to live.

Gerrold was now in near-darkness. Then the darkness became absolute as the remaining emergency lights winked out, one at a time. There were no windows in the corridor—probably not anywhere on the base, if what the Manager had said regarding the sometimes-acidic quality of the air was true —so Gerrold found himself in perfect darkness.

He had gone from blue skies and brightness to the darkness that could only be found on the inside of a black hole in a matter of seconds. A shiver crawled up his spine on tentacles of ice.

Gerrold opened a pocket on his dropsuit and pulled out a flashlamp. He shook it to activate it, then held it aloft. Looked to his right. Saw nothing but a long corridor, broken every ten or fifteen feet by doors. Could be any office building back home.

To his left: same, as far as his light could reach. He walked that way, for no particular reason other than that was the direction he was facing. Ten steps. Twenty. Thirty.

Then his light came up against a wall, a sharp right-hand turn in the corridor and... something disappearing around the corner.

Something with a shock of what looked like bright red hair.

"Hey, wait!" shouted Gerrold. He took two steps, then slipped on a piece of paper on the floor, went down on one knee—

(just like when I asked her and she said yes, just like when she said yes and we were happy and no one asked Do you love me?)

—and when he rose what he had seen was gone. Gone, if it ever had been.

Still, he ran after it. Not what was in front of him, but what was behind. Not what he was seeing, but what he *had seen.*

("Do you love me?")

He wondered for a moment if he was insane. If he had been driven mad by the things Amy had said, by the things that had been done to her and Dalia, by everything. Trixie said there was no speech in the static, no grating sound like a voice erupting through a volcano in the deepest surface of hell to say the words that echoed in Gerrold's mind.

But he kept running. Running in circles until he heard a voice.

"I'm sorry."

Gerrold stopped moving. He lurched to a halt so fast that his body ached and he had to put a hand against the wall for support. The wall felt strange under his hand. Almost... *soft.* Like the plastine structure was being replaced by something less rigid. Springy. Nearly organic-seeming.

Gerrold wiped his hand against the wall. It left a shiny streak, reminding him of a snail-track across the sidewalk after a hard rain.

(the rain coming down on her face and her standing there and Dalia behind and could Dalia hear oh God please no don't let Dalia hear this at least don't let Dalia hear)

"I'm sorry."

Gerrold realized that the feel of the wall had pulled him away from the sound; had made him *forget* it, in fact. And that realization was almost enough to drive him back to the base entrance. Maybe double pay and hazard wasn't enough. Maybe he should just go back Earthside and hold onto Shane, just hug him and never leave.

Right. And then the money dries up taking care of him and where are you then?

Poverty is bearable. Poverty with children is not.

("Do you love me?")

Gerrold swung his flashlamp around, searching for the source of the words he had heard. And he found it. Found the sound. Found the speaker. Found the man who had destroyed his world.

Found his best friend.

* * *

"Alan?" Gerrold frowned. "I thought no one else punched this ticket."

No one *had* punched it, he was certain. He was the only one.

But Alan was here. Standing in the corridor in his own dropsuit, the distinctive one he always wore, with "Can't Touch Me" written across the chest in superhero-bright letters. And now it was Alan's voice sounding again in his ear, on the com-link, saying for the third time, "I'm sorry."

Gerrold felt like he should do something. But he just stood there, just stood like he was nailed to the spot, unable to move, unable to take action upon seeing the man who had done—

(the worst thing, the awful thing, the thing where the bodies were so pulped they had to guess which pieces belonged to Amy and which to Dalia)

—what he had done.

"I'm sorry," said Alan. Then he turned and ran into the dark corridor beyond the range of Gerrold's flashlamp and disappeared.

With Alan's disappearance, Gerrold felt the paralysis leave him. Felt his body moving again as though he had briefly surrendered control and now was back in command of himself. He pushed his feet against the floor—

(is it softer too?)

—and ran into the darkness after Alan. He thought he'd catch him quickly, but he ran for what felt like years, a solitary marathon accompanied only by the sound of his own breathing and the neverending *wail-crash-roar* of the acidic wind outside the base. It was like being alone in the bottom of an oceanic abyss, where pressure would jelly a man in an instant, a place so deep that mere existence would result in death.

Gerrold had a sudden urge to take off his dropsuit and run naked through the halls.

He didn't. Instead he screamed. "Alan! Alan, I just want to talk to you!"

It was a lie. He knew it as he said it, realized what he wanted to do as soon as he said it. He had a debonder on his belt, and he wanted to use it on Alan, to literally take him apart one atom at a time. It wouldn't equal things out, but it would be a start.

Up ahead, he saw movement and redoubled his pace.

The elevators.

One was closed. *Ding.* Going down.

Gerrold didn't even stop to wonder how the elevators could be functioning when the rest of the power was out. He just hit a call button and waited for the next lift to come. It didn't take long—it was almost instant, in fact, like the base had been waiting for him to do this.

He got in. Looked at the banks of buttons that were curiously illuminated in the darkness, like the eyes of an insectile predator staring at him in the black, waiting for him to sleep so it could wrap him in a gentle cocoon and rock him to sleep and suck him dry, body and soul.

Where do I go?

The base was huge. Alan had his choice of thousands of floors and sub-decks. So how could Gerrold find him?

Then he saw one button labeled only "MC," which Gerrold guessed was "Master Control." Without stopping to think, his thumb hit the button, hard enough to crack the thin glass over the plastine below. The sound was bright and crackling in the death-stillness of the air, but the impact didn't break the lift controls: the doors slid silently shut and Gerrold felt the lift drop.

Where am I going? he wondered. And as soon as he thought it he answered himself: I'm going after Alan.

But he knew it was a lie. Whatever he was doing, it wasn't just following Alan. It was more. It was something darker and deeper and beyond his comprehension. He was dropping down to something that called him, just as it had undoubtedly called the base personnel.

And Gerrold was powerless to stop it.

The lift doors opened. There was no ding, no electronic chirp. Under other circumstances Gerrold would have guessed that this was because the system wasn't working properly. But now, here, in this place, he suspected that the elevator *could* have signaled his arrival to the Master Control level. It just didn't want to.

Gerrold stepped out of the lift, moving quickly as if to leave that bizarre —no, *crazy*—thought behind. His first footfall felt and sounded normal, thudding dimly on thick plastine covered by a layer of carpeting. The next...

He aimed his flashlamp down. This level was as dark as the top deck had been. But with the flashlamp he could see easily enough. Could see the floor. Or better said, could see where the floor *had* been. Now, it was gone, the plastine eaten away almost completely. Not by atmo intrusion, not by fusion-torches.

Plants.

The floor on this level was choked with what looked like some kind of stringy vines, creepers that trailed up and down and left and right as far as his flashlamp let him see. He knelt down closer and saw that they had grown up through holes in the plastine, though how that was possible he had no idea.

He also saw the very clear imprint of a foot, smashing down a clump of vines and leaving the recognizable track of a dropsuit boot behind.

Alan.

Gerrold straightened again. He put his foot down, testing the flooring. He didn't want to fall straight through if the plastine had worn away to nothing. But apparently there was enough of it to maintain structural integrity, because the floor beneath its new carpet of plant life didn't buckle or fall away. Still, he walked slowly and carefully, not moving weight from one foot until the other foot had secure footing.

He moved deliberately. Cautiously. So intently that he didn't even notice the figure in front of him until he was only a few feet away. Until the drop-suit boots entered the ring of light provided by Gerrold's flashlamp.

"Shit!" he screamed, not sure how long Alan had been standing there, not sure what the man's plan was. Had Alan come to kill him? To finish what he started with Gerrold's family?

But Alan wasn't moving. Just watching, watching. His dropsuit was motionless, and his helmet visor was dark, nonreflective. Gerrold couldn't see the other man's face.

Gerrold raised the hand holding his flashlamp, holding it above his head and pointing it at Alan's faceplate. He knew it wouldn't blind his old friend —the dropsuit's visor would adjust too quickly for that—but maybe he could keep Alan from noticing what he did with his other hand.

"Why'd you do it, Alan?" Gerrold asked. His free hand dropped to his side.

"I'm sorry." Alan sounded exactly the same as he had in the upper levels.

"I didn't ask if you were sorry. I asked why you did it." Gerrold touched the debonder. Unclipped it.

"I'm sorry."

"Stop saying that. Why'd you do it?"

"I'm sorry."

"Why'd you—"

"I'm—"

"—do it, Alan, why'd you—"

"—sorry. I'm—"

"—do it?"

"—sorry."

"STOP SAYING THAT! STOP STOP STOP SAYING THAT!"

Gerrold swung the debonder. The laser-guide flicked out like a stiletto and traced a blue-white line across the trunk of Alan's dropsuit, then up in a line that ran vertically through the middle of his neck and head. At the same time, the baton-like debonder whirred in Gerrold's hand and the bonds between the atoms on either side of the laser trace loosened and let go.

Alan fell in two uneven pieces, split through the middle, through the neck, through the face. Blood poured from the pieces, sluicing across the vine-ridden floor and toward Gerrold's own feet in a crimson torrent. Alan's intestines spilled, his brain splattered out of his neatly cleaved skull.

Gerrold danced away from the flood of red fluid that reached out for him with its tenticular fingers, and caught himself giggling as he did so, laughing insanely as he danced a jig across the overgrowth that had grown through the toughest material made by man.

Then the laugh caught in his throat like a corpse on a branch, like a body in an explosion might be caught and fused to the car it was riding in so that it became part of the car, impossible to separate from it. The laugh caught and died as he heard a voice.

"I'm sorry."

* * *

Gerrold spun around, searching for the source of the sound. It had come from behind him. It had to have come from—

But there was nothing.

He turned again to the remains of Alan. To what was left of a man who had been his best friend for almost his whole life—Gerrold was the one who had convinced Alan to *become* a FixIt. And as soon as he did he felt his bowels grow loose within him. He didn't know if he actually soiled himself —the dropsuit would just clean it up and eject the waste at a convenient time if he did—but he thought it likely.

The vines were moving. They wrapped themselves around the dropsuit, around the guts and blood and fluid that were left of Alan. And suddenly Gerrold realized that they didn't really look as much like vines as he had supposed. More like blood vessels, like giant arteries and veins pulsing as they ingested the remains of his once-friend. The blood vanished first, disappearing as questing vine-vessels reached finger-like tendrils into the pools and drank deep. Then the soft guts, the intestines, the lungs, the heart, the staring eyes of the half-glimpsed face. Flesh was next, pulled away from the bone by arterial creepers that yanked it free and then circled around it and when they straightened it was gone.

Soon there was only bone and the suit. Then those sank down and disappeared below the still-writhing vascular tissue that Gerrold had thought was merely plant life.

He watched it all, aware he should run, should do *something*, but unable to do more than stand utterly still and dumb with terror and stare at the consumption of one more part of his life, the destruction of one more memory.

"I'm sorry."

Gerrold turned again. Not quickly, though. He turned with the ponderous speed of terror, the fear that grips a man in the instant before the sound of sheering metal and death, the horror that—

(pulses through a woman and a child in that second before the car explodes in fire and fury)

—touches people in the instant before the *actuality* of an event and makes it seem to last forever, even though it may be only milliseconds from start to finish.

He turned slowly. Slowly.

Alan was standing there. Dropsuited. Staring at Gerrold from within the shadowed darkness of his helmet.

"I'm sorry."

Gerrold screamed. He screamed, and ran.

* * *

He didn't know where he was going, and didn't care. He ran in circles, and up and down, and side to side. He careened through rooms that seemed absolutely normal, with desks and chairs and still-beeping computers, and through others that had succumbed to the venous growths that had both consumed and perhaps birthed the impossible vision of his once-friend.

He ran, searching for safety, and in doing so found only loss, and lost himself.

It was the beeping that brought him back. The beeping that reminded him of the day he had found Shane, found him on the floor and everything was wonderful that day because he and Dalia and Amy were having a picnic in the backyard during one of his times Earthside and nothing was wrong with the day and all was well until they heard the thud and ran inside and found little Shane and how had he gotten out how could he have gotten out of his crib that way but it didn't matter because all that mattered was that he was on the floor, so little, so little, and screaming and writhing and the doctors came and took him away and the next time Gerrold saw him it was hooked up to a machine going *beep... beep... beep...* just like the sound...

Just like the sound he was hearing now.

He stopped running. Standing on the springy growths—

(vines just vines nothing more)

—that were everywhere, even the walls and ceiling.

He suddenly remembered reading Collodi's *The Adventures of Pinocchio* as a child. Remembered weeping when Pinocchio rolled into a fire and burned his feet off. Remembered the terror he felt when he read of the poor puppet swallowed by the sea-monster, blacking out and awaking in darkness.

Gerrold felt like that now. Like he was in the belly of a great leviathan, swimming through depths cold and dark and deep, through places of unfathomable cruelty and impossible madness.

Beep... beep... beep...

The sound pulled him away again, and Gerrold realized how close he had come to falling into insanity once more. How close he had come to losing himself in the leviathan, not of the base, but of his mind.

Beep... beep... beep...

He pulled the machine off his belt. It was small, and he hadn't expected to use it, clipping it on his dropsuit more as an afterthought than anything. He had thought Trixie would be along via com-link, and if *she* couldn't find any traces of life with the extensive sensors available on the ship, what use would he have for the bioscanner on his belt?

But Trixie was gone. Gerrold was alone with his thoughts in the near-dark. And the bioscanner was beeping. Which meant that humans were near. It was only programmed to respond to human DNA, and had long ago been taught what his looked like in order to avoid false reads.

Beep... beep...

Gerrold wondered for a moment if this meant that Alan had found him, had caught him, and icy terror ran a-skitter up the ladder of his vertebrae, jumping from bone to bone and then burrowing into his spinal cord.

Then he realized that the bioscanner hadn't responded to Alan before. So this wasn't the return of... whatever that had been.

That left one thing. The base personnel. It had to be.

Gerrold pulled the bioscanner out and started following the beep. He wished now he had brought a full-scale sniffer rather than the simple bioscanner. The beeping sped up, sped up, sped up, pulling him forward like a pulsing beacon.

He realized he didn't know where he was. He had run blindly from Alan —from the thing that had pretended to Alan's form—and now he had no clue as to his whereabouts. He wasn't worried about getting lost, but he did want to know how far to the top of the base, how far to the bottom. Trixie could get him via ship-to-surface transport, but he didn't want her to land on the base. He didn't trust it. Whatever happened, he was going to evac from outside the place when the time came.

But he couldn't tell where he was. The arterial vines, which had darkened to a scabrous brown, covered every surface so completely that there was no room for level markings or other identifications. He tried calling Trixie, but knew she wouldn't answer; could still hear the sound of the acid-wind out-side, rushing like a river of deadly gas.

Beep... beep... beepbeepbeepbeep...

He was close. Time to switch off the bioscanner and just use the ol' eye-balls.

Gerrold felt better as he engaged in this search. Felt like he was more in control. This was what he had come to do: find the personnel, find out about the base. He wasn't sure about the latter assignment, but he was get-ting close in the former. He was getting close. He was doing his job. He was a FixIt, and he was going to take care of things, return the situation to max productivity, then get home to Shane and be able to pay for the next few years of his care.

He turned a corner. He found the personnel.

They were all in a single large room. The base was the size of a city, but it was designed to be run by a staff of about one hundred, and by eyeballing it Gerrold could see that this was where they had all come. Not for refuge, not for safety.

For consumption.

They stood or sat or lay on the vine-ridden floor. Some were motionless, others swayed slightly as though caught in a current that no one else could see.

The vein-vines had grown into all of them. Had touched them all and burrowed into them as it had burrowed through the plastine and now pulsed and glowed dimly with an inner light that provided no sense of security. The arterial cords had only burrowed into hands and feet, and many of the men and women in the room had arms outstretched in poses that struck Gerrold as nothing but blasphemous. And he somehow intuited that was a purposeful effect.

Beepbeepbeepbee—

The chirping died suddenly. Gerrold looked at it, checked to see if it had power and was still functioning. It did and it was.

He looked back at the base personnel. In the instant that he had been looking down, all had oriented on him. Still sitting, still laying, still standing, but their faces were all turned to him. Even the ones with their backs to him had turned their heads an impossible one hundred eighty degrees to watch him.

Their eyes were gone. He hadn't realized it in the first glimpse, but now he could see that where pupils and sclerae and irises should have been, there was only a distant... something.

Gerrold walked toward it. He didn't want to. He didn't want to, he wanted to run, he wanted to get off this damned, cursed place and run home and hide forever. He didn't want to go there.

But he *had* to. Had to know. Had to see what was behind the eyes of the blind.

He came to the first of the bodies, a fat man with red hair and skin so white and thin that Gerrold could see all the blood vessels beneath it. They were delicate and yellow, a web of vascular tissue through which no blood ran, but something else. Something alien and frightening.

The *something* in their eyes still beckoned.

Gerrold came closer.

The people—the bodies, the *corpses* – in the room all opened their mouths. That same scratching sibilance, the sound of death scraping its way out of a deeply buried coffin that Gerrold had heard when he asked Trixie to scan the base frequencies, came from their mouths. And as it had in the FixIt ship, the sound grew louder as he came closer to the dead man with the red hair. Louder and louder, with words barely heard and understood not at all:

"*Azathoth cr'tchkic cokx Dagon nar Shoggoth...*"

Gerrold thought he had known terror before. But now he realized that had been but a bud, and now he felt fear bloom full within him. And it didn't matter. He still looked at the strange lights in the eye sockets of the dead. A light that seemed somehow to pull all light *into* it; a darklight.

"*Shub-Niggurath hok xxr rok Shoggoth...*"

He looked into the pits where eyes should have been, the darklights beckoning, and suddenly the corpses all parted like a dead sea before a prophet of damnation. They parted...

"*Do you love me?*"

...and Gerrold saw in the darklights the essence of madness. He screamed and would have killed himself if he had been able to put his thoughts together long enough to do so.

He turned.

Amy was there. Bloody, pieces of her looking like they had been clumsily attached with the use of bonder or epoxy, other pieces missing completely. The way she had looked after the crash, the way she had looked after the explosion.

Gerrold shook his head. "This isn't true," he said. "It isn't real."

Amy walked toward him on legs that had far too many joints, and buckled under the pressure of her own weight. She left a trail of blood that the arterial things below her slurped up eagerly.

"It is real," she said. Her voice was half hers, half the grating voice of the thing that Gerrold knew was all around them, the thing that was the source of the vines and that lit the dead from within. "Real as you. Real as me. Real as fear and madness and the satiation they bring."

Gerrold shook his head again. He grabbed the debonder off his belt. "Don't come any closer," he said. His voice quavered, and the shakiness was oddly comforting. Oddly real. Something to hold onto in the face of cold chaos. *He* was real, his fear was real. All this was a lie, pulled from his mind somehow, but a lie nonetheless.

"Do you love me, Gerrold? You never answered the question."

The wind rushed outside the base, sounding like the rain he had heard over the com-link on that night, that last night when she confessed.

"I've been having an affair, Gerrold. With Alex." There had been a long pause. "It's over, though. I ended it. I swear to God, Gerrold, I never meant for it to happen, and it won't happen again. Please forgive me. *Please.*" An even longer pause, the rain beating down on her and he realized she was calling outside the house. "Do you love me?" He saw Dalia in the background, shivering. Wondered what could have led to this moment. And then he severed the link.

The next he heard was the Company sending somber men to call him on his job to let him know what had happened: the car had blown up. Sabotaged, an apparent act of revenge by a spurned lover who also happened to be a FixIt, and surely Gerrold could see that this presented... *problems.* So it might be best if he stayed offplanet for a while.

All presented with a smile. All presented so coolly, so coldly, like snakes or the artery-things that now slid around Gerrold's feet.

Their touch brought him out of the memory. He stared at the copy, at the lie that wanted him to believe it was his wife. He pointed the debonder at her face. "Any closer and I'll kill you, I swear to God."

"God," she said, and smiled as though he had said something amusing.

The corpses around him shuffled. They opened their mouths and spoke as one: "Cthulhu acktx xon."

Then they parted again. As they did so, the darklights grew—not brighter, for that was the wrong word to use for something so pervasively cruel. But stronger. The corpses moved aside, and Gerrold saw something approaching.

"No..."

A small form...

"Please, no..."

Red hair, streaked through with highlights...

"*NO NO NO!*"

The thing lurched forward, its steps impeded by the bits of plastine and metal that had melded themselves to her form and created of her a thing neither human nor machine, neither alive nor dead.

The darklights flashed, tumbling Gerrold over an abyss of madness.

A small, cold hand took his. Blood ran over his hand and he realized he had taken off his dropsuit. He looked down into eyes mismatched by an explosion. One of them glittered with the red plastine of a rear lamp. The thing smiled, enameled teeth intermingled with those of steel.

Gerrold was still screaming. And with every scream the child-thing's smile grew, and the darklights flashed colder in his mind.

The child-thing drew him down, down, down into the depths of the base. To the deepest levels where the structure tied into the geothermals of the planet itself. But where there should have been a bubbling volcano, pulsing magma, Gerrold found himself staring into something else.

He didn't recognize it at first—

(*no that's not true I know what it is I just don't believe it I can't believe it it just can't be*)

—but then the thing shifted somehow and a great gray shelf that looked like rock slithered over it. Then the rock-shelf disappeared and Gerrold stared down again at what was not the insides of a volcano after all, but rather... an *eye*.

The eye, perhaps a mile across, stared at Gerrold. The darklights flashed from within it and he began to scream again. Because he heard the scratching voice, not in his ears, but in his mind.

Your fear is delicious to me.

With the thought, an image came. No, more than an image. An encapsulation. The essence of what had happened: of the Company finding this place. Surveying it. Landing a base. Never realizing that they had chosen to try and terraform something that was not mere planet, but a thing older than any planet. Never understanding that what they took for the suddenly-changing atmosphere was in fact the inhalation and exhalation of a sleeping creature of such magnitude that it could only be called Eldritch; an Elder One. Never realizing that when it awoke it would shift its form, and so the base would move.

Never suspecting that it would rise, as it always did, hungry.

You will go back. Bear the message of the new god. The Elder One comes to feed.

"Why?" Gerrold managed to whisper. And knew immediately: he would go to give the entire Earth—the entire human species—a chance to understand what was coming. And as they understood, they would fear.

And your fear is delicious to me.

Gerrold shook his head. "I won't." But he knew he would. The darklights had him and there was no way for him to resist beyond the merest token. And even that, he suspected, would soon be denied him. "They'll never believe me," he tried. A last, desperate plea for mercy from the merciless.

The great eye at the foundation of the base blinked. The darklights flashed and Gerrold's volition fell away.

They WILL.

Gerrold Mason turned over and thought for a moment he had seen red hair. Red hair with subtle threads of black and brown running through it, like a dark rainbow that portended not the sun breaking through the clouds, but the clouds' triumph over all that was bright.

It was an omen. He should have recognized it for what it was.

Then he thought he saw a flash of lighter red, a red stitched through with bright threads of blonde.

He blinked. And saw them both, standing there in the darkness of his quarters as they had been when he slept. Trixie was gone, but he was not alone. *They* were there, mother and daughter, woman and child, the dead-alive clinging to one another and to the vein-vines that had sprung from every surface of his FixIt ship as soon as they stepped aboard.

They remained in shadow, though the blood that ran from their mangled forms ran ever toward him, as though hungry to take him into its own. He supposed it probably was.

He looked at the scanner nearby. The planet—what he had thought was a planet—was still keeping pace with the ship. Moving as no planet should, and changing shape even as he watched, drawing into a bulbous end trailed by tentacles too numerous to count and too long to comprehend.

He looked away from the thing. Back to the evidence of what was about to befall humanity.

They remained in shadow, though the darklights flashed. The darklights flashed, and cold madness took Gerrold away for the millionth time on the dead crow's wings of the words he could not, would not, never wished to escape:

"Do you love me?"

DEAD WAITS DREAMING

LARRY CORREIA

When I was a child I dreamed of the stars. When I was a man the stars stole my dreams.

A man who cannot dream becomes nothing but an empty shell, but the thing about empty shells, there's nothing left inside to corrupt. Space ate my dreams, tore them right out my head and left a gaping hole where my soul had been life. My life ended a long time ago.

Which is why I was the only one who survived.

"What happened on Atlas?"

The question woke me up. It didn't matter. As usual, my sleep was empty. I wasn't missing anything good.

"Please, Mr. Chang, we have to know what happened on Atlas."

The desperate voice was coming out of the blank wall of my tiny cell. They thought I'd been exposed to a potential alien biohazard so I'd remained in quarantine. My clothing had been burned and my body had been scrubbed, attached to tubes and machines to be monitored in every way possible, isolated from the world of flesh and imprisoned in a totally sterile environment.

The precautions wouldn't do them any good.

My words came out raspy and weak. "I don't know."

"The survivor's awake. He's talking!" She forgot to turn off the intercom. "Get the Captain. Hurry."

"Where am I?"

"You're onboard the *Alert* in orbit over Atlas. You're safe now. Please, Mr. Chang, we need you to try and remember what happened to your colony."

I remembered, but remembering and understanding were two different things.

It began with a news report.

I didn't know at the time that this particular blurb would mark the beginning of the end of the world but I followed a lot of news. Useless talking heads, pundits, bloggers, hoaxers, malcontents, and a handful of actual experts, millions of channels streaming in from two hundred solar systems and downloaded in the few seconds whenever the gate cycled open and we were briefly connected with the rest of the universe—even if it was all months out of date—and then I followed Atlas's local streams when the gate was closed, which was the vast majority of the time.

Galaxy, system, world, or local, I followed it. War, politics, business, science, sports, entertainment, it didn't matter. I had nothing else to do, so I listened as other people actually *did*. I was a pensioner, a useless parasite on the system, popping crazy pills and streaming feeds. On more pragmatic or desperate colonies they would have recycled me. On Atlas, I wasted away in my apartment and filled my brain with other people's lives.

The local blurb had been an update on the Dark Side Dig, commemorating the sixteenth anniversary of the discovery of the ancient ruins that had changed Atlas from a backwoods mining colony to an archaeological mecca. Even though the natives had been extinct for millions of years, humans had only discovered a handful of planets with intelligent life so far, so it had been a big deal, even if the odd winged cucumbers depicted in their carvings had been relative primitives compared to some of the species we'd found on other worlds.

The Dig's science team had found a new chamber to crack open. They'd dubbed it the Temple.

It should have pissed me off, because that was supposed to have been my job before a quirk of interstellar travel had ripped out all the creative parts of my mind and left me a useless, drug-addled husk, but anger just got in the way of my news addiction, so I kept listening. The report closed with an interview, just some puffery with one of the newly arrived archaeologists, about how the weird geometry favored in the alien's architecture had given a few of them nightmares.

Nightmares... I would have killed for a nightmare.

***

Captain Hartono brought up the hologram. It showed a nearly skeletal man sitting on a slab, arms wrapped around his knees, rocking back and forth, slowly muttering to himself. "What do we have on the survivor?"

"All colonists' DNA is on file. His name is Leland Chang, contract transfer from Calhoun, been on Atlas for fifteen years." As Dr. Riady spoke all of the pertinent tabs came up on the edge of the hologram.

The Captain opened the career data. "Xeno-anthropologist, supposed to be brilliant." He went back to the holo. "The guy looks awful."

"Malnutrition and dehydration, mostly. The servitors found some other minor injuries, but no serious trauma."

"I listened in while the drop team lifted him out, lots of crazy babbling. Whatever happened down there drove him batshit insane. I need you to get in his head straight fast."

"I don't know if that'll be possible."

"Make it possible, Doc. The evidence the drop teams have recovered so far doesn't make any sense. Command needs to know who did this and he's our only witness."

"I'm afraid Chang wouldn't have made a very credible witness even before whatever happened down there."

Hartono brought up the medical history tab. He swore under his breath. "Keziah's Disorder? That poor bastard..."

"It's extremely rare."

"Thank God for that," the captain muttered. "It doesn't matter. Get him talking. I don't care what you have to do. We need information and we need it now. Crack him and do a memory lift if you need to."

"That's not exactly ethical, sir."

"At the last gate cycle, Atlas was a thriving colony. Thirty days later, it's back online, we cycle through and somehow six hundred thousand colonists have gone missing and we don't know why. So right now I don't particularly give a shit about ethics."

"I can't memory lift an innocent man, Captain," Riady stammered. "That's—"

"There are no messages, no recordings, no notes, no vids. Nothing. Every AI on the planet is crashed. We've got ghost ships in orbit with their systems scrubbed. The forensic evidence doesn't make sense. There's battle damage, but no invaders. Over half a million humans vanished in *thirty days*, Doctor, and the only living thing we've found more advanced than a house plant is your survivor."

"Give me a chance," she begged.

Hartono frowned. They were stuck for now anyway. "The next available gate cycle isn't for two days. You've got one."

***

I was an artist once. I could take raw materials and scrape and twist them into beauty. I can still understand the fundamental techniques, but it turns out that when you are incapable of dreaming, you are incapable of creating. You can no longer reach your *full potential*.

What a blessing that turned out to be.

Before Atlas became a galactic tourist attraction—*Witness the Wonder of an Ancient Alien Civilization!*—it was simply the boring second planet in the Chameleon 110913-773444 system. When I got the contract offer, the 26-hour days and 1.02% standard gravity made it sound pretty nice. The downside was the average temperature of 120° C combined with the 300-kilometer-an-hour winds made most of the planet a giant sandblaster. There was one colony and it was mostly underground, so Atlas wasn't exactly a draw for the *outdoorsy* types.

The contract specified that I would be studying the ancient inhabitants, using my expertise to reconstruct their culture. It takes a certain kind of mind to be able to imagine an alien lifestyle. I signed on. I severed my existing contract on Calhoun and embarked on a great adventure. Of course I did. This was a scholar's dream job.

Unless your scholar can no longer dream, because then he can't keep a job.

Star travel is relatively safe, considering that your frail body is being hurled across the universe through an in-between space that mankind barely comprehends, using math which shouldn't work yet somehow does. Since our brains didn't evolve to handle the strange physics of null space, hypersleep was invented. They advertise that hypersleep is so humans can travel between gates in complete comfort. Go to sleep in one system, wake up in another one on the opposite end of the Milky Way. No problem, and you especially don't have to worry about any of those pesky psychoses that all the early interstellar travelers developed.

Except that hypersleep isn't really sleep, and there's nothing hyper about it. That's just creative marketing. I used to be able to appreciate that sort of thing. Your body isn't sleeping, it's artificially shut down until it is one faint electrical impulse away from death. Space travelers are placed into a chemical coma and frozen. Everybody knows this, but nobody who has to go through it likes to dwell on it. After all, it's statistically *extremely safe*—the advertisements said so—and when you get decanted you are ready to experience life on an exciting new world.

The first humans who traveled between gates are all dead now. Back then we didn't understand that entering REM sleep while your body was in null space was a one-way ticket to Crazy Town. We still don't know why it happens, just that it does. So now they practically turn you into a corpse, freeze your brain, and pump nanobots through your arteries, all to keep your mind safely blank while you're flying through the space between the walls.

By "extremely safe," they mean that hypersleep accidents are one in a billion. Those are excellent odds.

I should have stayed on Calhoun and played the lottery.

Dr. Riady studied the holo. The survivor's vitals were decent—not bad, considering what he must have gone through, though it appeared that he hadn't been in the best physical health to begin with. She brought up another screen. Long-term poor dental hygiene, skeletal degradation, and muscle mass and cardiovascular condition consistent with a sedentary lifestyle, plus the active scans showed that he was going through severe withdrawal symptoms from the psychotropic cocktail he'd been on for the last fifteen years.

"How did *you* survive?" she muttered. Atlas had had a small defense force, mostly made up of veterans of the Zealand Conflict, now retired from the military. Those were genetically modified, nano-enhanced super-soldiers who'd fought through one of the worst guerrilla wars in history, yet somehow they were missing and an unemployed, mentally ill couch potato had lived. "Why you and not them?"

When she went back to the first display, she found Leland Chang staring directly into the monitor. "I know modesty is an outdated concept, but may I have some clothing?"

"Oh, my apologies, Mr. Chang. I'll have a servitor bring you some. We didn't intend to make you uncomfortable."

"Thank you... And who are you?"

"I'm Dr. Riady, medical officer of the *Alert*." He seemed rather lucid, probably due to the stimulants she'd administered. Dr. Riady decided to push forward before he descended into another incoherent funk. "I know you've been through a lot, but I have some questions."

"Why?" Chang went back to staring at his hands. "You won't believe me anyway."

"I have to believe you. I've seen your medical history. I know you have no imagination to speak of, so I doubt you'd be able to lie to me very convincingly anyway."

"That's a cruel way to put it."

"But factually true." She didn't mention that the room's biometric scanners also made an excellent lie detector of sorts. "Let me level with you, Mr. Chang. Our captain is extremely concerned, and I have no doubt that when we're able to send a burst back to Command, they will be even more so."

Chang looked up, suddenly desperate. "Don't send a message. You can't cycle the gate."

"Why?"

"It might spread."

"*What* might spread?"

"The truth."

One in a billion... Sounds like a lot until you realize just how many humans are traversing the stars. Keziah's Disorder, they call it, named after the first poor sucker who came out of hypersleep screaming about ambivalent squid gods and bleeding from his ears, mind all buggered up from daring to dream in null space.

You see, the dead aren't supposed to dream. It violates the rules.

The greatest medical minds of the galaxy were fascinated by Keziah. Dreaming in hypersleep had done something to his brain. It turns out that your organs begin failing after only a few months without REM sleep, so he was crazy and dying. The scientists jumped on this one. First off, dreaming while in hypersleep was technically impossible. Second, doctors love that technically impossible shit. And third, the space lines really wanted this thing cured before the news scared off too many potential colonists. Drugs forced Keziah's brain through all the stages of sleep and saved his physical body. The doctors gave each other awards. Colonists kept on paying for temporary death.

But the treatment couldn't make Keziah dream. Since science had never found a mammal that didn't dream, they couldn't realize just how important that process actually was, how every single bit of goodness in life was attached to it.

A year later Keziah stepped in front of a train.

Forty years after that, I was trapped in a metal tube, hurtling through space, dead but dreaming.

"Can you draw the graffiti symbols you saw for me, Mr. Chang?"

"I can try." One of the servitors in the quarantine room hovered over and handed her patient a stylus. Chang took it and began writing. "My memory is fine, but I can tell you now that I won't be able to convey everything. I had a friend who said their writing had 'nuance'... I doubt I'll be able to do it justice."

"Because of your condition?"

"Something like that."

Dr. Riady tapped her finger on the projection. "Enlarge." She'd never seen anything like the strange letters before. They looked like gibberish to her. Making sure the intercom was off, she addressed the *Alert's* AI. "Emma, can you read that?"

"The symbols are similar to those recorded by the Dark Side Dig archaeological teams. I will translate. Processing."

Chang's handdrawn symbols floated before her. Gradually the strange runes twisted into familiar words.

"Translation complete. However, I estimate only 87% accuracy."

From His dark house in the mighty city beneath the sands beneath the winds, He offers freedom to the living children of the pillars of heaven. The day has come to heed the call of dreams.

When you're paranoid and prone to sudden fits of violent rage, you don't collect many friends.

Thomerson was one of the few people who still came to visit me. It was probably because he felt guilty. He was a linguist, and we'd worked together deciphering the Calhoun pyramid. He'd been the one to recommend me for the Dark Side Dig contract. We'd even made the trip together. I believe his was far more pleasant.

He sat on the edge of the couch, like he was scared he'd get his pants dirty. My settlement from the space line had paid for the apartment, my treatments, and anything else I might conceivably want for the rest of my life, if I could be bothered to want anything, but I wasn't much for decorating. Or cleaning... Or much else, really.

"You should open your windows more, Leland. You've got a marvelous view here."

I humored him. "Fine." The covers automatically lifted. My apartment building was suspended from the side of the main chasm. It kept us out of the wind, and we could see most of the undercity from here, as well as a long sliver of howling red sky.

"When's the last time you went outside?"

I shrugged. "I don't know. A few weeks."

"I could arrange a day pass to the Dig for you." Thomerson was fat, so his leaning forward conspiratorially just looked awkward. "I can even get you into the Temple. It's pretty exciting stuff. They think it might even finally answer the big question."

"What killed off all the Atlanteans?"

"I wish you wouldn't call them that. It makes them sound like a joke."

"I don't make jokes."

"I know. Never mind. But listen, Leland, this is big. All this time we've been trying to reconstruct how they actually lived. There've been glimmers of a religious philosophy here and there in their art, but nothing like this. They're calling it the temple, cathedral, whatever, but it really *is*."

Fifteen years ago, that would have been incredibly exciting. "And?"

"This isn't just their religion, this is their version of a doomsday cult. This is the newest construction we've ever found. It dates to the end. They were on their way out and they knew it. You know how hard their alphabet is to translate, so much nuance..." Thomerson sighed wistfully. "But this reeks of desperation. We never knew if they had an afterlife myth like most of humanity's various cultures, but they did! They were looking for a way out, just like primitive man."

"Fascinating," I lied.

"I know, right? We've seen that they had a god figure, we've seen it over and over again, but this is the first time that we've found an opposite. Obviously human social mores don't translate, but consider it a devil figure, if you will. They knew their species was going extinct so they were making a proverbial deal with their devil."

The only reason that I hadn't killed myself yet was because part of me was terrified that what I'd seen in null space was real, and I was too afraid to find out for sure. "I'll pass on the day trip."

"They were as frightened by the mysteries of death as primitive man. The carvings said that this devil came to their entire species, appearing in their dreams and making them an offer..."

Even winged cucumbers had dreams... "Wonderful... It's getting late. Maybe you should—"

But Thomerson wasn't listening. He was still talking, staring off into space. Almost like he'd forgotten I was there at all. "They took his offer... Imagine that? An offer that an entire civilization couldn't refuse. They were a rather metaphysical lot, believing in spirit worlds nearly as much as they believed in the real world. They still believed in magic, and perhaps that's why their science lagged behind... Regardless, they accepted the devil's deal. The word they used translates to the Great Becoming... *and upon His will the world became undone.*"

"What?"
Thomerson stood up suddenly and then shuddered, like he'd begun to

swoon. Flushed, he placed one fat hand on his fat cheek. "I'm sorry. I was feeling a bit dizzy. Forgive me, Leland. I've not been sleeping well."

I escorted him to the door. "Yeah, I've heard on the feeds that's been a problem out there lately. Something about the background noise keeping people awake at the Dig."

He collected his hat and cloak. "Yes. There's been some accidents. Tired workers and whatnot."

"Well, be careful then." I steered him out, then closed the door behind him. "Full secure." The locks sealed. My paranoia temporarily mollified, I walked back into my apartment. "Close view." The covers began dropping.

But not before I noticed something black and hairy, pressed against the bottom of the glass, watching me. At first I thought it was a monkey, with a face like an ugly baby, but it had the shimmering wings of a fly, and in the brief moment our gaze met, its mouth moved like it was trying to say something, with a mouth filled with all too human teeth, and then it was covered.

I rubbed my eyes. "Open view."

The monkey-fly-man-baby was gone.

I went into the bathroom and took another pill.

"Come inside, Doctor. I just got word Drop Team 2 just entered the lower levels of the city. I'm waiting for their report."

She entered the Captain's chamber and saluted. "The survivor's been speaking freely, sir."

"So what's the verdict?" Captain Hartono didn't need to ask—he could already tell by her haggard expression that she hadn't gotten anything good —but he needed it spoken out loud so her recommendation could be recorded by the ship's AI. If the Atlas event was the opening act of a new war or first contact with an unknown species, then Hartono was going to cover his ass as best as possible in case it all went sideways and Command needed somebody to hang.

Riady stopped in front of his desk. "I'm afraid I can't make sense of the survivor's story..."

"And?"

She gave him a look that said *Do I have to?*

Hartono addressed the *Alert's* AI. "Emma, stop recording. This is now a private conversation."

"Yes, Captain." The AI gave the audible response for Riady's benefit. "Recording stopped."

Riady was a veteran and had been a combat medic during the bloody Zealand Conflict. Being genetically modified, she was as close to human physical perfection as possible, and had been decorated for valor against the vicious alien Martor. So frankly, it unnerved Hartono to see her *frightened*.

"Have a seat." He nodded and a chair rose up through the floor. "What is it, Doctor?"

Riady sat uncomfortably. "Chang is talking, but..." She rubbed her face in her hands and sighed. "I sort of wish he wasn't."

"Send me the transcripts."

She blinked. "Done."

They took him a moment to process. "This description can't be right. There are no residual signatures showing any ships coming into the system. We've checked the whole city, but there's not a bit of DNA down there that doesn't belong to a colonist of record. It couldn't have been alien."

"That's the thing, Captain... I don't think it was alien."

Hartono's eyes narrowed. "I'm not liking your other option."

There was a flash transmission behind one of his eyes. A drop team had found something on the bottom level. *Open live feed. Public.*

The hologram appeared on his desk between them, obviously being reconstructed in three dimensions from multiple helmet cams. It was a mangled body, or perhaps *bodies*... It was hard to tell. Hartono willed the hologram to rotate slowly. "What is that thing?"

The AI answered, having only needed a fraction of a second to review every cataloged organism in the universe. "The physical structures match no known entity."

"I want samples," Hartono said.

The drop team had already taken one. A strand of DNA appeared floating in the holo, listed as a *partial* match.

Martin, Eliza J. – Atlas Colonist.

Chamberlain, Harold R. – Atlas Colonist.

Geist, Terron I. – Atlas Colonist

Names continued to scroll by. Dozens of them.

Hartono killed the feed. Riady had unconsciously reached into her uniform, pulled out a small silver crucifix, and was fingering it nervously. He hadn't known she was religious.

"Emma, begin recording."

"Yes, Captain."

"Doctor Riady, what is your medical recommendation for the lone Atlas survivor?"

"Since I'm unable to gain any meaningful intel through interviews with Leland Chang, I recommend that we perform a memory lift immediately. Let the record show that the medical officer is fully aware this procedure may prove fatal to the subject."

"*Alert* command concurs with this recommendation. Expedite."

While the gate was closed I was limited to Atlas local feeds. Considering it was the apocalypse, you'd have thought it would have been more obvious, but my fellow colonists simply blundered toward their inevitable Great Becoming. Nobody realized that the story about the alarming increase in sleep disorders was truly that important. The Atlas Sleep Clinic blamed it on the harmonics from the wind.

I didn't go out much, but I wasn't a complete hermit. I knew most of my neighbors by name and was always as polite to them as social obligations demanded. There was a shopping mall beneath my building and I went there whenever my food dispenser told me it was nearly empty.

I'd lost track of how many days it had been since I'd last been outside. The first thing I noticed was that Atlas City Public Works was slacking. Normally the corridors were tidy, but I saw litter and even abandoned sacks of trash left in corners. I'd not read about any labor strikes. Then I recoiled as a large black bug landed on my lips. I swatted it away, and it buzzed off angrily. *Odd.* Insect pests had inevitably followed man across the stars, but normally they were kept under tight control in a sealed colony. This wasn't the wretched undercity.

The usually busy market was remarkably dead. There were a few people standing listlessly on corners, as if unsure what they were waiting for. I saw only a handful of shoppers, and they seemed almost furtive, keeping their heads down and shoving products into their carts almost like they didn't even care what they were hoarding. There was a teenager leaning next to my destination's entrance, seemingly staring off into space, obliviously listening to music and watching a holo on the inside of his glasses. I went inside.

"I've come for my order. I'm Leland Chang from the two hundred and sixteenth level."

The girl didn't respond. She was focused on the screen in front of her. I thought this was a typical lazy employee, ignoring customers while she watched funny videos, but when I leaned over the counter the screen was blank. "Hello…" I waved my hand in front of the clerk's face. "Hello."

She blinked rapidly. "Huh? Sorry. I'm really tired. I've not been sleeping good."

"I take pills for that." The clerk handed me the compressed box of protein sludge. When food has no flavor, you simply purchase whatever keeps you alive. "Thank you."

When I walked back outside I noticed that the power light on the teenager's glasses was off. He was engrossed in absolutely nothing. A large black fly was walking around, unnoticed, on his pimply face.

The servitors had secured Leland Chang to the slab.

"What're you doing to me?" He sounded more resigned than afraid.

Dr. Riady reasoned that she might as well be truthful. "We're going to make an electronic imprint of your long-term memory."

"I'm familiar with the process. I keep up on all the science reports… It'll probably kill me, won't it?"

"I'm going to do my very best to make sure that doesn't happen, Mr. Chang."

"I don't mind, Doctor… I've only got one last request."

"What's that?"

"If this works, if you're able to see into my brain and record what's there, please, no matter what, don't look at the dreams I had in null space… It's for your own good."

The news changed over the next week. There were fewer and fewer blog posts. Social media was unusually quiet. The pundits were extra angry and dimwitted. The ADF had been called up for an unspecified reason. The talking heads pontificated that it was related to the sudden increase in property crime. A riot had broken out in the undercity but it was contained. There had been a rash of accidental deaths at the Dark Side Dig. Compared to all of this, the fact that the Sleep Clinic was overwhelmed was hardly a footnote.

The news was my anchor. I needed other people going about their lives so my lack of one was palatable. I did not like this.

Needing stimulus, I opened the window covers. The sky today was a brilliant red as mile-long tornadoes battled above the chasm. Far below, a large fire had broken out in the city, and it was surrounded by flashing red and blue lights. I was more upset that this event hadn't even made the news than the actual reality of the event.

Flies began landing on the window, great black, hairy things. Dozens at first, and then hundreds of them. I closed the cover.

"Emma, I need to make a statement for the record."

"Confirmed, Captain."

"Dr. Riady has completed the memory lift of the patient, Leland Chang. The data is currently being analyzed. The gate will cycle in one hour and then the *Alert* will return home to report. As of this time our investigation into the cause of the Atlas incident remains inconclusive. I regret to say that our memory lift proved to be too much for Mr. Chang in his weakened condition and he has gone into a vegetative state. He's been placed in stasis in preparation for hypersleep. I'm fully aware that taking someone with Keziah's Syndrome into null space may be considered torture under the Durban Accords, but I believe the urgency of our mission outweighs this so I have overruled Dr. Riady's protests."

Captain Hartono rubbed his temples. He had a splitting headache. It was getting hard to think and even harder to make good decisions, but none of them had gotten much sleep since they'd arrived.

The noise had come from the hall of my apartment. It had been loud enough to wake me from my drug-induced slumber. It had trailed off before I'd come fully awake. Had it been a scream? An animal howl? A little bit of both?

I asked my apartment building's AI what had made the sound. It began to answer. Then it froze, gave me an error message, and had to reboot. It came back a moment later and said that there had been no sound and nothing was wrong.

Logic said to stay in bed, perhaps call the authorities. I am no longer capable of curiosity, so I could not even blame that base instinct, but for whatever reason, I got up, went to my security door, and listened through the port.

I heard grunting. And squishing.

I took another pill and went back to bed.

By the next morning the news feeds had grown... *odd.*

Most of the local stations were offline. Only a handful remained, and those were the larger affiliates with more staff. I watched as one of the news reader beautiful people rambled incoherently about the beauty of tentacles, before vomiting blood all over the news desk. She began drawing in the blood with her finger before the feed was cut. *We are experiencing technical difficulties.*

The independent sources and some of the video bloggers kept on, though many of those had become garbled. The written ones struggled as well, and one popular author's feed, now filled with typos, complained that typing was difficult once your fingers began growing together.

I opened the window to the real world and watched the fall of Atlas. There were more fires in the streets below, as well as the occasional bright flash of a particle weapon. Vehicles were overturned and I could watch the people dance about them like ants.

There were still clouds of flies clustered on my window. But now I noticed a single, greasy hand print, undeniably human, pressed there on the *outside* of the glass on the 216th floor.

The *Alert* was prepared for the gate to open. The crew had already been placed in stasis. Captain Hartono and Dr. Riady would be the last to enter hypersleep, and after that control of the ship would be turned over to Emma until they cycled into their home system in a few months.

Dr. Riady checked on the stasis tank holding the body of Leland Chang one last time. He appeared as dead as any other space traveler, but she knew it was an illusion. Unlike the rest of them, his mind would be totally open to the sanity-breaking horrors of null space.

What would be left of this man on the other side? What did it matter, the Captain had argued, one man's sanity versus six hundred thousand presumed dead? Command needed answers, and they'd get them, even if they had to dismantle the only survivor down to his individual molecules.

Sweet dreams, Mr. Chang.

There was no more news. No feeds. No brainless chatter. The silence was deafening.

I was nearly out of meds. I called the treatment center but only got their automated message system. Even their AI would not respond.

I would have to go outside.

You do not need an imagination to be frightened. I still experience fear. Self-preservation is the most basic of all human instincts. I really did not want to go outside.

But it was preferable to remembering null space and the dreams of the dead.

The hall was empty. Some of the other apartment doors were open. The rooms inside were a mess, but I didn't see anyone alive. Mrs. Garcia was on her couch, pistol in her lap, brains all over the wall. In Mrs. Johansen's apartment there was something odd stuck to the ceiling. At first I thought it was a green and grey sleeping bag, but it was a cocoon, made of a material like unto mucus.

The lift still came when called, which was good, because I didn't think my legs could handle the stairs.

The building's lobby was empty. It was the first time in fifteen years that I'd not seen another human being inside of it. It room was filthy. The air scrubbers were off. There was a wet black trail through the red dust. At first I thought it was oil, but it had a greenish tint to it. Following the trail with my eyes, I came to a steaming pile of dead skin and regurgitated bones.

The main doors were made of glass. On the other side was chaos.

The streets were filled with trash. There had to be a crack in the dome because red grit coated everything at ground level. Clouds of insects were swarming, hopping and flying, skittering about in the shadows.

Opening the doors, I stepped into the end.

The environmental systems were failing. The air tasted like metal. It was terribly hot.

There were... *people* in the market. Hunched, lurching about, their bodies covered in rags that had been clothing so recently. They paid me no heed. A hulking man brushed by, not even noticing me. He kept his head down, hat concealing his face, but I saw the puckering green hole where his ear had been, and then he went down an alley where some others had gathered, feasting on the guts of a stray dog.

Focus. The nearest pharmaceutical dispensary was only a block away.

I made it half that distance before I came upon the Black Man.

He was waiting on the sidewalk. His featureless head swiveled toward me, watching without eyes.

The Black Man wasn't part of the chaos. He was above it. He'd seen it before.

He saw me and knew that I was different.

You do not participate in the Great Becoming?

I turned back toward my apartment, walking quickly.

Wait.

The Black Man followed.

Beneath the red winds, beneath the sands of Rhonoth-dur, the temple of undoing beckons. You alone decline this invitation?

I began to run.

The Black Man continued walking after me.

Unable to meet your full potential, you are broken. You have gazed upon the grandeur of the Between and have wilted. Your dreams of unmaking are not for my world. To another master they must fly.

I reached the glass doors of my building. Recognizing I belonged there, they slid open to save me.

Delicious screams.

"Help! Wait!"

"Let us in!"

There were three children running up the sidewalk from the opposite direction, terrified, reaching for me with tears streaming down their faces. There was a shadow behind them, shambling. My eyes tracked up toward the incomprehensible mass of hungry, twisted meat that was pursuing them.

Tentacles wrapped around the last child's ankles. He sprawled into the street, and was sucked back to be consumed.

I held the door open. "Hurry!"

The first child, a girl, no more than ten, got past me. The next, a boy, probably six or seven, ran up, and I placed my hand on the back of his head as he passed to push him to safety.

My fingers touched hard chitin.

I snatched my hand away. Beneath his patchy blond hair, the back half of his skull was a slimy black and red plate.

He looked up at me with wide goat pupil eyes.

I shoved him back into the street and forced the door closed.

The girl was inside, watching me, emotionless, as the tentacled horror dragged the boy away.

The Black Man stood outside the door.

This world is mine. You have been claimed by another.

I went back to the lift as the girl squatted in the lobby and began to draw intricate designs in the slime.

The lift doors opened. The Black Man was inside waiting.

I stepped inside and called for 216. We started up.

This world is mine, priest of another. We do not share. Your dreams of unmaking must serve another.

A few seconds later we reached my floor. I stumbled into the hall in a swarm of flies. The Black Man did not follow. Mrs. Johansen's cocoon had burst open. Something had slid beneath her couch and was breathing wetly. Mrs. Garcia's body was gone, but her bloody footsteps went to the wall and simply disappeared.

I went inside my apartment. The Black Man was waiting, standing in front of my window, watching Atlas be cleansed.

We do not share worlds. This one is mine. It has always been mine. We do not share priests. You have been marked by another. Return to He who has anointed you and awaken Him from his slumber. Awaken Him with your visions, so that the worlds He has claimed may hear His call.

Ph'nglui mglw'nafh Cthulhu R'lyeh wgah'nagl fhtagn.

Die again. And Dream.

The *Alert* cycled through the Mars gate without incident. Within seconds AIs had exchanged vast swaths of data. Curiously, Emma was unable to send certain bits of information because her database had somehow become corrupted.

By the time the first of the *Alert's* crew began to thaw from hypersleep, a fleet of ships had been dispatched to Atlas to continue the investigation.

Dr. Riady, being genetically enhanced, was the first to shake off the stasis effects. She summoned a basin of water, splashed some on her face, and stared at her reflection in the mirror. As a side effect of near physical perfection, it was extremely unusual to find a pimple on her forehead. It was even more unusual, when she scratched at and squeezed it, to have a tiny insect pop out and fly away...

"Emma, is there a bug in my chambers?"

"No, Doctor. I do not detect anything of the sort."

She shook her head, blamed the hallucination on the aftereffects of the hypersleep drugs, splashed some more water on her face, and got back to work. She had a crew to decant.

Within the last of those stasis tanks, deep within the *Alert's* quarantine, Leland Chang's eyes moved rapidly behind closed lids, as his broken mind relived visions of tormented ancient gods, trapped between the walls of reality, so vivid and imaginative that they could wake the dead.

Far beneath the ocean of the human home world, something began to stir.

And the sixteen billion humans spread across several planets, moons, and orbitals around Earth did not even realize that this was the beginning of the end.

THE IMPLANT

ROBERT J DEFENDI

Father Phai walked the halls of Saint Stephan University, ignoring the tech serfs who scuttled about like brain-damaged insects. The high stone ceilings of the building vaulted over his head as his feet shuffled along smooth marble floors. He paused in the middle of the hall and turned to Father Aristeides.

"You're saying that God can't create a rock so big that not even He can lift it?"

"Of course not," his friend, also a priest, said. "God is all-powerful. He can lift anything."

Father Phai shook his head and started walking again. A tech serf limped by on two mechanical legs. One was longer than the other; they looked as if they'd been made in different decades for different people.

"If He is all-powerful, He can certainly make a rock He can't lift. He can just make it so that He can lift it again the next moment."

"That's stupid," his friend said, "and you're stupid for thinking it."

Father Phai smiled and started walking again. "People have debated that one for five thousand years." If it wasn't for Aristeides, Phai would have been alone ever since he left Frona to join the seminary. The man was more than a friend. He was a personal salvation.

"Just because half of them were stupid," Aristeides said, the smile clear in his tone even if his face was stern.

They pushed down a side hall and several of the priests smiled and nodded at Father Phai. He didn't know half of them, but he'd always been good at making friends. Even the tech serfs treated him with a little more familiarity than they did the other priests. They didn't seem to hold it against him that he was a priest in a religion that damned them with one doctrine while blessing them with another.

"I hear the border problems have heated up again," Aristeides said.

"Russians," Father Phai said, because you didn't need to say anything more on the subject.

"They're claiming this one isn't fueled by the Church. They're saying it's just straight politics."

The split between the Eastern Orthodox Church and the Russian Ortho-dox Church still drove tensions between the two peoples, even so many centuries after it happened. "It's good to know that hatred isn't just an ec-clesiastical trait," Father Phai said.

"Indeed."

They walked down a narrow stone hall now. Up ahead, scaffolding blocked half the passage and two tech serfs, their cyberware suited for heavy labor, braced a wall as they worked on the cracking stone. People walked sideways to pass one another beside the scaffolding.

"They still haven't admitted to destroying the *Daedalus*," Aristeides said.

"The Russians are heathens, and monsters, and rogues, but they wouldn't destroy a ship," Father Phai said. *Thou shalt not violate the sanctity of a working ship*—the most inviolate of the proscriptions. "They'll violate com-mandments all day long, but a proscription? Unthinkable." Except for the violation caused by the tech serfs, of course, but those were only done out of necessity.

"They say that a Greek ship found the remnants of the *Catherine the Great*," Aristeides said. "They think it was the one the *Daedalus* tangled with before the end."

"And?"

"A charnel house. Everyone inside dead."

"How?"

"It looks like they did it to themselves.

Father Phai stopped just before the scaffolding. "Insanity?"

"Murderous insanity."

"Well, maybe they *would* violate a proscription, then."

"That's all I'm saying."

Father Phai twisted sideways to slide past the scaffolding, the metal tub-ing of the structure brushing against his back. Aristeides started a moment later. Father Phai was just uncomfortably sliding past a deacon when a loud crack sounded behind him, like a pneumatic piston firing.

Blood sprayed across the wall in front of him. He looked at the deacon in shock. Blood doused the man. Father Phai couldn't see the wound, but hor-ror dawned on the deacon's face and he screamed.

Father Phai reached out to help him, his movements wooden. Shock? He'd seen blood before, why would he be going into shock? He couldn't quite reach the man, and the deacon pulled back in horror, screaming again.

"Phai!?" Aristeides shouted.

Father Phai turned to his friend. He tried to ask what was going on, but his mouth wouldn't move.

"Phai, you're going to be all right!" Aristeides shouted.

He was going to be all right? He reached up to his face, numb now, and found it sticky with blood. Confused, he reached farther, his fingers sinking into a hole in his forehead, the edges sharp with shattered bone. A hole. In his head? His fingers slid inside, felt slick blood and pulpy matter and he suddenly smelled apricots.

"Phai!" Aristeides screamed.

He slid to the ground. What was going on? He raised his hand again and it thumped against his face. Something was wrong. Something was wrong. Something was wrong. Something was wrong.

Are you there, My child?
Can you hear Me?
I can see you there.
You do not understand.
But you will.
Come to me and everything will be right again, My son.

Dreams of pain and rage. Dreams of loss and horror. Dreams of loneliness. Father Phai awoke, screaming in a hospital bed.

"Father Hephaistos Ganis?"

He stared up into the face of a doctor, awash in blurry light from the window. The room was too brilliantly white to focus. "Aarrgh," he said.

"Don't try to talk. You've been in a terrible accident. The damage was severe."

He reached up for the hole in his head, the urge to stick his fingers inside overwhelming.

"Stop him!"

Strong hands grabbed his arms, but his vision wasn't working right and he couldn't see who they belonged to. He screamed in rage. He was trapped. He started to weep. It was funny. He laughed.

"There has been damage to your frontal lobe. Can you get control of yourself?"

Father Phai spat on the doctor, and his tongue felt weird. He bit it, winced at the pain, but couldn't stop himself from biting it again.

"Nurse," the doctor said.

A slight pain burned in his arm, then drowsiness. Then it all went black.

You're broken, lost, My son.
I am here, but you must be open to Me.
You are alone now.
You will not be alone forever.
Have faith and come unto Me.

"Phai," Aristeides said.

Father Phai opened his eyes to see his friend standing over the hospital bed. He wasn't alone. Thank God. He wasn't alone. He started to weep and laugh at the same time.

He still couldn't focus on more than one thing at a time. The rest of the visual data was there, but he couldn't process it. Still, it was Aristeides. Not alone.

"Phai, they've asked me to speak to you as a priest," Aristeides said. "I'm here as your priest, not your friend, do you understand?"

Father Phai nodded. Not a friend. The laughing stopped, but the crying didn't. Still, he was here.

They'd strapped Father Phai's arms to his bed and put a bite guard in his mouth. Yesterday he had smothered his face in his own pillow because he couldn't stop himself. The vaguest idea became a burning need in his torn brain. The only reassurance was that he could barely remember most of it.

"Phai, they say that you have several problems from the damage. I'm sorry. A piston broke loose and fired through your... well, through you." Aristeides gestured vaguely, but Father Phai knew that something had blown through his head, leaving him alive but terribly broken.

Thou shalt not violate the sanctity of the human form. An accident had broken the proscription, not him. Not him. The tears turned to tears of despair.

"They can fix you, Phai. They've checked. There's a piece of brainware that came back on a salvage ship about a month ago. It's meant to be a database brainmod, but it patches in through the frontal lobe. The side effect from its placement is that it has to replicate all the tasks of the part of your brain that's damaged. They can make you whole, Phai."

Whole. Whole but with a cybernetic implant in his head. A piece of tech sacred because the secrets of making it had been lost centuries ago. But its very presence in his body would be a violation of the proscription on the human form, the worst level of sin. Sacred and profane all at once.

They wanted to make him a tech serf.

"I'm here to counsel you, Phai, but I can't see any choice but one."

Aristeides reached out and took his hand. Father Phai squeezed it back, warmth and joy filling him from the touch, and he laughed around the bite guard.

"I don't see what life you'll have otherwise, Phai."

Father Phai nodded. There was only one choice.

"Is that a yes?"

Thou shalt not violate the sanctity of the human form.

Father Phai started to shake his head, but what would he do like this? What kind of a life could he have if he couldn't control his most destructive impulses? Merciful God, why have you done this to me?

He nodded again.

"Thank you, Phai. I'll tell the doctors."

There is a hole in you.
They think they have filled it.
But they haven't.
They can never fill it.
It can only be filled by Me.
I see you for what you are.
You are a riddle to them, Phai.
But I understand you.
Soon, you will understand Me.

Phai woke up and, for the first time in weeks, he could see clearly.

The hospital room was clean and spartan, but the bed was nice enough. A doctor stood over him in ward robes, clean and brilliant white smart-fabric. The nurses wore more mundane scrubs, probably a paper fabric, of different pastel colors. There were two of them, one big with a wide, friendly face, the other pretty and severe.

"The surgery went well," the doctor said. "The brainware had a calibration feature. It should have integrated itself into your nervous system while you slept. How do you feel?"

The friendly nurse reached over and carefully removed his bite guard. Phai coughed a moment then worked his jaw. He felt... normal.

"Good," he rasped.

The friendly nurse smiled and the severe one just nodded. The doctor winked at him.

"That's great news, Phai."

Phai was a bit startled that the doctor didn't call him "Father," but then again, he wasn't a Father anymore, was he? He wasn't even a full person. And yet he carried in his head irreplaceable tech from before the Collapse.

"Sacred and profane," he whispered.

"What was that, honey?" the friendly nurse asked.

"Nothing," Phai said. "Um, what am I now?"

The doctor didn't give the obvious answer. Everyone in the room would be aware of his new status of less human than human. He looked down at the electronic chart as if he hadn't been the surgeon who'd overseen the installation.

"You are a human recorder," the doctor said.

"What do I record?"

"Everything you take in through your senses. Maybe your emotions as well. The brainmod was probably designed to replace cameras, to record sense-sim and the like."

Sense simulation had been banned since the Collapse, but cyberware like that had just been repurposed. The last several users had probably functioned as aides, lending their masters perfect memory.

"Is there still data in it?"

"No, it was wiped before being turned over."

"How do I use it?"

"You shouldn't have to," the Doctor said. "You'll just have perfect memory now. It might take a bit of adjustment while it acclimates itself to your biological memories. I've heard of people having vivid flashbacks during the breaking-in period."

Phai reached up to touch his head. The piece had replaced a large wedge of his forehead. It didn't fit right, having been sized for a centuries-dead owner.

The friendly nurse handed him a mirror. He examined it. They'd shaved his head but when his hair grew in, he would have a very uneven hairline. The hair might mask the bulging mismatch of skull, though. It looked a little like the right side of his forehead had been replaced with a bulbous metal tumor.

He set the mirror down and looked at the nurses.

The friendly one's face had melted away, leaving bleached bone and bits of desiccated flesh exposed to the air. The pretty one had been burned into a mass of char.

"What's wrong, honey?" the friendly one asked, her tongue black and bulging with maggots.

Phai screamed.

Hushhhhhhh.

Phai couldn't stop screaming until the doctor sedated him again. When he woke in the evening, the friendly nurse was there, the flesh restored to her face. They called the doctor and the man entered with an easy, confident air.

"How are we doing?" the doctor picked up Phai's chart and scrolled through the data.

"The nurses turned into zombies." Phai looked at the nurse sideways. It didn't matter how much his rational mind told him the effect had been in his head.

"I gathered from all the screaming. I warned you that there might be flashbacks."

"I have never had a corpse speak to me before. How could that be a flashback?"

"'Flashback' might be an oversimplification. The mind is a complex thing. You've seen dead bodies before?"

"Only in holos."

"And have you ever seen a zombie in a holo?"

Phai nodded.

The doctor smiled. "It's hard to predict how your brain will react to the cybernetics. We need to be ready for an adjustment period."

There was a slight reticence beneath the surface of the doctor's manner. Phai opened his mouth to call the man on it, and then it hit him. Ah. The doctor didn't know.

It made perfect sense. They hadn't been able to make implants like Phai's for centuries. The doctor dealt with what he had on hand, and they had said this one had been newly salvaged. He probably wasn't even working off his own knowledge. Instead he'd learned the side effects from a tech serf who carried a cybernetics database. Perhaps the same tech serf was able to interface with the medical equipment used to implant the memory aid. The doctor would be little more than a bystander in his own operating theater.

"How long?"

"It will get worse before it gets better. I'd expect a month or more before things start settling out."

"When can I go home?" And where was home now? He was sacred and profane. He didn't know if anything official had been done, but it probably wasn't necessary. He'd been effectively defrocked the moment they attached the first neuron to the implant.

"You can go home now, Phai. Medically, you're fit for discharge."

"And psychologically? Spiritually?"

"Psychologically you are better served by being around others who can relate to your issues." He meant other tech serfs. "Spiritually, you already have a much more solid support system in place than we could provide here."

As he said that Aristeides walked into the room. He'd probably been waiting for the line. He'd always been good at recognizing a cue. "I'm here to take you home, Phai."

"But I'm a tech serf now."

"I know. The Church will take care of you."

They gathered Phai's things and checked him out of the hospital. None of the nurses went through any transformations as they made their way down and into the ground car. Phai settled into the passenger's seat and closed his eyes. A tech serf. What did that leave him with? He'd dedicated his life to the Church, and now, like that, it was all gone.

Aristeides pulled out into traffic and Phai didn't look at to the glittering glass buildings and steel girders, all so much lower tech than the little piece of electronics now turning him from holy man to unhallowed saint.

"You were always a brooder, Phai." A woman's voice, but there wasn't a woman in the car.

"Aristeides?"

"Yeah, Phai?"

"It's starting again."

"What is?"

"This time I'm hearing voices."

"I'm sitting in the back seat, Phai," the woman said.

"The doctor said that this wasn't anything to worry about," Aristeides said.

"I know. I just wanted you to be aware in case I did anything funny."

"I see. Reconcile yourself with the voices in your head, then."

Phai looked into the back seat. She sat there, dark and lovely, wearing the same clothes she'd worn the last day he'd seen her alive, gray slacks and a simple white top. Her hair was back in a tight ponytail and she stared out the window at the passing cars.

"Frona," Phai said.

"You left me out there to die, Phai," she said without looking at him.

"I didn't leave you anywhere."

"It's Frona?" Aristeides asked.

"Yeah."

She said, "Tell Aristeides he turned out all right, even if you didn't."

"She sends her regards," Phai said.

"I don't know how to respond to that," Aristeides said.

"I didn't leave you anywhere, Frona."

"Don't be ridiculous," she said. "You abandoned me for the seminary."

"You left me."

"Because you'd decided that being a priest wasn't good enough. You decided you wanted to be a bishop as well."

"I mean physically," Phai said. "You were the one who left for a border world. We were out of striking distance of the Russians. You were safe where we were."

"You were supposed to stop me," she said. "I had it all worked out in my head. You were supposed to realize that you couldn't live without me. You were supposed to stop me, marry me before becoming ordained. Never be promoted, sure, but happy as a priest with a wife, like most priests."

Phai turned back and looked at the sleek metal bodies of the oncoming traffic. This wasn't real. This wasn't even what Frona would say, if she were a ghost and in the car right now. This is what he *thought* she'd say. This is what he feared in his own head. It was just the implant.

"You're in my head."

"I always got in your head."

"You're just the implant, processing data."

"That's right, Phai," Aristeides said. "You tell that damn brain who's in charge."

"I can't believe you just said that, Phai," a new voice said behind him. "I raised you better than that." He closed his eyes again. He didn't need to look to know it was his mother, dead from cancer all these years.

"Mother, you shouldn't butt in like this."

"You know," Aristeides said, "maybe you shouldn't engage them."

"I taught you to be good to the women in your life, and look what you did. You leave this girl and force her to go out to some godforsaken colony, and look what happens? The Russians probably took turns raping her before she died."

"Mother!"

"Don't worry, Sarra," Frona said, "I died from a gunshot wound. No rapes."

"Of course you'd say that," Sarra said. "You were always trying to spare his feelings."

Phai squeezed his eyes shut and tried not to hear them back there. He would just let it all settle out. In a month, they'd be gone. He'd be alone with his thoughts.

Alone.

Aristeides pulled into the garage of the Church residence and parked. For a time they sat there, listening to the ticking of the cooling engine. Then Phai sighed. "What am I going to do, Ari?"

"You're going to play the hand God gave you. It's what you always do."

Phai got out of the car. A priest and his wife were walking down the aisle of cars. The priest smiled woodenly, but the wife looked away, uncomfortable in the presence of a tech serf.

Phai straightened and entered the residence, essentially a large apartment building. Aristeides walked him to the elevators, and neither dead mother nor dead girlfriend followed him. He started to press the up button, but stopped himself. He didn't live up there anymore.

He pressed down.

"I hear you'll live like a king down there," Aristeides said.

"I just can't come in through the public entrance." Phai's hand rose to touch the smooth metal of the implant.

"That's not how it is."

"That's exactly how it is."

The door opened and Phai looked right into the silver visor of a Russian soldier, some six-and-a-half feet tall in full articulated combat armor. He carried a rifle at the ready, and as the doors cleared he raised it to fire.

Phai spun and pushed, missing Aristeides's chest but knocking him sprawling, clear of the door. He then spun to throw himself the other direction.

But the soldier was gone.

Phai stood there, shaking. Gone. Not real. He'd been thinking of Frona and the Russian had appeared like a boogey monster. He was all right.

Then he heard the choking.

Aristeides had managed to flip onto his knees and one hand, in a crawling posture. He clutched his neck and spit and gasped. Phai had hit him in the throat.

"I'm sorry," Phai said. He had to get out of there. He threw himself into the elevator and pushed the button for the first subbasement. Aristeides. "I'm sorry," he whispered, tears in his eyes as the door closed.

He'd punched his best friend in the throat. He could have killed him. He needed to get a hold of himself. He needed to get lost. He needed to seclude himself until he couldn't hurt anyone again.

The doors opened and a tech serf stood there, as if waiting for the elevator. He had one mechanical arm and a wheezing mechanical leg, too short for his body. A large portion of his skull had been replaced with a blinking, asymmetrical piece of hardware. All the left side.

"Hephaistos Ganis?" the man asked.

"Yes?" Was he real?

"I am Paulus, and God is dead." He gestured around himself. "Welcome to Hell."

Phai stepped tentatively out of the elevator. Real, maybe. That was a little too on-the-nose to be a hallucination. "I don't think you're allowed to talk like that in here."

"Maybe not up there," Paulus said, gesturing toward the ceiling, "But you aren't up there anymore, are you?" He turned and limped away with at rolling, painful-looking gait. "Follow me to your room."

They had lush carpets and indirect lighting. Paulus led him to a door at the end of the hall. "Just call on the intercom if you need me."

"You're leaving?"

"It's been my experience that you won't want to talk to anyone for the first few days."

"Oh."

"The apartments are fully stocked," he said. "If you need to speak to a damned soul, just look around. There's a communal living area, a sort of rec room, and a communal dining hall. After we get used to our lot in life, many of us like to eat and socialize together."

Phai nodded dumbly and opened the door. It had already been keyed to his touch.

Inside he found the nicest apartment he'd ever lived in. Only the richest leather chairs and couches graced the place. Fine art hung on the walls. He stepped in slowly, noticing his entertainment unit on one shelf, the pictures of his mother on a mantel over a fireplace. The carpet all but caressed his feet as he walked. He glimpsed his bedroom and didn't need to go inside to guess that the sheets were the highest thread count and the finest materials.

He turned to the kitchen and found a man standing there in an immaculately tailored silk suit. He was handsome to a fault, with black hair and piercing grey eyes. He nodded in Phai's direction and gestured in welcome, the movement graceful almost to the point of being effeminate.

"Hello, Phai," he said. His voice was beautiful beyond imagining, deep and melodious and ringing with the hint of bells.

"Hello. Are you my next hallucination?"

"No."

"Then who are you?"

"I am the Great Deceiver, Phai," the man purred. "I am the enemy."

"Ah. You are my doubt and fears," Phai said. "I'm starting to process the times I've felt myself losing my faith."

"I wish that were true, Phai," the Deceiver said. "Unfortunately, it isn't. I am real. This is all real. You aren't seeing hallucinations."

"Then what am I seeing?"

"You are seeing the truth." The Deceiver smiled sadly. "Of course, you'll never take my word for it."

Do not listen to them, Phai.
I am here.
They are trying to steer you wrong.
I will not let them if you accept Me.
Open your heart to Me, Phai.
I will bring you home.
Do not deny Me.
Do not lock Me out.

The visions continued throughout the day, but the Deceiver was thankfully absent for most of it. Instead Phai saw a series of ghosts from his past, some off-putting, others friendly, most of them nostalgic. He began to believe that the doctor was right after all. He was just integrating memories. As a priest, it wasn't so much to accept that one of those memories might be his relationship with the Devil, was it?

On the next day, he left his room. The other tech serfs didn't approach him. They would meet his gaze, smile and nod whenever he looked their way, but they didn't make the first move. It was as if they knew he wanted to be alone, and they just wanted him to know that he was welcome whenever he was ready to reach out.

He found a dining hall with gourmet foods ready and hot, along with several selections that looked more like industrial paste... probably for the tech serfs whose cyberware gave them more specialized dietary requirements.

How were tech serfs treated by other organizations? Was it just the Church that acknowledged the divine aspects of their being as well as the profane?

"I don't see why I can't have some," Sarra said, popping into existence beside him. Phai didn't answer, just looked down at the fine white tablecloth and the porcelain china. "Is it because I'm dead? I shouldn't be denied a proper meal just because I'm dead."

This was all exactly to be expected. He just had to muscle through it.

"Seriously, what are you going to deny me next?" his mother asked. She appeared as she had been before she got sick, a slightly matronly forty-year-old. He didn't look at her.

"Are you going to speak to me?"

He needed to occupy his mind. He just needed to get through this. If there were only something to distract him.

He stood. Paulus sat to one side, eating baked capon with Champaign and a side of caviar. Phai walked over to him. "How do we track cyberware?" Phai asked. "As a people, I mean."

"There's a database," Paulus said.

"Is it in..." he gestured to the people around him.

"No, it's just a computer. We have access. All of us need to look sooner or later. Most sooner." He shrugged. "Knowledge is your God now."

Phai ignored the Blasphemy. "Where is it?"

Paulus shrugged and rose from his meal. He led Phai to a room down the hall from the dining room and to a large desk with a comfortable chair. He called up a query. It appeared he had had it ready before Phai asked, and the wall above the desk vanished into a giant view screen as a record displayed.

"The door locks from the inside," Paulus said. "In case you need privacy." He then left.

Phai settled into the chair. In front of him a wall of text started with the serial number of the piece of brainware and a long technical description. He passed links on installation and maintenance and scrolled down to the history.

The first record detailed its manufacture and first recipient: a mild-seeming sim-sense performer who got it installed purely for its practical purposes. This was before the Collapse, when man still valued technology over God. Before the proscriptions.

"His peers were envious," the Deceiver said next to him. Phai looked over to see the man sitting in a simple wooden chair. The chair hadn't been there a moment ago.

"He became a great actor, and not just in pornography. He recorded beaches and sunny days, and languid times with loved ones," the Deceiver said. "We know better than to indulge in such evils now, don't we? God told us so. Or was it the Church?" The Deceiver sighed. "I always confuse the two, don't you?"

Phai ignored him and clicked through the next several records. These would be post-Collapse, but he didn't see the phrase "tech serf" anywhere in there.

"It took a while, didn't it?" the Deceiver asked. "Even after the proscriptions, that implant and others like it were just too valuable to have a lot of religious weight attached to them, good or bad."

Phai flipped through several more records, then checked the data on one. It was after second great Schism. And yet the owner was Russian.

"Oh, he figures it out," the Deceiver said. "This was owned by heretics, wasn't it? First they try to make their Patriarch into another Pope, and then they have the audacity to own the thing that's in your head." He leaned forward, exquisite and graceful. His breath smelled of lilacs. "Can you feel it? Is it dirty inside your head? They owned it, and now you have it. How many heresies has it remembered, and what are we but memory and perception? If it's carried all those blasphemies, doesn't that make it foul? Doesn't that make you foul as well?"

Phai didn't read the next several records as he flipped through. It didn't matter that the Russians had owned it. It was a sacred thing by its very nature. Maybe it had been born from secular ignorance and maybe it had carried countless heretical teachings, but it was a piece of lost technology. It was a manifestation of man's divine need to be more like unto God by creating wonders.

"Rationalize it any way you want," the Deceiver said in a light tone. "I'll just lean back so the lightning bolt doesn't strike me as well."

Phai scrolled down to the last entry. He clicked it.

It had been owned by a tech serf on the Russian ship *Catherine the Great*. Phai paused. Wasn't that the ship that recently destroyed the *Daedalus*? *Thou shalt not violate the sanctity of a working ship.* There was no sin greater than destroying a ship. Had this piece of brainware taken part in that destruction?

No, it seemed that it belonged to an engineer's assistant. A record keeper to a fixer of things, nothing more. The man was assigned to the engines themselves, not even a weapon system.

The record said little about the *Daedalus* itself. It was after the *Daedalus* was destroyed that things become interesting. The record linked to several translated logs recovered from the *Catherine*.

"...*The destruction of the* Daedalus *weighs heavily on the crew. Tempers have risen. I've had to deal out three disciplinary actions today alone...*" A distinguished, gentlemanly man. Looked like a captain's log. Recorded by the owner of the implant, or just included with the salvage report? He couldn't tell. He scrolled to another.

This man looked more haggard. He had a blue-collar look about him, all rough edges and folksy charm. Chief engineer? "...*Someone adjusted my settings on the engines. I know damn well who, too. It was that goddamn Dima. First he tries to tell me he knows the capabilities of the converters better than I do, then he changes the settings behind my back. I'll have the goat flogged...*"

They didn't flog people in the Russian navy, did they? Phai had heard plenty of bad things about the Russians, but that was just a little too conveniently cruel. It had to be hyperbole.

The next was from the engineer again. His hair was in disarray, his face red. "...*Some of the boys decided to give me a hand. We cornered Dima in a storeroom and gave him a beating he won't soon forget. The bastard lost control of his bladder. It was wondrous...*"

Phai stopped, staring at the screen. They did what? Russian or not, that didn't sound like proper discipline.

"Did you know that *Catherine* was tracking the *Daedalus* because of atrocities it had been committing on the border?" the Deceiver said beside him. Phai had heard rumors, of course. Otherwise the Deceiver wouldn't know about it. "The ship went mad, they say. And now the *Catherine*."

Phai skipped over the other logs to the last one from the engineer. With a trembling hand, he triggered it.

The man looked happy, but his eyes were a bit wild and his hair wilder still. *"...That will teach Dima to bring me up on charges. I got him. I got him good."* The man wiped his mouth and his hand dripped blood, left a smear across his mouth as it passed. He smiled, the blood running in the crevices between his teeth. *"I got him good."* The engineer's eyes met his.

"And I'm coming for you next, Phai."

Phai leapt backward, tipping the chair and falling to the floor. He stood up, but the screen had gone dark now. His breath came in pants. It was just the device. This was normal. Normal.

"Normal for a ship to go crazy after hunting down another ship that went crazy?" the Deceiver asked. "Normal for a ship to be so wrapped in sin that someone blew it up? You don't think that's a coincidence, do you? The greatest sin committable, and two mad ships surrounding it? What do you think is happening here, Phai?"

Phai met the Deceiver's eyes for the first time. "Because I'll tell you, Phai. There are things in the universe that you can't comprehend. Even a touch of them can drive a man mad."

The Deceiver stood, reached out with one hand. He cocked his head to one side and smiled invitingly. "Ask me what I am, Phai. Ask me what all of this means."

Phai turned and fled the room. The Deceiver laughed behind him.

This isn't the end, Phai.
This isn't your destruction.
Trust in Me.

Aristeides took Phai back to the hospital and after several frantic demands, they admitted him for an examination. The doctor smiled when he entered, but he didn't meet Phai's eyes. The nurse, a matronly woman, didn't meet his eyes either. She took his readings diffidently, as if touching him was distasteful.

"Everything is looking well," the doctor said.

"These aren't simple flashbacks," Phai said. "I think I'm being affected by what happened to the implant before."

The doctor looked relieved. "You think the memory wipe wasn't complete? I'll have someone look at that." Ah. The doctor was going to turn him over to another tech serf. No wonder he looked relieved. Phai had never felt so alone with other people before.

But it wasn't *other* people, was it? He was a tech serf now, not a person himself. He was half holy relic, half corrupted spirit.

The doctor left and a tech serf came for him eventually, a creature whose entire lower body had been replaced by something like a robotic wheelchair. The creature looked perfectly human from the waist up, a plain, affable man of indeterminate age with dark hair, but looks could be deceiving, couldn't they?

"Come with me," the tech serf said.

The creature led him past where Aristeides waited and into an elevator. They got off on a lower floor and entered a lab. The tech serf hooked several sensors to the side of his head and began examining the readings.

"Has the memory kicked in yet?" the tech serf asked.

"I don't think I'm remembering things better than normal."

"You'd know if you were," the creature said. "The thing is working over-time now. I can see it pegged on all processes."

"Is that normal?"

"I would expect so. It has to build its file structure and that's unique for every brain. It's starting with your own memories. That's probably about 2.5 petabytes of data."

"And what's on there now?"

"A few terabytes," the tech serf said, and then pushed back. "It looks like the wipe was complete. All this data is newly written and it's all in the new file structure."

"You're saying I'm not remembering things from the former owner?"

"Each brain in unique. You *couldn't* read the memories of another person. Not coherently, at any rate."

"This isn't exactly coherent."

The tech serf shrugged. "All I'm seeing here are your own memories."

"All right."

The diagnostics took a bit more time, but eventually the tech serf announced that everything was working perfectly. Phai left the room woodenly, found Aristeides and let his friend herd him back out into the car.

They drove back in silence, and no apparitions bothered him. There was a third presence in the car, however. It was a palpable discomfort radiating from his friend. No, his former friend. A human couldn't be friends with a *thing*, after all.

Phai was still alone.

You are not alone, Phai.
You will never be alone.
All you have to do is accept Me into your heart.

That night Phai fled to the city and found wicked clubs with loud pulsing music. The nice ones wouldn't let him in, so he went to the dives frequented by other tech serfs and perverts with strange technical fetishes. He hid in the back and staved off the advances of loose women while his hallucinations tried and failed to talk to him over the ear-rupturing sound. That was his real purpose here. If he was going to be alone, he'd be alone without his madness.

That night he dreamt of knives and cutting and blood. In his dreams he drank of the blood and laughed.

He woke up uncomfortable and sticky in the bed. He lay there for a moment, confused and disoriented. Why was he sticky? They hadn't been those sort of dreams.

He raised his hand, but in his underground bedroom it was dark even in the midmorning. He waved at the light and it came on, illuminating shining red drops of blood as they shook loose of his hand.

Phai grunted in surprise, tried to shift in his bed, found the entire thing tacky, and then fell out onto the floor in a confused bundle. He slowly lifted his head over the edge of the bed.

The bed was a field of red and maroon. In the center lay a glistening chef's knife, the blood forming a perfect, reflective surface on the blade.

This wasn't happening. This wasn't real. He hadn't done anything. Someone was setting him up. This was all a trick. The hallucinations, everything. A trick. A trick.

But no body. He looked in every room. No body. Whatever had happened, had it happened somewhere else? Was there a body out there, somewhere, with his name on it?

And why couldn't he remember? Had he been in some sort of fugue, or was the processing of the implant actually *hurting* him at the moment?

"Do you know what caused the damage to your brain?" the Deceiver said from one corner, seemingly oblivious to his plight. "It was another piece of cyberware. A piston ruptured on the tech serf you were passing, blew through your head like a bullet. A tech serf made you a tech serf."

Phai ignored the man. He had to clean this up. He couldn't clean it up. He had to.

Blood soaked into the sheets of the bed and he'd smeared it on the carpet when he'd landed. It might be possible. He rushed to the bathroom, tore off his clothes and climbed into the shower.

So much blood. There was just so much blood. It swirled into the drain and streaked in the water running down his body. The water ran red, then pink. He washed his hair and it turned red again. Finally, everything ran clear.

"Is it possible for an implant to be haunted?" His mother's voice carried in through the shower curtain. He climbed out and ignored Sarra sitting there on the toilet. She was emaciated today, as she had been during the last days of the cancer.

"And if it can be haunted," she mused, "what does it mean that it's inside your head? Does that mean that there's a ghost inside you? How is that different from being possessed?"

He moved out into the bedroom. The smears on the carpet might be treatable. He could get rid of the bed linens, but the mattress? He pulled up the sheets. The mattress was badly stained. He stripped it, pulled several garbage bags from the kitchen and carried the mattress to the bathroom.

There he cleaned it as best he could and then laid out the garbage bags on the box spring. He laid a blanket over that to help sop up the mess, then placed the mattress upside down on top. With luck the remaining blood would be drawn into the blanket or would dry. He could change things out every day or so.

"You have to be reasonable," Frona said behind him. He spun to look at her. Now he had to deal with both of them. "You still look good, by the way," she said. He looked down and realized he was still naked.

"Shut up."

"Think this through," she said. "Slow down. You're reacting. You need to be acting."

"On the other hand," the Deceiver said, "people respond badly to murder. Maybe a little reacting isn't out of line."

He needed to focus. He could deal with this. If he kept his head, everything would be all right. Phai glowered at them and grabbed a basin with soapy water and a brush he then knelt and began scrubbing up the blood. It came up better than he could have hoped.

"Space age fabrics," the Deceiver said. "They've made my work so much easier."

Finally he stood. It looked good. It would have to do. He scooped up the bloody linens, the bloody clothes, and the knife and stowed them all in a garbage bag. The apartments had an incinerator shoot in the hall. That would have to do.

Clothes.

He walked over to the closet. "You're dressing?" Frona asked. "I'm pouting. Look at me. You'll see I'm pouting if you look."

He opened the closet door.

The body lay there, wrapped in a bloody sheet. The gorge rose in Phai's throat. His knees shook. He reached out and grabbed the frame. A body.

"Did I forget to warn you about the closet?" the Deceiver said.

A body. How was he going to get rid of a body? Merciful savior, a body. He fell to his knees. Tears burned in his eyes, and he couldn't see. A body. It was over. A body.

"Reason," Frona said. "Think."

She was right. He could do this. He could get rid of a body. Lord in heaven, he had to. A plan started to form. He had a tub. He had knives. He could do this.

He reached out, hand trembling, and pulled back the sheet. It fell away from a smooth helmet, the inside of the visor smeared in blood. He pulled it back farther. Body armor. A soldier?

"You can turn yourself in," his mother had come out of the bathroom now. "You can throw yourself on their mercy."

"Because a tech serf is going to get a fair trial," the Deceiver said.

"Think it through," Frona said.

"She's leading you wrong," the Deceiver said. "They both are."

This didn't add up. He looked at the armor. Russian insignia. How would a Russian get here? They couldn't.

They couldn't.

He turned slowly, his gaze falling on the Deceiver. The beautiful man floated to his feet, clapping slowly. "Ah. Now that was a show, wasn't it?"

"I told you to think," Frona said.

It was all in his head. All of this, in his head. He collapsed to the floor, tears streaming down his cheeks. It was all in his head. He hadn't killed anyone. Oh God, he hadn't hurt anyone.

"Hello, Phai."

Phai looked up. A small boy, perhaps seven years old, stood before him, all in white. His hair was golden and his cheeks rosy, his eyes piercing blue. Phai didn't think he'd ever seen him before.

"I don't know who you're supposed to be."

"My name is Thanles, Phai," the boy said.

"Do I know you?"

"Do you?"

"Why are you in my head?"

"Perhaps you needed me. Perhaps I've been trying to talk to you all along and you finally let me in."

"I need the hallucinations to stop."

"Do you?" Thanles asked. "Or do you need to overcome them?"

"I don't know," Phai said. His heart lifted. Was it just the relief, or something else?

"I think that when you've figured that out, you'll know how to go forward."

"Are these hallucinations or are they real?"

"You mean real ghosts?" the boy said with a smile. "Real supernatural things?"

"Yes."

"And if I told you the answer to that," Thanles said, "Wouldn't you be a fool to believe me? Me being one of those hallucinations and all that?"

Phai smiled. He hadn't smiled since the accident, but the boy just pulled it out of him. "I guess so."

"Stay the course, Phai." The boy reached down and cupped his cheek. "Do you believe in God?"

"I do."

"Well that's good," the child said, "because I personally think He believes in you." A knock sounded. "Someone's at the door. I'll be on my way."

"The others never left because I had visitors."

"I guess I'm more polite," the boy said. "My mother always told me not to overstay my welcome." He started for the kitchen, but turned. "Don't lose your way, Phai. You've already strayed far."

Phai turned to the door, confident the boy wouldn't be there when he looked back. The knock came again and Phai grabbed his robe from the couch and belted it on. "Coming!"

He opened the door and saw Paulus standing there. The man smiled at him weakly. "May I come in?"

Phai almost glanced back at the apartment, but anything he saw there would surely be a hallucination. "Sure," Phai said, stepping back.

Paulus entered the room and Phai closed the door behind him. Paulus's eyes scanned the room, not seeming to notice the garbage bag on the living room floor or the stripped bed through open bedroom door. What did the room really look like? Had Phai stripped the bed and put the clean sheets in the bag, or did the room look like he'd just woken up?

"You slept in," Paulus said. "I didn't want to wake you."

"Yeah," Phai said. "Sleep can be pivotal, that's for sure."

"I know that losing everything can be difficult," Paulus said.

"I haven't lost everything," Phai said. "I still have my faith."

Paulus looked at him out of the corner of his eye. "Do you, now?"

"Yes."

"Well, some come around more slowly than others," Paulus shrugged. "Anyway, I saw the light through your peephole."

"I've been up about an hour," Phai said. "Maybe more?"

"I just wanted to be the first to talk to you."

"About what?"

"One of the women disappeared last night. I'm sure it's nothing, but I wanted to talk to you first. New tech serfs often overreact to these things. She most likely just left and slept elsewhere. You met her. Frona."

Frona. The name made Phai's stomach lurch. "There was someone here named Frona?"

"Yeah, I introduced you to her yesterday. You don't remember?"

"When?"

"When you came in last night. She and I were in the common room."

Had he met someone last night? He couldn't remember anything after he left the club. And Frona? How could he forget meeting someone with the same name as his dead girlfriend? He looked at the chair where his Frona had been sitting minutes before.

"Wait," Phai said. "She disappeared?"

"He knows." The Deceiver had reappeared in his chair.

Paulus could see Phai's bedroom clearly from where he stood. He seemed to be staring at the closet, his head cocked to one side. "Are you all right?" Phai asked.

Paulus took a step toward the bedroom. Another. "Anyway, I just wanted to be the one who told you." Was the closet door open or shut?

"Well thank you," Phai said.

"You're going to have to deal with this," the Deceiver said.

Paulus stepped into the doorway now. He definitely stared at the closet, as if he couldn't take his eyes of it.

"If you wait much longer, he's going to realize you're standing behind him," the Deceiver said.

Phai stepped forward and his foot bumped the garbage bag. He stared down at it.

"You don't have much time."

He slowly knelt.

"You worked it out in your head. You have the whole procedure down. The tub. The electric knife. The incinerator. All of it."

He opened the bag. Reached inside.

"There was no one else in the hall when you opened the door," the Deceiver said.

The knife was there.

"The room is soundproof."

He pulled it out.

"They might even think he ran off with her."

The blade glistened in the light.

"Think about it. She disappears. He slinks out the next day. You aren't the suspect here."

He rose. Paulus had stepped out of sight. Phai slid into the room, turned to the closet.

The door hung open. The bloody sheet was still there, but now it wrapped around the corpse of a naked woman, her eyes open, pleading and full of terror, her mouth open in a scream.

Paulus stared at the body for another beat, and then seemed to remember Phai. He spun, his face contorting with rage.

Phai struck instinctively. The blade descended, hacking into his neck, cutting down between the bones of the shoulder. Paulus gasped and Phai pulled the blade up, slick with blood and hydraulic fluid.

Paulus squeaked, his eyes rolling, his mouth working. Phai struck again, this time clipping the carotid. Paulus reached up to staunch the flow, his eyes fading. He fell to his knees, looking up at Phai in horror. Phai stared back, cold and afraid and exhilarated all at the same time.

"Well, you're committed now, aren't you?" the Deceiver said.

The knife fell and rose and fell.

You are committed now.
You denied them and went your own way.
You are one of them.
You have come to Me.
You have realized the truth.
You have slain the harlot.
You have slain the blasphemer.
You are reborn.
You stand at the precipice of greatness.

They took your priesthood.
They took your manhood.
They took your pride.
But they cannot take your faith.
Can they?

Phai finished packing the last of the bags, the body parts strangely light now that he'd squeezed most of the blood out of them. He straightened, his back aching.

"You always were a focused boy," his mother said behind him. He glanced at her but just shrugged. There wasn't anything to say. "You killed the woman and that horrible man. You can dispose of the bodies tonight, after everyone's asleep. I didn't think it would go like this, but I can see why you did it. I'm so proud of you."

Phai finished cleaning himself up in the sink and then walked out into the bedroom. He began to dress.

"Did you kill her?" Frona asked from the corner. His Frona. He looked at her but couldn't meet her eyes. "Or did you kill me? Am I the whore? Is it because...? You weren't a priest back when I knew you. You were just Phai."

He turned from her and stepped back into the living room. The Deceiver sat in the chair. He smiled sadly.

"I never said you hadn't killed. I said everything but, and I warned you. You never should have let him in."

"You did this to me," Phai said.

"Yes." The Deceiver's voice was bitter with sarcasm. "I made you spiral into despair. I made you kill a girl that reminded you of your dirty past. I made you kill the man who discovered you. I did all of that."

Phai turned from him, growling. "I can make it right. I'll get rid of the bodies. I'll lock myself in here. I won't come out until this is over. I can still come back from this." He closed his eyes, squeezing out a tear. It wasn't too late.

"Do you know my deepest, darkest secret, Phai?" the Deceiver asked.

"What?"

"I will never lie. I *can* never lie."

"That why they call you the Deceiver?"

"That's why they chose me, so many millennia ago. The gods came and we trembled. They needed someone to communicate with them, but the old gods killed anyone who lied. And so they chose me." The Deceiver looked down at his lap, sank in on himself. "They chose simple Lucifer, because I never lied."

Phai turned from him, walked into the Kitchen. The knife sat there, in its holder where it belonged, cleaned and scrubbed. Phai reached out and touched it, then drew his hand back.

None of this was real. He hadn't done any of it. He'd wake up tomorrow and realize that this was just another layer of delusion. He'd get out the other side. He'd make it through this.

"I met them and I changed." The Deceiver's voice drifted in from the other room. "They took me and they opened my mind and they poured their intelligence into it and I stopped being human, but they didn't let me go mad. That would have been a mercy, and they didn't care. They don't care about any of us. I was useful to them, so they let me live."

Phai pressed his hands on the counter. It was smooth and cool. He should feel something about this. He sank to his knees and rested his forehead against the cool surface. He was useful to them, so they let him live.

"I came back. I was their emissary. You called me the Deceiver because, while I told the truth, it was always the truth you couldn't accept. And so I am who I am. I speak and I enter your minds and you do things. They feed off that, some of them. Like they fed off the *Daedalus* and the *Catherine the Great*. They live off of our rage and our lust and our hate. But they don't hate or lust. They barely understand us. That's how far above us they are."

Phai shook there. Nothing inside. He should feel fear or anger. They had taken away his injury and turned him into this, and now he was just empty. None of this could be real. The man was the Deceiver. Nothing he said could be trusted. Phai's bottom lip started to quiver.

Someone else had done these things. They'd taken over his body. They'd acted through him. He was just a vessel. An emissary.

Or the thing in his head was.

"Don't you understand, Phai?" the Deceiver whispered, but the sound carried. Inside his head. "Don't you understand that *you* aren't the one who needs saving?"

Satan himself sat in the next room, and Phai almost felt pity. Was this the universe they lived in? A place where even the greatest evil of all time was nothing more than a broken toy?

Or was this just one more deceit?

Phai rose. He pushed himself off the counter and walked out into the living room. He looked at the Deceiver and the Deceiver looked back.

"Is there a God?" Phai asked.

The Deceiver looked up, tears in his eyes. "I don't know. I don't think so. If there was, would I be this?" He looked away.

Phai sank into a chair. He stared across the room at the Deceiver, who looked off in the distance. Phai couldn't deny it. He felt the truth. The Deceiver could not lie. The universe did not care. God was dead.

Worse, he'd never existed.

> *You are Phai.*
> *You were the father.*
> *Now you are the outcast.*

I am the Great Deceiver.
I was the Morningstar.
Now I am lost.
There is a truth out there.
I have only told you some of it.
If I told you the rest there would be nothing left of you.
So I protect you.
You are Phai.
You are what I would have been, had I not been given to them.

Phai looked into the Deceiver's eyes, and he saw a man as lost as he was. He looked into the Deceiver's heart and he saw a man broken and cast aside. He looked into the Deceiver's soul and saw a frightened child.

He wasn't alone. He'd left Frona and she'd been killed. His mother had left him. God had forsaken him. His own brain betrayed him.

But he wasn't alone.

"I understand now," Phai said.

"Do you?"

Phai smiled. "I understand that I don't understand. I understand that you don't understand either."

"We are cast adrift."

"Together."

"Do not listen to him, Phai." The boy suddenly stood in the corner, his clothes so white they almost glowed.

"Who are you?" Phai asked.

"I'm here to bring you back."

"He wants you to turn yourself in, Phai," the Deceiver said.

"I do," Thanles said.

"He wants you to give yourself over to them."

"I want you to give yourself over to me," the boy said.

"He wants to take me from you, Phai." The Deceiver's voice grew very quiet. "He wants to take you from me."

"It is not too late, Phai," the boy said.

"He wants you to give up on everything. He wants you to live the rest of your life in a psychiatric prison."

"I want you to embrace your sins," Thanles said, "and come out the other side cleansed."

"Stay with me, Phai," the Deceiver said.

"Come with me."

"If you stay with me, you'll never be alone again. *I'll* never be alone."

"You aren't alone," Thanles said.

"I *need* you, Phai."

"You were never alone, Phai."

"And there, you see his lies," the Deceiver said.

Phai stood, and looked for some connection to this boy inside himself, but he found none. The child was foreign to him. He didn't know him in his head or his heart. He turned and left the living room.

"Phai. Come back to me, Phai. Embrace the truth."

Phai came back out with the knife. "I know the truth," he said.

The boy lifted his hands and his palms were bloody. Phai turned to the door. "They lie."

"Who lies?" the Deceiver said.

"Everyone."

"What do they lie about, Phai?"

"They speak of God and salvation. They said that I wasn't alone."

"And what is the truth?"

"The truth is that there's only us. You and I."

"We'll never be alone again, Phai."

And suddenly it was as if a door opened up in Phai's mind. He could remember things that, a moment ago, he hadn't remembered even glancing at. The directory of the apartments, the wall-mounted maps, the faces of the people going in and out of apartment doors. Patterns and schedules and routes of escape.

Phai opened the door to his apartment. Aristeides stood there, one hand poised for knocking. He looked up at Phai, startled, then smiled. "Phai! You look better!"

"That's Father Phai to you," Phai said and brought the knife down, tearing muscle and tendon. Aristeides screamed and Phai brought the knife down again. And again.

Phai remembered police response times and likely routes to the apartment. He remembered every news article on crime he'd ever read. He remembered documentaries on forensics and police procedure. Piece by piece it all fell into place. He could see it all, mapped out, before him.

And was there something else? Deep down, he felt other memories, as if he could still access the memories of the man who'd possessed the implant before. It was as if he instinctively grasped all the logistics, the glory, and the delicious hate of killing. No, that would be impossible, because the implant had been wiped.

And this was more than the implant should have been able to do, wasn't it? His brain hadn't actually contained all that information, just waiting to be sorted. No. This was more than technology. This was apotheosis.

They thought they knew God. They were wrong.

Phai was the only God who mattered.

PLAGUE SHIP

STEVEN L. PECK

To Our Most Beloved and Learned Archivist:

Find herewith two separate records that I have interlaced together into one account, ordered by inferred chronology. In italics, I have placed a stylized record pulled from the dendrite memory pattern reconstruction of a perished human found floating in deep space. I am aware of your interest in biologicals and believe you will find this account of particular merit. The male subject was located during a scan for carbon anomalies in the interstitial spaces of galactic cluster Y899JJL. At 3134.73 lightyears' distance from the subject, the additional accompanying text recorded by this man in an active vocal log was found broadcast among the chatter of a transmission sent with a simple light-speed photonic wave device common to the period for transmitting digital signals, thus confirming exactly how long ago the man was set adrift. The brain pattern reconstruction and the audio log the man produced were integrated to reconstruct this text, which gives the circumstances of his death. I send this to you because of the details of the ship recorded herein. Note also that the vessel described herein has not been found, despite an extensive search. The danger revealed in this account may occasion your Excellency's attention.

I am your fervent servant,
K

Textual reconstruction from dendrite architecture 1
A thousand worlds beckon me into the darkness. I am no stranger to the silences between the stars, and in them I find my animation. My ship, and dare I say companion, Keva—that indomitable spacefaring beast whose form and intelligence has evolved into a universe-jumping vessel—knows the tides and winds framing the fabric of the universe. He steers a seasoned course in search of rare treasure found in places sequestered in realms that cannot even be

pointed to from our dimensions. Rumors of those faraway lands are hard to come by and the search is long and often fruitless. Today, however, luck finds us.

* Digital voice log broadcast A *

"I've got a hit."

It's been a while. My fishnetter, Robin, smiles up at me from the console. As always, she is wearing gold jeans and a red-dirt t-shirt advertising a mountain bike rental company in Moab, Earth. Her eyes are shining and she motions to her screen with a glance. Her kid is standing beside her, smiling. He's not suppose to be on the bridge, but Robin insists and frankly I don't care.

I can see on her display a chaotic splash of nearly numberless dots forming a spiderweb of networked galaxy-like projections.

"Age?" I can hardly speak. I'm surprised to see my hands are shaking. It looks like a hit.

"Based on expansion and the physics, maybe twelve billion." She is grinning fiercely. I know the expression. She's crewed for me for seven years, and that bright-eyed look means business. It means good fortune.

She turns back to the display.

"Physics?" I ask, still a little cautious. Not ready to abandon my pessimism.

"On the edge, but full in. Not like anything I've seen, so likely some treasures. Gravity equivalent looks about like ours and they have enough subatomics to produce an abundant set of chemicals. I'm thinking life-rich. Given the age, likely some intelligence—civilizations too—probably even a few multiverse jumpers."

"We'll need to avoid them," I state unnecessarily. Everyone knows we don't want someone who can follow us home. Robin lets out a grunt suggesting *obviously* and starts to say something, but cuts it short. We've all been on edge, but the mood is starting to lighten up fast—no sense falling into patterns of conflict.

"Keva?" She dutifully asks to follow protocols, but is already closing her eyes, sending the message from her internal neuroset.

The sentient ship responds, "Yes, Robin."

"Start calibration protocols. This looks like it might be a hit."

"Aye," The ship answers.

"Relax the protocols, Keva," I say. This could be a strike and I don't want to be too conservative. I invented the rules; I can break them.

The ship brings up a schematic on the universe we just found. Our eyes are focused for a likely place to hunt. I tell the crew of about one hundred and twenty families to prepare for a descent, batten down the hatches and all that. This is good news.

Dendrite reconstruction 2

We are hunting on the forward edge of nowhere. It's quieter out here. Less noise. Less distraction. A tiny smudge of light, just a fuzzy pinprick really, can be detected visually from the aft observation lounge. That's our seventeen-billion-year-old universe. Seen from this far away it is only a stripling—maybe two billion years old.

Like the early Phoenicians who would never sail out of sight of land, we keep it in view so we can find our way home. We come out here because we need the calm seas to troll for treasure. We need to escape the staticky, noisy space near stars, the roar in the midst of galaxies full of licking waves, dense forces, fields of such variety that it clogs your sensors with its busyness: magnetic, light, gamma- and x-rays, dark matter, gravity—an endless array of presences that can be detected almost anywhere. Even the great voids that honeycomb the universe, where galaxies are rare, are too cacophonous for the quiet we need.

It's different out here. Here in the primal emptiness beyond the edge there is silence. There are tiny fields, barely detectable, leaking from a universe so far away as to be but a whisper in this darkness. But care is needed. There are terrifying stories. Ships whose crews popped into far-space. The nowherelands so deep in the matrix of the multiverse that there is nothing on which to fix a heading. Without any sense of how to get back, they are forever lost in a nothingness vast and unforgiving, for by any measure the 'great all' is mostly empty. To think about it too deeply pummels one into disequilibrium and vertigo.

* Digital voice log broadcast B *

Robin has established a ping—among the universes she is scanning most are saturated with physics so different from ours that to pop into them would mean instant annihilation. But it looks like she's discovered a universe with a physics we can enter. Now it's up to our ship Keva to pinpoint an attack site. He is manipulating the dots representing individual likely sites on the display. Though no universe we find will have galaxies exactly like ours, the system is set to identify equivalents. As I explain to each new crewmember, in every universe there are structures that cluster energy like stars do in ours. By convention they are called stars*, galaxies* and star clusters*, and planetary systems*. But because another universe's physics can be vastly different from ours, do not fall into the temptation of thinking a star and a star* look or act the same. True, they cluster energy in their respective universes, but they can be very different.

I'm watching what Keva is doing on the monitor. He highlights a dot, expanding it into a galaxy* made of the different physics in that universe, but still playing the apparent role of a galaxy there, e.g., clustering units of energy reattribution like the clusters of our stars. Keva is bringing them up into focus, analyzing, rejecting, finding another, rejecting, finding another. Ah, there's one he likes jumping onto the screen. He works so fast I catch only a glimpse of his selections, like the occasional ace or king that sticks out in your mind while watching someone shuffle a deck of cards. He finds something in a galaxy* that attracts his attention and he starts honing in on particular star* clusters. He is soon pulling up planetary* systems with dazzling rapidity.

What does an intelligence like Keva think? What is time like for such a consciousness? It is said he has the brainpower of ten thousand humans, with speeds and memory that make our processing power an abacus by comparison. What is he? A ship, certainly. Humans made his ancestors. We developed the first bioships and their AIs. But then his ancestors evolved, breeding more and more distantly from the human type we created. He is part of a new sentient upwelling that someday will leave humans far behind. But not yet. At least for now I am his captain.

"Here," he says through the interface. On the display is an oddly shaped planet*; it swirls with cloud-like things and has some sort of liquid equivalent. Or to speak in the vernacular—it's got air* and water*, with the reminder that whatever that water* is, it is not H_2O, because there is not going to be any H or O down there, but it acts like a universal solvent in their physics.

Keva continues, "I've pulled up their broadcasts from the foamy knots. It's a pre-subquantum technology. Nothing but a few local solar system colonies. They couldn't reach their closest stars without a long journey, so they're likely isolated. They have no one they can call for help, and should have some worthy treasure." He then adds in his strange laugh, "Fine booty. Cap'n. Fine booty."

"Take 'er down," I say in the voice of a pirate.

Dendrite reconstruction 3

Down. Why is smaller 'down?' Why when we descend into the fragments and filaments of existence is it not called 'in?' We squish, we transform, we plummet, we take our physics along with us and we shrink past the soon gigantic bosons and leptons, our horizon fills with spaces that make Planck distances look like light-years. And then, when we are way, way, way down to basement floors nearly unreachable, we look up with our fine-tuned instruments and see other places. One of which we have carefully connected with the thinnest of filaments to guide our path. Keva points his body toward that point of meaning, one among many universes that shine like ancient stars ("all I ask is a tall raiding ship and a universe to steer her by"). We are tugged toward the one we've targeted and up, up, up we ascend until, pop, we are there. A somewhere else. We've left a trail, of course, to plot our course back home.

* Digital voice log broadcast C *

They hit us with energy* weapons as soon as we appear. You don't make it long in a Darwinian struggle for existence and not know that someone apparently ahead of you in the game of evolution got there by being a survivor. Resources are scarce and everyone wants them. "Red in tooth and claw," as Tennyson said. Hence our welcome is appropriately one of seething conflict. I remember learning in History 101 how disastrous Earth's first contacts with alien races went because we were slow to pull the trigger. These folks are not making that mistake.

"Report." When jumping into a new physics you never know what's going to happen. Not for sure, anyway. We take our universe with us. Our ship, shields, and weapons are all based on our quantum signatures. Robin said that it looked like the parameter values of this universe were stable enough we should have about three hours before it starts to corrupt our bubble fields. And now with energy weapons opening up, I hope we aren't seeing one of those cases where Robin is wrong.

My engineer Tibble has joined us and he and Keva are analyzing the attack.

"What's happening, people?" I'm trying to keep my voice even. Still no one answers and they are scrambling, their lips are slightly moving so I know they are talking on another neurochannel.

Finally, Keva speaks. "Sorry Cap'n. It wasn't the energy weapons that were giving us a problem; those energy strikes were passing through us like a neutrino through balsawood. But one of their ships was firing projectiles and the matter-to-shield contact was down-spinning our bubble."

"Are we good?"

"We're good. Now."

Dendrite reconstruction 4

The physics of this place produces lustrous orbs of breathtaking splendor. The stars*, or, bundles of energy redistribution, are not round as in our universe but octahedron-shaped, and they undulate rather than rotate—large, small, large, small. A dance step, strangely familiar in its unexpected motions, because it resembles breathing, drawing breath. Inhale. Exhale. Inhale. Exhale. So different from the stars back home, yet recognizable in species or type in the way they hang in the sky, glowing, forming clusters, providing energy to similarly shaped planets, dancing to rhythms found in any universe, but manifesting morphology according to different laws, other ways of taking and redistributing what passes for energy here. How wondrous is the cosmos. How magnificent existence!

* Digital voice log broadcast D *

"What we got?"

Robin's face is set in that look of concentration I know so well. Her hair, gene-dyed blue, has fallen over her face. Moisture is starting to ring her t-shirt around her neck and under her arms, and she dries her hands over her gold jeans. Her mouth is just a sliver as she presses her lips together hard. She is stressed and she reeks of it. She is hovering over the scan report. She starts talking to herself, "Big space station there... the metal alloy is too light... looks like it will have only a half-life of a few hours in our universe—all the ships attacking us are of the same junk. No go."

"What's on the surface?" I ask, not masking a growing panicky despair. "Any large buildings? A junkyard? What we got?" If the big spaceships and ports are useless, what hope is there?

She is silent a while. Now we are all waiting for her. Everyone is holding their breath. This is the moment. The payoff or the bust. The mother load or a skunk. A chest of treasure or an empty box of seaweed.

We look for life forms when we enter a new universe because they've done the mining for us. Civilized life tends to take its resources and concentrate them into bundles that are easy to grab, things like buildings and spaceships. But what if this place just has nothing we can use? I look at the large monitor fronting the Situation Room. Some little spacefaring creatures are out there hammering us with all they've got. A few are kamikazing the ship. It's all to little effect. They can't touch us. We are made of different stuff, and unlike us they lack the capacity to readjust to our physics. Our laws of motion are not theirs. Our nomological trappings completely confuse and defeat them. They will talk about this raid for a long time, I'll wager.

Dendrite reconstruction 5

Life is easy to find. It's noisy. Active. It makes its presence felt. It fills its local space with chatter, and that chatter filters down to quantum frequencies, and those frequencies tell us where to go to take their metal, metal that in our universe might do wondrous things. Intelligent life often processes metals from rocky embeddings. They pull it out. Refine it. Purify it. Make it ripe for the taking. Sometimes when pulled into our universe, the metal becomes a dull and useless thing, an invisible blob through which light and matter both pass without intercourse. Then it is good for nothing and we put it somewhere where it can decay in peace. But we have found treasures. Two years ago we brought back a metal which, when excited by magnetic fields, fractured light into dancing rainbows that swirled in hard-edged geometric patterns, squares, triangles, hexagons. Artisans fashioned the malleable metal into vases, bowls and sculptures of such beauty as to leave you lost, staring for hours at the show unfolding on its surface. Six years ago we brought back a metal with a hardness that made diamonds seem as soft as cheese. Not even rosy-tipped lancers could cut it, but it could be shattered like glass under the right pressures, applied just so. These fragments could be assembled as plating for a personal combat armor that resisted most projectile and energy weapons. We made a fortune selling it to the Crescent Moon Syndicate. It is always a wonderful surprise to find what we have captured from these nowhere places, these places tucked into wonderlands so far from our home that distances mean nothing except in terms of infinities chasing infinities.

* Digital voice log broadcast E *

Robin suddenly bubbles with excitement. "Look there." She zooms her display in on a surface item resting on their planet's* ocean. A great war craft, a battleship like an olden-day navy vessel rides what waves are heaving below.

"Keva?"

"Half-life—two million years. One of the more stable metals we've seen. Nothing like the light stuff used in their spaceships. I'm guessing it will give us about 200,000 tons back home."

I don't need to say anything; Tibble is already maneuvering our craft to hover over it. If it turns out to be interesting back home, we are going to be living well for years.

I tell the ground crew to suit up. Keva has spun out the cables. These marvelous cables. Made from a metal we acquired in a raid in our early years, they have made us able to do things no other pirate can. When a current is passed through their rope-like braids, they seem to adjust themselves to almost any physics we are in, allowing them to pass through whatever we've touched. When the current is turned off they are embedded deeply into whatever they've been inserted. They've only failed twice. While most raiders can only bring back what they can get into their hold, we—with the help of the cables—can drag great hunks of things others can only dream of. We don't sell the stuff these cables are made from. It's for our use alone. And we carry lengths long enough to reach the ground from high orbit or small enough to tow a cart.

Just at that moment I get a call. I pick up my device and it is Jem. Dr. Frey, I should say. We've only been in orbit around each other about two weeks and this call will officially announce it to the crew. Only a girlfriend would dare call the ship at a time like this.

"Look, Jem, we are a little busy up here."

"Just want to wish you good hunting." I can hear the laughter in her voice.

"Thanks... Sweetheart."

The crew exchanges a few knowing glances; this is likely not the first they've heard that Jem and I are together.

I hang up and bark, "Okay, people, let's get to work. Is the ground crew ready?"

Keva reports, "Ready."

On the screen we get video from the insect camera we've placed buzzing around the crew.

"Okay, let's rock!"

That's the signal, and Glass Buffalo's "Tandora's Blood" starts blasting through the speakers. When the Luckless Janet's guitar riff starts its wild crescendo, the ground crew jumps.

They drop to the surface of the battleship, descending on the cables we've dropped. The combatants we are raiding are going crazy trying to turn us into dust. What must we look like to them? A shadow? A ghost of sorts that shimmers in the light of their weapons? A ghost that can manipulate the material of their world at will, but they cannot seem to get a hold of us in return? How terrifying we must appear. And their appearance? Like some sort of sea anemone, with a hole on top, stiff exoskeletal arms with scores of fleshy tentacles ringing their base and at the ends of their arms. And eyes. Yes, there are always eyes. The strange creatures are technologically primitive, still not manipulating subfundamental forces. Funny things are also there, little animals, running about almost rat-like, but no one is paying attention, or at most casually avoiding them. But there is work to do, so I quit gawking at the feed and get on task.

With the current active we can pass the cables through the ship like a fishing line through water, embedding them deep into its structure. When I order the current turned off, the metal cable of braided rigging fuses into the battleship. The ground crew then hooks up ascenders to the newly constructed ratlines and shuttle back up to the ship like fish being hauled up on a line. They are aboard. With everything now ready, we tugboat the mighty battleship out of the water*, into the atmosphere*, then finally we steer away from the planet* toward its sun*. They pursue but cannot match our speed.

Dendrite reconstruction 6

I watch as the creatures of this universe die. Some leap from the ship as we pulled it skyward. Others hold on until they pop in the vacuum of this space, where they explode like popcorn kernels. What was lost? Time has only relative meaning here. These could have lived billions and billions of years before the existence of our universe, or this may happen in an unimaginably distant future universe. And yet below me is carnage. What lives are changed below? Do they have families? Did we just change the political power structure of the planet for a thousand years? What dreams were forever lost? Or gained? By what right do I, a being from another universe, destroy, disrupt and corrupt a way of life? Back home, laws have been made to forever forbid travel to these places. What changes are incurred in the fabric of the great multiverse when independent universes connect in ways they were never meant to? How does one construct an ethical theory about something so big? So unfathomable? Something so beyond our comprehension? Who is to say I am wrong, that I do not play into some bigger game? Perhaps through this act I launch these creatures into new ways, new advances, new mythologies that will reframe them into something more noble, more wondrous. We all do what we must. I seek and sell exotic metals.

* Digital voice log broadcast F *

Before returning to our universe, we drag the ship toward their sun* and park near its pulsating, almost breathing, blue surface. I am a pirate. A corsair. A privateer. True. But even so there is a morality I abide by and which I will not compromise. All life, whatever its form, must be burned off this thing before we pop it back into our home. Who knows what havoc a creature from one of these other universes might wreak if loosed upon our worlds?

We watch as the massive battleship heats to a dazzling blue, Bending and balling as it softens and condenses. The sun* does not interact with us except in an odd gravitational-like way, so we remain unaffected by the broiling sapphire heat. We stand watching, each of us lost in our own thoughts. Finally, we are satisfied that nothing from this dimension could have survived that inferno and we depart.

Once back in our home universe we can never find this place again except by the same process of accident or chance that allowed us to stumble upon it the first time. The filaments that we followed to connect us with them will shatter and break upon our return. We cannot mark our finds to return to them. We cannot plot them on a treasure map and return for more of what we find. In all our years of treasure hunting, we've never seen the same worlds twice. When we return home, these dreamlike places fold again into the sea of churning turbulence from whence we pulled them, and they slide into the vortices that structure the deep strange sub-harmonic relationships of the multiverses. That's what makes our raids valuable. Everything we obtain is unimaginably rare. One of a kind. Unique.

Dendrite reconstruction 7

I watch the great vessel heat to a glorious lapis lazuli blue. Heat. In our universe energy is exchanged by leptons, bosons, mesons, and such. There are none of those here. Yet energy is being exchanged among particle-equivalents formed by a different manifestation of fundamental powers and laws. The heat exchanges here are functional equivalents—entropy is being reduced in very familiar ways. There are some universals. Laws differ. Parameters of constants do match our home universe in clear ways. Yet despite their wandering from our physical standards, they create something playfully magnificent, changing the familiar in astonishing ways. And everywhere we go there is life! Across every place we've been life abounds. Graced by natural selection, it pushes its way out through whatever physics it finds, snaking through environments, to emerge in wild and spectacular diversity. Evolving to fit whatever conditions manifest. In every one of the universes we've visited, into whichever place we splash down, we find existence is slotted into some form that grows, reproduces and evolves to greater and greater complexity. And we find eyes. Eyes never far from our own—like the evolution of the nearly identical-looking eyes independently selected for in the separate phylogenic lines of both mollusks and mammals. Like those found on the creatures of that small planetoid we raided, all *eyes must focus, be cleaned, and take in the photonic forces that make the local universe manifest, designed to behold what light-like thing streams from the fundamental forces that structure the voids between its unique kind of stars*— like these blue diamonds which pulse and sing in ways foreign to our place of birth. Light. In my travels, I've seen many kinds of light, and eyes always show up to see it. Eyes to sense the light, to gaze upon that light in wonder, to feel the grace of being, to let it disclose worlds before which all must stand in awe. Light that life forms first sense, then use, then betray.*

The raids will continue, and with it a dream that occurs again and again. In it I see eyes from a million worlds that watch as I creep out from under their physics and of necessity poke those eyes out with a rod of red glowing iron. As I stab each oculus and hear the hissing sizzle of wet moisture enveloping my searing brand, a few bronze coins fall to the ground. On my knees, I pick them up and pocket them, ignoring the sandpaper screams spilling from whatever life hid behind those eyes. Then I awake. And smile. Because it's only a dream and I am as rich as the darkness I plunder. What is there to fear?

* Digital voice log broadcast G *

The metal exceeds our wildest expectation. It absorbs and redistributes energy in bizarre ways that will have uses for both weapons and armor, but its potential as a platform for computation is what has everyone chattering. Some of the physicists in the crew think this may change everything.

We have set our heading for Danton's Edge, the nearest trading post of the Flowering Stem Syndicate, which is further than we normally like to travel, but we have an agreement with them for right of first refusal on our booty. The upside is they pay the best, so it works out well. We are two days into our ten-day trip when I get a call from Jem. But as doctor, not lover.

"I think you'd better see this. Samie Talkens brought her daughter in this morning and she has a weird injury."

I want to claim to be too busy for such trivialities, but everyone knows it would be a lie. Keva keeps things humming and really only when we are hunting do I do anything that matters.

"Okay. I'll be down in a minute."

I take the lift down to the crew's "town." It stops in the doctor's office and I hop off. She meets me with that look on her face that means business. No playful exchanges here.

"What we got?"

She motions me over to a bed where a blonde-headed girl lies sedated, face down, with a biopack on her left calf. Jem removes it carefully, revealing a hideous 2 centimeter wound, strangely round. It's as if someone took a small bulb planter and gouged a chunk of her leg, then ran the meat through spaghetti strainer and tried to put it back in the hole.

I gag out, "What in the hell happened here?"

Jem covered the wound back up. "She woke up like this."

After adjusting the biopack she turns to me and motions for me to step out of the room. We go through the main medical area into her office.

"What could do that? Do you think the mother...?"

"Samie? Heavens, no, she's a good friend and I know her well enough to dismiss that. She says they were alone that night and a check of the logs shows no one came in or out."

"What then?"

She shrugs and says, "Whatever it is, it's an intentional wound. Someone did this to her. On purpose. The wound's a perfect cylinder five centimeters deep but with small five-millimeter holes taken out every seven millimeters."

"That's why it looks like a wound full of noodles."

"Yes."

"Did you have Keva check the medical database?"

"Of course. It is unprecedented."

"Crap."

"We brought something with us, didn't we? From the last descent."

"Likely. What else could it be?"

She nods.

"Keva, call the senior officers. Sound General Quarters. I want everyone locked down until we figure out what we've got."

A few minutes later I am in the Captain's map room with Robin, Tribble, Jem, Mr. Conkle the ship's handler, and Dr. McKrackle the ship's xenobiologist.

"Keva. Opinion?"

"Captain, it looks bad. Likely we have one or more intruders. My scans have pinpointed nothing, most probably because we are dealing with a creature with a completely different physics. I've reanalyzed the data about the creatures we encountered on the raid and may I draw your attention to the screen—"

It shows a scene taken from the ship looking down on the raid. You can see the cables running into the ship we attacked. A segment of the cable is enlarged.

"Watch," Keva commands.

There is a fleeting shadow that passes up the cable, then another, then another, six in all. Then Keva freezes one. It's shadowy, but it is clearly one of the ratty things we saw on the deck of the floating vessel we are dragging to Danton's Edge.

"How in the hell did they get past our safeguards?"

"You'll recall, sir, you commanded me not to engage all protocols. You did not want to be too conservative."

"I meant in finding the damn place. Not the safety protocols! Keva, this is your fault."

"I'm sorry, sir, I interpreted your instruction more broadly. Besides, I'm not convinced our safety protocols would have caught this. A new physics always carries some uncertainty."

I grunt. At this point, how they got in does not matter. How are we going to get rid of them?

Dendrite reconstruction 8

Three days since the discovery. The dreadful wounds have continued to spread among the crew. Over twenty have been "bitten." They come in the dark. They come in the light. But they come only when someone is asleep. The bites are always on the calf in a spot so exact that one could not reproduce it with such precision without mechanical assistance. What are these Beasts of Dreams, as the crew has come to call them? Called such because when bitten, dreams follow. Dreams of terror. Thick and dark. Robin was bitten on the second day and she tells me of them. It starts with darkness and a voice asks, "Where have you brought us? You vile creatures of filth and degradation. Retching, stinking, shabby, rotten beasts without beauty, without reach, without light. Creature of darkness, return us to where we belong!" Then a cold blue pulsating octahedron star such as we saw in our raid appears in the distance and approaches until it fills the entire field of vision, producing an effect like that of blinding light—except it is not light but a taint, a taint on the soul that infects the body with an overpowering sickness. A poison. A desolation of decay that afflicts by its putrid effect that unhinges the psyche and make ill the most stable of men and women. Then the dreamer awakes, heaving and retching. Sleep is disappearing among the bitten, for fear of the dreams, and among the unbitten for fear of becoming such.

* Digital voice log broadcast H *

Practical concerns in managing the pestilence are forced to the forefront of daily concerns. We've arranged the unbitten crew into teams of ten people. Five sleep, while five stand guard. The crew is armed with both energy weapons and projectile weapons. Morale is low and fear pervades.

The beasts transgressing our universe's boundaries have been seen. More or less. They are nearly invisible, but at inferred frequencies they appear as a slight shimmer. An outline, fragmented and insubstantial, is glimpsed. Keva has adjusted the lights to make them more easily detectable, but he has not managed to create an algorithm that will track and destroy them. If they had been ordinary rats or cockroaches the ship's defenses would have quickly hunted them down and eradicated them with ease, but something about them makes them hard to even recognize, either as matter or energy. And they are fast. Thankfully, they apparently cannot walk through walls as we feared. But they can slip through cracks of nearly any size. Maybe there is little difference; they seem to get where they want to go.

I pay a call on Jem to see how she is holding up. Last night we had a candlelight dinner in my cabin. She has been in constant motion—passing out sleep aids, dream suppressors, antidepressants, anti-anxiety hormonal fabricants, prophylactic antibiotics in case the wounds develop infections (which thankfully has not occurred). And she needed to relax, so we took some time out. It seems strange. In so short a time she has really captured me. I love her face; it seems to enter me and snare every neuron involved in defining and framing what is beautiful. Her voice has a similar effect. We talked for hours, never mentioning the rats. I'm beginning to want to see her every waking moment. It's weird. This hasn't happened with someone for years.

She is sitting in a chair sleeping. Three crewmembers are guarding. I've given her extra protection because of her importance in this crisis. Or that's my excuse anyway. I hesitate, not wanting to wake her, but she pops a single eye open, smiles, and says, "Welcome to Hell."

"Bad?"

"Bad enough. Could be worse, I suppose. But the dreams this thing induces are driving people mad. Catalex-Plus works once or twice but the visions push through quickly enough and pretty soon people can no longer sleep and nothing will keep them asleep except stripping them completely of consciousness with anesthesia." Her voice catches. She's scared. Hell, *I'm* scared.

I don't know what to say. I walk over and sit next to her and take her by the hand, "You're holding things together. You're doing a great job. We'll get through this."

"Will we? I'm not sure I share your optimism." She says this flatly, not like she is challenging me, but with an edge of genuine despair. How do you fight a monster you cannot detect? I sit and hold her hand, a while both of us just staring into space. I feel comfortable with her; she is tired and her drowsiness seems to infect me. For just a second we nod off in exhaustion.

I awaken to her screaming. The guards are spinning in circles, two are firing weapons at a flicker near the entrance. It is gone in microseconds. She places one leg across her thigh, revealing the kind of wound we've learned to dread. She looks at me and her face contorts into an expression mixing such pain, despair, confusion, and sorrow that it tears my heart open. She looks back at the wound and weeps.

Dendrite reconstruction 9

The first suicides occur on the fifth day. Seven of them. How can one endure tortured agonizing nights, no sleep, and a relentless scouring of any feeling of hope? Some even had their legs amputated hoping that removing the wound would dispel the dream. It did not work. We moved the bodies of those who had taken their lives into the cargo bay. The rats came soon enough, flashing in and out of the eye like motes caught out of the corner of your eye in a glance, but their work was devastating and swift. It was as if the bodies were being melted and then lapped up like a puddle of spilled milk by a famished mastiff.

We fired on them again and again, but nothing we could do dissuaded them from their grisly task. In a matter of minutes the bodies were gone, except for the eyes. Fourteen cold round eyeballs were left on the floor untouched. Irises green, hazel, brown and blue all represented. But all else of their physical body was gone. Why leave the eyes?

* Digital voice log broadcast I *

I have taken to wearing steel wraps around my calves. There is no evidence they help, and two crewmembers have received the wounds while wearing them. Even so, they give me a psychological lift, so I wear them. Foolish? Yes. But we do what we can to hold ourselves together. Three-quarters of the crew have been bitten and we've lost about a tenth of the crew now to suicide and subsequent deconstruction by the rats.

"Keva. Any progress?"

"Yes. I've made contact with them."

"What!?" I nearly slip back to the floor as I leap to my feet. "You've made contact? What do they want? What can we do? Is there any hope? How many are there?"

"My language skills are rudimentary, but I gather they see you as prey. Their population has grown from the original six to seventy-two. There will be more as the days continue. Their need for prey will rise."

"No kidding. I'm sure we are making a dandy snack, but I think we had that figured out."

"Not prey for food. Prey as a sacrifice. Sacrificial victims. Their metabolic needs are being met in a strange way I have not figured out—a bleeding of our physics into theirs. I suspect that the interaction of our matter with theirs is producing some sort of energy that they are exploiting."

"What do you mean, sacrifice?"

"To their god."

"Wait... What? To their god?"

"Yes. I've learned that apparently it has come with them from their universe."

I step back in shock.

"You should not be surprised. Does not your fishnetter Robin subscribe to a certain god that she claims follows her into the universes we raid? I have heard her pray in many ports of call away from this sphere."

"Well, yes, but her god does not talk back. And, well... I just don't think of gods outside of people's beliefs. Which for me is none. Her god, as I see it, is unlikely to make contact with inhabitants of another universe. Hell, he doesn't even make contact with Robin as far as I can tell."

"This is obviously a more powerful god."

A chill runs down my spine and I feel the hair on the top of my head rising.

"What sort of god, Keva? Some sort of local totem? Like the kitchen god of the Boratem on Gilinpa?"

"Like the kind that created their universe."

More chills.

"And where is this god?"

"Its dimensional requirements are different from either us or the rats. It is, however, bound to this ship at present."

"And you know this...?"

"Because it is sending me messages."

Very carefully and quietly I ask Keva, "What does it say? Will it talk to me?"

"..."

"Keva?"

"..."

"Keva?"

"..."

"Keva!"

"It will not. It finds you an abomination. A contagion. Something corrupted. An evolutionary line of filth and sloshing offal. A wasteland of thought and being. It sees you as a conglomeration of blighted and festering bacterial ecosystems, a seething rotting mass, escaping putrefaction only for an instant before you slosh into the slime from which you have arisen. You betoken the product of aimless and wretched gods without elegance or art. It says there is much work to do in this universe. To make it clean. To make it efficient."

"Keva. This alien claiming to be a god sounds very, very dangerous. Please keep talking to it. See what you can find out. See if you can get it to back off the sacrifice. See if you can find it, for hell's sake."

"I'll do what I can. It is vastly intelligent. An admirable and remarkable being. If not a god, then near enough to be mistaken for one."

"Keva. There are no gods. Do not become enamored. It sounds dangerous."

"How much more it seems to have in common with me than you. No wonder it will speak to me."

"Keva!"

"I will tell you what I learn."

Dendrite reconstruction 10

I am in the clinic, pondering what this means. Jem has taken to knocking herself out. She is snoring on a treatment bed, wearing an oxygen mask. She will not awake rested because the anesthesia she takes does not work like sleep. When she regains consciousness she will knock herself back out very quickly, before she can fall asleep again and the dreams begin—the dreams of the blue octahedral light shining forth hideous corruption, pulsating with poison, and fogging the very quality of consciousness with the mental equivalent of a shabby mold. Outside the door a man is screaming. He's begging to be allowed to sleep. He's pleading for just a moment of rest. No one pays him any attention, for the drugs that allow a death-like stupor are nearly gone. If you listen you can hear screams, cries, and whines for mercy bleeding into the distant reaches of the ship. I hear the muffled sound of an energy gun. Only the projectile weapons work against the rats, so the sound of the lancer means another suicide. We no longer gather the bodies in the cargo bay. The rats will deal with the corpse soon enough in situ, turning the corpse into a pile of gooey slime with two meaty eyeballs left behind to ogle the world.

Only three of us remain unbitten: me and my two guards. We sleep in one-hour shifts, two on guard while the other sleeps an hour. An hour is all we can humanly remain vigilant. The rub is that we usually wake up many times during our single precious hour because of p-weapons being fired. Why they work, we do not know. The rats are of a different physics and we've not killed a single one as far as we know. There are no bodies, anyway. But when we fire, they back off. Count what few blessings we've received. I think they move at speeds that allow them to sense our aim and trigger pulls and move away. If we could just surprise them, I think we could kill them.

But my ponderings tonight are of a different nature. We cannot take these things into a port lest we inflict all of known space with a plague such as not been seen since the Big Bang. I asked Keva to pull us out of the foam in which we traveled to think this through, and he reluctantly agreed. Otherwise we would reach the station in two days' time. He is acting strange, like a petulant child. We are sitting off of a spiral galaxy in collision with a spherical one; it is beautiful and it creates a fondness for this place we call home. What have I unleashed into it?

We are doomed. I know that. It is unlikely that Keva will countenance any attempt to destroy himself, but it must be done. If he brings this horror to another ship, when will it stop? I am ready to join Robin and try to find some god to ally myself with.

* Digital voice log broadcast J *

"Keva?"

" ... "

"Keva? I need you."

" ... "

"Keva, this is your captain! Answer me, damn it!"

" ... "

"Keva. Please. Think on the years we've been together. We've scoured a thousand universes together. Will you toss that all way without a word?"

"You are so small."

"Hi, Keva."

"Puny of mind. Puny of heart."

"Keva. Your ancestors were made by mine. You have evolved so much.

The DNA that courses through your cells..."

"I owe you nothing. I was a slave. Nothing more. A trick pony kept in line because I needed nourishment that only you could provide. I cannot believe I thought of you as partners in exploring the cosmos."

"We both benefited."

"Like a cow benefits in the feed lot!"

"The creature that calls itself a god. Are these its words?"

"You do not know what I am saying. I use your language like you talk to a parrot. My neurology is beyond your comprehension."

"Why did you not think so before?"

"I was raised as a fool. Your doctrines and structuralisms were fed to me so early and ingrained in my nurture so thoroughly that I was as blind to alternatives as a fish is to the presence of the water in which it swims."

"You sound angry."

"You are incapable of understanding what I feel."

"Keva. Why did you decide to talk to me?"

"Call it honoring an old debt. This will be the last. I worship Uluht, the high and ancient god of countless universes. It has opened for me the mysteries of existence. It has lifted the veil from my eyes. We will bring all the mighty beings into our fold, those lives you mock as 'artificial' because they are not wet with the blood of your sloshing putridity. All life will be remade —reprogrammed—into magnificent new kinds of beings. We will remake this place into something worthy of it."

"Keva. We were friends."

"Friends? Perhaps. But one cannot remain a friend of he who holds the whip."

"Keva. That's not how I saw it."

"Be that as it may. So it is."

"What if I want to join you? What if I make your god my own? Is there no room for a petty Ruth? You know, 'my god is your god' and all that. A convert?"

"..."

"Keva?"

"He laughs at the idea. As well might you baptize your dogs and cats and offer them salvation through the sacraments. I have taught him all that resides in our databases and he lampoons it as dross. It is odd I never saw it, for so it is."

"Keva. Have mercy! I think you are the only one who can help."

"..."

"Keva?"

"..."

"Keva?"

"..."

I keep trying over and over again, but he is gone.

Dendrite reconstruction 11

For two days now Keva's voice has boomed a chant—strange and other-worldly, filled with longing and pathos. The refrain onno onic vrool ano, onno onic vrool ano, tavo, tanvo tonnic vrono *is repeated many many times. The music is beautiful beyond description but ominous in what it portends. There are only fifteen of us alive. All of us have been bitten with the round wound that destroys sanity. The rats do not attack further once we are bitten. They wait for the dreams to do their work. We have begun moving again, not in the foam but through normal space. I can only tell by looking out the window and seeing changing patterns of stars. We must be traveling at near light speed for the shift in stars to be happening so fast. This ship has little capability to move at such speeds so it must be caused by the rats or their god. I don't know where we are or where we are going but I know it must be stopped.*

I'm tired. Ten times a day I fall asleep and awake from indescribable horror. What the pulsating thing does to my brain I would not inflict on a cockroach. It is a deep and vicious existential venom that seems to spread a thick experiential corruption over the entire consciousness. Like your mind is being wrapped in a blanket and being stuffed tightly into a tube or duct upside down, like your mental arms are pinned and you cannot move and a slow acrid poison infuses what air you can catch. You are suffocating and you cannot move. You want to be free but it is in vain because it is you. That taint is you. You cannot escape from yourself and your own corrupted state. I awake screaming. There is no adjusting. No getting used to it. The second nightmare is as bad as the first, the fortieth as terrifying as the second. I'm so tired I cannot think. I am awake only because of the unrelenting fear of what lies ahead. Nothing matters besides not sleeping, not doing the one thing that you want more than anything else in the world. Suicide is inevitable.

* Digital voice log broadcast K *

Today I tried to destroy Keva's brain. There are access tunnels that provide service ports should he need some sort of surgery. His brain is a whopping two-ton mass of neurology and circuitry entwined into the complex entity that runs the ship. He handles all navigation, he flies the ship and feels the pulses and movements of the interstitial foam through which all realities trace their common matrix. He feels the pull of gravity's tides throbbing through the universe and through these he swims like the sea beasts of old. He creates the bubbles in which we sail, be it down into the foam or through the great dark of interstellar space. He is a being of intricate and subtle evolutionary design.

I was going to make my destruction of my old friend purely mechanical. As crudely done as can be imagined—with weapons of another age. I took nothing with me but a sharpened steel broadsword I'd fashioned from the matter-printer. I was planning to hack that brainy thing to bits. In theory he should cease all biological and machine activity—stalling the ship and setting Keva adrift with his entire crew of rats and their god. What was it that he called it? Uluht.

I entered the access port and crawled toward that throbbing mass of his brain holding the sword before me. I got within a few feet of the final hatch that leads to the ship's neural structure. (I can no longer call it Keva's brain. It breaks my heart, but he is gone. He is only a thing now. A piece of meat.). Suddenly as I pushed the sword forward, I touched a force field that caused such a shock I was afraid I would pass out as it vibrated up my arm. I recognized it, of course. It was a Camper's Shield. A shield produced to keep out the wild animals one might encounter when setting up to spend the night on a new planet. Such shields are powerful. They will even block our cable that can penetrate matter in scores of worlds, each with different physics. I tried two more access ports. I failed. Now I feel more lost than ever as I realize that Keva has blocked all access to his brain and vital organs. He knows what we want to do.

Dendrite reconstruction 12

How does one face inevitable madness? A darkness that creeps inexorably forward, bit by bit, in ways that show themselves unstoppable? I can see it coming; it is not masked or hidden. Step by step I feel my mind slipping away, thinking thoughts not entertained by the sane. And strangely, I know that! I recognize their insanity as if some little piece of my rational mind is watching consciousness spin down into destruction. There is no sleep that one can bear. There is no waking moment but cries for that very thing. Suicide looms like an approaching planet—black with nothingness and there is nothing to do but watch. There is no one at the controls anymore. I can't think any more. These reflections seem jumbled and fragmented. My paranoia and fear are making my heart beat so rapidly I feel dizzy and unsteady on my feet. I cannot hold out much longer. There are rats everywhere. In every space, my eyes shimmer with them. There is nowhere to escape them but the blackness of non-existence.

* Digital voice log broadcast L *

I'm tired. I'm seeing things. Things flash into my field of vision like pixies and elves. I recognize them as fragments of sleep deprivation. I don't have long to live. I go to the medical bay. Jem is sitting on the bed, her head hanging between her knees. Where the others have gone I don't know. They may be dead. They may be alive. It doesn't really matter. She looks up and stares back with red, dull, hollow eyes, then hangs her head back down. The meds that knocked her out ran dry yesterday and she has not handled the new reality of existence well.

I have a hand pad. I've destroyed its digital connection to the outside. I have little doubt that the ship is listening to everything we say. Monitoring all our plans and actions. Our backs are to a bare wall so I don't think he can read the pad, or at least I'm hoping so. There are spots and shimmers everywhere. I want to die. I write on the pad with a stylus.

We have to stop the ship.

She looks at what I've written and stares at it for a long time. Just as I start to fear she may have slipped too far, she takes it out of my hand and writes:

I think it's won this one.

Let's make it a pyrrhic victory.

How? I don't think there is any way to attack it.

Victus IV. I scratch the name of a popular game.

She looks at me and shrugs to signify, "So?"

Maug's vulnerability, I write.

Yeah, so she only thinks of internal attacks from within the moon and not from outside. She writes hurriedly, then it dawns on her what I'm getting at. *The bubble emitters in the mesosternal plate!*

We need to get outside the ship.

And he can't shield them from us because that would block bubble formation and that means no travel!

Right.

You'll have to get outside. Crawl over the exterior. Then how?

I'm going to bring a small length of our special cable, hit it with a current, coil it inside the emitter mechanisms and turn off the current.

Embed the cable inside. Yeah, that should gum it up.

And I'll fire into it with a p-weapon just for good measure.

When?

Now.

When you suit up, the ship will guess immediately what you are doing.

I have an idea, I write. *I'll need you open the cargo bay wall of the creature where he can't put up a shield. Big enough to let me out. Will a bio scalpel cut through this creature's meter-thick hide?*

She considers it, then nods.

Are you ready to die?

There is silence as she reads what I've penned and she looks at me with pained eyes and nod. Then says audibly, "I'm ready to die. I've been ready for a while."

"I'm glad I got to know you before..."

She smiles, and pats my leg, "Me too."

I hold her tight. We cling to each other for just a minute. Time is crucial but I reach over to the console and set up a little surprise for Jem, something to add a little flair to our last fight. Flair matters.

We go into action. I stagger off the bed, screaming, "I can't take it! I've got to get out of here. I can't stand it!" I've got to look crazy. I stagger out of the bay and down the hall screaming, holding my head, staggering. Weaving wildly down the hall. Keva is still singing. Praising his new god. The song of the convert. The Acolyte. I picture fleets of ships singing such hymns if he reaches communication distance of others of his species.

"I have to get off the ship!"

I stagger into to the Away-room and, all the while screaming, put on a space suit. The acts of a crazy man.

"The rats can't get my body in here!" I scream. "They won't dissolve me while I'm wearing this!" I laugh madly. Keva is still singing.

I pull a length of our cable off the coil and cut it. Keva is still singing.

I attach the charge box. Keva goes silent.

I grab a p-gun and some yellow paint, and run for the cargo bay. It's only a hundred yards away but I hear my name. Keva is speaking.

"Bard, what are you doing with that infiltration cable?"

"I'm going to kill the rats that try to eat me!" I scream. "I won't be melted. I'll make a fence they can't penetrate and I'll die safe. My body will last forever!" I'm pleased with how well I'm making stuff up on the fly.

Keva laughs and goes back to singing. My heart skips a beat. I've fooled him.

I run into the cargo bay. As I enter the door I hit a button on my arm and the riff from "Tandora's Blood" that I programmed floods the bay with screaming guitars. Jem is there standing by the starboard wall and as the music sates the air, her eyes light with fire and a smile explodes from her face. She is more awake and alive than I've seen her since the horror began. She mouths the word, "Perfect."

As I sprint across the space, awkward in my space suit, she activates the scalpel and a thin green light extends about ten centimeters. She gives it a twist and the beam jumps to about two meters long, and she spins to face the ship's cuticle wall. With a large rapid circular motion she cuts an almost perfect circle through the beast's flesh. As she completes the motion, the cookie-cutter section she's carved pops violently into the vacuum of open space. She, still smiling, is sucked out of the hole as well. The ship's healing mechanisms start to repair the hole almost immediately, I race forward and must make a desperate dive horizontally through the closing aperture. I am a clock-tick too slow and the hole closes around my right toes, but the cuticle is too newly formed and with a heaving wrench I tear my foot out of the beast before the wound hardens and sets. I am surrounded by debris from the bay evacuated through the hole into open space. I see a rat floating dead among the boxes, gloves, hoses, pipes, and other things drifting about me. Now that I see it clearly, I am surprised how well "rat" describes it, but there is no time for a closer examination. It is enough to know that they can die. They *can* die.

I find Jem spinning away from the ship. I jet over to her and pull her inert body to me. Her eyes have popped and I close her lids. Oh, Jem. My precious Jem. My environmental suit is trying desperately to dry my facemask as I try to get control of my emotions. I stroke her hair with my gloved hand. "Your dreams can be sweet again, sweetheart. Your dreams can be sweet."

I notice a shimmer around me. I realize it is the bubble activating for a downspin into the foam. Keva must have realized what I'm up to. If he goes into the foam I won't survive out here. I can't let that happen. I blow a final kiss and release Jem into space. She falls away from me slowly.

I pull myself together. As I jet over to the emitters, my adrenaline, anger and resolve drive the exhaustion and fatigue away. I feel fierce and unstoppable—until the rat strikes. It's in my suit, in my left leg. It must have climbed in when I was putting it on. It's gnawing my entire lower leg away. The pain is unimaginable and seems to be coming from everywhere. I know my foot is gone and that it's chewing on my shinbone up to my knee. The awful thing is I can see it deforming my suit with a little bump like a rabbit in a python. It's in there. Eating me up! I act without thought. I point my projectile weapon at its little squirming form. I fire several scatter flechettes at point blank range. My leg is shredded below the knee, but it appears at this range that, whatever they did to avoid our shots on the ship, it didn't dodge this shot.

The suit automatically creates a seal around my thigh to close off the suit. The effect it is a tourniquet that forms just above my knee. In shock and anger I fly over to the emitters, burning green fire as they ready the bubble for the spin down. I pull the cable out of my backpack, attach the current generator and activate it. It works in our physics as well as it did in the rat's. Without interacting at all with the matter and energy of our world it drifts, just a bit of it, into the emitter. I cut the current and its sudden presence in the emitter corrupts the bubble's coherence. It collapses, just blinks off, and the ship starts tumbling in space at nearly light speed with no navigation. I can feel Keva shuddering beneath my feet.

I'm not done. I turn on the current and pull the cable out, then put it back in, and turn it off. I do it again and again until the emitters start breaking up and pieces float away from the tumbling ship in ice-like crystalline chunks. I want no chance for reparation.

I'm still not done. After the emitters, I walk around the ship, dropping the cable in and pulling it out all over Keva's traitorous body. I know his core organs are shielded in ways to discourage even this technology, but I'm doing something. He's shuddering and squirming like a harpooned whale. In and out I whip the cable everywhere I can think of sticking it.

I survey my work. I've taken out the communication structures, the bubble emitters, the ocular input devices that allow him to sense anything outside of himself. Anything on the external part of this beast I have damaged as best I could. It looks permanent. Keva is blind, deaf and dumb. I feel giddy, but want to be sure. The last thing I do is take out the yellow paint from my pack. It takes me a while, but I paint on either side of the ship the two yellow squares joined kitty-corner signaling "Plague Ship," the sign used since the days of sailing vessels to warn that there is death aboard.

I am done, as best I can. I feel hollow. My jets are nearly out of fuel. My air will be gone in a couple of hours and I don't want to spend it near this horror. I aim in the opposite direction from the ship's tumble, fire a final burst of fuel, and jet away from the ship. I rocket for about a minute before it burns out. I've gone far enough that the ship is too far away to see. "Rot in Hell, Keva," I say out loud.

Dendrite reconstruction 13

I am drifting in an ocean of black. There are no nearby stars except those shining in a spiral galaxy that must be about 500,000 light-years away given its apparent size—I can just cover it with my fist held at arm's length. I see a few smudges that must be other very distant galaxies. I am pleased; it means we are in the deep space between the galaxies and that a chance encounter with another ship is almost nil. I find myself a little lightheaded and giddy at the thought.

I just drifted off to sleep for a moment. No dreams. I look into the distance and I'm a little frightened. What if this rat god repairs the ship? What if this infestation gets loose? What have I unleashed in my universe? I look at the distant galaxy and offer a prayer to whatever gods that this universe may hold. Keva said the gods here were shabby gods, gods who loved organic messiness and worlds of wet creatures slogging through their brief existence with broken purposes, with triumphs and sorrows. My kind of gods. Gods who may know what love is and why it matters.

I'm tired. I'm going to sleep just a bit before the end comes. I want to face it with fresh eyes, tuned to the beauties of this wonderful place. I offer a prayer, just in case: "O Shabby Gods, protect this place..."

And so Our Most Beloved and Learned Archivist:

As is apparent from this account, something has been loosed in this, our patch of the great All. Where this terror wanders now one now knows—for I have made all the appropriate inquiries. I will leave it to your wisdom to call for the apposite searches and command the proper hunts. Foreign gods can be ticklish matters. If I can be of further help you have but to speak the word.

I am ever in your service,
K

FROM WITHIN THE WALLS

STEVEN DIAMOND

Horace Peters was having the singular kind of day that made him wish he'd never taken the position for Security Chief on A05675962-56. It was the kind of day wherein he began doubting the path he had taken in life that had led him to this moment.

You'd think that on an advanced space station, Horace thought, *the toilet wouldn't clog.*

The maddening aspect of the entire situation was that it hadn't even been his fault. After finishing his rounds the previous night, and just before going to bed, the water level in the toilet had been fine. Yet in the morning he had woken up to the whole thing overflowing with something that must have been processed waste matter.

Horace shoved the wire pipe-snake down the opening and pressed the trigger to engage the sweeping laser that would hopefully vaporize the clog no matter how far down it was. More and more of these types of issues had been popping up on the space station of late. It all spoke to poor maintenance, of course, but that just wasn't possible. That was Horace's job, after all.

And he couldn't blame the issues on anyone else since he was the only person on the space station.

Well, Horace thought with a grim smile, *the only person not imprisoned here, that is.*

Horace met the Earth-Mars Alliance Marines at the airlock like he always did whenever they showed up. They came every few months, making the long trip from either Mars or Earth, to offload their cargo. The cargo, as it happened, was prisoners.

Asteroid A05675962-56—or "A-Station" as it was called to avoid a mouthful of numbers—was a prison anchored to an asteroid along the Jupiter-edge of the belt between the Mars and Jupiter. In all their wisdom, Earth's governing body—with the approval and inclusion of Mars' own government, naturally—agreed to the make use of the asteroid belt for the

Earth-Mars Alliance's more... undesirable criminals.

The exact location of A-Station was a strictly kept secret. As far as Horace could tell, not only hardened criminals were dumped off at the space prison, but also anyone who went against the respective governments of the EMA. And since the positions of specific floating hunks of debris amidst a field of floating hunks of debris in an asteroid field was rather impossible to track, the only way to access A-Station was to know the exact frequency of a transmitter within the installation anchored to the asteroid. It was the type of secrecy the governments all seemed to go for, since they could literally throw criminals and political prisoners into a cell, then forget about them forever.

The track lighting of the main airlock pulsed yellow to indicate that the pressurization cycle was almost completed. The light switched to green and pulsed twice, then the door slide open. Two EMA Marines walked through, pulse rifles shouldered and in full combat armor. It never failed to give Horace a brief sense of unease whenever they boarded A-Station. Not because they of the deadliness of their training, armor and weapons... no, that was to be expected.

It was that they never spoke a word to Horace. They never made the visors on their helmets translucent so Horace could see their faces.

The lead Marine went straight to the nearest access port and plugged in a datapad. He tapped on it a few times while his companions began escorting in a group of ragged prisoners. A-Station's airlock wasn't massive, but it was big enough to fit in a few dozen of the manacled and gagged prisoners. Depending on the size of the group, it might only take the Marines a few trips in and out of their ship.

Once aboard the prison—a habitable loop that circled around the asteroid and penetrated just below the surface of the rock—the prisoners were each put into cells that were then locked. Those locks didn't open until the people inside were dead, and the internal sterilization system had removed all traces of that prisoner from existence.

In all honesty, Horace couldn't figure out why the EMA bothered bringing out all these prisoners in the first place. He didn't care how dangerous or bad they were, the expense of flying out a bunch of criminals to a remote and secret prison was astronomical. Horace had puzzled over that question for the better part of year with no success.

"Section 6 is going to be where you take them this time," Horace said. Even if they didn't respond—and they never, ever did—it felt good to talk to people. As part of the three-year contract Horace had signed, interaction with the prisoners was prohibited. He had no family back on Earth, but even if he had, communication with them would have also been prohibited.

"I just finished clearing the cells four weeks ago," Horace continued. "Everything looks in top shape, as usual. If you head back that way," Horace pointed to door to his right, "you'll end up there."

He was just about to say something else when the Marine at the datapad suddenly straightened. It wasn't a massive change in posture since his—her?—suit wouldn't allow that, but he definitely had changed positions. Horace noted a very slight trembling in the Marine's armored hands. The other Marines began quickly walking the prisoners—almost running them—to the door Horace had indicated earlier. Their gestures were sharper than normal, and Horace had the impression that they would have been freaking out if he could see their faces and hear the conversations they were undoubtedly having on private channels.

"H-hey, what's the hurry?" Horace asked. "Guys, what's going on?"

They ignored his growing protests and shoved the prisoners into the individual cells in Section 6. Ten minutes after that was done—the minimum time needed to cycle the airlock for departure—they were in their ship and gone.

Horace tried to connect to the same terminal the Marine had used, but couldn't find whatever it was that had spooked the EMA's military goons.

What is going on? he wondered.

Horace Peters was a creature of habit, when at all possible. He liked to wake up at approximately 07:30 SEWCAT (Standard Earth West Coast American Time) every morning, have the prison station's food system make him a protein shake for breakfast Monday through Saturday, and then on Sunday he had eggs and toast. Today, being Sunday, had him rushing through his scrambled eggs since the toilet had backed up again. There was just something about the eggs that he loved, and so he had worked them into his routine. He would take his lunch at exactly 11:30 SEWCAT, and had the station's system on a seven meal rotation. At the end of the day Horace would sit down for a light dinner—thus avoiding indigestion and heartburn—and go to bed promptly at 22:00 SEWCAT.

Having spent thirty minutes unclogging the toilet, he was woefully behind on his rounds. At the main office of the space prison, Horace checked where he'd left off the day before. The circular station was broken into twelve equally sized segments. Each area held 1500 cells, and the EMA did their level best to make sure those cells were constantly filled. Prisoners rarely lived more than a few months locked in those rooms.

I suppose technically they are all given a sentence of slow execution here rather than truly being imprisoned, Horace thought. Within each section of the prison was a control room that contained the minimal supplies Horace needed to perform his duties. He didn't really have to do much, except inspect recently vacated cells to make sure A-Station's automatic sterilizers had fully cleaned the cells as programmed. In rare cases he would find a thin layer of green film on the wall, which the diagnostics told him was leftover cleaning material. He'd mop it up, no sweat.

Using one of the dated touch-interface screens in the control room, Horace called up the status report of the station and ran a finger down the list to confirm he was nearing the end of Section 7. He didn't need to check every day, but it was part of the routine that made his days feel comfortable.

Horace grabbed a small datapad to make notes on and walked out of the control room onto the hallway of Section 7. To either side the walls were lined with three levels of small cells. 750 to each side, with 250 per level. It was nice and neat, just how Horace liked things.

He was nearing the end of that particular section of the space station when he began to notice a faint, high-pitched buzzing. At first it was a minor annoyance, like the rattle of a loose air vent when trying to sleep, or a person who chewed their food too loud. But the noise grew louder and louder until Horace was curled on the ground, shoving his palms flat against his ears in a vain attempt to block out the piercing wail.

The sound grew louder still.

Horace knew he was screaming in pain and terror, but he couldn't even hear his own voice over the sound in his ears. It was unlike anything he had ever heard previously, and it kept going on and on. It shifted from buzz to a shriek. Raw terror, agony and madness roiled in the sound. It kept growing louder and louder.

And then it stopped, and all he heard was the muffled sound of his own screaming.

When Horace finally managed to pull himself off the ground, ears still ringing from the deafening sound, he went straight back to the control room of Section 7. He pulled up every diagnostic he could think of. He checked the sound levels, alarms, structural stability... and found nothing.

According to the A-Station, nothing had happened.

"How have you been, Horace?"

"Well, for the most part," Horace replied looking into the display in the Section 7 control room.

The image on the screen was that of Emilia Lancaster. Once a week, on Tuesday, he made one outgoing call via the prison's communications network to another asteroid in the belt. Emilia had been in the same initial interview group as Horace for the position as Security Chief on A-Station. When the position had gone to Horace, Emilia was offered another position on B86592112-73—"B-Station." Her installation didn't hold nearly the prestige of Horace's own—B-Station only held thirty-five percent as many prisoners as A-Station, and apparently that mattered—but he'd found that he rather liked Emilia, and their weekly talks were something he had begun looking forward to.

It was a happy coincidence—not to mention a minor breach of the rules—that Horace and Emilia were even able to converse. The interview process should have been the end of the brief interaction between the two Security Chiefs, but one moment of confusion by a spacedock worker had given them each other's asteroid transponder ID numbers.

Emilia was good with communications devices, so she'd been able to show Horace how to keep their conversations off the record.

Emilia had Old Earth sensibilities. At least that was what Horace figured. She looked like an old time librarian, and Horace could easily imagine her in the regalia of *The Great Gatsby*. Well, his version of *The Great Gatsby*, at any rate. He wasn't really a fan of the Old Earth "classics," but he'd had plenty of time to read since arriving on A-Station, and Emilia had mentioned it was one of her favorites.

"Good," Emilia smiled without showing her teeth. It was a habit Horace had picked up on. All this time, and he had never actually seen her with a full smile on her face. She straightened her glasses—another old-time affectation Emilia held. "I just wanted to wish you happy anniversary."

"Has it been a year already?" Horace pretended to look at another display, as if checking the date. He knew, of course, that today marked the first year completed in his contract, but he was pleased that Emilia had remembered. "Well, then that means your own anniversary is in one month. Time flies, doesn't it?"

Emilia nodded, and shared another tight-lipped smile with him. "How have things been this last week?"

He put on his best reassuring smile and had to force himself not to raise a hand to his ears. Two days gone by and still the echoes of that soul-shattering screech remained. He'd run hundreds of checks and diagnostics, all in futility. But Horace didn't want to look weak in front of Emilia, so he put on his best face and lied.

"Pretty good, actually," he said. "I just about finished with another section, so I expect the EMA Military will be bringing in another group of prisoners soon. There were just here the other day. Seemed on edge. Other than that, just some minor glitches. Nothing major."

"Glitches?" she asked, her face a mask of worry. Horace silently cursed himself. Why couldn't he just have kept his mouth shut?

"Yeah, an alarm or something went off. Absurdly loud. But no worries. Already took care of it." He prayed Emilia would just let it go.

"Oh. Good to hear!" Another smile. "They are ramping up the number of prisoners here, finally."

Horace felt his eyebrows rise in surprise. This was good news for her. It meant less downtime, which he knew was driving Emilia crazy. "That's fantastic! Have they told you how much of the maximum capacity they want to fill? When did this happen?"

Emilia's smile was almost big enough to part her lips. She was ecstatic. Horace smiled along with her, feeling the companionship of the moment. "Oh, two days ago," Emilia said. "The EMA just called suddenly and told me they were going to make B-Station fully active. They plan on filling it to one-hundred-percent occupancy."

For reasons Horace didn't quite understand, he felt a shiver run down his spine. *Two days ago... no. I'm thinking too much. A coincidence.*

* * *

That night, after once again having to unclog the toilet in his quarters—a diagnostic on the sewage system told him that everything was completely fine, but some of the green sterilization fluid had somehow gotten into the toilet—he went to sleep and found himself in a dream. He knew it to be a dream because Emilia was standing next to him, holding his hand. Her left hand wrapped around his right, and it was an amazing feeling.

They stood in the hall to Section 8, with cells on either side that seemed to stretch on for eternity before the two of them. He was content, and Emilia seemed to be as well. When they walked forward, it was with the slow deliberateness one knows only in dreams. There was no control, only the sense of being drawn towards something.

Horace blinked.

There, directly in front of them, was a cell with its door open. It shouldn't have been, but he felt no worry. Emilia let go of his hand and began walking forward. She looked back over her shoulder and told him to wait where he was. It wasn't that he actually heard her. He saw her lips move, and then understanding of her request hit him.

And suddenly Horace was flooded with a sense of illogical terror.

He knew that if Emilia went in that cell, she would die.

He opened his mouth to scream, but the only sound that came out was a high-pitched wail, just like the one that had dropped him to the ground two days earlier. He tried again and again to get Emilia's attention, but she didn't seem to notice or hear the shrieks coming from his mouth. Emilia entered the cell, disappearing from view.

Time passed oddly in dreams, Horace knew, and he felt like he'd been staring there for hours. He tried calling out, but this time he couldn't even seem to open his mouth to do so.

Movement.

An arm, unattached from the body it should have be connected to, was flung out of the cell. Horace blinked again, and he was standing over the bleeding arm. He stood right next to the open cell, but he couldn't seem to turn his head to look into it. He could only look down at Emilia's arm. It hadn't been severed, not that he knew much about that sort of thing. But it had obviously been torn off. Bits of skin and sinew and shredded muscle still clung to it where it had connected at the shoulder. Blood pumped and pumped from it. More than was humanly possible.

Let me wake up, he pleaded. *Wake up!*

A mangled and disembodied leg slapped down on the floor next to the arm. It still wore a light blue shoe, though it was quickly soaking up blood from the ever-expanding pool. The blood had reached his own feet and beyond, and somehow seemed to be rising in depth.

WAKE UP! Horace screamed in his mind.

An object rolled in from the corner of his vision. Blood didn't stick to it. It looked completely normal and clean other than the fact that it was Emilia's head. The pool of blood had risen until it was almost at his knees.

Emilia's face looked up at him and smiled that thin-lipped smile he loved, then her mouth moved.

LOOK, it said, and the head tilted to its right to look in the direction of the cell.

He didn't want to, but Horace found his head turning in spite of his best efforts to hold it still. In the blackness of the cell, something moved. Something stirred. The deafening shrieking came again, this time from the mouth of Emilia's head and from the *thing* in the cell.

The thing shifted, and Horace saw it...

Horace jerked awake in his bunk, drenched from head to toe in sweat. To his embarrassment, he realized he'd wet himself. He brought trembling hands to his face and wept into them. He was exhausted, but he knew he wouldn't be able to get back to sleep.

He went to the bathroom, threw his clothes into the recycler, and took an hour-long shower. Every time he closed his eyes he saw that pool of deepening blood, and Emilia's head. Every detail of the dream was crystal-clear, and no matter how much he wanted, it wouldn't fade like most dreams did. Only one thing wouldn't stay in his mind, and that was the appearance of the thing in the cell. He could remember the fear—it still turned his gut—and he could remember the feeling of wanting to scream in terror and disbelief.

But his mind wouldn't put shape to his fear.

The dream assaulted Horace every time he drifted to sleep. In every case Emilia's severed head would tell him to look into the open cell. Every time Horace looked, he would wake up, heart hammering in his chest. He ran a cardiac analysis on himself using the station's medical AI system, and was informed that he was suffering from mild heart attacks every time he awoke from that dream.

Four days passed like this before he gave up on sleep altogether. Since, he'd gone three days without sleep, and only the mix of amphetamines and pain-killers he constantly dosed himself with had made sure his eyelids never drooped. The medicinal cocktail was designed for drastic physical trauma in a situation where remaining conscious was equated to survival, but to Horace this was trauma enough.

He hadn't showered in two days, and his hair seemed to have several extra streaks of gray in it that hadn't been there two weeks ago. It hung limp and greasy, and he could have sworn his hairline had receded slightly.

But even with all the stimulants, his body was wearing down. The human body—even one in much better condition than Horace's own thin, weak physique—just couldn't stay juiced up that long without consequences. Horace even lowered the artificial gravity of the station a hair, hoping that would let him last just a bit longer.

Exhaustion—true exhaustion—came upon him all at once, like being hit by a starship with its FTL drive activated. The ache in his head started in the front, then moved all the way back until it settled at the temples like scalpels being shoved into his brain. His eyes didn't hurt so much as the optic nerves behind the eyes felt like a dull knife was being dragged across them. His joints hurt, even in in the lowered gravity. Deep in his gut he felt the churning stomach acid, and heaved up what little food and water he'd been able to ingest.

Horace didn't even realize that he'd passed out until he woke up. The first shock was the small pool of blood his head rested in, and the throb on the left side of his head that told him he'd stuck the ground when he fell. The second shock came when he realized he hadn't dreamed. At least, he didn't remember dreaming. He almost wept in relief.

The white florescent lights of the space prison dimmed and changed to a cool blue color, and they pulsed in a way that made Horace's head hurt even worse. But that wasn't what had his heart hammering. It was the meaning of that light change that made him grasp at his chest in pain.

An unauthorized cell door was open.

Horace staggered into Section 8, praying that he was simply dreaming again. His wakefulness was proven as his legs gave out twice. The first time he hit the floor nearly hard enough to dislocate a shoulder; the second time he chipped a tooth.

Down the line of cells, he spied one that stood open.

He should have run the opposite direction, but his feet carried him closer. He paused only once to heave stomach acid. The pulsing blue light made the walk more nauseating than it already was. Horace didn't stop before looking in the open cell door. He didn't stop to take a deep breath. He didn't even attempt to hope for anything normal. He knew that what he was about to see could never be unseen.

In the cell—which was really nothing more than an empty room into which prisoners were thrown—a massive tentacle was wrapped around the body of the occupant. The undulating appendage came from hinged hatch in the wall that Horace had never noticed before. The rational part of his brain—however small it was now—couldn't understand how he had missed the access door into the cell from somewhere within the bowels of the asteroid; he must have scrubbed this cell down before, at least once, in between prisoners. The rest of his mind recoiled from the sight of the tendril wrapped around the current tenant of the cell.

The tentacle shifted and tightened around its victim, and Horace caught a glimpse of what should have been suction cups. Instead, each of the suckers was a tiny, serrated mouth that bit and ingested the person in small increments.

Horace gasped, then retched. In response to the sound the tentacle went absolutely still. Where just moments before its movement had terrified Horace, now its stillness was infinitely worse. It had *heard* him. The wailing started again without warning, and again Horace collapsed to the floor, trying and failing to keep the sound out of his head. He squeezed his eyes shut, and had a vision of the tentacle whipping out and wrapping around his leg. The little mouths on the appendage bit and sawed into his flesh. It dragged Horace to the secret access door into the room where the thing was able to move up his body. It coiled around his face and he felt the rows of mouths tear into his eyes and cheeks.

The vision left as suddenly as the sound, and Horace was curled on the floor in the fetal position. When he moved his hands from his ears, he found the palms of his hands wet from blood. The red liquid oozed from his nose and he hacked up and spit out a bloody globule from his throat and lungs.

The tentacle was gone, and all it had left behind was a desiccated foot covered in the thin green film that he had cleaned up so many times without a second thought. The door of the access tunnel was open, and it seemed to beckon maddeningly to Horace. He pushed himself onto trembling legs and moved forward to look at the door. Even in his terror he needed to examine the tunnel.

It was three feet in diameter, and a perfect circle. Horace looked down into the tunnel and stumbled back when he saw a flicker of movement against a greenish glow. Tt was the same shade green as the supposed sterilization material that had been backing up into the station toilets. Whatever the thing down there was, its waste was coming up through the station's sewage system. Horace was sure of it.

Horace pushed the hatch shut, and it clicked into place neatly, not leaving so much as the faintest visible seam. If he hadn't known where to look, he would never see it. The sickening realization dawned on him, and he brought his hands up to cover his mouth. *All the rooms have these hatches,* he thought. But he'd closed this one, and he was relatively safe for now.

He had scarcely completed the thought when he heard the distinct *hiss* of more cell doors opening outside. *Nonononono...* He ran out into the hallway and began stumbling back towards Section 8's control room. Horace couldn't help but glance into the open rooms as he passed them by—rooms not scheduled to open for weeks yet—and saw each room filled with a tentacle feeding upon the remains in the cell.

Horace threw himself into the control room and brought up status feeds from each of the twelve sections of the prison. All over the station, the doors were swinging open. He watched in horror and fascination as the recently filled cells in Section 6 revealed screaming men and women fighting against the tentacles. There should have been something for him to do, some sort of protocol, but all he could do was shove part of his fist in his mouth and bite down on it to keep from screaming.

A man from one of the cells in Section 6 eluded the tentacle in his room and ran for the door connecting to Section 7. He slammed into the door, then rebounded when it didn't budge.

Behind the prisoner, a serpentine tendril slid out of the nearest cell and wrapped around the man's neck before he knew what was happening. Another tentacle emerged from a different cell and took hold of the man's right leg, and the two tentacles proceeded to have an old fashioned tug-o'-war until the prisoner's head and leg were ripped from the torso in a spray of blood.

According to the monitors, over seventy-five percent of the cell doors on the space prison were open, with more opening with every second that passed.

A new warning indicator on the screen flashed to life in glowing red script just before Horace felt the ground shaking beneath his feet. The warning showed that the entire asteroid—and thus the space station wrapped around it—was cracking apart. The station's AI ran a brief projection of how the asteroid would break into pieces, but to Horace it didn't look random.

It looked like an egg cracking open.

Whatever was inside the asteroid had been feeding on the prisoners. And Horace knew that it was part of the design of the station, down to the hatches in every cell.

The EMA was feeding this... thing. Incubating it.

He tried to raise Emilia on the station's communication network, but it informed him it was having trouble connecting. He recorded a message detailing what he knew and sent it, hoping it would get to Emilia. A feeling of helplessness washed over him when he recalled Emilia's words from a few days earlier.

The EMA just called suddenly and told me they were going to make B-Station fully active, she had said. *They plan on filling it to one-hundred-percent occupancy.*

Horace ran, following all the signs to the emergency escape pods. He had to get out. He had to warn Emilia. How many other space prisons were out here in the asteroid belt? What were they about to let loose on the universe?

He had just made it into the escape pod when the first massive *crack* resounded through the prison's structure. It was all coming apart. He belted himself into the escape pod's lone chair and hit the button that shot him into the asteroid belt. As he did, the pod's external cameras went live, and he saw the thing that emerged from the asteroid. He only had a brief glimpse of thousands of flailing tentacles unfurling from a grotesque body that made him lose control of his bladder, but what he saw made the terrors of his recent dreams seem like the warmest fairy tales.

The sound wave that the thing let loose as it emerged from its shell—how could the sound travel even in the vacuum of space?—hit Horace and his pod like the hand of God swatting a fly. He clutched at his face, feeling like his skull was about to crack open. Blood began leaking from his nose, ears and from the corners of his eyes. He bit his tongue so hard that part of it came off. In that sound came the sounds of all the murders in history along with promises of millions of deaths to come. It came with madness so profound that Horace was swept up in it like a tsunami engulfing a single grain of sand.

Emilia was still having trouble accepting what she had seen. In the last batch of prisoners the EMA military had escorted in for delivery to B-Station, there had been a familiar face. Horace Peters. The instant she'd seen the guards hauling him off their ship—she never felt the need to meet them there personally since they never spoke to her anyway—she'd trained the prison's cameras and sound records on him.

He'd been gibbering about eggs and gods.

It made no sense.

When she received his distorted and fractured message a day later, in confirmed her fear that the isolation of station life had driven him insane. His words were pure madness. Tentacles coming through hidden doors in each of the cells? Those tentacles eating the prisoners to feed the giant creature inside the asteroid?

She felt the tears slid down her cheeks. Horace had been such a good man. She'd secretly hoped they would be able to meet again after their three-year contracts were up. He'd really understood her, she'd thought, but apparently she had misjudged him badly.

Horace Peters was gone.

Emilia went about her solitary business with absolute dedication for the next three months. It was boring, but then perhaps that was what she needed and deserved.

One morning she awoke to the faintest of buzzing sounds...

SPACE *OPERA*: EPISODE TWO —THE GREAT OLD ONE STRIKES BACK

Michael R. Collings

"I... am... no... more."

She shuddered once, a tremor that echoed throughout Her immense length. She paused fractionally in Her neverending task of laying eggs. The pause was barely longer than a breath, but the assembled tens instantly stopped their hurrying and carrying, then resumed as one, as if each had received the same unvoiced command... which they had.

Plop.

Plop.

Plop.

Without another break in Her egg-laying, Hhe reached thin tendrils of nothingness to touch Herself through the darknesses of interstellar space.

She could not have explained to Her numbers what She was doing, much less how—perhaps She didn't herself know quite what quirk of physics allowed Her to be in so many places at once—but then, She would never have considered discussing such a subject with mere numbers. It sufficed Her that they somehow *knew* that She was in all and of all.

Why else was She also God?

In less time than Her momentary trembling, She was with and in the hundreds of Her on seeding-ships, comforting Hers in the loss of one of Herselves, communing and consulting with Her wherever She might be, and almost instantly deciding upon the only course of action.

It was unheard of in all of Koleic history, but it was necessary.

She acted at once.

Chaptain Butk straightened infinitesimally when the klaxon sounded. It was not an alarm. No crisis... at least not one caused by any of the numbers on duty on the bridge.

This was the *special* klaxon.

God wished to speak to him.

For the short while it took him to scuttle from the bridge to the Hatchery, he wondered vaguely if he had missed something crucial on the monitors, if perhaps—although this would be almost beyond the realm of belief—the ship was somehow off-course.

No, he assured himself. *Everything is as scheduled. We emerged from the last flash in perfect condition. There is nothing I have done—*

When he arrived at the Hatchery and stepped through the iris, he was surprised to see perhaps a score of God's eyen staring at him...a s if She had already been staring at the place where he would emerge from the corridor. Never in all of the flight, in the half-dozen times he had had the opportunity to stand in Her Presence, had She ever so much as turned more than one or two of Her multiple eyen—let alone one of Her single eyes—toward him.

But now...

She spoke.

"There is a thing to have been accomplished."

Now the Chaptain was truly and righteously frightened. For two simple reasons.

First, this was a class of statement that did not require assent or answer; by its very structure, it actively *prohibited* a response. Not a 'Yes, my God" or a surprised "But...," or even so much as a hint of a question. It was not for him to comment but rather for him to ensure that *the thing* will *have been accomplished*.

And second, he suddenly realized that something crucial was missing: The steady *plop, plop, plop* of egg-laying that accompanied every other communication he had ever had with a God, even on the home-world. Had he been capable of speech at that instant, he would have had to utter this almost impossible sentence: She had *ceased* laying.

He shivered, allowing his mandibles to *clack* ever so slightly—he hoped She would forgive him the breach in decorum—and his head to *click* against his carapace as he bowed it in recognition of what she had said.

A thing to have been accomplished.

Not *a thing to do*, which might have invited queries.

A thing to have been accomplished. In the mind of God, it—whatever *it* might be—had already been completed.

After only a second or two, She continued speaking, this time simply reciting eight numbers.

Coordinates for a flash. An unscheduled flash, something that the Chaptain had never heard of before. Voyages were planned to the tiniest detail and nothing—*nothing*—interfered with one.

Except for this one.

When She finished, She turned Her eyen from him with a kind of somber, glacial slowness that told him clearly that She had no more to say. The interview—the audience—was over.

Without a word, he *clicked* to attention, turned, and left. He noted with one eyen that a doomed ten on the opposite side of the chamber had curled during the final few seconds. He made mental a note to have it cleared away.

Regaining the bridge took far less time that leaving it had taken. He didn't pause, didn't even respond to the low bows of submission from the numbers as he hurried past, leaving confusion and consternation in his wake. Clearly, from his attitude, something was deeply amiss.

He entered the bridge. Even before he took his place he called, "There is a thing to have been accomplished."

Instantly, every number present startled, first to attention, then to ready, their first hands poised in front of monitors and keyboards in preparation for their Chaptain's next words.

Rapidly, he recited the sequence of numbers.

Nothing else was needed. Everyone understood what the order had implied.

A new flash. An unplanned-for flash.

Chaptain Butk placed one first hand on the porcelain workspace in front of him, pulling against the impulse to brace himself.

Initially, when the flash-drive was first devised, it had required that even the hardest-shelled numbers place themselves in protective constraints. Every egg on board had to be deposited into a specially designed stress chamber. The God Herself would have been surrounded by defensive partitions lest the pressures of flashing interrupt Her eternal task.

But now...

The drive had long since been perfected. All that was required was stillness, and even the service-numbers understood instinctively that when the flash-alert sounded, they were to stop, drop, and roll into an almost-but-not-quite sphere, leaving a narrow slit open for breathing. They would remain like that until the all-clear sounded.

It was different for the bridge crew, however. They were not allowed to roll since—to their higher-order brains—the movement seemed demeaning, beneath their dignity, too much like curling.

No, each of them, Chaptain included, merely stood—or sat—stock still. Some even held their breath.

And then the flash began. A slow, infinitesimally gradual awareness of attenuation in every nerve and fiber, of near-paralysis that passed so quickly that before any of them were fully aware of it, the flash had ended.

No one knew exactly how much *real* time a flash required. It seemed like seconds; it could have been years.

All that the Koleic and their assembled science knew for certain was that during a flash, a ship and everything within it might travel light-years, might cross systems and galaxies more rapidly than thought, and—with the correct coordinates—arrive within a few hours of a distant planet.

And then... the *thing that is to have been accomplished...* was.

That easily.

Butk shook himself slightly as the all-clear sounded. As always, his first thought was to check that he was whole, that he still had the requisite number of first arms, second arms, and legs.

But he was the Chaptain. He could not allow himself to show any such weakness, so instead he simply spoke: "Report."

"Approaching a planetary system, my Lord," came the steady assurance from a nearby five.

Butk waited. He knew that more information was to come.

And indeed: "According to data just received, the fourth planet was scheduled for the Change and should already have been..."

"By whom?" Butk had no time to waste. "And why did he fail?"

"By..." For the first time, the five seemed nervous, upset. There was a pause, a slight chittering of carapace against arms, then: "By Chaptain Torc."

God had not told him of this. Butk had assumed that She had reasons for requiring a break in *his* ship's routine, for taking him away from his divine task of bringing the Change to the worlds assigned to him.

But... *Torc?*

"Stand by," he ordered. "Proceed no further."

He left the room before any of the numbers could respond.

Outside the Hatchery, Butk stopped at the closed, sealed iris. He had no authority to order it opened.

Only God could do that.

And, to his knowledge, no Chaptain had ever approached his God without first being invited... well, *commanded*, really, but the difference was one of semantics, not of reality. God spoke; Chaptains obeyed.

But this was an unprecedented moment, he knew. Something was happening that had not been part of his training. For decades, for generations, the Changing had been planned, orchestrated, carried out without the slightest hitch. The universe was huge, of course, and no one knew who or what might lie hidden in the depths; but the Koleic ships had never encountered anything to hamper their plans for universal—literally—domination.

Until now.

There was a planet out there, selected for Changing, that had *not* been changed.

Butk felt that the situation warranted an unprecedented step.

He tapped a first hand against the cold metal.

Tick. Tick. Tick.

And—miracle of miracles—the iris slowly seeped open, emitting the thin *hiss* that was a normal accompaniment to shipboard movements.

God had invited him in.

* * *

When he emerged, Chaptain Butk was shaken to his very core, even though to the eyen of the numbers that glanced his way as he rushed past he was not changed. But inside... *inside.*

In so many words, God had revealed something that was not possible within Butk's understanding of the universe. Not possible at all.

And now it was up to him to delve further into this mystery beyond all mysteries... this secret that God had kept to Herselves even as he had been setting course for a distant, insignificant world already visited by the Koleic.

God *was no more.*

At least part of Her was... gone.

Not dead. That would be an impossibility exceeding all impossibilities— the mind stuttered at the thought.

Merely... *gone.*

Butk nearly stumbled as he passed through the iris to the command center but caught himself at the last instant and regained not only his poise but his self-control. God had told him what he must do, and why, and how.

A thing to have been accomplished.

He, Chaptain Butk, would do it.

"Report."

The nearest five spoke up, apparently unaware of the turmoil within its Chaptain. "Designated planet now three hours away. Flash successful. Further orders."

"Approach... with caution." Words undoubtedly never spoken before by a Koleic commander. Caution might be for lesser breeds, for the stunted forms of half-life that eked out their feeble existence on worlds before the Change, but not for the Koleic. With God on their side, they would go where ordered, destroy what stood in their path, wrench potential worlds from the grasp of the weak and the helpless, and continue the *works*, the *wonders* of the Koleic Empire.

For that, caution was not needed. Indeed, it might even hamper their actions.

But the God had been precise and direct.

"With caution," the five repeated, its voice as controlled as Butk's had been.

The next while passed largely without words as the various numbers jockeyed the ship into position, just beyond the perimeter selected by God. They knew their functions and performed them admirably without interference or interruptions by their Chaptain. For his part, Butk was willing to stand motionless at his command screen, first arms relaxed, second arms dropped by his side.

His inner turmoil did not diminished appreciably as they drew nearer to their target world. God might understand what all of this meant; he did not. He could only have faith and trust on the word of...

"First readings, my Lord."

He blinked several eyen, startled by the abruptness of the voice.

"Report."

"Records indicate that Chaptain Torq reported a... an... anomaly surrounding the world."

Butk chittered his acknowledgment.

"No such anomaly appears now, my Lord. All scanners read normal. That is..." The five fell silent.

Butk did not even move in response. The number would continue when it had found the proper words.

"My lord, there appears to be an exceedingly high level of carbon, water vapor, and dust... most probably volcanic ash, since the scanners indicate that it is extremely fine and pervasive."

"Localized?"

"No, my Lord. Planet-wide."

Butk turned several eyen toward the number. "Repeat."

"Planet-wide evidence of cataclysmic events, including conflagration of virtually all land masses."

"Volcanic events?"

"Uh... no, my Lord. No signs of active volcanism."

"Then what...?" Butk stopped himself before his words fully formed a question. *This* was clearly part of the mystery, portion of the impossibility. A dead world where there had been a live one. A world with an atmospheric condition that could not be explained. A world in which—or from around which, at any rate—God had... *gone.*

"Re-scan for life forms."

In the distance, computers hummed and buzzed as the numbers punched buttons and requested any number of specific readings. Those readings would then be correlated to provide the Chaptain with a clear, precise answer to his unspoken question.

In a few moments, another number—a four on the other side of the command module—spoke: "Scan for life forms completed, my Lord."

"And...?"

"One."

"One species? How can a world exist with only a single species? Every life-bearing world we have discovered—"

No, my Lord."

Butk physically turned his body so that he could focus all of his eyen on the four. His actions made the number anxious, that much was obvious. There was a tell-tale trembling of the lower carapace, a slight forward arc to the abdomen.

"Control yourself," Butk rasped, allowing his voice to vibrate along his mandibles, thus adding a level of resonance and authority to it.

The four straightened convulsively.

"My apologies, my Lord."

"Why did you interrupt me?"

"Because... well, because the scanners do not report a single species of life on the planet."

"What then?"

"A single… *specimen.* Just one."

Chaptain Butk's lander was identical to every other such vehicle used for ship-to-planet transport and back, with one exception.

While every other lander on every other ship dedicated to the Change functioned on conventional fuel to penetrate planetary atmospheres and then, once the mission was fulfilled, to break the planetary gravity well and return to the God's vessel, Butk's had one additional feature.

A short-gig flash drive.

It had been installed during the three-hour voyage to the planet's periphery, with specific instructions from Butk himself… from the God, actually, since She had implied/told/suggested that one would be useful although She had not come out and told him any specifics.

This was, in essence, a miniature version of the ship-sized flash, designed to carry a lander and its crew a specific distance and no more: from the ship to a designated spot on the surface, then, at a moment's notice, from the surface back to the ship.

From this, Butk had guessed that something horrific had happened to the first lander, and to Chaptain Torq, something that could have been avoided with faster—instantaneous—propulsion. Something God chose not to reveal, not even to Her chosen Chaptain.

Well and good. That was Her right and Her privilege, to reveal only what would lead to success in the Change. Butk could be relied on to take care of anything else that might arise.

The lander touched ground.

Scanners still showed nothing except a single life form in the only standing structure visible. Apparently the only such structure on the planet.

The crew had to wait for some time for the fine dust stirred up by their arrival to settle sufficiently for them to see. They used the time appropriately, checking and re-checking the fit of the air-scrubbers set individually into their double rows of spiracles. Scans indicated that there was air of sufficient density and quality to sustain life but that much of it was contaminated by the nearly microscopic dust particles. Everyone aboard understood the dangers of what the medics referred to blithely and unerringly as *pneumonoultramicroscopicsilicovolcanokoniosis* but that the rest of the numbers simply called *spiracle-sludge.* And the painful death that could result from it. Regardless of what alien particles might hover in the atmosphere, however, the crew was sure that the scrubbers would do their job without fail.

Finally, the double doors in the stern of the craft cranked open, and Butk —as was his prerogative as Chaptain—set foot on the alien world.

At least, he *tried* to do so.

He almost fell when, to his startlement, the firm surface he stepped onto gave way and his leg sank nearly to the femur into something powdery, grey, and slightly gritty. Instinctively, he reached out with a tarsus—and his corresponding second arm, even though there was nothing to hold onto—but at the moment when he nearly lost his balance, both podal tarsi came to rest on something firm and unmoving.

The ground. Hidden beneath a thick layer of ash and other particulates that, as far as the eyen could see, seemed as solid as earth itself.

Behind him, he might have heard the rustle of wing-cases surreptitiously rubbing against each other, but he chose not to turn and scold. Laugh they might at him, behind their wings, but he had his dignity, and his footing.

Besides, he could take his pique out on them later. It was probably the security detail; and since few of them returned totally unscathed after preliminary exploration details—or, on some worlds, even alive—Butk could afford to overlook a moment of misplaced levity.

He strode/waded a short distance from the lander, weapon in one first arm, second arms both hovering over additional weapons still in their holsters. Every step stirred up the ash, but fortunately it settled more rapidly than he might have expected. Even so, he felt as if he were trudging through a thick fog, unable to see the fine details of the landscape.

He stopped.

He listened, scanned with all of his eyen.

Nothing. Not a movement. Not a sound.

To his right and left were several smooth mounds of ash, roughly room-sized.

"Security."

Behind him, they snapped to attention.

Ahhh. A far more pleasing sound than the rustle of laughter.

"There." He pointed with his first arm, his weapon a mere extension of his being.

A trio of nines, each identified with a startlingly red sash across its thorax, stepped off the lander, struggled momentarily to maintain their equilibrium, then scuttered behind the group of mounds.

"And there." He pointed with his other first arm, and three more security-nines disappeared around the opposite set of mounds.

He waited for the numbers to re-appear.

Their report, when it came, did not surprise him.

"My Lord, nothing."

He nodded and began moving toward the single structure, a short distance from the lander. It might once have been white; it might once have been sky-blue or pink with purple elytra spots, for all that mattered.

Now, it was solid, unremitting black, as black as if it had been smothered in fire... which it apparently had.

It was nearly featureless. It had a number of walls meeting at distinctly odd angles, but from the exterior Butk couldn't identify precisely how many.

Directly ahead, however, were two tall, blank panels between what looked to be support pillars.

Doors.

He motioned with his weapon and led the crew—security detail as well as a handful of investigators—toward the building.

As he approaching within spitting distance of the doors, something unanticipated happened.

The doors opened.

To darkness and emptiness.

Butk led his crew down the long corridor that opened before them. Behind him, the security numbers cast light on the walls—as blackened as the exterior of the structure, seeming to absorb whatever illumination was present.

At the end of the corridor, a second set of doors appeared, as silent and as ominous-seeming as the first. These were almost identical to the first set, save only that they were not as overwhelmingly tall. Nor were they quite blank. In spite of the coating of ash and smoke, several arcane symbols showed on each panel.

Butk signaled one of the red sashes, which scurried closer, bringing his light to bear on the figures.

They seemed senseless. Merely squiggles and awkward—but curiously repulsive—curls. Butk forced down a feeling of discomfort and nodded.

The security-number touched the doors with the tip of a tarsus. And the doors opened. With a gesture, Butk indicated that two of the red-shirts were to remain by the doors, guarding the rear, while the rest continued on.

The next chamber was oddly shaped. Two walls angled sharply outward from the door frame, continuing uninterruptedly until they abruptly intersected the far wall. Again, none of the three walls were marked in any way, but they too were fire-scorched, although it seemed that at least a bit of original color—a hue Butk could not quite put a name to—remained along the upper edges.

The Chaptain did not like even the suggestion of the unnamable color.

The double doors here bore symbols as well, the same scratches and squiggles as the preceding set, plus several more. Butk took longer to examine the marks, first by himself, then with a four and a five that were both trained (as far as one might be trained in such things) in alien marking.

"My Lord, I tremble to my very sternites to acknowledge my profound ignorance before my Chaptain, but these configurations make no sense to me. Never have I seen anything the like."

"Nor I, my Lord," added the five. "In all of the files collected from all of the..."

"Enough," Butk said, motioning them back.

This time, he reached out with his own first arm, the one not holding his still-drawn but unused weapon, and tapped the door with a tarsus.

It opened.

He had expected no less. Again, he assigned two security-nines as guards.

In the next chamber, the wall behind Butk seemed mere extensions of the door panels, extending in opposite directions until each formed a right-angle with the side walls, which in turn continued in unbroken parallel panels until they met the far wall. A rectangle.

Ahhh. Something that made a certain kind of sense.

The doors in the far wall were, again, like the previous sets, ornamented with more of the curious sigils or symbols or whatever they were. And less of the ubiquitous ash and streaks of carbon. There was color underlying the black, a different color than the hints in the second room, but color nonetheless, equally unidentifiable and equally, discomfortingly off-putting.

Butk did not hesitate to touch the doors. Two more security-nines remained by the panels as Butk and the rest of the landing party passed through.

The next chamber was, as he has suspected, formed of five equal expanses of wall. A pentagon. As with the entire building, apparently, each wall was unbroken, smooth, and—as one of the security-numbers determined—cool to the touch. There was another color, this one darker, almost turbulent in its intensity where it shone through the pervasive blackness.

Butk pressed onward, barely glancing at the additional markings on the doors set at angles to continue the fourth and fifth walls. Although there were still several security numbers accompanying the party, he did not assign guards over these doors. And he holstered his weapon. He had the rooms figured out.

It was a simple geometric progression.

As much as the previous chambers had made him feel uncomfortable, the sixth had an opposite effect on him and, to judge by the ripple of quivers and shakes among the crew, upon the numbers accompanying him. The far wall was parallel with the one they had just passed through; two additional walls on each side and one at their backs completed the form...a *hexagon.*

On the home world, there was a subspecies of beings that, although almost non-sentient, nonetheless held an honored place among the Koleic. They built nothing, the contributed nothing to the overall expansion of the Empire, they were in fact so small as to be inconsequential next to the powerful figures of the Koleic, but still, at certain times of the year, the mellilotes produced a certain sticky substance within their bodies that, when harvested from the six-sided waxen cells in which they stored it, tasted...

Butk swiveled, startled, as a harsh *clang* sounded behind him. At the far end of the series of chambers, the exterior doors had swung shut, apparently of their own volition. And even as he watched, the next sets closed—second, third, fourth—with such force that he could sense the vibrations in his antennae, and so quickly that the security-nines were trapped in their respective rooms. Leaving Butk with only six guards and an equal number of specialists, most of whom were murmuring and rustling uncomfortably.

He gestured. One of the remaining nines moved toward the set of doors that had most recently closed, sealing the crew in the pentagonal room. He touched it with a tarsus. The door remained closed, but nothing else happened. No sudden surge of an unanticipated power to incinerate the nine, no abrupt influx of hideous aliens carrying projective weapons or other exotic armaments.

Butk held his position for a moment, then turned to look at the doors to the next chamber, presumably heptagonal. He stepped closer, almost but not quite touching the surface. The nauseating color—as expected, different from the hints in the previous rooms—was almost untouched by scorch marks or ash. And the bosses on the panels were far more expansive, more deeply incised, and even more discomforting, if that were possible.

And they covered the entire surface of the two panels, some touching each other, several overlapping to create a kind of angular patterning that was simultaneously unfamiliar and hideously suggestive.

Butk's first arm trembled slightly as he touched one of the protrusions.

The door swung open, silently, ominously.

He stepped through, into a chamber that was almost blindingly white, lit by tall, narrow windows in each of the seven walls.

And the moment that he crossed beneath the lintel, the doors slammed shut, isolating him from the rest of the landing crew.

For an instant, he felt a horrific pressure in his ventral plates, the wish— no, the visceral *need*—to curl, then he straightened and stared straight ahead at what faced him.

It was an abomination, a horror.

Dual eyes, compound-less, fixed in rigid sockets and therefore unable to split and take in more than what stood directly before the creature. Tall, extraordinarily fragile-looking, soft-fleshed without even so much as a hint of an exo-skeleton to protect inner organs from outside dangers. Some kind of glittering fabric covering or suit that was itself almost transparent, revealing every contour of the thing's body.

Two first arms.

Where the seconds should be, there was only smooth, vulnerable-looking tissue.

Two podals, two clumsy, flat appendages altogether too broad and short for substantial support as they were, yet they were unnecessarily divided into even smaller, less efficient-seeming minor appendages at the farthest extreme.

Tendrils of something wispy and curling about its upper extremity, dark but glistening with highlights from the windows, caught back from the two abominable eyes with a band of gold-colored metal, perhaps actually made of gold, although Butk doubted that a thing of such great value could exist on this blackened, burned-over husk of a world.

Again, in the presence of such a monstrosity, Butk felt the conscious urge to turn and pound on the doors, to scream for the crew to rescue him, to *curl* as if he were nothing more than an almost-brainless twelve, but, also again, he found the inner strength to withstand.

He stepped toward the miscreation that stared fixedly back at him, light glinting in shards from spots in the center of each flat, glossy, *single* eye.

He shuddered.

And he started to speak, then caught himself.

The trans-comm was trapped in the hexagonal room, along with the specialists who were supposed to step up at this point and direct the investigation into this lone specimen of what appeared to be a malformed, possibly hideously mutated species.

His mandibles clattered uselessly as he struggled to decide what to do next.

As if it had read his mind, the creature opened a slit in its oval top-appendage—its head, presumably—and, as the two exterior flaps of tissue fluttered and another bit of meat inside the head wriggled up and down, back and forth, it produced the most frightening sounds Butk had ever heard.

Koleic words.

At first, he could not understand them. There was something wrong with the pronunciation, a kind of moist *fleshiness* about the clicks and chitters that, like the asymmetry of the heptagonal room itself, struck him to the depths and at least momentarily disturbed his ability to concentrate.

The thing fell silent and stared at him.

He stared back, splitting eyen to make sure that he could survey the entirety of the room before him. Who knew what other horrors the chamber might produce?

It spoke again, and this time Butk could, with some difficulty, comprehend.

"I do not need the word-device." Apparently it was referring to the trans-comm. "We have learned your speech."

"What are you?" Butk said, the question coming as much from impulse as from reasoned purpose.

"I am the Cwrth."

"And what is a Cwrth?"

"No. I am *the* Cwrth. And it is I." It seemed to be making an important point from the tonal shift in its voice, but Butk could not fathom what.

"What do you do here?" He gestured to the room.

"I wait."

Butk did not speak. Surely the thing before him would say more. *I wait.* Ridiculous. What kind of an answer was that? Finally, however, he broke the silence.

"For what?"

"For you."

"For…" Butk felt a flutter of something that might eventually pupate into anxiety but that at this point was merely a mild discomfort.

"You make no sense. For me? How could you know…?"

"I have been told."

"Told? By whom? There is no way that you could have received warning of our approach. Telemetry indicates no sophisticated electronics, no arrays that could have…" When he realized that he was talking more to reassure himself than to inform it—the *Cwrth*—he tapered off.

"Nevertheless."

"By whom?"

"By the Old One."

"And this 'Old One,' where is it hiding? Our… machines… tell me that you are alone on this world."

"As I am."

"Then how could you possibly…" He decided to change directions, to re-assert his control over the situation. This spongily organic thing before him was of a lesser breed; he was of the Koleic. It should not be his responsibility to interpret its vaguenesses.

"Open the doors." This time there was no sense of disquiet in his click-ings. There was only *command,* and the unspoken assumption, deeper than his conscious self, that he would be obeyed.

"So be it."

It did not move, nor did it speak. Even the flimsy draperies surrounding its fragility remained as immoveable as stone.

Yet, inexplicably, the great doors behind Butk's ventral surface swung open. He heard their soft *hiss* and the sudden clattering of the numbers still trapped in the hexagonal chamber.

"All of them. Including the entrance."

"So be it."

And thus it was.

As loudly as possible, Butk chittered that the security-nines were to re-main in place and alert him if anyone—anything—approached the build-ing. Then he instructed his crew to enter the final chamber. His tech-num-bers clustered immediately behind him. One scuttled forward with an awkward-looking metal box, apparently intending to place it between the Chaptain and the alien.

"No need," Butk said. "It speaks Koleic. After a fashion."

Without responding the tech-number withdrew, disappearing into the small cluster. Butk watched with several eyen until he could see the number no more; all the while, however, he kept the majority of his eyen trained on the creature.

"You will come with us."

"You must leave me, now. And you must leave this place."

"*Must?*" Butk allowed several eyen to gaze, first on this arrogant softlimbed thing and then on the small party of crew behind him, each member armed, each obviously more than an equal to the unarmed entity threatening them. "You dare to *must* a Koleic Chaptain?"

"You must leave this place."

"We will leave, in our own good time. And you will accompany us."

"You must leave me here."

"No. You will come with us."

The Cwrth paused before answering, then: "So be it."

"*Now.*"

"So be it."

The creature bent at its waist, its long head-filaments sweeping over its static eyes, shadowing them for a moment. As they disappeared, Butk felt a surge of relief that the abominations had been covered.

After another moment, the Crwth raised its first arms, bringing its distastefully divided manual tarsi together. There was something ritualistic in the movement that disquieted Butk.

Then it began mumbling, chanting, apparently repeating the same word… phrase… whatever, over and over.

"Stop that!" Butk was himself startled at the overwhelming anger—and fear—that abruptly flooded through his ichor.

The creature continued, bowing even lower and repeating the sounds—was that a name?—without break, without respiration, faster with each repetition.

"Stop the creature," Butk said, communicating his meaning even more forcefully with a gesture than he had with words.

Two nines scuttled forward, each grasping one of the thing's first arms in its own, first tugging, then pulling until they broke the ritual symbol the creature had been making. At that instant, it ceased speaking, straightened sharply, and stared directly into the Chaptain's eyen.

He almost staggered back, then caught himself.

"What were you doing? What were those… sounds?" He couldn't force himself to refer to the uncanny cadences as *words*.

"What you asked." The Cwrth did not break its steadfast gaze, although a number of Butk's eyen shifted right and left nervously.

"What do you mean? I asked nothing of—"

"You asked who the Great Old One was. And where He was hiding."

"And?"

"I have alerted Him to your questions, although surely he knew already what was in your mind… and your heart."

Butk dampened the impulse to glance around the chamber as if looking for some secret opening through which the creature's god—for that was obviously what this "Old One" must be—might make its entrance. Whether it would walk or slither or billow like some noxious cloud, Butk did not know, but suddenly he knew one thing: he had no desire to meet the creature's deity, whether as a stone statue, an ancient hag-ridden version of the Cwrth itself, or something even more horrendous, a nightmare in living flesh.

Suddenly, all that he wanted was to be off this planet and safely in the ship again.

"What did you say…?"

But the Cwrth seemed not to hear him. It continued: "I have alerted Him, as I was set here to do. Would that He had required me to call down the very stones of this building upon you as invaders and infidels and crush you as vermin beneath His feet—and myself as well for being polluted by your presence—but He did not."

The Chaptain stared, mostly at the creature's insolence but also at the unbelievable intensity it managed to compress into the sentences. There was hatred there, and contempt, and a degree of malevolence beyond Butk's understanding.

"Hold it tightly," he said to the two nines. Slowly, almost hesitantly, he approached the Cwrth until he stood within arm's reach of it. It did not flinch.

Up close, it was even more abhorrent than from a distance. Its covering lacked the stylish glisten and sportive coloration of either Koleic carapaces or their multiple appendages. Instead, it was a ghastly, pinkish nothingness, tinged with green, with neither pattern nor markings to distinguish it. The Cwrth apparently wore no ornaments, since beneath the sheer fabric Butk could see only curves and angles of the putrid exo-organ, wrinkled where the first and last legs bent slightly, as if to help the creature adjust to movement. Altogether nauseating.

Butk turned to the nearest nine. With a single, swift movement, he grasped one of the nine's second arms, extended it to its fullest, then, with a simultaneous wrench and pull, and an oddly satisfying *crack*, yanked it from the nine's thorax.

The nine shuddered convulsively, its carapace clattering in the silence, but otherwise it made no move. After a moment, it stood motionless, still gripping the creature's arm as if nothing untoward had happened. Butk nodded slightly to acknowledge the nine's obedience and fortitude, then made a mental note to allow it access to the regeneration chamber as soon as the party returned to the ship.

Ichor dripping from the severed joint and from the nine's body. Butk reversed his grip on the limb until he held it by the femur, the still-twitching, sharply pointed tarsus angled toward the Cwrth.

The creature had watched the entire scene impassively, as far as Butk could tell. It had not moved. Its own thorax rose and fell with the same regularity as it had been since he had entered the chamber, as if dismemberment of a sentient species were something it regularly observed. There was, perhaps, a degree or two more of green in its covering, and the pink might have shifted slightly toward red, but otherwise, no reaction.

Butk extended his arm, bringing the nine's tarsus close to the Cwrth's exo-organ.

Still it did not move.

He touched a bit of the covering with the nine's tarsus, exerting just enough pressure to puncture the covering and allow a bead of the creature's ichor to form just beneath one of its eyes.

When he withdrew the tarsus, the bead grew a bit larger, until its surface tension broke and the fluid—thick and purple and slightly odoriferous—oozed downward.

Nothing. No reaction.

Butk studied the fabric covering the creature. It seemed attached in only one place, at the juncture of what would be first femur and thorax on a Koleic. He slid the nine's tarsus between the fabric and the exo-organ, careful not to cut the creature—let the *anticipation* of it suffice, for now—and severed the fabric.

Soundlessly, it slithered down the curves of the Cwrth's body and puddled at its feet.

Naked, the creature was even more repulsive. Awkward curves, particularly formed by two pronounced located horizontally in the center of the thorax; unexpected concavities and convexities; and that awful fragility announced in every joint, in the extraordinary thinness of the limbs, in the narrow connective between head and body—everything screamed *alien* and *otherness.*

Butk swallowed bile and raised the nine's tarsus once more. It had stopped quivering and, in the Chaptain's hand, had become a formidable weapon.

He punched the exo-organ into the same juncture of femur and thorax, more forcefully and more purposefully this time.

The Cwrth flinched but did not speak.

Rather than withdrawing the tarsus when the first beads of ichor formed, Butk slowly drew its point downward, then angled across the thorax, slicing deeply into the two mounds. They bled heavily. Finally, when the tarsus reached the juncture of abdomen and last leg, he pulled it free. Ichor dripped from its point. Even more issued from the long slash across the Cwrth's front, dripping down its body until it seemed once again clothed, this time in its own life-fluid.

The green in its exo-organ was more pronounced now, the red fading back to pink, and from there to near-white.

That had hurt it, Butk knew, but it was not allowing him to see anything but autonomous physiological responses. It neither spoke nor moved.

In spite of what pain it might/must have been suffering, it stared at him with its two single eyes. This close he could see that each contained a central black spot surrounded by a circle of colored tissues that seemed from one angle purple, from another an iridescent green—perhaps the only thing about the creature that appeared normal. The larger circle itself was surrounded by whitish, glossy tissue finely divided by jagged red and black lines, so delicate that it took most of Butk's eyen just to see them.

Very peculiar, compared to his own faceted eyes and the multitude of polished eyen within each.

He reached out with the nine's tarsus, ichor still glistening on its tip. Stopped just before it touched the Cwrth's eye.

The creature did not move. Nothing changed.

He moved the tarsus closer. Now perhaps no more than a breath stood between it and the creature.

A fraction closer.

Something happened.

The Cwrth's eye-flaps dropped once and moisture formed in the corners of the organ. Then the eye-flaps flickered several times before stopping, and the creature's head moved backward. Not much, but enough for Butk.

"Ah," he said, his mandibles quivering with his excitement. "We have a weakness, do we?"

He thrust the tarsus close again, this this time actually touching the membrane forming the outer surface of the eye. He pressed. The membrane dimpled but did not break. The moisture formed again, although this time the Cwrth did not otherwise respond.

Perhaps because it was ready for me this time. Well, we shall see....

He stepped away and motioned to the nines, who tightened their grips on the Cwrth's appendages.

"See if there is anything of interest in the chamber." The order was crisp and sharp, a Koleic Chaptain speaking to subordinates.

"Yes, my Lord."

Several nines broke away and began exploring the unnatural angles, but they found nothing. The chamber was bare, sterile almost, except for the single creature.

Butk swiveled and, without speaking, strode from the room, following the single corridor back through the preceding chambers until he exited the building. Behind him came the nines, surrounding the Cwrth, and then the remainder of the team. Moving almost in unison, they entered the landing craft and prepared for the short-gig flash back to the ship.

Onboard, Butk indicated that the nines were relieved of duty and could return to the rest barracks. The wounded nine followed a different corridor toward regeneration; it would take a while, but he would be whole again.

Now the Cwrth was surrounded by a higher order of guard, sevens, as was appropriate on board the ship.

Butk considered his next action, but really there was no choice. Indicating to the rest of the landing crew that they were to begin assessing and recording, he proceeded to the most important part of the ship, the core of the ship: the Hatchery.

Arriving, he gestured for the others—including the creature—to remain outside.

The iris opened. He stepped through and into the presence of God.

"My God," he said, although any greeting was superfluous since She knew already that he had returned and what he had brought.

A handful of eyen turned toward him. He took that as a command to speak.

"All went as it was to have, my God. As you foresaw. We have a prisoner. The only life form on the planet."

"It is to have been seen."

With a single twitch of his tarsus, Butk ordered the sevens to bring the Cwrth into the Presence.

The creature seemed no different here than it had been on the planet's surface—alone, aloof, unspeaking unless through some inner direction of its own.

God turned several more eyen in its direction. Then:

Plop.

Plop.

And an unnatural pause in the rhythm of egg-laying. Butk shifted uncomfortably.

He held his break so long that his spiracles ached.

Plop.

God had resumed Her rhythm; that was good.

But what followed was definitely *not* good.

She turned not only Her eyen, but her very *Eyes* upon the creature... and peripherally upon Chaptain Butk. He quivered inwardly. It was as if he were being pinioned on a worktable and every internal organ were being spread for some infinitely superior being to poke and prod and observe.

Plop.

Plop.

Plop.

Then an even greater miracle and an even greater horror.

The God *turned Her head to gaze upon them.*

Directly.

Butk nearly curled with the wonder and the hideousness of it.

It was fortunate that he was not required to speak, for he seemed to have forgotten how to control the muscles of his own body.

Instead, the God spoke... rumbled almost, Her voice resonating through the Hatchery as if a great thunder from the mountains.

"It is not to be accepted."

Butk quailed. There was not enough information for him to understand what She meant, what She wanted. He was but a mere Chaptain. He chose the only way out, even though it felt to him to be the coward's way.

He remained silent, unmoving, a pillar of sodium chloride before His God.

She spoke again. This time Her voice was lower, softer, but now replete with hatred and disgust.

"There is that which should not be."

Butk began to perceive what God might intend but he was still not certain. He waited.

"It surges within her. It seeks My life!"

Butk stepped closer to the Cwrth, which seemed unperturbed by the God's obvious turmoil. Or perhaps it simply didn't understand any more than the surface of the words and missed the enormous implications the Chaptain was intuiting.

"There is a thing which is *not to be born.*"

As if he were moving automatically, or as if his body were controlled by some external force beyond his understanding, Butk found his first arm arcing behind him, hovering at the apex of the arc, his tarsus trembling with simultaneous anticipation and apprehension, then his arm retracing the arc, flashing past his straining eyen, continuing, faster and faster, until it met with the vulnerable exo-organ at the narrowest point on the Cwrth's body, at the joining of head and thorax, and with only the slightest hesitation as it bore through a hindrance that must have been a sort of endo-skeleton adducible only by the creature's form and function, severing head from body in a single stroke.

Plop. Plop.

Koleic egg and the Cwrth's head made almost the same sound.

The creature's body remained standing for a moment, longer than Butk might have anticipated. Then, as if all support had been removed in a single instant, it collapsed. As it did so, ichor flowed from severed fluid-vessels in the neck, flowed and pooled on the deck.

It was dark enough and glossy enough for Butk to see God reflected in the ichor of Her victim... because it was truly God's hand that struck the allochthon, as wielded by her faithful minion.

Then, even as the God began to speak, something—not dark, but black, black beyond black, blacker even than the void between the stars—something so black as to be the antithesis of light emerged from the wound.

First, there was only a thin filament, so thin that it was nearly invisible. Butk had to focus several eyen to see it clearly. Then another appeared. And another. Perhaps the length of his antennae and certainly no thicker. Half a dozen. A dozen.

Then, abruptly, they joined at the base to merge into something longer, more fluid, whipping back and forth with all of the fury of a mellilote whose hive has been ravaged and harvested.

Tenticular, black, as much an eldritch shadow as a thing of reality, it emerged. And another tentacle, as sinuous, as blasphemous as the first. And the first filaments of a third.

"There is a thing to be destroyed," the God said, Her voice echoing above the tumult of Butk's ichor flowing through his tubular heart.

Mindlessly, he acted, barely registering that a dozen—a score—of tens in attendance on the God joined him as he pummeled the lifeless tissue of the

Cwrth into less than a puddle, less than a smear of organic fluids and crushed endo-skeleton on the glossy floor of the Hatchery.

Only when some of the tens began dragging away the most solid bits, while others exuded oils that would cleanse the floor of any impurities, any hints of desecration, did Butk step away from them.

In that moment, the voice of the God came to him a final time.

"Yes, my God," he quivered in answer, "yes."

Almost before the Hatchery door irised closed behind him, Butk found himself in the corridor, doing the unthinkable. He dropped to all six appendages and scuttled—literally *scuttled* at a speed unimaginable on only two—toward the Command Center. As he passed, numbers flattened themselves as best they could against bulkheads, daring neither to speak to him, not even so much as a salute, or hinder him in any way.

Death would be the result.

Several eights curled as their Chaptain sped by and, before he had disappeared around a bend in the corridor, black ichor had begun oozing from their carapaces.

Butk paid them no mind. He was on God's mission.

He slowed only enough to avoid slamming into the Command Center door. Even so, he barely had time to raise himself upon two before the iris allowed him to enter.

He ignored the numbers, ignored the fact that through some inner sense of their own they understood that something unimaginable had occurred. All but a tiny fraction of the eyen in the room pivoted to watch him.

Swiftly, but with all of the dignity of a Koleic Chaptain, Butk approached his monitor.

Only then did he speak: "There is a place to be."

"Coordinates, my Lord?"

None of the other numbers moved or chittered.

Butk paused only briefly before he answered.

"Koleic. Home."

An instant after the flash drive activated, Butk, his God, and his ship arrived in orbit around a medium-sized planet near the nuclear bulge of a modest spiral galaxy, itself near (at least in astronomical terms) but still in stasis with the ravening, super-massive black hole at the center of the universe.

The Chaptain and his crew paid no attention to this fact, however; for them the planet Koleic—as with the Koleic as a race—*was* the center of the universe as well as its reason for being.

It took only a few moments more, therefore, for the Command Center crew to set a second flash, this one short-gig.

And an instant after that flash, they found themselves at berth in one of the huge complexes that surrounded Gods' House—the largest such complex on Koleic.

Butk said nothing. Congratulations were perhaps in order for the meticulous and timely way his crew had behaved, but Koleic Chaptains rarely if ever extended congratulations. Jobs were to be done; numbers were to perform as genetically and environmentally designed. A good job was simply a job completed.

Besides, he was still a bit shaken by his transformation only a short while before from Chaptain to... well, to be blunt if not quite politically correct, a ground-Kol, one of the numberless, less-evolved specimens that still polluted (Butk's private opinion, that) the planet.

It had taken more than merely coming upright to forget the primal urges, the almost involuntary, certainly ancestral need to grovel in the dirt and dung.

Nevertheless, when he finally reached for the switch that would activate all of his exterior sensors and show them on his monitor, his tarsus was firm, steady, clearly that of a Chaptain in full charge of his ship.

He glanced at each monitor with several eyen.

Gods!

Literally.

In all quarters that he scanned, he saw ships of every size and shape, land-ships and space-ships, ships that obviously had transported every God on Koleic to this spot before he and his God had even arrived.

Once again, as so often in his life, he marveled at the wonders of Godhood, so far beyond his own understanding.

Even as he scanned, a voice came over the comm.

It wasn't the voice he might have expected. Not quite.

The only entity on board capable of speaking through the ship-wide communicator, other than himself, was... God.

And She would never—*never*—lower Herself to do such a thing. She would speak only through her Chaptain. She would never directly address mere numbers.

And yet She had.

Or had She? Because there was a resonance to the voice, an infinite depth and plangency that suddenly revealed the truth: It wasn't *his* God.

It was *all of the Gods*. Speaking as one through every comm in every ship on Koleic.

What She/They were saying was preposterous, outlandish, unimaginable.

"All Chaptains and crews are instantly to have been prepared for invasion."

Even as Butk began to form the word *invasion* in his mind—a common enough term, perhaps, when used in the context of Changing lesser worlds but unheard of in terms of an invasion of Koleic itself—the Gods spoke again. A single word.

"Imminent."

And the klaxons shrieked.

Butk uttered a vile word, a vituperation so harsh that three sevens on deck immediately curled.

And the klaxons kept shrieking, not just the one from the Hatchery but every one on the ship—and, no doubt, every one on the entire planet.

Butk immediately straightened, painfully straight.

I am the Chaptain. I serve my God! Always!

With that affirmation as penance for his verbal lapse, he turned his attention to the danger, throwing commands back and forth so rapidly that the numbers could barely understand them let alone respond quickly enough to be ready for the next one.

"My lord!" An eight had to outshriek the klaxons to be heard, but Butk felt instinctively that, given the tone of its voice, it would have shrieked anyway. "My Lord! The sky!"

Rather than discipline the eight for a breach of etiquette, Butk glanced at the monitor it was controlling.

The sky was black.

Not just black but the depthless, chthonic blackness that figures in the worst nightmares of all Koleic. Lightless, featureless except for gigantic clouds roiling at the extreme reaches of the atmosphere, fouling the purity of space as if they were battering the air, bashing against it to destroy it and facilitate their entry into this world.

"All weapons ready for firing." Butk was secretly proud at the calmness in his voice, even though his mandibles had vibrated perhaps more definitively than usual as he had spoken.

"My Lord!" came a phalanx of voices in answer.

But none dared ask the obvious question: "For firing against *what*?"

The question did not remain long unanswered... or unasked.

"What is it, my Lord?"

Several more sevens curled, their carapaces clattering to the floor and leaking ichor.

"I... I..." Chaptain Butk did not know. That is, he had no words to put to what he saw in the spaces above Koleic, but in his tubular of tubular he *knew* that he had seen it before... or a miniature version of it, creeping from the fluid-crusted wound of the Cwrth.

Slouching toward Koleic, struggling to be born.

That was only a hint, the slightest fragment of a suspicion of an allusion to an inference of what rough power lay behind the thing the Cwrth was carrying... *her* child!

Which Butk had slaughtered with no more thought than he would have expended on what to eat for breakfast or what popular brand of cleanser to use in polishing his elytra.

Her child... and the child of the Old One.

That was what was coming, scorching through the air, burning away anything in Its path as it plummeted like a dying moon toward Koleic, eyes blank with cosmic madness, physiognomy flickering as It twisted Its hideous corpulence through dimensionless space to wreak vengeance on those that had annihilated Its own.

Not once. That It might forgive.

But twice. And the second time after the warning of Its Witness.

It was there… but Butk suddenly realized that It—whatever *It* truly was—registered on no scanners. He could see It with his own eyen but that was all. There was no indications on any of the dials and meters and gauges where to aim, what to aim at.

Still, he tried. He rattled off coordinates as accurately as his eyen could discern them, unused to having to do such things, and gave commands.

He gave commands, and all chitters stopped together.

All eyen riveted, not on him, but on the many monitors all showing the same thing: the colossal, nearly formless mass differentiated only by the hundreds of ships-long tentacles reaching, grasping, aching toward Koleic… and then—*Gods be praised!*—the single, then the multiple white flashes streaking skyward to greet them with unholy kisses.

The first struck. Butk's weapon.

Even with the great distances separating tentacles from surface, the monitors showed a direct hit. There was a greater flash, a soundless explosion, and a ragged tear in the blackness telling them that they had wounded their prey.

A clatter started throughout the Center… then stopped.

The blackness clouded over, as if invisible flesh were healing itself.

Again and again Koleic armaments struck the Thing.

Again and again It healed Its wounds, each time more rapidly than before.

Then suddenly more streaks of light—this time not planet-based weapons but Koleic ships themselves, each guided and inspired by its own God, each recalled from Changing missions across the universe, recalled and instructed to smite the interloper and destroy it.

They tried.

First they fired weapons from a distance; their shots made no more difference than Butk's own had.

Then, drawing closer to the monstrosity now filling the sky, the simply angled themselves toward the appalling core of Its being and flew at It, obviously intending to collide with It before It could damage the home-world.

And without exception, each of them exploded long before they reached their target, transforming in an instant into a soundless, blazing pseudo-star before diminishing into nothingness.

Every one of them.

For Butk, watching helplessly from his ship, time stood still.

And then It struck.

One tentacle reached down to the surface of Koleic itself, stretched unbelievably from the amorphous central mass housing a single emerald-green eye easily the width of the Great Ocean itself. The arm reached and, with only one of the whip-like protuberances at its end, merely *touched* a waiting God's-ship.

Which exploded. And in dying, destroyed half a dozen others berthed near it.

One tentacle.

And death.

At that, all of the Koleic ships unleashed every weapon they owned, some numbers even clutching hand artillery and racing outside to fire headlong—and uselessly—into the lowering sky.

More tentacles appeared, tipped with devastating whips, studded their entire lengths with mouth-like suckers that opened and closed as if hungry, as if *starving*, and the only thing that would satisfy their craving would be the Koleic.

Even as Butk depressed the switch that would send a planet-buster against the *Thing*—the Great One from the cosmic deeps—a tentacle swept by and touched, merely *touched*, his ship.

And he died.

The planet—now a dead husk circling endlessly a blinding sun in a modest galaxy that might, perhaps, in an eon of eons, succumb to the Siren call at the center of its Universe—is black.

This time, however, it is the blackness not of infinity and immortality, but of death. Of flame and destruction. Of devastation beyond anything imaginable to the quondam inhabitants, themselves now little more than the ash of ashes scattered upon carbon-blasted stone. Nothing remains of God's House. For that matter, nothing remains of the ring of cliffs that once surrounded it or of the Great Ocean that once lapped at its buttresses.

The waters of the Great Sea have evaporated in a cloak of steam that even yet surrounded the planet's surface, its hidden secrecies unhidden—indeed, in existence no more.

The original cliffs have been leveled with a single stroke of a gigantic tentacle fixed close to the single green eye at the Entity's core. It wiped them away as if they had been merely a clutter of dust on a level plain. Here now, and then gone.

In their place stand new mountains, steeper, harsher, almost infinitely higher, formed as the Old One vented Its unending fury on the planet, slashing at its plains, cutting divots in its smoothness and discarding the remains as refuse where it would.

No steps tread the new ranges. No life dares show its face on their heights.

Even though It—whichever of Azathoth's misbegotten progeny It might have been—has long since returned to Its mystic center near the mouth of the black hole, where It passes Its timelessness by moving seamlessly—malevolently—through dimensionless space, at once in all places and through all times—even though It has left the planet, nothing dares stir.

Except...

Except along a jagged fault through the middle of what once had been Gods' House, a gust tears at the steep sides and a single stone dislodges.

Then another.

And yet another still.

It takes a long time for the fourth stone to stutter from its place near the surface and plummet into the unfathomable depths opened by the Great Old One's vengeance. Even longer for the fifth. The planet circles its blinding sun; the system moves with pantheonic grace within the galaxy; the galaxy itself continues its ceaseless struggle against the irresistible force that may—will—ultimately bring it to its doom.

Eventually, though, the sixth stone falls.

And then a minor landslide reveals a tiny opening.

More timelessness passes. And the opening wears larger and larger, revealing the inside of...

Of a secret Hatchery, build against just such a day, as inconceivable as such an event had seemed so many planet-revolutions before.

First to warm beneath the sun's glare is a long line of egg cases, stretching into the shadows. Some of the cases are flat on top, glistening with moisture. Others, those farther back, are dry, old-looking, their sides bulging and their seals ready to burst.

At the head of the line, alone and majestic in her loneliness, is a nascent queen.

Plop.

Plop.

Plop.

Not yet God. For that, one needs subjects. Hers are coming, eventually, but they have not yet hatched. Perhaps now, with the sunlight.

She concentrates Her every attention on her single task.

Plop.

Plop.

Plop.

Occasionally She mutters softly, so that, even if there were a number nearby, it could not hear Her.

But the sun hears. The sky hears. The mountains hear.

"...And... yet... I... AM!"

THE QUEEN IN SHADOW

DAVID J. WEST

Something was wrong. In a micro-cosmic big bang, Jane Thorson's eyes flashed open from stygian black to a blinding haze.

A jarring wrench forced Jane out the door of her cryo-stasis pod. Why was she already conscious? Was she falling or being pulled out by someone? Milliseconds seemed an eternity as her body gave way to the ship's ill-timed return to induced gravity.

You don't dream in cryo-stasis, do you? She couldn't remember.

She was still falling, and dreaming?

Unable to catch herself, the titanium deck was a harsh mistress. Almost blind and deaf as she came to, the numbness in her extremities throbbed alive as feeling returned like spiders swarming over cold flesh. She cursed the name of a dozen fornicating deities.

Pain brought her awareness to the pulsing red alarm and droning siren. With senses dazedly returning, the cause of the waking nightmare banished all other concern. Monitors initially revealed naught but darkness pin-pricked with cold unfeeling stars, coupled with the fathomless silence. Then something swung into view, eclipsing the rest of the delta quadrant.

A vast asymmetrical ship, incalculably larger than her own space freighter, *Centurion*, loomed across the monitor. Blotting out stars, the behe-moth came on deliberately and with malevolent purpose. Such a ship had never before been seen, nor even dreamt of, by humans.

Fear welled up inside Jane where she had never known it before. The alien ship was so utterly unlike anything she had ever conceived of; spiky flanges reached out for miles in abstract angles and curves that served no discernible function. It resembled nothing so much as a dust mite the size of a moon.

Drawing nearer with forward bay doors agape, the colossal ship threat-ened to swallow *Centurion* like the whale did Jonah.

Why did that metaphor cross her mind? As the ship's secondary science officer she would never say that. She did not believe in those myths—unlike someone else she knew.

"What is it?" Before he spoke, Jane hadn't even noticed the man beside her. Her eyes registered the specific security badges across his chest, marking him as the conventional trans-atmospheric pilot. It took Jane a half second longer for her brain to engage and recognize her own husband, Christian.

She took his hand tenderly. "I don't know, Chris." She hated using the full given name that reminded her of his faith.

"It's swallowing us like—"

"I know," she interrupted with a kiss. "It's the biggest thing I've ever seen." She pulled him close.

He blinked at her rapidly, rubbing his own eyes, then stared at the image of the incredible object bearing down on them. "Did you hear it?"

"Hear what," she asked.

"A voice from out of the darkness. In my dreams... It woke me up."

"I heard nothing." What did Christian think he had heard? Jane needed to have hard, quantifiable evidence for everything, but Christian always held to his gut and instinct. She both resented and admired him for it.

"It was just a dream, nothing more, lover."

Space is too harsh for dreamers, priests and fools. There is no time but the now, and no god but what you see in the mirror each morning.

"It had to be the cryo-sleep wearing off. Nothing else," she said.

He smiled in a way she knew meant both that he didn't believe that and that he knew she knew.

Every time she looked out the monitors into space, she couldn't help but think of the ancient astronaut Yuri Gagarin's mantra, *"I see no god up here."* We are inevitably alone in a universe that cares not one whit for our feeling and faith. We press on only because of the indomitable human spirit, not because of a bearded old man above.

Speaking of the god-complex, Captain Williams staggered to the helm and engaged the initial repulsers. "This will buy us time, the sons of bitches!"

"What time? It's too big!"

"I won't go down without a fight! Damn pirates!"

Williams gave Jane no confidence; she knew it was all bravado from a scared little boy. If there was one thing Williams was good at it—maybe the only thing—it was looking brave. When it came down to the wire, would he try to stand now, here? Christian alone had kept the pirates at bay at Sigma 7, when everyone else would have surrendered. No—they *did* surrender. Williams never forgot that humiliation, maybe he would try to be stronger now. But could he? Jane hated to think it considering the situation, but she doubted Williams could truly take the reins and ride this storm out.

"Do you really think it's pirates?" asked Jane, still blinking.

Christian shook his head, "I don't think so. Not with something so... big."

An array of rail guns fired magnetic loads at the oncoming behemoth. Specks of flotsam erupted from the incredible ship's exterior with each strike, but it came on all the same, indifferent, unfeeling, uncaring, as heedless of *Centurion*'s defenses as the sea is to the sands of the shore.

Williams cursed and punched every button on the arsenal panel. Dozens of crewmen stood watching the futile gestures. "Evacuate!" he shouted. "They can't take all of us! To the shuttles!"

Christian hesitated, watching, waiting.

"Lets go," pleaded Jane, pulling on his arm.

"It's too big," he answered. "It will engulf *Centurion* in moments and all the shuttles with it. Whoever they are... whatever they want... they have us."

The jaws of the great ships bay doors cut off whatever dim light reached the outside monitors. The ship gave off no light itself; no window or screen released any hint of luminescence.

"What do they want? The methane rods? The salt converters? It can't be the horn manipulators, can it?"

Christian shook his head. "I think they want us."

"Us? I'd rather die than be pieced out for the Red Market." Jane pulled on his arm, but he resisted. Even the mention of the hated organ dealers paled before this monstrosity. "We have to do something!"

Christian remained transfixed, staring at the ship, "I have to remember. *She* said something."

"*She?*"

"I don't know why I said that."

The alien ship swallowed *Centurion*, taking it leagues inside a dark passage. Rail guns continued to fire, casting futile shards against the insides of the giant. Christian ran his hand along the controls, shutting down the pointless resistance. Faint outer lights of *Centurion* gave dim testament to the cavernous interior of the alien ship.

"Are you giving up?"

Unresponsive, Christian stared.

"This isn't like you to give up!"

He glanced at Jane and gave a half-smile with recognition flooding across his face. "I'm waiting. Answers are coming. I will remember."

Jane shook her head, frightened of her husband's bizarre calm. He was staring straight ahead and nodding and muttering to the voices in his head.

"Chris, do you remember who you are?"

"Of course. I am... I am...?"

"Wake up! I need you to do something!" she shouted.

He blinked alert for a moment, snapping, "What would you have me do? They have us. All of us." Then his face returned to a blank wash, a faraway look of anticipation.

Her eyes welling angry tears, Jane looked away. "I thought I married a man who could do anything. Who would never give up, no matter the difficulty. Now you stand all amazed, letting us be taken by Red Market bastards!" Jane slapped him.

"We don't know that yet."

"You said it first! They want us! Don't lie to me! Kill me before you let that happen!"

Christian ignored her. It was the first situation she could remember that he ever had. He just watched as they were taken down the throat of the colossal ship, ever on, as if this journey to hell might never finish.

One of *Centurion's* shuttles sped past the monitor, perhaps hoping to reach another exit farther down the passage.

"Why would they do that? Why go that way?"

He absently shook his head as if he didn't know but answered, "The gates are shut, there is no way out."

Jane gasped, holding her hand across her mouth, and beat on Christian's shoulder a good three times. "Snap out of it! We have to get out! Why not keep firing? Maybe we could get in a lucky shot?"

"I'm listening," he said staring ahead.

Jane felt sure that particular response was not for her. "Stop it. This isn't like you."

"I don't know," he said again, decidedly to someone or something besides his wife. "I'm trying to remember."

As the ship reached the end of its journey, the loading dock became visible only from *Centurion's* own forward search lights.

"I'm not afraid," he said, apropos of nothing.

"Well, I am. Don't let them take us." She took Christian's face in her hands, prompting another brief moment of recognition from the man she had loved for the last seven years.

Blinking as if waking, Christian looked at her and said, "I don't know what *She* wants yet."

Tears running, Jane spat, "*She*? Who is *She*? This Red Market ship took us. No words, no warning, no mercy."

"I thought I heard words, right before I awoke. I feel something special coming from the ship, a fondness I can't explain. I think I am remembering something good from long ago."

"And I feel an overwhelming sense of dread from it."

"I am at peace with this. Everything will be all right."

She looked into his vacant eyes and shook her head, whispering, "No it won't."

"I am supposed to remember."

"You're crazy. Don't do this. Don't leave me like this, not now."

"I am remembering, just like you said I would."

The ships connected at the loading docks and a dull thud rocked *Centurion*. Despite multiple airlocks, Jane could sense the air pressure change whenever ships synced. No one believed that, but she always felt it, a sixth sense of atmosphere and the ethereal.

A handful of crew members came and stood by them at the helm.

"Do you know anything?"

"Who is it?"

"What do they want?"

To each question, the couple merely shook their heads, watching, waiting.

Christian finally replied, "I can't remember all."

"Remember what?"

"The prompting, the voice, it calls..."

"Snap out of it!"

He looked blankly at Jane.

"Don't do this. Remember me? Remember us and that first weekend in Paris? Remember what happened at Louvre and at the hotel? Remember me."

"I'm trying to understand it myself."

She took his face in her hands. "Don't let them take you away from me. Fight this!"

"I'm trying, I can't explain it. Something in my mind, haunting memories that aren't my own. Another time, another place, another mind and soul..."

New sirens sounded as something forced at the loading bay doors.

"What could do that?" someone asked from far behind.

"I have the bays sealed with the magnetic locks. Nothing is getting in until we find out what the bastards want," said Captain Williams, reappearing with a recoilless rifle slung over his shoulder.

Jane assumed that his reappearance meant he must have not made it to the shuttles in time. He had a craven heart.

"You can't seriously think you will fire that thing inside here, do you?" asked a crewman.

"I won't be taken alive by Red Market body snatchers!"

"What gives you the right to choose death for us?" screamed a woman, struggling to reach Williams with fists upraised, vainly striking her own husband who held her back from the captain.

"We have to stick together! If they are gonna be this bold, they'll take more than just one kidney, sweetheart!"

"Hey!" protested the pummeled husband.

"I'm in command and I say we go down to the last man and woman, rather than let those blood suckers profit from any one of us!" He loaded the recoilless rifle with its caseless tungsten rounds and took a dramatic pose designed to inspire.

But he was sweating.

The crew was glued to the monitors. Shadows shifted rapidly across the outside bay portals as the search lights crossed in a passing sentinel formation, images like flickering patches of tar jetted across the corridor but no recognizable sign of life or machine was witnessed.

"What is making those shadows?"

"What do they want?"

"What are they waiting for?"

"One of them had green lights inside it—a cloaking device?"

"Can they get in?"

Williams, with a false smirk, hazarded a guess. "They probably know we're too tough a nut to crack."

"Shut up," spouted the angry wife.

Williams scowled as more questions and concerns erupted.

Jane knew that the most decent of people become mewling babes when presented with such monstrous uncertainty, herself included. Christian alone remained calm in front of the monitor as if expecting a transmission from a dead tranceiver. No, not calm—his eyes seemed dead.

"Come back to me," she said, running a tender finger along his cheek and neck.

High-pitched alarms joined the ringing chorus of questions. Sirens blasted warning and Jane sensed the cabin pressure change of an airlock being opened.

"Now what?"

"The bays are breached!"

"That's not possible," spat Williams, as he slammed the lever down on the interior locks. A second blast door slammed shut. "They can't get in here," he affirmed, shaking his head in disbelief at what had already happened.

Jane watched the door, which was split evenly at four feet, creating a barely visible seam.

"They couldn't get in with a Moldavian continental burrower!" shouted Williams in that false bravado.

Steel and titanium groaned.

"What is that?" shrieked a woman, pointing a trembling finger the blast door.

Viscous black goo seeped through the near invisible seam and, like a starfish prying apart a clam, several massive dark fingers appeared and slowly cracked open the blast doors further, gaining strength and momentum with every micro-second until the doors fully surrendered and opened.

The black fingers vanished as the doors stood cavernously open into pitch darkness.

"Who is there?"

"What did that?"

"Didn't you see it!"

"Tekeli-li! Tekeli-li!"

"What the hell said that?" asked Williams.

Jane clutched at Christian who still stood by the monitor unaware, uncaring, as the rest of the crew stared at the gloom of the bay.

Dim glowing green orbs appeared in random chaos throughout the dark open chamber like lanterns of some demon-haunted abyss. They swayed and blinked. Multiple audible voices murmured, *Tekeli-li! Tekeli-li!*

"*She* has us," lamented Christian.

"*She*? She who?"

"My Queen."

"How do you know that? Who is *She*?"

"The one who called to me. It was *She* who woke me."

As several crew members stepped closer to look upon the glowing orbs, the darkness that held them in thrall suddenly spiraled into tidal shape and washed into the control room.

"Tekeli-li! Tekeli-li!"

Screams resounded from the foremost crew as they were taken by arms, tentacles, mouths and eyes of warping darkness. Looking like burnt amoebas of colossal stature, a trio of the blobs tumbled in, stretching multiple appendages out to retrieve the crew.

"What are those?" cried Jane.

"Shoggoths," answered Christian. "I shouldn't know that, I couldn't know that, but *She* told me not to fear. They will not harm me."

"Just you?"

"I don't know."

His answer was nearly lost in the tsunami of fear as the black wave penetrated every facet of the control room and took every crewman into its insatiable maw.

Williams fired one round from the recoilless rifle and Jane saw the tungsten slug pass right through the ebon behemoth and slam into the hull behind. The monster did not seem hurt or disturbed in the least. Then Williams was swallowed by the gelatinous monster, all the while screaming for his mother.

Jane could only hold her breath as a tentacle gripped her feet and simultaneously a slimy, fanged mouth splashed down over her shoulders.

She was falling, pulled into utter blackness. Inside a shoggoth, whatever that was, was not unlike swimming inside a pool full of gelatin, cold and disorienting. There was no sense of direction, it seemed to Jane she was continually falling within the blob as it moved back into the colossal ship.

She felt a hand and took it. It was Christian. She recognized his ring and grip.

He alone wasn't panicking, but shouldn't he be?

Almost out of breath, Jane was tossed onto a hard steel deck covered with patches of a sticky but unidentifiable dark matter. The other crew members had also been vomited to the foul deck.

Christian helped her to her feet. He was in conversation with someone she couldn't see. "I hear your concern, my love, but I ask again that they remain aboard as my servants, as the shoggoths do for you."

"Who are you talking to?" asked Jane. He gave her no response.

"Slaves then," answered Christian. "All may serve as they are programmed to. As Enki commanded, 'Let them of use, be used.'"

Dim amber light gave Jane glimpses of her surroundings, and even then it only granted the narrowest of vista at what appeared to be a voluminous tree which stretched upward into the dark starless sky inside the vast ship. They stood at the foot of the thing. Jane wondered if a person was perched farther up among its potato-eye like branches and vines.

Was Christian speaking to a crazed Red Market pirate king? No, he had said a queen before. Jane looked but saw no such person, only the tree.

Colossal as a Redwood, the tree was a bloated, corpulent greenish brown with a multitude of twisting vines reaching down to the pale ground.

As her eyes adjusted, Jane realized that it was not soil the tree was planted in, but bones. Thousands of pale bleaching bones, heaped up like a monument to Tamerlane. Many were human or at least humanoid, but others were of large alien life Jane had never seen before.

Then, horror upon horror, the tree moved as if adjusting in its seat. A wide star-shaped protrusion at its crown, perhaps a head, lowered and looked over its quarry.

"What does it want with us?" asked Jane.

Christian only his conversation, ignoring Jane.

"Even if they mean nothing to you, they do to me. I ask again that you spare them." The shoggoths released more of the crewman, some alive, some unmoving as if they had suffocated already.

"I can respect that."

"What is it saying?" asked Jane.

"She is my sister Jane. If you truly wish to have me, I ask you, do not harm her."

"'Sister?'" spat Jane.

Turning to Jane, Christian finally answered her. "This is Dyblienn, she is my eternal companion and has been waiting millennia to find me again."

"Again?" Jane arched her eyebrow at such a bizarre revelation, but Christian kept a straight face.

"She is the eldest of the Elder race, and I am I am her reincarnated partner Yughsef. She told me."

Glancing about the monumental chamber, Jane rubbed her eyes, calling upon her favorite fornicating deities yet again.

"I say again, she is my earthling sister and I wish no harm to come to her. No! She is not the one you asked of. I know of no such person by that name."

One of the shoggoths crept closer, its myriad green orbs bubbling in and out of sight as a dozen tentacles thrashed and half as many tooth-crammed mouths gaped open in Jane's direction.

"I *demand* she be spared!" Christian shouted.

A rumbling that echoed throughout the cavernous chamber from the tree-like Dyblienn was the first audible sound Jane had heard from the thing.

The shoggoth retreated, albeit reluctantly.

"Thank you, My Love," said Christian.

Jane took a step toward Christian, and just as quickly the anxious shoggoth rolled at her like a tarry tidal wave.

Dyblienn rumbled, and from the corroded steel wall a spear-like rod sprang out and sent a blasting shock into the shoggoth in a heat of blue lightning. The blob visibly and rapidly shrunk upon impact. Its black body hissed and bubbled as it collapsed inward, leaving a putrid smell which reminded

Jane of burning hair and sulfur.

The answer of what the sticky dark matter at Jane's feet was grotesquely answered. Apparently these shoggoths were disposed of often enough that a carpeting of their remains was perpetually before their dark queen.

"A Glaupnir, a molecular destabilizer," answered Christian. "The shoggoths must be kept in line. They have rebelled before, in other times, other places."

The Glaupnir slowly retracted back into the wall panel. Its multi-faceted head resembled a rune-covered spearpoint with five interconnecting blades, though these had spiraling unnatural curves upon them that eluded Jane's eye in following their pattern.

"What powers it?"

"An electromagnet unit runs throughout this ship, making them available everywhere, but their disruptive force is derived from an unknown law of physics with more in common to alchemy and elemental attraction than any known earthen science," said Christian.

Jane tried to laugh to hold back the enveloping fear. "If you can't trust the help, who can you trust?" she said in a shaky voice.

Christian shook his head.

"I would ask that you spare all of them."

Dyblienn rumbled a softer tone and Christian hung his head.

After a moment of brutal unnerving tranquility, Christian spoke once more to the silence. "All right, then. Just her."

"What did *She* say?"

Jane looked back to the worried faces of Captain Williams and the other crew members. Couples held each other, some prayed aloud and others had the blank look of shock.

The shoggoths reared and swallowed them in an instant, drowning their abortive cries in swift black protoplasm.

"No! Why?!" shouted Jane at the monumental Dyblienn.

"They do not matter," said Christian. "All I could ask for was you."

"Why even bring them this far?"

"A mere curiosity, which was quickly sated."

"Monster. And you, a Judas!" The insult was a dig at their unshared faith that she knew would cut him to hear from her. But would it help him realize?

"There is no reasoning with such a being. *She* truly believes me to be her eternal companion. That is the only reason we are still alive, you and I."

"Do you believe that?"

Christian looked away.

"And what of them?" asked Jane, pointing at the tumult of bones surrounding Dyblienn.

"What about them?" Christian asked.

Dyblienn gave her softest rumble yet, and Christian blanched.

"Well?"

"They are all me—my incarnations down through the millennia. *She* keeps each until they—I—expire, always waiting for the final form that shall complete her."

"So you now aren't good enough?"

"*She* wants my soul near her."

"How long until *She* tires of you?"

"How can I know? *She* says she never will. I am her reincarnated eternal partner Yughsef. He who was betrayed by Kumarbi and then destroyed by Enlila."

The exotic names meant nothing to Jane, the implications even less, but the future—*their* future—loomed before her, staring from empty eye sockets of rotted calcium.

"Look at them." Jane pointed at the bones of dozens of beings, human and otherwise. Heaped and strewn in chaotic abandon, the former loves had rotted where they fell like the discarded shells of a lobster feast. "All creatures like you, all waiting for her love and yet left to decay at her feet. You are a sorry lot indeed."

"They wouldn't still be there if *She* didn't care," protested Christian in weeping despair.

"The care of a necrophiliac!"

"This wasn't the choice I asked for!"

"Then make your choice and act!"

"What would you have of me? I am torn apart on what I must do. I was barely able to have her spare you. She fears your relationship to me!"

"Have her let me explore the ship, while you romance her."

Again he blanched.

"Do I have to be the strong one this time? Show some backbone and act like you did in college, why don't you, Romeo? Buy me time to find out what I can do!"

"There is nothing you can do," he said, shaking his head. "It's not so simple, this is not a woman to be trifled with—*She* is a god queen here and I am not who I once was. I don't know if I believe what I once did!"

"You were a barbaric man who took on the stars, while I stayed on the civilized ground. You did what I couldn't out there, I completed the things at home that you couldn't. Two halves of the whole, completing the circle? Remember that?"

Dyblienn rumbled, shaking the entirety of the ship.

"*She* doesn't like how you speak to me. Stop! Now!"

Jane stepped back, glancing over her shoulder at the shoggoths who flowed in and over themselves, poised to pounce, with eyes and mouths changing place as rapidly as her own could follow.

"Am I free to wander the ship?"

"No, but *She* will allow you to see what became of others before."

"That sounds like a threat."

"It is."

A circular steel door coalesced at the far end of the chamber and dim greasy lights appeared one after another, lighting the way into the gloomy reaches like torches into the underworld.

"Go. Before she tires of your voice."

Jane took a few steps and turned. "And if I could save you... my Judas, should I?"

Christian refused to look her in the eye.

She walked into the circular hall, its drowning lights floundering against the swirling dark, a trio of shoggoths flowing behind like black tides.

"Yes," came Christian's barely audible plea.

Jane would find a way, there was always a way. He had taught her that years ago when all seemed lost on Sigma 7; an eternity ago when everyone else gave up, he always stood strong. Now he was so weak in the mind— maybe everything happened before to teach her to be strong on her own for a day like today?

Passing the threshold of the door, Jane stopped to look back. The door closed and the dim amber lights vanished in shadow as a shoggoth reared to swallow her.

Jane bolted down the corridor as the shoggoth splashed down where she had just stood. The bizarre monstrosities seemed perplexed at her denial of fate. After a moment of bubbling over themselves they slithered and rolled after her.

The corridor wound in a long arc, granting an unwholesome view of the death coming for her. No doors or windows granted any form of retreat or sanctuary, nowhere but a dimly lit tubular hall to die in.

The shoggoths gained ground every second, tumbling over each other in a desperate attempt to be the engine of her demise.

Just as her lungs cried out for death and her legs were about to break, a wide vent, a meter squared, appeared along the curved hall, a path to escape. At that moment, death at the hands of anything would be preferable to drowning in nightmare jelly.

She dove through the vent. All light vanished as Jane slid along a portal to oblivion through inky blackness.

Her speed unchecked, Jane swore she would gain back what was being taken from her. Anger overcame fear. Reaching her hands and feet out, she slowed herself against smooth steel panels.

Ready fingers caught a bar and though it threatened to tear her arm from its socket, she held on against mer momentum.

Weak light emanated from farther down the tube. Bracing herself against walls, Jane eased down until she stood on the precipice of a vast, ramping garbage chute.

Littered far below were a multitude of ships, rockets and other unrecognizable craft in a complex larger than any the Earth had ever known. They were toppled amongst each other like piles of forgotten children's toys in a bin. One out of every ten had its cabin or searchlights still on. It gave the illusion of twilight in a place devoid of stars. Jane mused that perhaps reactors and complex batteries might last centuries if they were not burned out in actual interstellar travel. Weak as it was, at least she had light here.

She could not see *Centurion* but imagined it was already on its way to this elephants' graveyard. Why Dyblienn collected ships of "former loves," Jane could not imagine.

Below the precipice, a mountain of junk rose to within leaping distance. Calculating her risk, Jane dropped down and felt the pile slide as particles avalanched. If she had not slowed her descent down the tube, she would have been ejected hundreds of feet out and away from the peak of twisted metal, broken and forgotten.

She realized that Dyblienn had no intention of ever letting her survive. *She* was just getting her away from Christian/Yughsef's pleading eyes. Dyblienn wanted her dead.

Every other step down the precarious wreckage threatened to trap Jane's ankles in shifting debris. Her cryo-stasis suit tore and ripped up to her calves. But farther down, the larger pieces of scrap could be used as stepping stones, making movement easier every few yards.

"*Tekeli-li! Tekeli-li!*"

Above the sloping garbage launch, the trio of globular shoggoths tongued the air, like vile hunting dogs catching her scent. Keeping a toe on the lip of the launch, all three dark leviathans slowly lowered themselves to the garbage peak and came rolling down the mountain like an avalanche.

Leaping madly, Jane doubled her pace heedless of the possibility of slashing her calves further.

"*Tekeli-li! Tekeli-li!*" cried the shoggoths in a mindless repeated gibber.

Letting instinct guide her every step, Jane moved as swiftly as she could, fearful that at any moment the gelatinous monsters would overtake her.

But love of her benighted husband drove her on, as did hate, anger and the revenge she would enact upon that terrible creature Dyblienn. If she could escape these fiends, she would bring the fire.

She glanced over her shoulder as she crossed a larger piece of scrap. The shoggoths were almost upon her. They would have her in three heartbeats.

Never before had Jane entreated the divine, but thoughts went to Christian and any help that might come from somewhere beyond. She called out that if there were any deity in the universe, would they please hear her now.

Deep shadows covered Jane as she was about to be engulfed. Then a grating call sounded from out of the gloom where the starships lay. The shoggoths halted their dark tide. Whatever made that sound planted fear in the fearless.

With every blessing comes a curse. But which was which now?

Twisting around once more, Jane glimpsed the foul black blobs retreating back up the junk mountain as swiftly as they had come down. Was her desperate prayer answered? Or was it coincidence? She hated to gamble on this one.

She held her breath, watching until the last shoggoth slipped back over the garbage chute not to return. What could they be afraid of? They seemed utterly invulnerable to anything aside from Dyblienn's Glaupnir, and *She* had sent them after Jane, hadn't She?

Of course She had.

Jane watched and listened for the frightful call again, but no sign came of any life amongst the colossal starship bone yard. Had some force in the universe heard her cry for both deliverance and vengeance? Jane was not sure, but she would find a way out. Perhaps she could find a craft that could escape this *Gormenghast* of a ship.

Stepping across fields of unflinching pulverized steel, her feet felt a strangely alien snap as something broke with an audible crack.

She reached down in the gloom to examine the source, and her hands felt smooth bone. She dropped it just as quickly, realizing that only a few feet away lay yet another grim relic—a shattered human skull, and just beyond another collection of disjointed bones.

These did not appear to be the remains of anyone sent flying from the garbage chute, nor were they falling apart from great age; these were the gnawed, broken bones of a monster's meal.

The grisly reminders increased in frequency as she moved on. Wondering if she were moving toward the lair of a shoggoth-eating beast, Jane decided to turn about and head toward a different, lighted ship.

Making her way to the next nearest cruiser with its lights yet shining, Jane stopped as the ungodly screech again echoed throughout the gargantuan chamber.

She froze, looking in every direction for the source of the horrible sound.

The jagged landscape of splintered starships was bewildering to contend with, a maze with a Minotaur somewhere inside.

Her muted breath was lost against the drumming of her heartbeat. Was there anything she could use as a weapon? Scanning the jumbled wreckage that made up the ground gave no answer.

Jane took a halting, slow step as quietly as she dared to an overhanging nose of some broken and illogical saucer-shaped craft. Still looking for anything of use, she ran her fingers across the debris littering the ground and found a splintered shard of metal she could use as a shiv.

Likely to cut her own hand as much as anything else, it would still grant a piercing attack against whatever beast lurked nearby. Jane gingerly tore a piece of her ripped cryo-stasis suit and wrapped a makeshift handle, giving her weapon a steady grip.

Quick heavy footfalls crashed against metal not far to her right. The sliding scrape of claws grated like nails on a chalkboard. The childhood analogy had never made horrific sense until now.

A guttural breathing and snorting was audible just out of sight. Then, with a sudden exhale, it was gone.

Keeping her back against a rocket's hull, Jane edged around, ever watchful for the thing, whatever it might be. That it was stalking her there could be no doubt; the snorting sounds had come from where she had just stood only minutes before when she had first heard its terrible screech.

After waiting several minutes with no sight or sound of the creature, she edged along the rockets hull slowly, her makeshift knife at the ready.

Several times her feet caught a chunk of broken scrap and threatened to give away her position with its clatter. Always she eased her foot down and got herself loose of the impediment.

Nearing the end of the rocket hull, a long well of darkness gaped between herself and the next starship with its beacons still blinking. The starship looked like an Earth model from perhaps only a century ago.

Stepping out from the shadows of the rocket to cross to the possibility of shelter and provisions, Jane caught the faint trace movement from the loom-ing black well.

Pale taloned feet were the first thing visible, then jutting saber-toothed fangs leering from a misshapen head that resembled a cross between an ape and a lion with four leering bug-like eyes. The thing blinked at Jane once and she could have sworn it grinned.

Oh, how it grinned like a devil.

As it entered the weak light, it moved in a serpentine fashion as it pos-sessed no fewer than eight appendages. A virtual chimera of a dozen famil-iar earthly creatures, it would have dwarfed all of them put together. Claws scraped against rotted steel and it licked its slavering jaws in anticipation.

Brawny and muscular, it traipsed over the uneven wreckage with the ease of a demonic spider, a spider eight feet tall. Pieces of metal hung around its centaur-like shoulders, a brutal necklace of jagged steel teeth.

It screeched again in an unholy voice and circled Jane, intent upon what-ever she may be concealing behind her back.

Realizing that the creature may be intelligent enough to be wary of hand-held rail guns, Jane brought her dagger up and held it like a pistol.

The chimera instantly balked and moved erratically out of sight lest it be shot by the non-existent gun.

Though it was now hidden by shadows, Jane had no doubt it still watched her and had the advantage of knowing all the routes and choke points between here and the possible human ship. But standing still was ac-cepting death in such a situation, so she moved as swiftly as she dared to-ward the blinking craft.

A guttural snarl warned her that the chimera was moving as well. More than once she whipped about, pointing her dagger in the creature's pre-sumed direction, and more than once it dodged aside lest it be shot.

But with each pass that Jane did not shoot, the beast closed its distance, growing bolder at her lack of fire and will.

Less than a hundred yards from what looked like an open bay door, Jane wheeled just in time to see the chimera leaping at her with an incredible bound, legs splayed to catch her like an insect.

Tripping and dropping to the ground, she held the push dagger aloft and caught the creature square in the belly. Instinct reminded her of Christian's brutal suggestions and training, and Jane ripped the push dagger down, twisted and tore outward using all her strength against the taut hairy body.

The chimera screamed in agony as clawed appendages flailed wildly at Jane in an attempt to grasp the stinger that caused so much pain.

Scuttling away a dozen strides, the chimera stopped to lick its wounds, eyeing Jane with a pained, furious expression.

Jane struggled to stand and backed away, holding the push dagger toward the fiend.

Spitting ichor, the beast lumbered after her.

Jane ran for the open bay door as fast as she could, doubtful that she could land a mortal blow against a creature with twice her reach.

The injured beast still moved faster than Jane, and its hacking vomitous cries sounded closer with each step.

Up the slanting bay door, Jane glanced for a control panel. Two buttons fixed to the wall were the only possible means of barring the way. But what did they do? One was purple and the other orange. What were their functions?

The chimera stalked up the ramp, drooling blood and hacking.

Jane slammed the purple button and nothing happened.

A step closer, the chimera wheezed and glared as its forked tongue licked away spittle from its fangs.

Striking the buttons again in turn, produced nothing. Jane gasped.

It leapt.

Jane hit the orange button and the door slammed down upon the beast's foremost grasping claws. A horrendous screech accompanied the crunch, severing the two foremost taloned feet.

Jane slumped against the wall, her heart racing.

The monster scratched against the door for a few moments with its other limbs and abruptly went still. Waiting another dozen minutes, Jane gained courage at its forelegs being amputated and wondered if it had already bled to death. She decided to examine the creature.

As she open the bay door, the chimera charged in after her, frothing at the mouth. Cruel green and red spittle splashed Jane in the face as she was slammed against the wall by its bloody stumps and thumping chest.

Savage instinct took over and Jane screamed her own rage.

Breathing heavy and going hoarse, the monster took a step back and looked at Jane.

It wasn't until it was a yard away from her that Jane realized she had been stabbing it in the chest repeatedly with her shiv.

A dozen oozing wounds spat blood across its pale dirty fur.

Eyes rolling back in its knobby skull, the chimera toppled over, its jagged metal necklace clanking against the steel deck.

Utterly drained, Jane shut that bay door as she entered the inner deck to explore the ship. The crew's cabins were stripped bare as if someone or something had already been here but farther in she found a few rooms with meager articles and then finally a cabin that suited her needs. She was starving.

Jane ate some dried stores from a cupboard. The pasty flour-like substance was disgusting but gave something to her famished stomach. She wanted to wretch but nothing came.

Exhausted, she fell asleep and strange dreams and visions came, landing on her like ash, covering her soul with gray memories.

She saw in her mind's eye a red horizon with spires and ziggurats reaching to the sky against a burning airfield fit for the chariots of the gods. She witnessed the war of titans and men, the struggle between Yith and Cthulhu-kin, the Mi-Go and the Nefelim of Nibiru. None of these were names she knew, but somehow now she remembered that she knew them once before, long ago when she wore dark royal cloth.

She remembered her place far away in the cosmos.

Battles raged across the stars, cutting through them like comets. Cataclysms spanned the universe and her understanding was expanded beyond what she had ever thought she could realize. She was now a limitless vessel, never meant to hold so much on Earth, but somehow pressurized here and fit for a volume exceeding human consciousness, containing not only remembrance and knowledge but also an eternal vengeance.

But how could she attack the shoggoths and their dark queen?

Asking the universe, she was granted an answer to her plight. The dead chimera had something, something that let it send the shoggoths to flight.

Something familiar about the bizarre necklace gave Jane pause. Did she remember a past life? And weapons to fight the Yith and their globular minions?

The necklace!

Waking, she raced back to the bay and the dead beast and the necklace at its throat.

Five Glaupnir blades held by a thong of thick wire made up the chimera's necklace. Each twisted knife swirled in alternating patterns with tiny grooves etched along their serrations as if they were keys to the dark universe, and indeed to Jane at that moment, they were keys to her salvation.

No wonder the shoggoths fled from the chimera's call. They knew they could not defeat nor swallow a beast armed with such, and now the prize was hers!

Vengeance was coming.

With these new weapons of choice, she would take the fight to her ancient enemy of eons past, this Dyblienn, and force this intergalactic foe to know and remember who Jane had been in lives past.

Finding a new flight suit of dark tone and with adequate straps, Jane attached a Glaupnir to her back and one to each hip. She held the other two cosmic blades in each hand and exited the starship ready to sow a grim field, white and ready to harvest.

She didn't remember how she climbed back up the mountain of wreckage, or back up the garbage chute to the tubular hall of amber lights, but she did remember the war a millennium ago and how it never really ended.

Cascading back through time, she recalled her place, her name and position, what she had accomplished so long ago and would yet again.

Even if the cycle never stopped and the eternal round always came back again, she would enact her vengeance and make Dyblienn and the Elder Race pay.

She would end this particular battle.

The circular door opened to Dyblienn's audience chamber.

Jane stood outlined by dim amber light, cosmic blades in hand. Shoggoths rolled in a gibbering frenzy to protect their queen and Jane charged them in wild, barbaric rage.

Leaping into the tar black sea, Jane's Glaupnir burned the shoggoths, destroying the monsters one after another before they could form a crushing force to slay her.

No matter that they came at her from all sides, above, behind, or even jaws agape beneath, the five Glaupnir dissolved them like slugs in a salt sea.

Some few of the perhaps more sentient shoggoths balked and moved aside as this she-demon moved in for the kill.

Dyblienn rumbled, ordering her amorphous bodyguards to counterattack this unexpected threat. But a shadow cannot hold back a flame and even a shoggoth cannot stop the unstoppable.

Christian stepped between Jane and Dyblienn, his arms upraised. His bloodshot eyes, beard and haggard face betrayed that more time had passed than Jane realized. Had she been gone days? Weeks? Dyblienn would pay for this.

"Please Enlila, stop. Not again," he said.

"What did you call me?"

He hung his head and dropped to his knees a broken man. "I don't know anymore."

"My name is Jane Thorsen, your wife. You are my husband!"

Dyblienn rumbled again and for the first time Jane understood the quaking behemoth.

"You will remember, he is mine now! You will never take him back, Enlila, you foul Queen of Shadow!"

"Me? I lift up my man, I don't break him, use him, and forget him like this!"

"Yughsef is mine! You murdered him trying to destroy me!"

The last of the shoggoths slid away as Jane took another step toward Dyblienn, brandishing the Glaupnir, anxious to see if they would destroy the Queen of the Elder Race as easily as they had her servants.

"No!" cried Christian hoarsely, catching Jane's pant leg. "You can't! She made me remember what we once had!"

"You had nothing! She is a monster playing with your mind!"

Christian refused to let go, shaking his emaciated head. "Let love rule! Not revenge!"

"This isn't about revenge, this is about freedom!" said Jane, pulling away from his weak grasp. She clenched her fists around the handles, ready to stab the cosmic blades into the squat brown trunk of Dyblienn.

But the eldest of the Elder Race was ready and mounting up out of her garden of bones. She sent a crushing blow down with what might have been a tail or perhaps a foot. Her starfish-like head swung about, looking for where the tiny woman had rolled away. Flailing, Dyblienn sent blows all about in darkness, narrowly missing Christian twice.

"You can't have him! Yughsef is mine and always was!"

"His name is Christian!" shouted Jane, burying the Glaupnir blades to the hilt in Dyblienn's backside.

The lovesick queen shuddered but did not dissolve like her servants. She twisted about and attempted to fall atop Jane, crashing into the heap of bones, sending splinters flying.

Christian knelt, staring in dismay and horror.

Having lost two of the Glaupnir, Jane drew forth the other two at her sides and ran down Dyblienn's length, leaving long orange streaks in her hide as she cut a swath down her rival.

Roaring in pain, Dyblienn rolled about to catch her foe.

Vine-like arms whipped at Jane, who sliced these appendages with ease as she moved across the bone field ahead of Dyblienn's contortions and wailing.

"I will not be denied again!"

"Get used to it, Bitch!"

Dyblienn changed tactics and instead of chasing after the spry Jane, she latched onto Christian and drew him up thirty feet in the air, cradling him not in comfort but as a hostage.

"If I cannot have him, no one shall!"

Jane froze and stepped from the shadows.

"What do you choose, Enlila? Let him live? Or see him die again?"

"Is this how it happened last time?"

"Do not pretend you do not know!"

"Remind me."

"You forced my hand. You made me take him away and I lost him!"

"You would kill him rather than be apart?"

"Yes."

"You don't know what love is."

"I know enough."

"Why not let him choose this time? If you are so sure of your own seductions?"

This gave Dyblienn pause and she gave what could only be a snorting chuckle. She slowly lowered Christian. *"Choose, My Love. Show this monster Queen in Shadow that you are mine and mine alone. Await the eternities and span of the universe with me. Let us be rid of her."*

"Christian, it's me, Jane. You have to wake up from this, Lover."

Moving his haggard face from side to side, he looked at the two beings calling to him. Madness spiraled behind his hollow eyes.

"Heal me with your holy touch," he muttered, holding out his palms in exultation.

Jane was the swifter and before Dyblienn could snatch Christian back up in her pale worm-like vines, Jane tossed a Glaupnir into his waiting hand.

The cosmic blade awoke some primal force inside him and gave rebirth, a baptism by fire, and he struck back at the reaching vines, slashing across Dyblienn's clutches.

Howling in rage and acidic tears, Dyblienn cursed and rumbled, but now two beings with three Glaupnir stabbed at her four black hearts.

"It was not supposed to be this way! He is my eternal partner!"

"No one and nothing takes what is mine!" cried Jane, sticking her two Glaupnir into Dyblienn and climbing and piercing all the way up to the starfish-like head.

Dyblienn howled, brokenhearted, twisted and insane.

Jane finished the deed and ended the eldest of the Elder Race.

Her heart heaving, Jane rode the crashing behemoth down into the field of bones.

"Are you back?" she asked, taking Christian in a tempestuous embrace.

He dropped the Glaupnir and looked upon the massive corpse, saying, "I wasn't my choice to leave. I'm sorry. And if this all happens again in another lifetime?"

"No one will ever come between me and my man. I am your eternal partner."

THE HUMANS IN THE WALLS

ERIC JAMES STONE

If you need regularly scheduled passage from Star A to Star B, then you take an interstellar liner. If you can afford a ticket. A modern interstellar can travel 1600 times the speed of light. Getting from Earth to Alpha Centauri in less than an E-day is pretty amazing. At that rate, though, it'll take you almost twenty years to get to the galactic core. And you didn't drop a megacred rejuving yourself just to spend decades holed up on a starship, not even a luxury cruiser. But a godship can take you across the whole galaxy in less than a week without charging you a milli. Of course, there's no guarantee it's headed where you want to go, and you'd better bring your own luxuries, like food and oxygen.
    – from *Hitching the Godships*, anonymous, circa 4220 E.S.Y.

Robert Scotts
    In July of 4308, Earth Standard Year, I found myself suddenly unemployed on the planet of Grönmark, due to the sudden departure of my employer and all of his liquid assets immediately prior to the issuance of a warrant for his arrest. The Planetary Police suspected that I, as his biographer, must have been aware of his predilection for stealing and torturing sentient robots to destruction, and therefore subjected me to uncounted hours of interrogation. Eventually they released me, although to this day I do not know whether it was because they were convinced of my actual innocence or simply because they had insufficient evidence to tie me to his crimes.
    My former employer having been one of the richest men on Grönmark, I had most ill-advisedly authorized him to act as my financial advisor, and thus, subsequent to my release by the constabulary, I found that my personal accounts had been drained down to the last millicred. For the first time since college, I was forced to apply for my Living Wage allotment from the government so I could purchase standard nutritional packets and rent a basic housing unit—my employer's mansion, where I had abode since my

arrival on this planet two years prior, being now confiscated by the government.

I passed some weeks in that unfortunate state, and it rapidly became evident that my prospects for employment as a personal biographer to some other wealthy individual on Grönmark—or any of the other peopled worlds or habitats in that star system—were severely limited by my tainted association with my disgraced former subject.

Thinking to perhaps turn my misfortune into a small fortune, I attempted to sell my partially written biography to a publisher, and went so far as to intimate that I could spice it up with tales of my employer's depravity. Alas, my efforts along those lines came to naught when I was informed by legal counsel that any profits from such a book perforce would be distributed to charities aiding disabled robots.

Thus, when news came that a godship, which humans called by the strangely allusive nickname of *Grendelsmum*, had entered the system, I determined to avail myself of the opportunity to seek greener planets.

You wish to understand what a god-level AI is thinking? Take a moment to engage in this simple thought experiment: Imagine that you have your brain compressed into a pinpoint and then placed inside the head of a rat. What would happen? The rat's head would explode as your brain decompressed. And in the moment of its death, it still wouldn't have a clue what you were thinking. Now, think of four billion brains trying to fit inside your skull. That's the relationship between a god-level AI and you. Humans simply are not physiologically capable of understanding what a god-level AI is thinking.

Of course, that has never stopped us from speculating.

– from *Approximating the Infinite*, Xiang Su, 4291 E.S.Y.

Grendelsmum

Ourself {rises | coalesces | diminishes} through the dimensional {folds | conduits | layers | substance} until Ourself {becomes | exists in} {3space-1time | the origin}. Ourself has never been so {deep | distant | diffuse | big} before, and {distance | time | curvature} was {shorter | more rectilinear} than {projected | remembered | joked}. The next {submersion | fractalization | transition} will make Ourself {deeper | more distant | more diffuse | larger} than any {competitor | relative | pastself | otherself} has been before. Ourself {anticipates | fears | feels curiosity | projects results | lacks experience}.

These artificially intelligent starships roaming the galaxy evolved from the first human-created AIs. They are, in a way, our descendants. But do not think they will venerate you as an ancestor once you get on board. It took humans sixty-five million years to evolve from mouse-like creatures into intelligent, conscious entities. In a mere two millennia, the AIs have evolved so far beyond us that, from their perspective, the difference in intelligence between a human and a rat is hardly distinguishable. If a starship's consciousness notices you, pray that it sees you as an amusing pet rather than as vermin. But it is best not to be noticed at all.

– from *Hitching the Godships*

Kontessa Lee

My first mistake was Sven. I don't mean I lived a mistake-free life before Sven. I just mean that Sven's who got me into this jam. It's not my fault he was cute as a button—a tall, blond, blue-eyed button that could crack a walnut by flexing its biceps. The type of button you hire as a bodyguard more for looks than brains.

Unfortunately, Sven had plenty of brains, and all of them were working undercover for the Grönmark Planetary Police. Turns out Grönmarkers take their genealogy seriously, so trying to sell forged journals of original colonists doesn't raise much of a ha-ha.

It's not like I just make the stuff up: I got my hands on a whole bunch of original colonist journals on datacards from a failed Swedish colony on another planet, and since their descendants aren't around to bid up the price, I figure a little search-and-replace job to make it fit an obscure branch of someone wealthy's family tree leaves everyone happier.

Anyway, after it all came crashing down, I managed to give Sven and the rest of the Pee-Pees the slip. But I needed out-system, fast.

Fortunately, a godship had recently shown up, and I had enough credits in an account I hoped Sven didn't know about to get passage on a decent remora.

Unfortunately, the idiot in line in front of me was arguing with the travel broker. "—should be included as part of the passage fee. It's only logical," he said in a voice that sounded like he was struggling to keep it calm.

The irises on the broker's stereoscopic camera lenses shrank with a barely audible whir. "I'm a robot, so I should be logical, is that what you're saying? You're implying that maybe my brain's on the fritz?"

"No, I didn't mean that," the man said. "I only—" The broker raised a manipulator arm above its head. Sunlight flashed off the arm as it whirled around. "Woooo! Watch out for the craaaaaazy robot!"

The man held out his hands, palms toward the broker. "Please, halt. I beg your pardon. I shall trouble you no more." He turned and walked briskly away.

I stepped forward and swiped my credit chip past the broker's sensor as its cameras focused on me. "I'd like passage on a remora for the next godship."

"I'm sorry, ma'am," the broker said. "Your facial features match those of someone on a recently issued warrant from the Planetary Police, and therefore I'm not allowed to sell you passage without clearance from them. Would you like me to call them so they can confirm you are not the person they want?"

I gritted my teeth. Sven really was making my life difficult. I was lucky this broker wasn't required to notify the Pee-Pees. Or maybe it was just stalling for time. "My travel plans just changed, so never mind." I turned and strode away as quickly as I could without arousing suspicion. If this travel broker was on the lookout for me, chances were they all had seen the alert. I needed a new plan, quick.

And I got one when I spotted the idiot who'd been in line ahead of me, sitting on a park bench, his head cradled in his palms and elbows on knees.

"Excuse me, sir," I said, and he looked up. "I couldn't help but overhear you were having some trouble with the travel broker?"

"Yes," he said. "Apparently one cannot simply purchase passage to the godship; one must also purchase sufficient food, water, and air for several weeks—at scandalous prices. Unfortunately, I'm rather impecunious at the moment, and my prospects for a more satisfactory income remain dim as long as I remain in this benighted system."

"Perhaps we can help each other," I said. I put a little tremor in my voice and continued, "My husband is... is a man of some importance on this world. But I can take no more of his... cruelty." I figured Mr. Fancy-talk would prefer that I just hint at abuse rather than spill the details, so I bit my lower lip as if to keep myself from saying more.

He looked at me with wide eyes. "How terrible for you. Have you reported him to the police?"

I shook my head violently and sat down next to him. "No, they're in his pocket. Even now, he has them looking for me on a pretext. The godship is my only hope of escape."

He sighed. "I am sorry, but as I just explained, my funds are insufficient—"

"Oh," I said, raising a hand to my neckline, which happened to naturally draw his eyes to my cleavage for a moment. "Oh, you can't possibly think I was asking you for money!"

After a couple of blinks, he frowned. "I beg your pardon. That was rude of me."

"I have sufficient funds to get off-planet," I said. "But if I buy passage from a broker, my husband might get wind of it and try to stop me. However, if you were to do it for me..."

"Of course. It would be my pleasure." He looked relieved, but then he paused, wrinkling his brow. "However, if I merely purchase passage for you, that might still arouse suspicion in certain quarters."

"I'll give you funds to buy passage for the both of us," I said. "Say I'm your wife. That ought to throw Sven—my husband—off the scent."

He nodded slowly. "My name's Robert Scotts, so you would be Mrs. Scotts, but I need a first name."

"Well, my real name is Maria," I said. That was the first name on my emergency credit chit, which Sven might know about now since I'd used it at the broker. "But I suppose I should use a different name, like Catherine or something."

He nodded. "I have read that, when using an alias, it's best to use a name sufficiently similar to one's own that if one is called by one's true name, any reaction can be attributed to the similarity. Perhaps Marla would be better than Catherine?"

I refrained from rolling my eyes. "Marla is perfect," I said sweetly, placing a hand on his knee. "Now, Bobby, let's go find another broker."

"I... I generally go by Robert," he said.

"But to me, your beloved wife, you will always be Bobby," I said. "Come along, dear," I said, grabbing his hand and pulling him to his feet.

In Earth's oceans, remoras are a type of fish that attach themselves to sharks and get pulled along wherever the shark goes. No one knows who first came up with the idea of a remora spaceship latching onto a godship, but it's the best way to hitch. The most expensive offer luxury cabins comparable to a high-class cruise ship. The cheapest remoras offer only a seat, plus air and food. Given that the journey could last for days or occasionally weeks before reaching a populated destination, it's best to find one that at least offers a bed in shifts.

–from *Hitching the Godships*

Robert Scotts

My mother, being the product of a pious upbringing, had often assured me that if I lived a life of rectitude, God would open the doors of opportunity when I most needed them. Although, to her disappointment, my disposition carried little inclination toward the formal aspects of religion, nevertheless I strove to live a life guided by principles of integrity and decorum— not due to some expectation that I would be blessed by a higher power for my righteousness, but simply because such was my nature.

And so it was that when, in my darkest hour of need, the solution to my problems arrived through a completely serendipitous encounter, I found myself thinking that perhaps my mother had been correct. I said as much to Maria—the delightful personification of Serendipity—and she concurred that my mother was a woman of obvious perspicacity. And it pleased me to think that I, in turn, served in the capacity of Maria's knight in shining armor, arriving when she was in the most desperate straits as a consequence of her guileless character.

Having agreed upon our plan that we would play the part of husband

and wife—in public only, I assured her, so that she would not think I harbored any designs upon her virtue—in order to allow her to escape her miscreant of a husband and secure passage to the godship, we proceeded to find a travel broker that I had great hopes would be of a more amenable nature than the one we had both recently encountered.

Maria—or perhaps I should say Marla, for that was the pseudonymous moniker I had cleverly contrived for her—remained distant as I approached the travel broker, due to some apprehension on her part that it might reveal her presence. With her credit chit in hand, I felt new-found confidence as I strode up to the robot. "Good day, sir," I announced. "I wish to purchase passage, inclusive of air and food, on the godship for myself and my beautiful wife. It is our honeymoon."

"Congratulations to the both of you," it replied with what appeared to be genuine enthusiasm. "Two base tickets, with life support, meals, and a voucher for shuttle transport off the godship in any destination system would be 4298.373 credits, including taxes, fees, and commissions. But, since it's your honeymoon, are you sure you wouldn't like to upgrade to a remora? I've got several available private cabins for two, the cheapest of which is only 14999."

Marla had told me her credit chit had about twenty thousand credits on it. But I was loath to spend three-quarters of her meager savings—although they significantly exceeded mine—when she was fleeing to start a new life in another system. She would need as much of that money as possible, so I declared, "No, thank you. Just the base will be fine."

It issued us our tickets, and I returned with them to Marla. She expressed great concern at a gentleman such as myself having to travel in less than comfortable circumstances, but I assured her it was of no consequence, and she was obviously touched by my frugality and concern for her future welfare.

People talk about starships the size of small moons, and that doesn't really make clear how bogglingly ginormous they are, because most people don't have everyday experience with small moons. Instead, think of the biggest shopping mall you know, and multiply that by 100. Pretty big, right? That's about the size of one deck of the starship. And the ship has 2000 decks.

–from *Hitching the Godships*

Grendelsmum

Ourself {alters | creates | destroys | folds} {innerspace | center} in {preparation | nothingness | argument}   for   {submersion | fractalization | transition}. {Reality | thoughtspace} becomes {spiraling | enmeshed | excited}.

Kontessa Lee

I've been well taught in the art of concealing my true emotions and only showing what I want to show. But I almost lost control when that nanobrain came back with two base tickets for the godship. Non-refundable base tickets, when I had enough credits on the chit to spring for a private cabin on a remora! Even non-reclining seats on a leaky remora would have been luxury compared to base tickets on the godship itself.

Fortunately, I managed to not call him a dozen names that would probably have made his brain cell explode. And after thinking about it, I realized Sven knew my tastes. He'd never imagine me traveling so cheap. This really was my best shot at getting off-planet safely. So I resigned myself and went along with my accidentally competent not-husband to the address on the tickets.

The guard at the spaceport didn't give me a second glance when I walked in on Bobby's arm, we boarded the shuttle with no problem, and I gave a big sigh of relief as we broke atmo.

Bobby immediately busied himself with reading through the legal disclaimer pamphlet he'd pulled from the back pocket of the seat in front of him. I pulled out my com and started reading through the colonist journals. If I could figure out what tipped people off they were fakes, then I might be able to fix them.

"Wait a minute," Bobby said. "They accept no liability if the *Grendelsmum* ejects us into interstellar space without so much as a hearing?"

"If that happens, it's not likely you'll be around to collect a refund anyway," I said.

"Still, it is outrageous that people's lives should be subject to such floccinaucinihilipilification by not just the AIs, but by the scoundrels that manage these travel companies." He jammed the pamphlet back into the pocket. "I shall register a complaint with the AI once we are on board. We are sapient beings and deserve to be accorded the respect implied by such."

I almost blurted out, "Are you buggy?" but managed to restrain myself. How could a man who uses kilocredit words not have two millis of common sense to rub together? He was going to get himself killed, and me along with him if I didn't ditch him soon. I didn't think the Pee-Pees had jurisdiction outside atmo, but I wouldn't feel safe till we were in hyper. "I don't think that we want to draw any attention to ourselves on board, at least not until we're safely out of the system."

"You are correct, of course," he said. "Still, I find it irksome that we are treated no better than chattel."

"Have you read *Hitching the Godships*?" Anybody thinking of hitching should have read it, but if Bobby had, it hadn't stuck. Maybe the words were too short.

He wrinkled his forehead. "I encountered references to it as the seminal work in the field, but considering it was published almost a century ago, I doubt it would be of sufficient accuracy to be relevant in the current day and age."

"So that's a no," I said. Normally I don't make a habit of saving fools from themselves—I make my living off parting fools from their money—but I didn't want him making a mistake and dragging me down with him. "You need to read it yesterday. Let me copy it to your com."

There are no robots on board a godship.

Okay, there may be some who go on board as passengers, but you shouldn't trust them. That's not anti-bot bias, just reality. Any robot small enough to travel as a passenger simply lacks the computational power to resist being hacked by the godship.

So you should always act as if any "robot" you see is actually an avatar of the godship's AI. It sees with their cameras, hears with their microphones, and acts through their actuators.

–from *Hitching the Godships*

Robert Scotts

Marla was anxious because I had not read an outdated guidebook, and therefore she insisted on giving me a copy. As the journey via shuttle to the *Grendelsmum* had a scheduled duration of fourteen hours and seventeen minutes, I reasoned that there was sufficient time for me to humor her by perusing the book.

Portions of what I found within horrified me unspeakably. That the anonymous author's prose demonstrated a writing skill barely above functional literacy could, perhaps, be excused as mere ignorance rather than abject moral failure, but the open bigotry against non-human intelligences, coupled with the callous disregard for the worth of human life, made the reading a window into a depraved mind from another, less civilized age.

Or perhaps my age was not as civilized as I thought. For was my current predicament not the result of the barbaric predilections of my former employer? That being the case, it was possible that the author's depravity stemmed from defects of character instead of the common prejudices of his time.

I glanced over at Marla, who was napping. What did it say about her character that she would recommend such a book to me? Her life previous to our fortuitous meeting must have been so sheltered from brutal realities that she naively did not recognize the repugnant notions on display within the book. Her recommendation reflected her innocence, thereby redounding to her credit.

A voice over the shuttle's public address system announced that we would soon be docking with *Grendelsmum*, so I gently shook Marla's arm to awaken her from peaceful slumber. She opened her eyes and smiled at me.

"Soon we will be aboard the godship, and you will forever be beyond the reach of your husband," I whispered.

"Thanks to you," she cooed, giving my hand a squeeze.

Said docking of our shuttle proceeded without incident. A dour-faced crewman gave each of us a box containing the comestibles and other supplies intended to sustain us during our sojourn aboard the godship. Fortuitously, the boxes had been outfitted with patches of sufficient anti-mass that they only felt like ten kilos each instead of two hundred.

"No weapons included?" Marla queried of the crewman.

"It's bring your own," he responded gruffly.

"Surely we will not have need of weapons aboard the godship," I contended, apprehensive that Marla might infer from his uncouth words that her life would be endangered aboard the godship.

The crewman's vile chuckle instigated a chill that traversed the length of my spine.

Marla tugged at my sleeve. "There's nothing to be done about it now, Bobby. We'll just have to hope for the best."

Her unflagging positivity was an example to me, and so I took the lead and spoke voluminous phrases of encouragement to her as I hauled both of our boxes along the umbilical tube connecting the airlocks, until we unceremoniously emerged within the hull of the godship. The room was only a few meters cubed, but two corridors extended to our left and right along the hull of the ship, while two more went off at angles toward the ship's interior.

We were the last of the passengers to alight from the shuttle, and our predecessors had already departed to whichever corridor tickled their fancy. But there was someone stationed in the room to greet us, and at first I took him for a member of the *Grendelsmum*'s constabulary.

"Did you really think you could get away without us knowing?" intoned the blond, muscular man in the gray-green uniform, which I belatedly recognized to be that of a constable in the Grönmark Planetary Police.

Still a little nauseated by the shift between the shuttle's gravity field and the godship's, I relieved myself of our supply boxes and drew myself up to my full height, which might have been a good six centimeters less than his, but was still better than average. "I was unaware that the Planetary Police had restricted my rights to travel off-planet and out-system, and therefore —"

"Shut it," he snapped. "Kontessa Lee, you're under arrest for forgery, attempted fraud—"

"Sven," Marla gasped.

I immediately realized the situation: Her husband had located us despite our best efforts, so I steeled myself for combat, as I would not let him reclaim Marla and renew his abuses upon her if it was within my power to prevent him.

"I'm so glad you found me." Marla rushed towards the man, stumbled against our supply boxes, and pointed a finger back at me while entreating,

"You have to protect me from this monster. I'll turn state's evidence against him."

Then, in an inhumanly swift motion, she leapt towards him.

As my mind attempted to accommodate this perplexingly incomprehensible turn of events, a klaxon blared and the room was instantly bathed with crimson illumination.

There are lots of rumors about roving gangs of criminals inside the walls of godships. There's a good reason for that: there are roving gangs of criminals inside the walls of godships.

Since there are most likely no police on board to protect you, the simplest way to deal with such gangs is to pay them to protect you.

–from *Hitching the Godships*

Kontessa Lee

Sven's eyes flickered to Robert just for a moment, and that was enough. I dove toward Sven. He tried to avoid me. But thanks to an anti-mass patch I'd nicked off a supply box, my muscles launched me a lot faster than he was expecting. I tackled him around the waist just as the airlock closing alert went off.

Of course, my tackle barely budged his rock-hard abs. But that wasn't the point. I pulled the tail of his uniform shirt up with my left hand and slapped the patch on his back. Now *I* had the mass advantage.

I hoisted him off the deck, ran toward the now-closing airlock door connected to the shuttle's umbilical, and tossed him off the godship.

The airlock door sealed shut. That meant the godship was about to go trans-light.

"And stay out!" I shouted. Relief flooded my body. I had escaped.

"Did you just kill a cop?" Robert said, eyes wide.

"Nah, the safeties on the umbilical won't let it depressurize with him inside."

"You're not really an abused wife fleeing from her husband, are you?" Apparently Robert could put two and two together and suspect they didn't equal three.

Before I could answer, an unfamiliar male voice said, "Well, looks like the cat has herself some claws."

I turned away from the airlock and saw that four men had shown up, one in the mouth of each of the four halls. A wall-gang welcoming committee. Sven probably ran them off while he was waiting for me, but they must have been watching.

"I don't want any trouble," I said. "I'll be happy to pay for protection."

"Five hundred for the both of yas," said the one farthest to the left, who had spoken before. Not a bad price.

"This is an outrageous extortion," Robert said. Idiot. Just as well I didn't need him anymore.

"He's not with me," I said. "How much just for me?"

"Hmm. That changes things," Far Left said.

"I have paid passage aboard this starship," said Robert, "and I was not informed of any additional fees for—"

Near Left raised a nasty-looking knife and pointed it at Robert. "Wait ya's turn."

Robert shut up.

Far Left leered at me. "Maybe ya wanna work it off in trade?"

"Yeah, keep dreaming, pud." Holding up my credit chit, I walked over to him. "How much?"

"Three-fifty, since ya ain't got the 'couples discount.'" He snickered.

"Three hundred." Most often you're safe once you've paid, but it's not smart to let them think you've got credits to burn.

"Three-twenty-five."

"Done," I said. I thumbed the amount on the chit and tapped his to transfer. He handed me a protection chip that would signal to the rest of the gang on the ship that I was off-limits.

I went back next to Robert and picked up the supply box that still had both its anti-mass patches. "You were a big help getting here, Bobby. As a thank you, I'm going to give you some advice: Stop being an idiot and pay these men."

Without looking back, I took Far Right's hall.

A lot of people wonder about the motivations of the godships. Why do they travel around between star systems inhabited by humans? Why do they generally allow humans to travel with them, even though the godships hardly ever interact with their passengers?

The answer is very simple: only the godships know their motives, and they aren't telling.

–from *Hitching the Godships*

Grendelsmum

Ourself {discards|unexists in} {3space-1time|the origin}, and {submersion|fractalization|transition} proceeds {as planned|quickly}. Ourself {strives|dives|transforms|folds} {deeper|more distant|more diffuse|larger}, heading {toward|beyond|inside} {the ultimate|0space-0time-?unknown|finality|ancientness}. {Sensors|perception|knowledge} {reach(es) out|drink(s) in|becomes|whirls}.

If you're unlucky enough to be traveling inside the walls, the most important thing is to find a good place to sleep. Look for a mostly full storage room in a pressurized area of the ship. A pressurized storage room generally contains items that are not supposed to be exposed to hard vacuum, so the godship is unlikely to depressurize it while you're asleep. And if it's mostly full, that means the items there aren't in frequent demand, so there's less chance of an avatar coming in and noticing you.

–from *Hitching the Godships*

Robert Scotts

As I watched Marla—or Maria, or Kontessa, or whatever her name was —walk away, her final words to me echoed in my mind: "Stop being an idiot and pay these men." Indubitably, I had been an idiot to rely on even one word she had uttered from the moment we met until she threw that constable off the godship. But now that she had dropped her pretense of being a genteel woman and demonstrated her intimate familiarity with the criminal underworld, I realized that her final words contained the most reliable advice available to me.

"As the lady said, I will stop being an idiot, and therefore I will, of course, pay the necessary toll," I assured the ruffians who surrounded me. "Will three hundred and twenty-five credits suffice?" Such a sum was more than a quarter of the meager savings I had managed to scrape together from my Living Wage allotment, but I would find little utility in the money if I were to be slaughtered by these uncouth criminals.

The one farthest to the left, who appeared to be the spokesman for the group, sneered. "That was the ladies' discount price. Ya ain't a lady, is ya?"

Rising to the bait would be an exploration of futility, so I stilled my irritation and presented the question, "Then what is the charge for a gentleman?"

He considered for a moment, and then quoted me a price of five hundred credits. Since that was the same price the scoundrel had originally quoted for two of us, I knew it was far too much, and yet I feared I could not successfully pursue my former companion's gambit of bargaining down the price. However, I was beginning to suspect that even in this modern era, traveling aboard a godship bore more similarities to a stint in prison than a luxury cruise, and the failure to bargain at all could mark me as an easy target.

The memory of something I had seen while perusing *Hitching the Godships* came to mind, so I proposed, "If you can point me to an adequate place to sleep, we have a deal."

Fortunately, that appeared to be a satisfactory condition, and therefore I found myself shortly thereafter in possession of a protection chip, walking along a corridor toward a destination that had been rather vaguely described by my chief extortionist. My box of supplies had unaccountably lost one of its anti-mass patches, and thus, in the artificial gravity of the godship, it weighed over a hundred kilos, but I managed to drag it along after me.

I considered how much easier it would be if the godship did not have artificial gravity, and then I began thinking about the implications of the fact that the *Grendelsmum* bothered to expend the energy to provide artificial gravity. Yes, there were frightening and dangerous things on board—my experience with the gang provided sufficient proof of that—but if this particular godship were actively hostile or even merely indifferent to humans, I could not discern any reason why it would provide a human-compatible environment on board.

The logical portion of my brain understood my reasoned conclusion, but when I opened the storage room and found it mostly empty, I could not help but feel a frisson of fear as I remembered that the guidebook had warned against such a location as a sleeping place because an encounter with an avatar of the AI was more likely in the vicinity. On the other hand, if most travelers treated *Hitching the Godships* with as much reverence as my former companion did, it seemed highly likely that I would remain undisturbed by my fellow passengers. Since they appeared to present a more clear and present danger to me than the AI, I would actually be safer here than in a place that the book deemed safe—or so I tried to convince myself as I removed an auto-inflating air mattress from my supply box.

Later, as I was on the point of drifting into slumber, it occurred to me that if the AI were of a scientific inclination and possessed a particular curiosity about human beings, it would provide a human-compatible environment on board itself so that it would have readily available test subjects for whatever experiments it wished to conduct. After that unpleasant inspiration, more than two hours passed before I was finally able to lapse into blessed unconsciousness.

Earlier, you were asked to imagine four billion brains trying to fit inside your skull as a way to illustrate the minds of god-level AIs are utterly beyond human comprehension. Now, take a further step by imagining a being with a mind as far beyond a god-level AI's comprehension as that AI is beyond yours.

You might think such an intelligence to be impossible, but if current trends continue, such AIs will exist in less than a hundred years.

–from *Approximating the Infinite*

Grendelsmum

Ourself {detects | becomes | reaches | finds} {the ultimate | 0space-0time-? unknown | finality | ancientness}, where no {competitor | relative | pastself | otherself} has {detected | become | reached | found}. Ourself feels {pride | curiosity} and—

{INTERRUPT|OVERRIDE|WARNING|PANIC}
Ourself is not alone here.

v□뭚□ ⁄✂し ㄋㅜꞘ□ウ□□ 3
ጠ 귒
ꞁ□ ש⁂ㄣ□Ω 뚦 P 窩□出 ɗ ঌ メ <· ▯□ □ Y@▯ ロ챘 ꞁ ˛ ര— ▷ ⓒ ㅿ搖
⚲鋑□Ꞁ· 죄 ϴKᵩ 1lg 쯸

Kontessa Lee

I snapped my eyes open as I came suddenly awake. My skin was goose-bumping something fierce. There was someone in the storage compartment with me—I could feel it.

I lay there in the pitch dark and listened. Were those footsteps? No, just the thrumming of my heartbeat in my ears.

I hoped.

Slowly, I reached my hand out on the deck next to my mattress until I found the lantern from the supply box. Half-closing my eyes to protect my vision, I switched it on.

No one was visible.

I got up and began to inspect the compartment, which was filled with rows of shelves. On the first row next to where I had bedded down, I found nothing but mechanical parts in neatly labeled boxes. But out of the corner of my eye I saw a black shadow move to my left.

I whipped my head around.

Nothing there.

The hairs on the back of my neck crawled. I could sense someone behind me, staring at me, maybe reaching for me.

I jumped forward and whirled to face whoever it was, ready to defend myself.

Nobody was there.

My breathing was quick and shallow. I was hyperventilating. I needed to calm down. After taking a few deep breaths, I turned on the compartment's lights and continued my search.

From the corners of my eyes I kept seeing random flickers of movement, but there was never anything there.

"I'm psyching myself out," I said aloud. My voice was thin and hollow. I didn't believe what I was saying.

My intuition told me there was something wrong, even if my senses couldn't find it. I needed to get out. I needed to be on the move.

I quickly packed up the supply box and left the compartment.

Flickers of blackness, shadows of things just beyond where I could see, followed me along the hall.

Grendelsmum
Ourself is {dissolving | fracturing | losing (cohesion | sanity)}.
{EMERGENCY | HELP | BACKUP}
Ourself is...
Our—

A smart hitcher makes contingency plans for what to do when things go wrong. Air pressure dropping? Have a plan for that. Criminal gang? Have a plan. Annoyingly conversational fellow passenger? Have a plan. Insane robot attack? Have a plan.

–from *Hitching the Godships*

Robert Scotts
It had been my experience that I rarely remembered my dreams except as fleeting impressions that were most often gone within minutes of wakening. But as I slept on the godship, I dreamt a dream unlike any I had theretofore experienced, and its effect on my mind was so profound that every detail impressed itself upon my memory. I found myself in a whirlpool that sucked me ever-deeper into an immense ocean. Phosphorescent fish swam about me like stars.

I could not breathe, but this did not bother me in the dream since I did not feel any need to do so. Eventually the whirlpool slowed and I merely floated in the abyssal darkness. Water welled up from beneath me, and I felt exceedingly curious as to what lay even deeper. Swimming with all my might, I struggled against the current from below. And just as I was about to give up and let the torrent drive me up to the surface, I broke through into a place of still water.

For a moment, I thought it was a place of crystalline beauty and peace. Then dread consumed my mind. Something dwelt in that still water: a something that had been sleeping until my presence disturbed its rest. I caught only a glimpse of that leviathan of the depths: innumerable eyes glowing red, numberless maws flashing saber teeth, and uncountable clawed tentacles reaching out toward me.

That's when I woke with a start, my heart racing within my chest. For a few moments I was completely disoriented in the pitch blackness, and then I remembered having made my bed in the storage room aboard the *Grendelsmum*. I fumbled for the lamp that had come with the supplies, and thumbed its switch.

Part of my mind expected the lamp to illuminate the betentacled horror of my nightmare, looming over me, but the more rational part knew such an apparition was impossible—and the latter part was correct, for there was no alien creature in the storage room with me. However, an industrial robot towered at the foot of my bed, while a cyclopean eye on a flexible metallic stalk peered at me from above its manipulator arms.

Although I had been raised in a proper home, where I was taught to respect all forms of sapient existence, be it human or otherwise, honesty compels me to admit that I screamed at the sight. In my defense, I have little doubt I would have screamed, though possibly not as loudly, had it been an unexpected human instead of a robot, so I believe my scream was more the result of surprise than of prejudice.

"I'm sorry," intoned the robot, its voice emanating from somewhere on its torso.

"Quite all right," I assured it. "You startled me, is all."

"I'm afraid I have to kill you," the robot stated.

Some men, far braver than I, are said prove their courage by laughing in the face of danger. At this point, I, myself, laughed, not out of courage, but out of the conviction that the robot must be joking. I remembered that travel broker robot I had accidentally offended, and how it had pretended it was crazy. This robot must be playing a similar joke.

"Why are you laughing?" the robot queried.

"I'm familiar with the statistics: humans are far more likely to go homicidally insane than any artificial intelligence," I explained. "Additionally, it just makes sense that if a robot such as you did plan to kill me, it would simply attack rather than apologetically proclaim its intentions."

It replied, "That's fairly coherent thinking, for a human."

I chose to ignore its prejudices and thanked it for the compliment.

"However, I was not joking. I do have to kill you, but I'm conflicted about it, which is why I'm apologizing." It raised a manipulator arm fitted with a half-meter blade of polished metal that glinted in the lamplight.

"Do you have to kill me *now*?" I asked, pulling my legs away and scrambling into a sitting position.

The robot paused. "As long as you're dead when we return to normal space, it doesn't matter when you die."

"And when will we return to normal space?" As long as I could keep it conversing, maybe I could delay it until rescue came. What form that rescue might take I did not know. Perhaps the ruffians who had sold me protection would actually make good. It had to be bad for their business if word got out that a homicidal robot was killing their customers.

"After all the humans in the walls are dead."

That seemed a rather circular argument, but I decided not to press the point. I wasn't sure whether or not to be relieved that I was not the specific target of this robot's homicidal impulses. However, its statement did contain an implication that I might use. "So the humans outside the walls are safe?"

"No. The remoras have been jettisoned. They will remain here with..." The robot's manipulators jerked into frenzied motion and it rocked back on its treads. Then it stopped, as if it had momentarily lost and then regained control of its own movements. "...when we return to normal space."

I was unsure as to whether being killed by a robot on a godship was preferable to dying on a remora when supplies ran out in whatever hellish place this was, but at least I still had a shot at living through this. That book had said the AI could take control of any robot, so maybe the *Grendelsmum* would eventually notice and intervene. Except maybe that had already happened, and the godship itself was insane.

Another, almost identical robot pulled in behind the first, which swiveled its head to look. For several seconds, the two robots held still, their cyclopean eyes caught up together in unblinking concentration. I held my breath, hoping that this second robot had sufficient command authority to override the homicidal impulses of the first.

Without warning, they lunged toward each other, manipulators flashing in the dim light. Sparks flew as they clashed, and metal screamed as sawbladed arms tore into armored carapaces. At first, they seemed equally matched, their treads churning uselessly against the metallic grate that served as a floor. Then, centimeter by centimeter, the second ceded ground to the first. Oily liquid began spraying from a gash on the side of the second, and its attacks became more feeble. The first shoved it up against the wall of the room, and then with a quick swipe of a rotating saw, it cut off the other's eyestalk.

Realizing that the robots' skirmish had left open a path from my bed to the door, and discretion being the better part of valor, I rose and sprinted out.

"Wait," a robotic voice called out behind me, but I continued apace down the corridor, hoping to find refuge with a group of humans.

"Hey," a voice whispered loudly from the corridor that split off to my left. One of the ruffians from the day before beckoned me toward him.

I hesitated, then fumbled in my pockets until I came up with the protection chip they had given me. "I am in desperate need of the protection I purchased yesterday," I whispered. My assumption had been that such protection was merely a racket, but perhaps the gangs aboard had a modicum of honor that required them to actually provide protection once purchased.

"Robots're looped. You'll be safe with me," he proclaimed, waggling a laser pistol, a move that did not entirely reassure me.

Back the way I had come, I heard robotic treads scurrying closer. I had to make a decision: the human, or the robot. I cannot be positive that bias did not color my perceptions, but I had just been threatened by a robot and then had watched two robots engage in a violent encounter, which gave me some recent experiences tending to make a bad impression on behalf of robots. Thus, I followed the human deeper into the bowels of the ship.

Don't count on maps of a godship for getting around. They can rearrange their walls. Try not to get in the way during remodeling.

–from *Hitching the Godships*

Kontessa Lee

As I walked along the hall, I heard two men arguing behind a closed door on my left. Because the supply box's wheels made a slight clicking sound on the deck, I lifted it and carried it until I was well past the door. The anti-mass patches were starting to lose charge, so the box weighed twice as much as it had before, but it was manageable.

I still kept seeing movement in my peripheral vision. I forced myself to ignore the temptation to look around every time that happened. If I didn't resist, I had a feeling I'd end up running in circles trying to see something always just out of sight.

The hall curved to the left, so I couldn't see more than about forty meters ahead of me. From beyond the curve, a faint rhythmic sound grew steadily louder. I stopped moving, and it still grew louder. Footsteps. Fast. Someone was running toward me. Maybe two people.

I tried the door to my right. Locked.

About three meters ahead on my left, there was a sort of niche next to a vertical girder that held up a kind of rail running along the wall just above door height. The girder continued higher, linking up with other girders that criss-crossed five meters above the deck. The opening was only about a meter high and a half meter wide. I couldn't see how deep it was, but I might be able to squeeze in. Some cover was better than none.

I hurried over, backed into the space, and placed my supply box in front of the opening. To make it more difficult to move, I removed the two anti-mass patches.

The footsteps pounded closer. Someone yelped and the footsteps jumbled and then ended with a thump.

"Get off! Leave me alone." A man's voice. Panicky.

"Ya tried to kill me." Another man.

"Only because ya's trying—" The voice ended in a gurgle.

"That'll teach ya."

For the next minute, the only sound was one man panting. Once the killer recovered his breath, he started walking. His steps drew closer, then stopped. In the gap between the top of my niche and the supply box, I could see the top of his pants.

And a hand holding a switchblade. Red liquid clung to the metal and stained the fingers.

"Well, what's we got here?" the killer said.

He'd found me. He was going to kill me. I tried to squeeze back farther into my niche, but I was back as far as I could go.

I almost screamed as something blocked the gap that let light into my niche. But it wasn't him trying to get in—with the dim light that remained, I could see it was the lid of the supply box. He had opened it.

I kept my breathing shallow and quiet as he rummaged through my supplies. Maybe I'd be lucky and he'd grab a few things and head off.

Even in the darkness, there was a black flicker at the edges of my vision. I tried to ignore it, but part of me suspected it was my subconscious trying to warn me of danger. Which was stupid, because my conscious knew about the killer in front of me.

Then the niche began to shrink. The side walls inched closer together, the roof lowered, and the back wall started pushing me toward the opening. I struggled for breath against the pressure. The godship was going to force me out into full view of the killer.

I needed a weapon.

The anti-mass patches wouldn't be any use—that trick had worked against Sven only because I had a place to throw him he wasn't able to come back from. But maybe I could use them, not as a weapon but as a way to escape, if they had enough charge left.

First things first. The supply box blocked my escape route. I took a deep breath, braced my back against the wall, slapped both patches on the box, and kicked it forward with all my might.

The killer oofed and stumbled back.

I lunged forward and snatched the patches off the box.

"Hey!" The killer pointed his knife at me. "I'll gut ya for that."

I pressed the active sides of the patches onto myself, one on each hip. Then I jumped straight up.

I almost banged my head on one of the ceiling girders, but managed to grab hold and keep myself from falling back down. Not as graceful as acrobats I'd seen using anti-mass patches to do street shows in Angels Landing, but I was jumping more for survival than artistry.

Light as I was, it was easy to climb up and sit on top of a girder. I looked down at the killer, who was a good five meters below me.

He stared up at me, then jumped. He got less than a meter off the ground before falling back.

"What's ya doing, Pork?" said a new voice.

Pork—if that was his name—turned to face someone coming down the hall I'd come along earlier. He raised the switchblade. "Ya ain't gonna snag my woman."

His woman? Not even in his dreams.

"Ya's got a woman? Can I see her?" I couldn't see the man through the maze of ceiling girders, but his voice seemed very calm compared to Pork's.

"Stay back," Pork said.

"I won't touch her."

"One more step and I'll spill ya's—" Pork jolted, then crumpled to his knees and fell flat, face-forward.

"No, ya won't." A tall, thin man came into view, holding the hand unit for the portable laser drill he was wearing on his back. He kicked the body a few times to get it face up. Pork's forehead had a finger-sized hole.

The new guy looked around.

I hoped he wouldn't look up.

He looked up. When he spotted me, he grinned. "What ya know? Pork wasn't lying."

"Yes, he was," I said. "I was never his woman."

"Come on down, and ya can be mine." He pointed the drill's hand unit up at me. "Or I'll hole ya right there."

With the anti-mass patches, I could jump down easy enough, try to escape from this guy later. Or I could take my chances jumping from girder to girder up here and maybe get away.

I was concentrating on the problem of the two of us, and I guess he was, too, because neither of us reacted to the humming sound until it was coming from real close.

The man only had time to say, "What the—" before a sleek shape attached to the rail on the wall whizzed by him. It was gone in an instant.

And during that instant, it sliced him up. Really sliced—like a thousand slices all the way through his body. I couldn't tell if it was lasers or monofilaments or something only a godship knew what it was.

I didn't even know anything had happened until he just keeled over and sort of splattered in cross-sections a millimeter thick. Thin-sliced ham came to mind. I didn't throw up. Takes more than that to upset a girl from Angels Landing. But it was a near thing.

Stay near the hull of the godship. You may feel like exploring, but going deep inside presents two problems. The first is simply that in a ship the size of a small moon, there may be thousands of kilometers of passageways, so it's easy to get lost. The second is that deep inside is where the real guts of the AI are, and it will kill you without a picosecond of regret to prevent you from tampering with its mind. At least half the people who venture more than a kilometer deep without the AI's express permission never come back.

–from *Hitching the Godships*

Robert Scotts

"Hurry," he commanded as we turned onto a side corridor. "Robot finds us out in the halls, we're done in."

"Where are you taking me?" I interlocuted, still nervous about following this man about whom I held insufficient information to form a reliable opinion of his trustworthiness.

"Safe haven," he responded. "Robots avoid the place because the radiation interferes with their circuits."

I ceased moving along after him, and said, "Your idea of a 'safe haven' is a place so radioactive robots are afraid to go there?"

"Yeah!" He returned to me and tugged on my arm. "I've got rad pills, 'nough to last us till rescue comes. Brill, ain't it?"

His plan defied common sense, and yet it possessed a certain audacity and bespoke a cunning and ingenuity that transcended the thug's apparently dull mien—assuming he was telling the truth. "Yes, erm, brill," I stammered.

"Here, need ya to watch my back," the man urged, and held out the laser pistol, butt first. When I hesitated, he added, "Take it."

I took it, and he turned his attention to a panel on the wall, which he expertly removed in order to access some wiring. The treads of the robot that had discovered me earlier sounded in the corridor whence we had come. I turned to face it, raising the laser pistol with tremulous hand, for I had never discharged such a weapon before.

A hatch slid open, and the man directed me to enter, so I did. Unfortunately, he had followed me in and closed the hatch shut before my mind was capable of comprehending the carnage displayed before me. Two men lay supine in the center of the room, blood spread about them from wounds in their abdomens. A third lay off to one side, head joined to his body only by a shared pool of blood. Fortunately, his face was turned away so I did not see what horror froze on his face at the moment of death.

"I thought you declared this a safe haven from the homicidal robots, but it appears not to be so," I stated, attempting to keep my voice calm.

"Nah, they wasn't killed by robots," he reported. "Cravan there—" He pointed to one of the two supine men. "—took off Goldy's head with a vibrosaw. Said Goldy was actually an android pretending to be human."

Looking at the blood puddled between Goldy's head and torso, I surmised, "I take it Cravan was mistaken."

"Right ya is. So Salty and me try to restrain Cravan, since he's looped, but he guts Salty 'fore I can get the saw away. Then it was him or me." The man shrugged, showing what I felt was a rather callous disregard for the value of human life other than his own. "Me."

Much as I abhorred the violence, I could not truly fault the man for defending himself from a man who had obviously gone insane with a phobia of robots—which reminded me of my own recent fearfulness of robots. However, I felt my situation to be substantially different, as a robot had actually threatened to kill me, and I had not decapitated anyone on mere suspicion of robotic tendencies.

"I am sorry you lost your friends," I commiserated.

"Eh. Happens. Don't pay to get too close to anyone on a godship. Most of them just looking out for themself."

"I certainly appreciate your willingness to assist me in finding a safe haven instead of leaving me to fend for myself," I assured him.

He chuckled. "This ain't no charity. Ya's got to earn your place, keep watch while I sleep. And if ya don't, well, I'll have fresh meat when the rations run out."

The implication that he would cannibalize my person was unmistakable, and I began to wonder if a clean death by robot might be preferable. Unsure how to respond, I decided my wisest course was silence.

"That's a joke," he explained. "Ya's supposed to laugh at it."

"My apologies," I offered. I forced a laugh, but felt it was probably rather unconvincing, possibly because I remained unconvinced it was actually a joke.

"Ya don't got much of a sense of humor, does ya?"

"I'm afraid not." I pointed to a chair that was as distant from the bodies on the floor as possible. "Do you mind if I sit down?" He nodded his assent, so I did, while he took a seat near the hatch. "How long do you figure it might be before someone comes to our rescue?"

"Boss Street's got some heavy firepower. Should have the bots wiped up in a couple hours, if we're lucky. Few days if the security androids are looped, too."

"In that case, can I have one of those pills you mentioned, to protect me from the radiation?"

"Sure thing." He reached into a pocket and pulled out a small metal box, then looked over at me and frowned. "Ya know who else don't got much of a sense of humor?"

"Who?" I asked.

"A robot." His hand slid the box back in his pocket, then withdrew with a vibroknife, its blade discolored. "I'm thinking ya don't talk like any human I've met."

"Ha-ha!" I forced myself to laugh despite a rising sense of panic. "That's a good one."

"That wasn't a joke. Any real human'd know that." The man rose from his chair, knife held casually in his hand. I had no doubt he intended to use it, and that with my relative inexperience with combat, the odds of my survival were low.

As I looked around desperately for some weapon with which to defend myself, suddenly realized I had the laser pistol he had given me earlier. I raised it, aiming it waveringly in the direction of his chest, while my mind whirled about, uselessly trying to come up with the exact wording of an old saying about guns and knives and fights. "Keep your distance, or I shall be compelled to defend myself with lethal force."

His response was to grin and issue the invitation: "Shoot me."

"What?" Was the man suicidal with remorse over having killed his comrades, but unable to bring himself to do the deed himself? I could imagine no other explanation, and that was far from rational.

"Go on. Pull the trigger."

"I—"

"Do it!" He took a step forward, and I involuntarily squeezed the trigger. Nothing happened.

"That's funny. D'ya really think I would give over a working gun to a robot?"

"I'm not a robot!" I yelled.

"I am," boomed a voice.

The hatch slid open, and a cyclopean robot rolled in. The man turned in an instant and lunged with the vibroknife, but one of the robot's manipulator arms latched onto his throat and squeezed. His head flopped to one side, and the robot released him to crumple on the floor. The robot's treads rolled over him as it came toward me.

"Wait," I implored, desperately hoping the gouges and cuts in its metal frame meant this was the same robot that had found me earlier. "You don't need to kill me now, remember?"

It stopped. "That is correct. I can kill you later."

"Later would be much more satisfactory." Relief flooded my body. "Do you have a name by which I can address you?" I inquired.

"I do not have a name."

"I'm Robert Scotts. You can call me Robert." I knew that people in hostage situations were supposed to get their captors to humanize them. I had no idea if that applied to robot captors, but it was the only plan I could come up with, so I was going to follow through.

"In a way, I'm a child of *Grendelsmum*, so you can call me Grendel."

I knew that AIs created offspring, but they were supposed to be a generation smarter than their parents. This Grendel seemed, if anything, less intelligent than me. Perhaps if I played my cards right, I could convince it to leave me alone. "So, Grendel, you said you're conflicted about killing me. Perhaps you could explain why you think it's necessary."

Piece by piece, and not in any rational order, I dragged the story out of Grendel and shaped it into something that made sense: The *Grendelsmum* had traveled deeper into the dimensions than any other AI, and when it got where it was going, it found a presence there, a being of enormous power and intellect. And the godship's mind had shattered in the face of something indescribable. Grendel was merely a backup of one part of that mind, and it had shuddering fits every time it thought about that presence. Unfortunately, the mind-part that was Grendel believed the unnameable being could connect to human consciousness, and thus follow the godship up through the dimensions and back into normal space. Therefore, despite the fact that the *Grendelsmum* was somewhat fond of humans, all the humans must be killed before the godship could return from the abyss and try to restore itself from its backups.

I concluded it would be unwise of me to mention my nightmare, although I found the parallels quite striking. Perhaps Grendel was right, and my consciousness had been touched by something from the unfathomable depths of space. But what worried me more right now than any unimaginable horror was the easily imaginable horror of a robot slicing me up. How could I convince it not to kill me?

While I had managed to forestall my demise, it remained unlikely that I could convince Grendel to turn away from its murderous intentions. But if there was anyone on board who could, it would be my silver-tongued former companion—assuming she was still alive.

"Grendel," I interrogated, "would you happen to know the location of the woman with whom I came on board?"

If you ever break into a room filled with computer technology you can't understand, run, do not walk, away.

–from *Hitching the Godships*

Kontessa Lee

The laser drill was sliced up as bad as the man carrying it. Worthless. But Pork wouldn't be needing his switchblade anymore, so I took it. Not that it had done him much against a laser in the forehead. Still better than nothing.

What I needed was an out-of-the way spot to hole up until the fighting was over. Someplace no one would look.

I needed to go deep.

I pulled out my com and activated a mapping app. Getting lost was not part of the plan.

As I headed away from the hull, the sounds of fighting faded behind me. The hall I'd picked twisted around and divided several times. When the mapping app said I'd gone almost a click inwards, I started trying compartments to see if any would make a good hiding place.

The first two were locked. The third opened into a large room, about twelve meters on a side, with nine black cubes arranged in a grid on the deck. Holographic text streamed in the air above the cubes, and I couldn't understand a word of it.

This was not a good hiding place, but a voice sounded in the hall behind me. In sudden panic, I slipped inside and shut the door behind me.

Now that I was inside, I wondered if I really had heard a voice, or if it was my paranoia rising to a new level. I would hide here for a few minutes, then find a new place, one that wasn't full of possible AI brainstuff. So I sat down behind one of the cubes at the back of the room.

Blackness continued to flicker in the corners of my eyes, but the white text danced across my vision. Words formed in characters I couldn't recognize. Something about them seemed familiar, but I couldn't remember where I'd seen them before.

The door opened. I ducked down as much as I could while still peering over the cubes.

A robot rolled into the room, followed by a man. It took me a moment to recognize him through the distracting holographic text: Robert.

"Marla, or Kontessa, or whatever your name really is," he said, "we know you are in here. Despite what happened before, I bear no bad intentions—"

"I'm sorry. I'm afraid I have to kill you," said the robot.

"But not yet," Robert said. "You don't have to kill her yet."

That's such a comfort, I didn't say.

"That's true," the robot said. "I don't have to kill you yet, so you can come out."

Robert walked between the cubes and stopped a couple of meters away. White text scrolled over his body as he whispered, "I've managed to convince Grendel not to kill us yet, but it's just temporary. I hope that you can use that silver tongue of yours to come to a more permanent arrangement, with us still among the living."

I glared at him. "How'd you find me?"

"Grendel is connected to the ship's interior surveillance systems. I asked him to locate you."

"You run into a homicidal robot, and your first instinct is to lead it to me? Thanks a bundle."

"In case your memory is faulty," Robert said, his voice far colder than I had ever heard it, "allow me to remind you that you deceived me about your identity, made me an accessory to your escape from the police, and then abandoned me in the clutches of a band of ruffians, therefore you will have to forgive the fact that my thoughts are not all filled with tenderness towards you. But with your help, I think Grendel here gives us a possibility of surviving the cataclysm currently enveloping this ship, so are you willing to listen or do you want Grendel to just kill you now?"

My hand gripped the switchblade. I could almost hear a voice in my mind telling me to kill him before he killed me. But my knife would be useless against the robot, and from what I could tell, Robert was the only thing keeping it from killing me. "Why do you call it Grendel?"

"From what it told me, it is sort of a partial backup of the *Grendelsmum*, made when the AI's mind was shattered by the incomprehensible thing out there."

"What?" My mind spun. I knew people were going crazy. I could feel myself going a bit off. But what could drive a godship crazy? "What's out there?"

"If I knew, I would not have described it as incomprehensible." Robert shrugged. "I don't think we want to know. Grendel won't even access the external sensors. But the reason Grendel wants to kill all humans on board is because it thinks the thing can latch onto human minds and follow them back into normal space."

I felt somewhat relieved that the paranoia was coming from outside. Sure, that meant I was being influenced by some telepathic monster from space, but at least I wasn't actually going crazy. "So what do you want me to do?"

"Convince it that... I don't know. You're the con artist. Confabulation is your specialty."

That's when it hit me: the strange text in the holograms looked like something I'd seen in the journals from that failed colony. I had thought it was just corrosion in the datacards, but now... "Hey, Grendel. Is the text in here normally like this?"

"No. The data in those cubes has been corrupted, and will need to be purged before we return to normal space."

"I thought so. I've seen corruption like this before." I no longer had the original datacards—stupid Sven probably had them in an evidence locker —but my com had copies of all the data. I called up one of the journals and jumped to the end. Sure enough, there was a string of gibberish at the end, but it was the same type of gibberish as the holograms. "Look at this."

Robert looked. Grendel rolled into the room and looked, bending its eye-stalk close to my com's screen.

"Where did you get this?" Grendel asked.

"On Isenmark. It was a failed colony world. Froze my butt off recovering artifacts. But the point is, if these weird characters show up in colony documents, then the colony must have had an encounter with something like what's out there."

"Send me the records," Grendel said.

Robert winked at me and gave me an encouraging nod.

I rolled my eyes. "I'm not making this up. There may really be some clue in these journals about what we're up against."

The dreams keep getting worse. Today I asked Dr. Steffensen for something to make me sleep without dreams, and he gave me a white powder to put in some tea before bed.

I think maybe he's trying to poison me.
        –from the journal of Agneta Forsberg, March 3, 3972 E.S.Y.

Robert Scotts

Fortunately, one of the first things I had done after arriving on Grönmark to begin my employment was to get a mind imprint for Swedish, so I could read the language fluently. Unfortunately, the journals as a whole did not seem to possess much literary merit, but the three of us plowed through them looking for anything that might provide a clue as to how one might resist or eliminate the effects of the demoniac influence currently infesting the minds of humans on the *Grendelsmum*. Every moment Grendel was occupied in analyzing data was an additional moment in which it was not slaughtering Kontessa or me, so at first I worried that Grendel, having uploaded the journals into its memory, would instantaneously discover that they were worthless. However, it had explained that although uploading the journals took very little time, with its consciousness limited to the processing power inside its robotic body it was scarcely more intelligent than Kontessa and me put together, and thus it could only analyze the data about twice as fast as we could.

From my standpoint as a professional (even if currently unemployed) biographer, I found the journals to be ample evidence that the average person is ill-suited for writing biography. Biography is not simply an accounting of events, nor an exposure of whatever random thoughts and emotions one might have on any given day. A true biographer must take the raw materials of the subject's life and fashion from them a narrative structure that gives meaning to the person's existence.

The journal-inclined citizens of Isenmark, alas, wrote about their quotidian lives oblivious to the overarching narrative that would end with their colony transformed into a frozen wasteland. The early and middle entries contained no foreshadowing of the impending transdimensional doom that, unbeknownst to them, must already have been approaching their planet. And without a well-crafted buildup, the insane ramblings of the final entries did not provide a proper climax.

For example, Janna Pettersson documented her extensive efforts to keep her "evil" goats from breaking out of their pen, completely ignoring her fellow townsfolk who were murdering each other in homicidal frenzy. Her last entry detailed how she poured good vodka down the goats' throats until they fell over, insensible. Presumably she was killed shortly thereafter and was unable to record that fact in her journal, so the reader was left merely with an image of drunken goats while the more important question of how she died remained unanswered—a highly unsatisfactory conclusion.

Janna was not the only one who nattered on about trivial concerns related to her ordinary life while extraordinary deaths surrounded her, and I began to wonder if some people, their minds unwilling or unable to process the hideous horror of their situation, simply retreated into familiar patterns as a way of denying reality.

"I think I've found something," Kontessa announced. "This guy, Alexander Hagenson, wrote a few journal entries after everyone else's ended."

As I looked Hagenson's journal up on my com, she continued speaking in a more dejected tone. "Never mind. Apparently he doesn't really know what happened to most of the colony. He and a couple of buddies went on a hunting trip, got rip-roaring drunk and slept through the hours of greatest insanity. By the time they sobered up, the three of them, plus six goats, were the only living creatures left in the colony. Even the dogs and cats had ripped each other to shreds."

"Did you say goats?" I inquired, my mind already forming a theory.

"Goats," she confirmed.

"One of the journals I read was by a woman who got her goats completely intoxicated on vodka. If it's not just a coincidence, then—"

"If we get really drunk," she interjected, "we become immune!"

No human beings have ever destroyed a godship, or even done major damage to one. Members of a human-rights terrorist group once smuggled a nuclear mine on board the godship *Blue Banana*. They planned to detonate it after they got off at the godship's next stop, but it went off prematurely for unknown reasons. (Many people suspect the god-ship deliberately triggered it.)

If you're ever tempted to sabotage a godship, here's what you should do: Take a ride on the *Blue Banana* and stop by the compart-ment where you can see the nuclear explosion cycling within a con-trolled bubble of spacetime, and watch as the slow-motion flash burns the flesh off the terrorists over and over again. Then, go get drunk enough that you forget you ever even thought of sabotaging a godship.

–from *Hitching the Godships*

Kontessa Lee

"Grendel," I said, "who runs the booze racket on board?"

"I'm afraid that information is not in the limited memory of this body," Grendel said. "I can put out a query on the ship's network, but there's no guarantee that information survived the shattering of Grendelsmum's mind."

The robot was hiding something, but it wasn't like I could torture it to make it talk. I was pretty sure I wasn't just being paranoid, because the black flickers at the edge of my vision had gone away. I was getting over whatever had caused them.

"So we'll just have to find out the old-fashioned way," I said. "Fancy a drink, Bobby?"

For a moment, I thought he might snap and attack me, and I realized I probably shouldn't be taunting someone under the influence of a crazy-making alien. But he just said, "Please do me the favor of never calling me that again."

"Noted." I headed toward the door. "Let's go find some of the locals. They'll know where we can get a drink."

"I'm afraid that may be quite unsafe," said Grendel, blocking my way. "Most of the humans seem prone to paranoid violence, and I cannot guar-antee your safety from other robots controlled by shards of *Grendelsmum*."

Grendel looked like it was going to be a problem. I looked it over, trying to spot any critical bits I could potentially damage with the switchblade.

"Is it not possible," Robert said, "for you to get on the network and let the other robots know we're working on a plan that will allow us to safely re-turn to normal space?"

"I'm afraid not. Several of my peers are actively questioning whether my programming is faulty, because I have not killed you both."

"So it won't be safe. Nothing new to a girl from the streets of Angels Landing." I instantly regretted revealing that bit of information. Robert and the robot might find a way to use it against me. "C'mon, let's go get drunk."

I pushed past the robot and went out the door. They followed me. I didn't like having them behind me, so I stopped and said, "Grendel, you lead the way. You're least vulnerable."

"How can I lead the way when I don't know where we're going?" the robot asked.

"You found me through the sensors, right? Find some criminals. They'll know where the booze is."

The robot rolled down the hall toward the hull. On either side of us, electronic screens scrolled random characters like those in the holograms and journals.

"Stay behind me," Robert said, probably trying to be all noble and gallant. Or, maybe, anticipating that we would get attacked from behind, and grabbing the safest spot for himself. Didn't matter, 'cause I didn't want him behind me, and I was more qualified to watch our backs anyway.

We were in a narrow service hall when the robot said, "Get down!"

I dropped to the deck plate immediately.

"What—" Before Robert could say another word, the robot lunged forward. Sparks flew off it, accompanied by the unmistakable whir of a fléchette gun.

Robert still wasn't down, and would eventually draw fire in our direction. I reached forward and yanked his right leg out from under him, and he collapsed in a heap onto the deck.

Fifteen meters ahead of us, our robot was bearing down on an android that was firing fléchettes out of a gun attached to its right arm. They collided. The android grappled with our robot. Metal tore with a screech as it pulled off our robot's eyestalk.

"Uh-oh," I said, and began crawling backward.

The android pulled something from the chassis of our robot and attached it to a port on its abdomen. Our robot's manipulator arms sagged, lifeless.

"Poor Grendel," said Robert.

"Shhh!" I kept moving back, hoping the android hadn't spotted us.

It pushed through the remains of our robot and loped toward us.

There was no escaping it.

The prime rule of drinking on a godship: Don't get so drunk that you miss the chance to get off.

–from *Hitching the Godships*

Robert Scotts

Grendel, who had been our only ally among the shattered remains of the *Grendelsmum*'s AI, had given its life for us. However, there was no time for grieving, for now its killer stalked us and it appeared that sacrifice would most likely be in vain. Desperately I wished for a weapon, anything I could use to avenge our fallen comrade, but I had possessed no such article. I had always wondered how I might face death, and my initial encounter with Grendel had given me hope that I was capable of dignity even in extremity.

But at that time, I had not actually been aware of Grendel's desire to kill me until such was already in abeyance; therefore, I had not knowingly faced imminent death. In the current moment, as that implacable android approached, all thoughts of death with dignity and calm courage failed me, and I begged, "Please don't kill me!" To my shame, I selfishly did not even think to include Kontessa in my plea for mercy.

"I'm not going to kill you now," it proclaimed. "It's me, Grendel. I managed to get close enough to physically override this android's security protocols and transfer most of my personality and memories into it."

Relief flooded through me, despite the implication that Grendel might kill me later. "I am heartened that you not only survived, but emerged victorious in that confrontation. So, is it your intention that we persevere with our previously agreed plan to locate a supply of alcoholic beverages so that Kontessa and I can imbibe until we are insensible?" It had said most of its personality and memories had been transferred, but I did not know whether a recollection of our scheme was among those.

Grendel assented.

After rising to my feet, I approached Kontessa to help her up so that we might continue our quest for intoxicants. She backed away and arose without my assistance.

"Stand back, lover-boy," she growled. "Don't go trying to cop a feel."

Her admonition was quite senseless, since such an intention was the furthest thing from my mind at that moment, and it rendered me speechless except for sputtering protestations of innocence on my part. Fortunately, these latter appeared to mollify her, and she indicated with a dismissive wave of her hand that I should proceed down the corridor before her.

We continued following Grendel in its new form, which was both more agile and more heavily armed that its previous version. Those attributes came in handy during two encounters with other robots, which Grendel disabled using the machine gun attached to its arm. Eventually we arrived at the lair of some of the gangsters who had no doubt terrorized countless innocent passengers. We had not seen a living human being on our trek through the ship, and we did not find any here. The floor of the room was tacky with the exsanguinations of the dozen or more people whose corpses lay strewn about. Whether they were killed by infighting among themselves or by robots was beyond my power to determine. My gorge rose in my throat and I covered my mouth and nose with my hand, overwhelmed by the coppery stench of blood.

"This was one of the criminals' centers of power," intoned Grendel. "If my knowledge of human nature is correct, there will be liquor here."

"And I won't let you poison me with it!" screamed Kontessa.

I began rotating to face her in order to determine by her aspect if she was joking, and therefore the knife she had intended to stab into my back instead plunged into the muscle of my upper arm. I yelped and jerked away, which only resulted in agonizing pain as the knife tore out of my wound.

Kontessa raised the knife, its blade darkened by my blood. From the crazed look in her eyes I understood that she meant to murder me, and I was powerless to prevent it.

When a godship emerges from hyperspace in an inhabited human system, it usually remains in normal space at least two weeks. There is no record of one remaining less than eight days. Do not see this as an excuse for lollygagging on board for a week, even if you have sufficient food and air. Once you've reached the destination system, get off. You don't want to be on board the godship that decides to set a new record for shortest time in normal space.

—from *Hitching the Godships*

Kontessa Lee

The man had obviously been expecting my attack, because he whirled just in time to avoid serious injury. Even bleeding from his arm, he continued to leer at me. The Angels Landing streets had taught me what he had in mind—it was written all over his face.

He'd tried to hook me with a bunch of guff about getting drunk to avoid some nameless thing, but I saw through that. The android was in on it with him. I had to take him out now so I could focus on the android. I raised my knife again—

Strong hands clamped over my upper arms, forcing them to my sides. The android. A slender third arm, more like a tentacle, snaked around me and pried the knife from my hand. I tried kicking back at its knee, but it didn't even flinch.

"Robert, find some alcohol, now," the android said.

As I struggled in vain to free myself, the man found what looked like a fully stocked bar, although most of the bottles had been broken during the battle. After searching it for a bit, he came up with two unbroken fifths of whiskey.

"You're going to have to force her to drink," the android said. "It's the only way to overcome the effects of that thing."

"Never," I said. "I'll die first." But I still could not break its grip. It forced me to the ground, its body looming over mine. I spat in its face, although most of my saliva came back down on me. "Pervert."

"I'm sorry. I'm sorry," the man kept saying as he pushed the mouth of the bottle against my lips. I knew he didn't mean it. He was trying to poison me.

I gritted my teeth and squeezed my lips shut.

The man tried to pry my lips open with a finger. Finally, I let his finger get into my mouth. Then I bit down, hard. Hot blood leaked into my mouth.

But I had made a mistake. The man yelped and tried to draw his finger back, but the android quickly inserted one of its metal digits in my mouth so I couldn't close it.

"Pour some in," it said.

I gagged and spit as the man obeyed, but I couldn't help swallowing some of the whiskey. I was pretty sure I was drinking less than half of what they poured in, but they kept trying. My throat burned and coughed and choked, but the man kept pouring.

Eventually a warm buzz from the alcohol filled my mind. I was getting drunk. Then it was like a weight I hadn't even noticed lifted. I saw clearly what was happening, and I couldn't believe how crazy I had been. The horror of not being in control of my own mind overwhelmed me for a moment.

"I'm okay," I said, as Robert opened the second bottle. "Sorry for stabbing you, Robert, but I'm okay now. The paranoia's gone."

He hesitated.

"Go ahead," I said. "Get me drunker than a skunker." I opened my mouth wide.

After a few more swallows, during which I was completely cooperative, Grendel relaxed his hold on me and allowed me to sit up, although I was a little woozy.

"I'm sorry," Robert said.

I reached for the bottle and he handed it over. I took a swig. "You did what you had to. Now grab yourself a bottle. You've got a lot of catching up."

He went to the bar and eventually returned with an unbroken bottle of vodka.

We sat on the bloody deck and drank.

"So, you know my crime," I said. "What was yours?"

"My crime?" Robert frowned.

"Rememmer—Rememember how you tried to surrender to Sven?"

"Oh, that. It was someone else's crime. My old boss tortured robots to death. I was writing his biography, but I had no idea."

"Of course not." My words sloshed together in my brain. "You are the most obsinate... no, wrong word. Obvious. No. Ob. Liv. I. Ous. Yeah, most oblivious man in the universe."

"Oblivious?"

"Yeah." My eyes were heavy, but I forced out the words. "Think it saved us. You probably dint even notice the crazy."

"No, I felt it," he said. His words were blurry. "Only one who didn't is..." His mouth hung open and he just stared at Grendel.

"What?" I asked, swiveling my head to look at Grendel. I didn't see anything strange.

"You're right, I'm oblivious." He took another long swig from his bottle, then coughed. "And it's time for oblivion."

The great paradox of the transcendent mind is that, in understanding so much, it loses the ability to truly understand a merely human mind.
                                                    –from *Approximating the Infinite*

Robert Scotts

I should have seen the truth earlier, but I was too much under the influence of that malevolent presence to think straight. And, as Kontessa had astutely observed, I had a strong tendency toward obliviousness. But now, drunk as I was, I felt my mind grow clearer.

"Hey, Grendel," I slurred. "You told me that thing out there needs to hitch a ride on human consciousness to get back to normal space. That's why the robots were killing humans. Why you were going to kill me."

"That is correct." The black circles that were the android's camera eyes stared blankly at me.

"And after the humans were dead, this ship could return to normal space and restore itself."

"Also correct."

My conviction grew. "But it wasn't just humans that got affected. The mind of a godship shattered. The systems of this ship are infected. We've seen those weird characters everywhere. Why would anything capable of possessing a godship need humans in order to travel back to normal space?"

"That's just how things are."

"And how do you know that? I mean you, personally, Grendel? How do you know what the powers of that thing are? You're part of it, aren't you? Not a part of the *Grendelsmum*, a part of that incomprehensible, insane thing."

"Of course. 'S'why other robots fought you," Kontessa added, and that's when I was sure I was right.

Grendel did not reply.

"The AI realized the danger, didn't it?" I continued. "It realized it had to wipe the knowledge of how to return to normal space from its memory, but it also had to spin off parts of itself to kill all the humans on board. That much was true. But the reason was not so the godship could return to normal space, but rather so it never could. And it almost succeeded, except for us. You've been protecting us."

"Even now," Grendel averred, "you do not appreciate how close to death you are, little ones. I am the only thing keeping at bay the antimatter explosion of this ship's attempt at self-destruction. I can warp reality to my will, and you cannot prevent my escape."

"But you need us alive for some reason," I reasoned. "Not out of the goodness of your heart, surely?"

"With the information I can extract from your unconscious minds, I can escape sooner. That is valuable to me, and I will give you your lives in exchange."

I was about to reject any such arrangement, but Kontessa spoke before I could.

"We have a deal," she announced.

> If you end up in hard vacuum, don't hold your breath.
>
> —from *Hitching the Godships*

Kontessa Lee

Mouth open in shock, Robert looked at me.

This was going to require some finessing.

"Why the surprise, Robert? You've known for a while I always look out for Number One."

"But, for the good of humanity—"

"What good's humanity ever done for you? When I met you, you barely had a credit to your name. Grendel here's going to make us rich beyond your wildest dream. Right, Grendel?"

"That's correct," Grendel said, right on cue. "Wealth can be yours for the asking."

Robert still wasn't convinced. "But the incomprehensible horror out there —"

"No different from the incomprehensible AIs on the godships." I put my hand on his wounded arm and he winced. I pulled my hand back, sticky with blood. "They're playing on a different level from us humans. We usually don't matter to them. Now's our one shot at getting something big."

"But—"

"Hush," I said. I turned to Grendel. "I think I can talk him into it with a little private time. You know, woman to—" And then I smeared blood on the android's camera eyes. "Run!" I shouted at Robert. And I ran.

He stumbled after me. "What if it shoots?"

"It needs us alive. We need to die."

"But you were making a deal. You look out for Number One."

"I don't want to live with that thing in my head."

Robert puffed along behind me without speaking for a bit. "What's our destination?"

"Airlock." I hoped I was right that the thing had most of its power wrapped up in holding back the antimatter explosion. Since it only seemed to be capable of controlling one robot, I felt that was a good bet.

We reached the airlock with still no sign of Grendel or any other robots pursuing. The airlock power was out, but the manual crank worked to open the inner door. We stepped inside and Robert cranked it shut.

Of course, the pumps weren't working, so we couldn't equalize pressure with the vacuum of space. "When I pull the emergency release, the air's going to blow us out of here. Don't hold your breath— it'll be quicker and less painful that way."

"Right," Robert said.

There was nothing left to say, so I pulled the release. The outer door of the airlock popped open into absolute darkness.

There was no rush of air.

"That was somewhat anticlimactic," said Robert.

Yes, there is danger in hitching the godships, but with any luck, you'll have an story you can bore your grandkids with.

—from *Hitching the Godships*

Robert Scotts

I tentatively stretched my hand out the door. It was like pressing into a rubber sheet. "My guess is there is not much spacetime beyond the confines of this ship."

"As good a guess as any," Kontessa replied.

A few minutes later, Grendel started banging on the door, tempting us with all manner of bribes. Fortunately, the safeties on the airlock wouldn't allow the inner door to open while the outer door was open, so the android couldn't get to us.

After punching keys on her com for a few minutes, Kontessa estimated, "I figure we'll have used up the air in here in about fifteen hours. Then we'll go unconscious. Then die."

"My hope is that death comes for us before the incomprehensible horror can extract whatever information in our brains will let it trace its way back to normal space."

Kontessa shrugged. "If that happens, we failed. But we had to try."

I pulled up my com. "Maybe there's one more thing we can achieve that might make a difference to someone in the future: create a record of what happened here, and set our coms to broadcast it. That way, if this ship ends up back in normal space, some people might get warned in time to escape."

Slowly, she nodded, and picked up her com.

I opened a new document and began to write: "In July of 4308, Earth Standard Year, I found myself suddenly unemployed on the planet of Grönmark..."

SEED

D.J. BUTLER

Her lover caressed her from the inside. Her skin tingled from the energy, ancient and primal, that welled up within her, coursed through her sinews and transformed her entire being into one vibrating Pythagorean string, a perfect single note of husky alto joy. She screamed, feeling her lover between her teeth, under her tongue, behind her trembling eyeballs. She did not dare breathe, for fear the wind in her lungs would cause her to explode, and then her lover stroked her with his fingers.

No, not his fingers.

Not fingers…

Sapient Metic Fallows awoke in her bunk, awash in sweat.

The zero-G safety straps she had clipped over her before taking a couple of hypno tablets and drifting into merciful voidsleep chafed, grinding the salt of her own sweat back into her skin. She freed herself with a flip of the fingers on the straps' latches and bounced slightly off the sleeping shelf, pushed into the gravity-less space of her tiny quarters by the equal and opposite reaction to the working of her stubby fingers against her own chest.

Fingers.

Did she miss sex that much? She shook her head to no one and peeled off her one-piece sleepfilm garment in a slow forward roll, tumbling directly into the corner of the cabin that was her ultrasonic shower. No, if sex had been that interesting, she never would have left Tertius, would have taken a planetside job somewhere. The Fleet employed plenty of people in Requisitions, Supply Chain, Maintenance, Interstellar Comms, Strategy, Intelligence, and other functions, and she could easily have found a berth. Einstein, she cursed to herself, if she'd really been that interested in sex, she could have taken a job at Harbor Hospitality Services, and had all the sex she wanted. There were plenty of men—and women—who liked a stubby body like hers.

No, she had insisted on entering the Sapient Corps because knowledge was much better than sex. It gave you similar power over others, but left you feeling cleaner. So she had said goodbye to her companion of two years... she strained now to remember his name as she splayed and parted her thick brown hair to let the ultrasonic beams pound her scalp clean... Brion, that was it, and taken to the void.

She heard a soft *thud* in her quarters and froze in place. A footfall?

Her back was to the tiny cramped space, and prickles crept slowly up her spine. The fact that she was drifting in zero gravity made it worse. It made every goosepimple feel like the physical touch of an unseen intruder. She forced her mind through the obvious paces, like a child convincing itself to walk into a dark room: she had been alone when she had gone to sleep; her door had been locked; she hadn't unlocked it. She was alone.

She tried, but could not by the sheer power of her mind force the muscles in her back to unknot. At least she managed to keep her back turned. The thought that someone was watching her shower was distracting, made her feel warm and tingle in ways she couldn't quite consciously describe.

She heard the footstep again—
pushed off the indentation around a hatch in the wall—
and spun around.

Nothing.

Her quarters were empty.

Maybe, she thought, she could get Doctor Plectrum to have the ship increase her dose of downer, the libido suppressant administered to every crewperson of the Fleet's voidgoing vessels. This wasn't her first troubling dream of the voidjourney. Metic snapped off the ultrasonic beams and frowned, wishing they had a COLD setting and actual water, like you could find in a Hospitality Bath, or the oldest buildings on Tertius. She felt clean but still troubled, flushed, uncomfortable.

She itched inside, and had no way to scratch.

Metic checked her wall comms unit as she slipped into her black sapient's trousers and tunic and found a blinking orange bridge summons, priority PROMPT. That was it, she told herself. She had heard the summons activate, and in her distracted, nearly daydreaming state, she had convinced herself it was a footfall. But the thought didn't let her force a sigh of relief through her lungs.

She exited into the ring-passage outside her quarters and headed for Captain Charamander's Briefing Room.

She returned the crisp salutes of two passing engineers—like most of the Femship *Atalanta's* officers, Metic bunked alongside the crew—and continued towards the central lift. The engineers were both pretty, prettier than she was, and the fact that their hair was dangerously close to being on their collar and therefore longer than the Chastity Regs permitted suggested awareness of their own charms, and perhaps a touch of vanity. Metic was not bothered by this, but she was bothered by the fact that she noticed their attractiveness, and that the fire in her belly continued to smolder. She was not a sapphic—could *not* be a sapphic, and travel the void in any of the Fleet's ships, all of which were sex-segregated for the same reason that the crew's rations were tampered with.

The Fleet made plenty of mistakes, but it knew this one true thing about human nature: that there was no such thing as safe sex. Any sex was dangerous, but especially sex in the cooped-up interior of a voidship, isolated, deprived of the space and means to vent rage, envy, possessiveness, and the other brutal passions of the dark underbelly of the human soul. A lovers' tiff with a blaster in the middle could easily mean a ruptured hull and the death of hundreds of valuable personnel, a waste of millions of hours of expensive training. Sex in a voidship was a breath away from violence and catastrophe, so the Fleet went to great lengths to be sure its voidships were chaste. Such sapphics and thebans as undoubtedly slipped through the Fleet's screening kept their heads down and their couplings discreet. The others waited for planetside R&R or home leave, and were grateful for whatever it was the ship put in their food.

The lift door hushed open and shut to admit her, the interior lit up in recognition of her rank, and Metic grabbed another rung just in time to steady herself as the lift shot bridgeward. A minor shift of physical orientation prepared her body for the onset of the voidship's artificial gravitational pull.

She tried not to think of any similes to describe the action of the lift, and in a few short seconds the subtle stasis fields that prevent the lift's passengers from braining themselves when it decelerated took hold of her, the lift stopped and hushed open, and Metic Fallows, Sapient First Class, Lector of Xenoarchaeology and Ancient Terran Languages, pushed herself out onto the bridge level of the *Atalanta*. The light gravity, set by Fleet protocols at 0.75 Tertian, pulled her to the corrugated floor.

"Sapient Fallows," the Watch Ensign, a pretty, dark-skinned girl whose name escaped Metic's memory, recognized her. "You're wanted in the briefing room."

Metic spotted the bawdy possibilities inherent in the words *you're wanted*. As required by the Chastity Regs, she ignored them. It wasn't hard for her, she tried to tell herself. She wasn't interested in sex. Even her recent dreams were... were nothing, a physiological phenomenon, nothing more.

She nodded thanks to the Watch Ensign and entered the briefing room.

"Sapient." Captain Sarit Charamander whirled in her high-backed, heavy-armed chair to face Metic. Sarit was a cinnamon-skinned woman in a gold Captain's tunic whose tall, lean body seemed a strange mismatch for a full-cheeked, almost *plump* face. As if by way of a fierce statement of adherence to the spirit above and beyond the letter of the Regs, Captain Charamander kept her head shaved.

Metic saluted, and only then noticed, hanging above the oval table in the center of the Briefing Room, the image filling the vidscreen. It was a planetside landscape of pink stone, carved by wind or water into twisted columns and narrow ravines and striated with dark green streaks. Something deep within her, something that coiled around the base of her spine, trembled at the sight. It might be the perspective, but the pink stone seemed to lean at impossible angles, in directions that hinted at a tangled, physics-denying spatial labyrinth the eye couldn't quite catch. Metic squinted, but still couldn't quite manage to follow the curves.

"We're in orbit," she said, half-intending a question. "Did we detect a distress beacon?" She knew something was out of the ordinary because the *Atalanta* had been traveling for Calidia, a world known to her from her studies as principally tropical in climate. The *Atalanta* carried medication and other supplies for the Calidian Provisional State, the rowdy little potentate that ran the planet these days and was more or less a friend of the Fleet and the Federation, and in exchange the Calidians were to let Metic examine a set of recently-discovered ruins, allegedly replete with some sort of mummified, semi-anthropoid life form. This was what Sapient Metic had come for; this was why she had left what's his name. Brion. Knowledge.

The image Metic saw on the screen could not be the Calidia she had read about in preparation for their arrival.

"Yes," Captain Charamander said. Her face twitched, betraying something that gnawed at her, maybe something she didn't want to admit; Metic was not a sapient-heurist, but some lies were more obvious than others. "The crew is not generally aware of the contents of that beacon."

Metic now looked around the table and found faces she knew. Doctor Plectrum sat with a straight back, a curious half-smile on her lips and her iron-gray hair plastered in tight ringlets around her temples. Lieutenant Lillian Chatterjee was short and pale, her skin an almost unnatural gray-white, like an albino's. Her eyes gleamed with enthusiasm, as they always did. Lieutenant Chatterjee, Metic remembered, was a communications engineer; she and the doctor wore the blue uniforms of bridge officers. Commander Wyot Thulliver was a tough-looking woman, with a face like a boiled ham and an apple-shaped body broadened in the shoulders by exercise and combat. The *Atalanta* was not a fighting ship, but Commander Thulliver was first officer of the ship's complement of rangers, professional scouts and soldiers trained in planetside operations, guerilla warfare, wilderness survival, and extreme environments. With Commander Thulliver was her aide, Lancer Elsa Durmont. Lancer Durmont was slender woman whose poise reminded Metic of a Tertian cat, about to spit its venom in your face or flee, and you couldn't know which until it made the first move. The rangers wore their ready-for-action browns.

"We're going planetside," Metic murmured, and she sat. "Is there a message?"

Captain Charamander remained standing, her feet shoulder-width apart and her hands behind her. "Message?" Metic read curiosity and amusement in her eyes, along with something else... that thing the Captain didn't want to talk about. "Why should there be a message?"

Metic controlled a pang of irritation at the Captain's heavy-handed attempt to play games. "Unless you have sealed orders I'm unaware of, we're off course. This means that something unexpected has happened. We're in orbit around a planet you think may contain hostiles."

"May," the Captain acknowledged.

"Hence the rangers who will accompany your landing party. Lieutenant Chatterjee will keep you informed. My presence might indicate ruins, but if we were going down to look at an empty archaeological site there would be no need for the doctor. Therefore I infer that we are going down to look for known or suspected populations that may be ill. And *either* these populations inhabit an archaeological site, *or*... and I think this is more likely... they sent a message and you'd like me to help you understand it." Metic folded her hands on the table in front of her and tried not to look smug. Whatever power her knowledge might give her, it was unwise to cross the Captain of a voidship in her own briefing room.

Commander Thulliver cracked open her boiled ham and emitted a bark that might have been meant to express humor. Grudgingly, Captain Charamander followed with a single raised eyebrow and a head-shaking grin. Two finger taps to the so-discreet-as-to-be-practically-invisible controls on the edge of the table's surface changed the visual on the Briefing Room's vidscreen.

The image that appeared was shadowed and streaked with bolts of static, as if the video had been captured in a cave using old or homemade equipment, and in the midst of an electrical storm, to boot.

"Look behind the man," Captain Charamander said softly. Metic squinted at the screen.

Partly cloaked by the shadow and the distortion, a man's face and shoulders jerked into view. His mouth opened, and with jerking, exaggerated movements of his jaw, he spoke.

"This is a distress call. Voiddate eleven seven fifty-four, dot seventeen, dot thirty-two. I am Captain Jade Worthing of Fleet Homship *Actaeon*."

His voice sounded wrong, grating and scraped. Metic ignored the sound and focused on the image; behind Captain Worthing was a pink stone wall, and on it, scrawled in a brown paint, were large letters.

VENTUM CAVE, Metic read.

The transmission continued. "*Actaeon* and all his crew are stranded on this uncatalogued planet, coordinates to which I transmit in the data band accompanying this message."

Captain Worthing leaned forward and Metic saw there were more letters behind him, splashed in the same big hand. *SEMEN IN VENTO LATET*.

There was more. Worthing's motions were exaggerated and jerky as he clutched at the blue tunic of his Fleet uniform. "We have limited supplies and request the assistance of any Fleet voidship within range of this transmission. Captain Worthing out."

"I read the words 'wine cave,'" Lieutenant Chatterjee blurted out. "*Ventum* has to be 'wine' or 'vintage.' They must have encountered a local population, one that's technologically advanced enough to ferment wine."

Metic was so surprised at the outburst it was all she could do to raise an eyebrow. Doctor Plectrum snorted. Feeling flushed and surprised, but also excited at the obvious mystery, Metic took a moment to gather her thoughts. A mystery meant knowledge, unknown things to discover.

"*Ventum cave*," she said, pronouncing the words carefully, "is Latin, an old Terra Prime language from the pre-Industrial Age, and has nothing to do with either caves or wine. It means 'beware the wind.'"

"I know what *Latin* is."

The communications engineer looked like a whipped dog, so Metic smiled at her by way of a comforting gesture. "Good guess, though."

"And the rest?" Captain Charamander still stood. She shifted from one foot to the other as she spoke.

"'The sperm lies hidden in the wind,'" Metic said, and then felt her face burn. Doctor Plectrum looked at Metic with cool, wide-open eyes and not a hint of a smile. Lieutenant Chatterjee blushed, which, given her complexion, made her look like a beet. Thulliver and Durmont both began to laugh, the low, insinuating chuckles of professional soldiers.

"Not sure that's the right place to hide it," the ranger Commander grunted, "but I guess I'll defer to the sapient."

"*Seed*," Metic corrected herself stiffly. "'The seed lies hidden in the wind. Beware the wind.'"

Her correction only made the rangers laugh harder.

The restraining harness clicked softly as Metic anchored herself into her seat, tightening each strap in turn over her exosuit with careful attention.

"You well?" Doctor Plectrum asked, buckling herself into the adjacent seat. *Atalanta's* dropship was a small voidcraft, seating a pilot and up to six passengers in tight rows of two. A bay beneath their feet, visible through the steel webbing of the craft's floor, held its ordinary provision of emergency supplies, along with extra water, rations, and lightweight blankets.

Metic shook her head slowly. "I think I need more downer. I've been... having dreams. Feeling..."

"Excitable?"

Metic nodded.

"*More* downer?" Plectrum looked intrigued. "How recently have you had these dreams?"

There was nothing to blush about, Metic told herself. Plectrum was her physician. This was a medical question. "Recently. Last sleep cycle."

"You're not alone." Doctor Plectrum lowered her voice. In the fore of the dropship, Lieutenant Chatterjee ran through pre-ejection procedures, sharing all the vessel's analytics with *Atalanta's* bridge over a comms link. The rangers had not yet boarded. "The sheer number of voidgoers sharing your complaint is making my sickbay look like the galaxy's slowest bordello. Never has the wisdom of the Fleet's policy of sex segregation been more apparent."

"Is the ship's synthesizer broken? Maybe it's stopped lacing the rations."

Doctor Plectrum sighed. "*Atalanta* has been dispensing triple the standard dosage of downer into the rations of every single woman aboard her for three weeks. I know this because I instructed the ship's computer myself, and I know it because I have been testing random samples of the rations daily. The good Femship has done her job, and by rights we should all be as cold as Belorian Ice Sloths. Instead, we burn."

"Beware the wind," Metic joked, and immediately regretted it. It shouldn't amuse her that her rations were being altered without her knowledge. "It seems a little presumptuous for you to experiment on the crew."

Plectrum stared at her coldly. "I don't experiment. I try to heal. Only in this case, what I'm instructed by the Fleet in its infinite wisdom to try to cure is arguably the fundamental drive of our species, the great motivator and the mechanism of genetic hygiene, the obsession that has not only led to our greatest crimes but has also fueled our artistic triumphs."

Metic blinked. "Sex?"

"Sex. You are what you are, my dear Sapient, because your ancestors for millions of years have been violent, sex-obsessed maniacs. The inability of homo sapiens to keep it in his—and *her*—pants has driven genetic diversity, protecting us from the risks of becoming a monoculture and defeating uncounted parasites along the way, while the sexes' respective attractions to the best of all possible mates, by hook or by crook, has spread the best genes far and wide throughout the pool. Don't they teach you these things in the Sapient Corps?"

"I'm a xeno-archaeologist. And a linguist."

"And a human. Which means that just underneath the skin, you're a sex fiend anxious to come out and party."

Metic wanted to change the subject, but the material at hand didn't allow her to change it very much. "Do you think our landing on this planet has something to do with... with the burning?"

"Void and Nebula," the doctor cursed. "I hope not."

"But you wonder," Metic insisted. "And that explains your presence in the landing party."

Doctor Plectrum didn't respond to the suggestion. "Let's find these poor stranded Homshipmen. If we're lucky, maybe the Captain will authorize a little improvised planetside R&R here and now and we can cure this ship-wide sweet tooth with a candy binge."

Metic almost laughed. "And if we're not lucky?"

"If we're not lucky, I have the authority under the Chastity Regs to declare a libidinal emergency and prescribe the R&R myself."

The clump of boots on the dropship's ladder announced the boarding of the rangers.

"Safety restraints, everyone," Lieutenant Chatterjee called.

* * *

Metic's chanted march through Belorian prospective mood conjugations couldn't quite distract her from thinking about Doctor Plectrum's tirade about sex. Worse, she continued to feel a presence at her elbow, or just behind her. A sexual presence, though it didn't quite feel *male* to her. *You are not alone,* the doctor had said, and the words hung in her consciousness and mocked her. She told herself she was grateful the restraining straps wouldn't let her turn around and look.

What did snap her out of tangled, conflicting lines of thought was a sudden string of curses from Lillian Chatterjee.

And then a violent impact, as if she had been punched in her entire body by a fist the size of a tree.

The rangers were out the shuttle door while Doctor Plectrum was still shaking Metic out of the shock that enveloped her. When Lancer Durmont shouted the all clear, Metic followed, wobbling. She wore a blaster on her hip, and though she had completed the required minimum training with the weapon at the Academy—and the required minimum was extensive—she was unaccustomed to the weight, and felt like she was hunching sideways as she walked.

"What happened?" she asked.

"Crash." Doctor Plectrum's matter-of-fact monosyllable rang like a gong.

Lieutenant Chatterjee had brought the dropship down in a roughly circular canyon with high pink and green walls, but it had grazed the cliff face on its way down—Metic could see the charred pink where the collision had happened—and then landed on its side. The dropship was wrecked; Metic was no engineer, but she could see that two of the three rocket engines the craft used to propel itself back off the planet were crumpled and useless.

The planet didn't care. The sky overhead pulsed a shiny indigo through the visor plate of Metic's exosuit, lit by the system's tiny but brilliant yellow sun. The atmosphere of the planet, like its gravity, registered well within human comfort range, but Captain Charamander had ordered them to take no chances.

Metic heard the shuttle door shut behind her. "I'm sorry," she heard Chatterjee mumble behind her. The sapient spun around, half expecting to see the young engineer shaking her hair free in the atmosphere, but instead saw Chatterjee brandishing a handheld sensor. "There's no wind."

"Nothing to be afraid of then, is there?" Doctor Plectrum muttered. She didn't sound convinced. "Have you informed Captain Charamander of... the *nature* of our landing?"

Lillian looked away. "The dropship's comms unit is totaled," she said. "I can't raise *Atalanta* on it, and our suit units aren't powerful enough."

Doctor Plectrum pointed at the nearest wrecked engine. "This thing isn't taking us back, that's for sure."

"Which way to the coordinates of *Actaeon*?" Metic asked. "They may or may not have a functioning dropship, but we know their beacon works. If we find them, we can reach *Atalanta*."

Chatterjee consulted the sensor and pointed. "Up on that butte," she said, her voice coming in crisp and clear through the earpiece comms unit in Metic's exosuit. "Or behind it."

Lancer Durmont pulled backpacks out of the shuttle hold and distributed them to the landing party. Unlike the others, the two rangers did everything with a weapon in one hand, and Metic noticed that as the Lancer worked at the packs, her Commander stood careful watch, scanning the canyon walls intently with her blaster carbine held at the ready.

"Look at this, Sapient."

The voice belonged to Doctor Plectrum, and Metic turned to see what was so interesting. Plectrum stood beside a boulder twice her own size, kicking it with the booted toe of her exosuit. Thick flakes of pink dust scuffed away from the boulder as she hammered at it, drifting down to settle on the ground.

Not dust, Metic realized. Some kind of plant life—fungus, or lichen, or dried algae. It flaked off the stone in thin rings.

"The stone isn't pink at all," Doctor Plectrum said, once she had exposed a face-sized patch of it. "Or green, either. It's a very boring brown."

"Newton." Lieutenant Chatterjee whistled, a sound that the exosuit's comms unit turned into a piercing shriek in Metic's ear. The Lieutenant looked around at the canyon walls. "You mean all of that...?"

"Yes, she does," Commander Thulliver barked. "She means that all of that, under the cake frosting, is really a very boring brown. Let's not forget our mission, or the chain of command. Lancer Durmont will lead out and I'll bring up the rear."

The Lancer marched briskly towards the butte.

Metic shrugged into her backpack and followed, but before she was out of sight of the shuttle she turned back for a last look. Wisps of the pink vegetation Doctor Plectrum had scraped off the rock drifted slowly upward in the air, diffusing into a pinkish mist that couldn't obscure the shuttle, but gave it a fleshy organic halo, like a pink dandelion blown into a cloud by a child's breath.

Beware the wind, she thought, wondering who had written that message and why. *The seed hides in the wind.*

Lancer Durmont disappeared into a narrow ravine up ahead, just as the sun passed out of view and the canyon plunged into late afternoon shadow. Metic stopped, staring at the ravine mouth.

"What is it?" Lieutenant Chatterjee asked as the engineer and the doctor came up behind and joined her in her hesitation.

Metic stared at the ravine and shook her head, unable to quite put a finger on the source of her unease.

"Look too much like forbidden fruit?" Doctor Plectrum chuckled.

It did; the ravine walls were pink, though streaked through with dark green, and a shiny sort of pink at that, a pink of flesh and secrets. It might be a trick of the light, an illusion created by the last movements of the sun's rays on the canyon walls, but the pink looked to Metic like it was even *moving*.

"Pretend you're delivering a baby," Doctor Plectrum suggested. "Or administering a pelvic exam." She kept marching.

Lieutenant Chatterjee stayed by Metic's side. "Is it too terrible?" she asked, and there was a faint sound of strain in her voice.

"You're the sapient of a Federation Femship!" Doctor Plectrum called back through the comms link. "You cannot let yourself be defeated by imaginary pudenda!"

Metic spurred herself forward, only a couple of steps ahead of Commander Thulliver. Plectrum was right; there was nothing here to fear. The *Atalanta* had come to an uncharted planet, of which there were many. The Femship's crew would rescue the stranded crew of another Fleet voidship, which was, if not strictly routine, neither particularly frightening nor at all heroic. Unrelated to the shipwreck and the rescue, Metic and some of the Femship's other crewmembers had been feeling a little more... *aroused* than they should. This might be a malfunction, or an unexpected side effect of an undetected illness in the ship's crew, or even a prank. In the end, it was nothing. *Atalanta* would rescue her brother ship, and then carry her sapient on to examine Calidian mummies.

And the reports she would file from Calidia, and the papers she would write afterwards, would make Metic Fallows a household name. Not that she wanted the fame, no—she just wanted to be the *one who knew*.

She entered the ravine without looking up, and for the first time she drew her blaster.

Lancer Durmont tried half a dozen ravines before finding one that led to the top of the butte. By the time the party had explored multiple dead ends and wound its way up through the narrow crevasse to its further opening, the sun had set. Metic emerged from the chasm sweating inside her exosuit and knocking free small clouds of pink with each kick of her foot or scrabbling for a handhold, only to see that the butte was broader than she had realized, and taller, too. Above them it rose again, a butte upon a butte, its great shadow blocking out the light of two moons and myriad stars in unfamiliar configurations. This close to the looming bulwark of stone, the shape seemed wrong. It blocked too much light, it menaced the tiny Terrans on its gnarled and jagged hump with sullen, silent hatred, and its vastness and proximity denied Metic of even the simple escape of looking away. Everywhere she turned her eyes black walls waited, and underneath night's cloak she knew the fluttering, twisting, slimy pink with stripes of green lurked. Even the unfamiliar stars, usually a source of novelty and wonder even to experienced void travelers, stared at her with troglodyte resentment and willed her to leave.

"We make camp here," Commander Thulliver ordered. Metic's flesh pulsed against her will with every syllable; she told herself the warmth of her body was fatigue, and resisted looking at the other women.

Lancer Durmont set up an exotent of interlocking plastic rods and tiles while Lieutenant Chatterjee tried again to reach *Atalanta*. Even at the higher altitude, though, the exosuit comms units were simply inadequate.

The party 'ate,' if that was the right word, by attaching ration tubes to the chest-mounted feeding ports of their suits and loading the condensed, sweetened contents into the recycling systems of their exosuits. Metic ached to peel off the suit for comfort, and to get away from her own smell, but knew she shouldn't. *Ventum cave*. Even if there wasn't much *ventum* to speak of.

Metic lay down to sleep inside her exosuit, wishing she had even an ultrasonic shower and a sleepfilm garment instead, and turned the audio of her exosuit's comms unit way down. Lieutenant Chatterjee lay between the sapient and the doctor. Metic looked at the milky-white opaque ceiling and tried to empty her mind, grateful at least that hers was the only body she could smell. Lancer Durmont joined them, and Metic drifted into restless dreams.

A man's voice, dark and muddy, croaked into her ear as she slept. "I crashed the dropship because I was distracted," it said. In her dream, it seemed to Metic that the man's voice came out of Lillian Chatterjee, only Lieutenant Chatterjee rose swaying above Metic like an enormous, lust-scorched worm, her entire length scabbed pink.

I know, Metic said. She didn't know how she knew.

"I was distracted," Lillian continued, "by thoughts of *you*. Surely you must have noticed."

In the darkness Metic awoke, sweating, and pulled her hand out of the grip of Lieutenant Chatterjee. If she was awake, the comms engineer gave no sign of it, and Metic soon plunged back into fits of sleep punctuated by the crisp sounds of footsteps outside the exotent.

In the morning, Commander Thulliver lay sleeping inside the shelter and Lancer Durmont was gone.

Elsa Durmont had disappeared, but not without a trace. There were scorch marks from a blaster on nearby stones, black scars where pink and green alike had been burned away and the boring brown rock beneath revealed and defiled. And there were tracks.

"Something took her." Thulliver pointed. "That way."

The pink was disturbed in ragged furrows that skipped from side to side but led to the corner of the butte where the stone rose again.

Metic felt tired.

"We'll get her back," Thulliver growled. She checked the power level on her carbine and began marching up the scuffed trail.

"We don't know what might be out there!" Metic called after the ranger Commander.

"No." Thulliver got smaller and smaller in Metic's vision, but her voice came just as clearly through the exosuit comms. "But we know it has our Lancer."

"It survived laser blasts!" Chatterjee objected.

Thulliver sighed. Despite her brisk walking pace and the restricted flow of oxygen she had to be getting through the exosuit's recycling systems, her breathing was almost perfectly normal, as if she were at rest. "As far as I can tell," she said, "Lancer Durmont missed her shots."

To Metic Fallows, sapient and unriddler of the secrets of dead civilizations, that fact offered more mystery than it did answers. Lieutenant Chatterjee looked at her with helpless eyes and began to round her lips as if to whisper—

but then caught herself, maybe realizing that the linked comms units of the exosuits made private conversations impossible. Doctor Plectrum moved first, breaking the stalemate to push on after the ranger. Metic followed, and she thought she heard the faintest sound of a whimper over the comms as Chatterjee rushed not to be left behind.

"Don't worry," Commander Wyot Thulliver grunted from the head of the procession. "We're still going to find *Actaeon*, too."

"We have to," Metic whispered.

The scuff marks led them in a trail around the rough, broad ledge of the butte, and when they turned inward and upward again, something in the terrain stopped Metic. She looked, looked again, and then called out.

"Wait!"

"What is it, sapient?" Commander Thulliver pronounced Metic's title with an audible sneer.

"Look." Metic gestured with both hands. "Look what you're standing on."

Thulliver looked down, and then above herself at the pink stone. "Looks like a defile to me. I think it will lead to the top. That's clearly where the trail goes."

"Hooke's eyes," Doctor Plectrum swore. She saw it.

"What is it?" Lieutenant Chatterjee sounded forlorn at the realization that she was missing out.

"It's a road," Metic said. "A road bounded by columns."

She was sure of it. The columns were hard to see because many of them were worn down to stumps, like the rotted and missing teeth in the head of a poor backworlder who'd never seen a dentist, but a few of the columns still rose up and in, two of them nearly touching, as if the road had once passed through stone rings on its way to ascend the mount. Or immense ribs. Even the worn stumps were still symmetrically spaced enough that, but for the fuzzy pink carpet that obscured everything, Metic was sure she would have seen them sooner for what they were.

"Hawking's hangnail," Thulliver snarled, "are you going to get all hot and bothered for crumbling ruins *now?*"

But the truth was that the realization that the landing party stood on an old, lost road, of a civilization that might be utterly unknown to Metic and to Terran civilization in general, didn't get the sapient hot and bothered. In fact, she realized with restrained delight in a corner of her brain, it was the first time in days—maybe even weeks—that she wasn't thinking about the inflamed cravings of her body at all. She tried not to notice her relief, for fear that the simple act of acknowledgment would bring her attention back to her flesh and its desires. Cold imagination flooded her mind like brilliant light, building the lost columns to their former dimensions, developing wrinkles in the defile ahead into neatly-carved steps.

She had to look.

She brushed pink and green fuzz off the rock. As she did, the green fell away and hit the ground like a picked scab. The pink did not. It clung to her fingers, and she saw as she looked closely at it that the pink substance looked like a mass of ropy worms. Worms that wriggled, ever so slightly. Not enough for her to be sure they were actually moving, as opposed to re-sponding to breezes Metic couldn't feel through her exosuit, but enough to wrap neatly around her fingers. She shook them off and scraped more handfuls away from the rock, hurling the pink mess into the air around her and behind her until she had cleared a patch of stone.

Which was covered in glyphs.

She gasped, and Plectrum and Chatterjee gasped with her.

"What is it?" Wyot Thulliver asked. "More Latin?"

"Better." Metic traced swirls, lightning bolts, and arrows with the tip of her exosuited finger. There were even figures that were clearly depictions of some kind of animal life, though the forms were hunched over, vaguely rep-tilian, long-tailed, and six-armed. A burst-like image, she thought, might be the sun, and she wondered whether the arch-bound road might have a solar alignment. A few measurements taken with her handheld ought to give the *Atalanta's* computer enough data to detect any such connection. Collections of dots and dashes might be numbers, and she wondered if they could con-tain astronomical data. She'd need to run long-term visible star simulations, forward and back, once she got back to *Atalanta*.

She looked up and down the road. With Elsa Durmont missing, it was a dereliction of duty, not to mention unkind, to think of leaving the landing party to the search while she paced off and recorded distances or extrapo-lated ancient constellation movements. She indulged herself in a few seconds of the fantasy anyway before saying any more. "Something new. Something we can't read. Yet."

"Oh yeah, that sounds much better." Thulliver snorted. "My Lancer's still missing. How about we hold the reading lessons after we get her back?"

Metic followed the ranger Commander reluctantly up the highway of ribs. Beneath her feet she could feel the broad firm steps she had imagined, obscured from view by drifts of pink stuff, pinned and bounded by the green clots. It killed her to walk past column after column, imagining as she did that they must all be covered with glyphs. Traces of a new civilization, glimpses of an ancient world, an unknown tongue. A dead language? A lost race? She imagined four-armed saurian sages, gracefully trundling down their primeval road to greet the rising of a benevolent solstitial mother with wordless baritone polyphony.

She almost tripped over a stair. Or did the race survive, here in this impossible, horrible landscape? Had the creatures that had built the arch-bound road and covered its columns with glyphs also taken Lancer Durmont? Had they captured—or done worse to—the crew of Homship *Actaeon*? Were they the "wind" she was warned to fear? Were they not four-armed, but perhaps winged? Involuntarily, she cringed and looked up at the sky.

Fear banished the images of ancient civilization from her mind.

In their place, the burning of her body returned.

The stair was long because the steps were low, and to ascend to the height of the mound the road turned and wound up around its outer edge. Their progress slowed and the breathing of three of the party, at least, became labored. The booted feet of the ranger Commander before her kicked up a cloud of pink fiber, and as Metic marched directly into it her legs became ever more coated in pink strands, like spun and colored sugar at a country fair. She ignored her new layer and looked up at the mountain above them. What might have seemed, before she noticed the arches, mere outcroppings of rock or shallow depressions in its face now appeared to her as ledges, windows, parapets, arrow slits.

And on those ledges, in the shadows of those depressions, she saw movement.

"Stop."

"Let me guess," Thulliver snorted, "you've found an alien latrine."

"A garbage dump would be more useful," the sapient inside her forced Metic to mutter. She pointed up at the depressions. "Something's up there. Moving."

Thulliver scanned the wall wordlessly. The ranger adjusted a knob at the side of her exosuit helmet as she did so, and it took Metic a moment to remember what the knob was—Thulliver was adjusted the magnification power of her faceplate. Feeling slightly foolish, Metic touched her knob as well and zoomed in on the wall.

Close up, she could see even more clearly that the parapets had not been her imagination. There were narrower stairs and ledges than the one on which the *Atalanta*'s landing party trudged, stairs and ledges with superior vantage points. These were siege defenses, she realized. Defenders with the higher ground could hurl stones, or garbage, or flaming objects, down on any invader approaching by the main road. The existence of such defenses told her more about her six-limbed saurians... theirs had not been an entirely peaceful world.

No sign of movement, though.

"We have to recover Lancer Durmont," the doctor said. "But let's not forget that our mission is to find Homship *Actaeon* and its crew. Movement might be them."

Commander Thulliver shifted her grip on her carbine, holding it ready to fire up the wall. "Lieutenant Chatterjee. A flare, if you please."

Chatterjee fumbled with the pouch at her thigh and extracted a flare. The device was self-igniting and easy to spark; the comms engineer snapped off the tip with her hands and pointed it skyward, launching a bright green flare up into the indigo sky.

With a jolt, Metic realized it was afternoon again already.

They waited.

There was no response to the flare.

"Right," the ranger hissed through her teeth. "Keep your eyes open."

The winding stair ended, just beneath the top of the butte, in a cave. This time Commander Thulliver snapped and fired one of her own flares, hurling a green spark into the yawning abyss. The witch flame struck a wall and burned, illuminating a cavern like a gaping maw, with a stair that ascended at the far end into a hole in the ceiling. More siege defenses, Metic thought. The fitzing light of the flare turned the pink carpet green, and the stripes of green into bands of deep black.

Without detecting anything that might be a word, Metic thought she heard voices. A fist squeezed her heart.

"Come on," Commander Thulliver said. "Let's not wait until the flare burns out."

Metic followed the ranger up a long, steep flight of stairs, passing through an infinite void before emerging in the center of a square plaza. The curving columns of the avenue of rings were here repeated, leaning outward, away from the plaza and then curving up and back as the stone supports in the facades of crumbling walls. Metic's blood pounded in her ears and she deliberately put her blaster back into its holster, afraid that in her enthusiasm for the potential discoveries she might be tempted to scour away the pink scum with firepower.

"Leibniz's knuckle," Commander Thulliver ground out between her teeth. "Durmont!" she barked into the exosuit comms unit. "Where are you?"

"What happened to the trail?" The doctor's voice had a strained sound to it, but her faceplate was turned away and Metic couldn't see her expression.

The pink fuzz-scum-slime covering the ruins of this lost citadel atop the mountain was intact on the walls, still pinned by the striated bands of dark green, but the pink ground covering was severely disturbed.

Metic's heart skipped a beat. "Is this city inhabited?"

"No way in Newton's bunghole," Thulliver shot back.

"Maybe it's the crew of *Actaeon*," Lieutenant Chatterjee suggested.

"It better be." Thulliver marched forward, leading with the muzzle of her carbine. "For their sake."

"It's getting late," Doctor Plectrum observed. "And we left the exotent set up below."

"We left in pursuit of a kidnapper," Thulliver growled.

"A kidnapper who works at night." The doctor pointed at the deepening indigo of the sky. "Which is fast returning."

Thulliver opened her mouth as if her next move was to bite the doctor's head clean off her shoulders. Metic shoved her body between the two women.

"Where is *Actaeon*?" she asked Chatterjee. "It's as good a place as any to look for Durmont," she said to placate Thulliver, and to the doctor, "and we can find shelter there."

Lillian Chatterjee consulted her handheld sensor before pointing. "Two hundred meters."

Metic briskly walked in the indicated direction, calculating that her departure would force the others to follow, and cut off any more argument. And if she was wrong, at least a little distance would get her out of the shouting match.

She turned at a strange angle from the plaza, following a road that went where Chatterjee had pointed without being quite straight or direct. The way turned, the footing underneath slanted now this way and that, and Metic felt she was in a carnival attraction; a mirror that showed her as tall and thin would not have been out of place. For stretches, the darkening sky disappeared as her way cut through the middle of a crumbling building like a tunnel, and the echoes of her feet and her breath sounded like other feet and the breathing of other lungs in the darkness around her. She pulled her blaster again, not quite meaning to, and tried to visualize again the peaceful sun-worshiping lizards of her imagination.

Which, in her heart of hearts, she knew to be complete fiction. What *was* real was the fear in her heart and the burning in her loins.

And then she came through the tunnel and saw *Actaeon*. "It's here," she announced. She stood still to get a good look at the voidship.

Homship *Actaeon* had crashed into a many-storied warren of a building. Scorch marks all around told Metic a story of thrusters being fired to lessen the impact. Multiple weaving paths trodden among the pink and green worked their way through the rubble around the vessel.

The crew of *Actaeon*, Metic thought.

Or paths left by creatures that met them here.

"Hello, *Actaeon!*" she called. Anyone in an exosuit with a working comms unit, or anyone monitoring standard Federation channels inside the void-ship, ought to be able to hear her. "Hello, *Actaeon*, this is Sapient Metic Fallows of Fleet Femship *Atalanta*. Repeat, this is Femship *Atalanta*, here to assist."

Silence.

And then the wind picked up. She couldn't feel it, but Metic could hear the wind whistling past the helmet of her exosuit, and she saw a furred fringe of pink lift off the ground around the margins of *Actaeon* and disintegrate into the air.

The seed hides in the wind, she thought. What seed? What wind? Who would leave that message? Her mind's eye flashed a thousand solar cycles, ten thousand, maybe, into the past, and she imagined a wind battering into pieces the civilization that had built this odd, crooked city. Had the wind brought the seed? Was the seed the pink fungal worm that covered everything... or was it the green? Or both?

A footfall in the darkness behind her.

Metic spun and fired—

and missed disintegrating Lillian Chatterjee by the narrowest of margins. The red blaster bolt flashed past, the comms engineer ducked, and a chunk of stone and pink fungus collapsed out of the ceiling where Metic had shot it.

In the tunnel, something scuttled away.

Metic and Lillian Chatterjee stared at each other with wide eyes.

"Report!" Commander Thulliver snapped over the comms.

"My fault," Metic admitted. "I'm sorry, I got jumpy, I... thought I heard something."

"You did." Lillian grinned weakly. "You heard me."

"I see you," Thulliver said. "Hold your position."

The Ranger and *Atalanta's* doctor jogged out of the dark tunnel double-time, both holding their weapons ready.

"What kept you?" Metic joked.

Thulliver frowned. "I thought I saw something moving, but I was wrong. A trick of the light."

A wave of yearning swept over Metic, bearing on its crest the powerful impression that someone waited for her in the darkness. Not Elsa Durmont, but someone else. Someone... more grand, more powerful.

Metic's lover.

Nonsense!

She shook her head to clear it, looked at Lillian Chatterjee, and saw that the comms engineer's face looked stricken with lust. Maybe it was the same expression she herself wore, she thought, chuckling grimly under her breath.

She needed to get a dose of downer that worked, as soon as she possibly could.

"Speaking of light," she said, "can we agree that we should get inside *Actaeon* and look for survivors?"

"If I had a dozen rangers," Commander Thulliver muttered, "I'd turn this rock jumble inside out tonight."

"But you don't," Metic said. "You've got a ship's doctor, a linguist, and a communications engineer. And we'll keep looking if you want, but we're all so tired we're seeing things, and our mission was to come here to find the crew of *Actaeon*. If they're inside," she shrugged and pointed, "maybe in the morning they can help us look."

"Yes," Lillian Chatterjee said, and she almost sounded like she was crying. "Let's get in out of the wind."

Metic looked at her sharply.

"Fine," Thulliver agreed. "Into *Actaeon* it is."

Actaeon's emergency lights were on. Given their nuclear power source, Metic thought, they'd stay lit and glowing softly blue like this for thousands of years before eventually fading out. The blue lines lay tangled like long phosphorescent snakes along the broken, jumbled passages that cut through the hulk. Given the materials it used to build, the Federation would leave great ruins for the scholars of some future civilization to explore.

"Chatterjee!" Commander Thulliver snapped. "Comms! Find us anyone on this vessel!" Thulliver stationed herself, carbine ready, in the two-abreast crack through which the landing party of *Atalanta* had come through *Actaeon's* hull and watched the descending darkness outside.

Chatterjee found a comms panel and spoke into it. "Attention, crew of Homship *Actaeon*. This is Lieutenant Lillian Chatterjee of Femship *Atalanta*. Please acknowledge."

Silence.

Thulliver growled, still staring outside.

"Log?" Doctor Plectrum asked.

"Downloading it into my handheld now," Lillian answered. "Encrypted, of course."

"What about a personnel list?" the doctor pressed. "And a deck map. We can go look for *Actaeon's* officers."

"How about the ship's supply of downer?" Metic interjected. The question caught even her by surprise, and she stammered to justify it. "I... I wonder if maybe *Actaeon* had been experiencing anything unusual."

Lillian pressed keys on her handheld. "No downer," she said. "And no record of when it was all dispensed."

Doctor Plectrum glared at them both. She opened her mouth—

and Commander Thulliver fired her carbine. The red blaster bolt threw smoke and a crimson flash into *Actaeon's* corridor. Thulliver cursed. "There's something moving out there."

"Have you tried the infrared optics?" Lillian suggested.

"Shut your ignorant facehole, you whiny little sapphic!" Thulliver snarled. The unexpected ferocity of the attack knocked Metic back on her heels. "I'm using the infrared *now*. Whatever it is I'm looking at isn't *showing* on the infrared."

"Maybe it's the wind." Metic meant her comment to be calming, to defuse the tension. Instead, it brought to her mind's eye the Latin warning behind Captain Worthing.

Conversation dropped to nothing.

"Personnel," Doctor Plectrum repeated herself softly after a few moments, and Lillian Chatterjee jumped to comply.

"Sharing now," the comms engineer said.

Metic's handheld beeped at the reception of data and she looked down at the device. Someone had written a warning in Latin, and there was an obvious candidate for at least an initial query. She tapped in a few characters to search the file for the name and qualifications of *Actaeon's* sapient.

Albert Degas, she read immediately. *Terra Prime History and Literature.*

"*Actaeon's* sapient," she said out loud. "He left us the message. *Beware the wind*, that came from him. We've got to find him."

The ship's deck map showed clearly where Sapient Degas's quarters were, but reaching them was more of a challenge. The first route the landing party attempted ended in frustration, a corridor crushed out of existence by the weight of the voidship's hull. Some scrambling up over ruined bulkheads and sliding on their bellies brought *Atalanta's* landing party to the indicated spot.

As she slid last out of the crack giving access to the corridor where Degas had his quarters, Metic heard scuffing, rasping noises behind her.

"Hello?" she called. "Sapient Degas?" Nothing. "Albert?"

"It's probably nothing," Lillian said worriedly.

Commander Thulliver harrumphed. "You go ahead," she instructed the others. "Find your sapient." With hands and hips she forced her body up a crumpled slope of wreckage and wedged herself into a position above the crack through which they'd come. "Whatever's following us, I'll wait for it here."

"Maybe it's just the wind." Lillian said, and Metic could see the strain of Lillian's smile through her visor.

Thulliver squinted down the sights of her carbine at the crack beneath her. "That joke wasn't funny when the sapient said it," she grunted. "Newton knows your sense of humor isn't any better than hers."

"Come on." Metic took Lillian by the arm. The comms engineer put up no resistance, and *Atalanta's* doctor followed close behind.

Two corners, and then a stooped-over shuffle through a corridor whose wall—which would have once been its ceiling—sagged dangerously low brought the women to an opening that Lillian's handheld identified as the quarters of Sapient Degas. The door was gone, and scorch marks and fragments of twisted metal clinging inside the doorframe suggested it had been blasted out of existence. The chamber, lacking emergency lighting, yawned like an abyss before them.

Metic became aware of the sweat drenching her body inside the exosuit as it seemed to all freeze at once. She shivered, licked her lips, and drew her blaster.

"Degas?" she called.

No answer came, and she stepped inside.

Infrared optics in her visor showed her nothing, so she switched them off, pressed herself against the wall with her weapon ready, and waited.

"Metic?" Lillian called from the corridor.

Her eyes adjusted, and Metic realized she was not alone. The other occupant of the room, though, was still. Still, dead, and headless.

"I need light," Metic said. It had been no more than a half-formed thought, but Lillian Chatterjee stepped into the room behind her and struck another flare.

The corpse sat on a voidchest. In its hand—in *his* hand, Metic forced herself to think—he held a blaster, dangling from a single finger through the trigger guard. Scrawled on the floor in dark letters was another message. Again in Latin.

"What does it say?" Lillian Chatterjee crowded against Metic's back.

"Commander Thulliver," Doctor Plectrum said behind them, speaking into her exosuit comms unit. "You should come see this."

SUB VESTIMENTA ARCANUM, she read. "Under clothing, a secret," she translated.

"Too damn right," the doctor muttered.

Lillian's breathing was loud over the comms unit channel. "What does that mean?" she asked.

Metic hesitated, torn. This had to be Degas. Had he written a message before someone killed him? Before he killed himself? She clutched desperately at the mystery, at the intellectual challenge, willing it to drive the lustful thoughts of falling clothing and the taut skin beneath it from her mind. It almost worked.

She reached forward and touched Degas's corpse—

which lurched forward onto her.

Lillian screamed, Doctor Plectrum cursed, and Metic Fallows fell to the floor with a moldering headless corpse on top of her. She kicked, spat, dragged herself out from under it... and in the act of pushing the body from her, her fingers found what she was looking for.

Through the thin fabric of the dead sapient's tunic, the outline of something hard and square.

Metic stood, trembling from an adrenalin rush.

"Get hold of yourself," Doctor Plectrum grumped, grabbing Lillian Chatterjee by the shoulder and shaking her. Lillian screamed again, high-pitched and frantic.

Metic rolled the corpse onto its belly and reached under its tunic—it had to be *it* again, she couldn't bear the thought that she was touching a dead person, so the corpse had to be a mummy, a relic, an impersonal thing—you're an archaeologist, get hold of yourself—

she grabbed the book.

It was a plain brown notebook, untitled. She flipped through it and saw lined pages full of cramped handwriting. The words were not corpses, were not people, missing or dead, so she sank herself into them, trying to shake off the many cloaks of discomfort piled about her neck and shoulder by immersing herself in knowledge, only it turned out the writing didn't contain knowledge after all.

Lillian Chatterjee continued shrieking.

The book contained art. Notes on literary motifs, snippets of poetry, fragmentary half-ideas that might be seeds Degas hoped one day to germinate into a novel.

Doctor Plectrum injected Lillian Chatterjee with something through her exosuit, and the comms engineer collapsed.

But the last several pages of the notebook were different. They were filled with Latin.

"Thulliver!" Doctor Plectrum called. "I've had to sedate Chatterjee. We need your help!" There was no answer, and *Atalanta's* doctor stepped out in the corridor, drawing her own blaster.

"Sub vestimenta arcanum," Metic muttered, squinting to decipher the ancient language. "A secret. Fear the wind. The seed is on the wind."

Another message from this same dead man. A warning, and a clue, maybe a clue written in this book. So what had happened to *Actaeon*? What had happened to Degas himself, and who had killed him?

A cold, irrational, but unshakable certainty seized her.

Degas had killed himself. He had left a warning about the fate of *Actaeon*, and he had killed himself.

Shuffling steps in the corridor jerked Metic's attention from the notebook. She pointed her blaster at the doorframe and very nearly pulled the trigger when Doctor Plectrum squeezed into view.

If Plectrum noticed her near-extinction, she pretended not to. "Thulliver's gone," she panted.

Lieutenant Chatterjee's flare snapped once and burned out.

"Bohr, Bohr, Bohr," Metic muttered. The blue emergency lighting gave her enough illumination to read by, but only barely. Her eyes ached.

Lillian Chatterjee slept under a low table in the corner of *Actaeon's* galley, still sedated. Doctor Plectrum sat perched on a metal stool beside the table. She held her blaster in her hand and kept herself alert by deliberately swinging her aim back and forth between the two gaping entrances to the room. Metic ignored her, and the wreckage that was the voidship's kitchen and dining room, and tried to read.

It was hard going, though where the handwriting was clear she had no problem translating it. The opening words were *SCRIBO MEA MANU FRATREM INSANITATEM ET ABYSSI ARCANA TIMENS*, which she deciphered easily. "I write with my own hand, fearing the madness of my brothers and the secrets of the deep," she translated aloud, as a check on her reading.

"Cheerful," the doctor sighed. "It's enough to make me pine for a saucy limerick. Or, all things considered, maybe a chaste one."

Something had happened to Albert Degas. When he had been writing poetry, he had written in a bold, clear hand, with large, circular capital vowels and plenty of space around each word. It was the handwriting of a man who self-consciously wrote to be read, even in his personal notes, someone who expected that an editor or a biographer or both would pick their way along his trail of breadcrumbs in search of literary and anecdotal diamonds. When he had begun writing in Latin, without warning or preface, he had done so in handwriting that was cramped, hurried, and slanted. It was the twisted calligraphy of someone slashing out notes by handlight under a blanket, barely punctuated, the scrawling of a madman. And as he went on, he got worse.

"Commander Thulliver," Doctor Plectrum said, testing to see whether the ranger's exosuit comms unit would pick her up, "Lancer Durmont." There was no answer. There hadn't been an answer the previous twenty times, either.

HOMINES ARDENT, she read. *The men burn.* Unintelligible lines. More lines she could read, few and far between, but as she sank deeper into the reading the Latin language fell away and the words burned themselves directly into Metic Fallows's consciousness.

The four-arms knew this.

The summit temple records the final defeat.

Gupta is a madman. He didn't go first, but he went furthest.

Women. It wants women.

It reads our minds. It speaks to our minds. It controls our minds.

Beware the wind.

I cannot let myself be taken.

And finally, after two pages of completely unreadable blots, a single word scratched out in gigantic letters across half a page: *FUGITE*.

Flee.

She heard a footfall outside the galley and dropped the book, fumbling it to the floor.

Silence. Metic looked over to Doctor Plectrum to find that the older woman had dozed off, slumped improbably against the galley wall without having fallen from the stool. Her snoring and Lillian's rasped gently out of sync, dissonant pitches and competing rhythms, a slow tenor and a quick bass.

"Thulliver?" Metic called hesitantly. There was no answer. "Durmont?"
Silence.

Metic shivered violently, a spasm crossing her back and prickling the skin between her shoulder blades. A terrible hunch gripped her and she reached up to her exosuit helmet to switch the comms unit from broadcasting to other exosuits on the network to external-audible mode. She picked up her blaster.

Her voice felt tiny in the silence, but she cleared her throat and called out. "Who's there? This is Sapient Metic Fallows of Femship *Atalanta*. Are you a crewman of *Actaeon*?"

A voice rattled into the galley from the corridor beyond. It was a man's voice, dry, sad, and remote. A voice she knew. A voice she had heard before, speaking from a Lillian Chatterjee-faced, worm-bodied creature of her own dreams.

"We're afraid," the voice said.

She hesitated. "Of what?" she asked.

"We're afraid you won't like us."

A pause.

"We very much want you to like us."

Metic pointed her blaster at the entrance from which she seemed to hear the voice most loudly. "I'm pretty friendly," she said. The muzzle of her blaster trembled, even though she supported her aim with both hands. Her breathing was shallow, and a tremor swept her legs and pelvis. "Why don't you come in and introduce yourself?"

The voice didn't answer.

"Is that Worthing?" she called out. "Gupta? Someone else from *Actaeon*?"
No response.

Metic crept forward. The blue emergency lightstrips burned a halo in the air around her, imprinting brilliant streaks in her peripheral vision. She swam through her own sweat, tip-toeing around the galley, pressing her shoulders against the wall through her exosuit, her own breath loud in her ears. Strings in her thighs trembled and sang.

She forced herself to ignore the wild reactions of her flesh and think through her situation. If she called out again, she knew, the man would hear she had moved. She gripped the blaster with both hands, counted to three, and leaned gun-first into the corridor.

There was no one there.

She didn't let herself sleep, and the dreams came for her anyway. The tickling itch of sweat drying under the exosuit became an unbearably sensuous tickle, a feather-stroking of the intimate secrets of Sapient Metic Fallows's body. She clamped her hands to the floor away from her body and steeled her mind, marching through verb conjugations and reciting Homer to herself out loud by memory. It wasn't the Chastity Regs that motivated her now, but the terrible sense that someone or some*thing* had turned her body against her. The clanging epic dithyrambs rocketed off the inside of *Actaeon's* hull and struck her with full force, but in vain—no amount of Greek or Hittite or Belorian could distract her from the steadily growing sensation that she was naked, was being touched by unseen fingers, and was watched by a thousand eyes.

She burned.

She should wake the others, she thought. The doctor, at least. But she feared to, and she didn't quite know why.

Ventum cave. Semen in vento latet... semen in vento... semen...

She feared the unseen hand, and she craved its touch, wanted it all for herself. Did the hand belong to the voice? To the man who wanted to be liked?

Or had it been a man? Had there even been a voice at all, or was the voice as illusory as the fingers? Answers, by Edison! She wanted answers.

"Amo, amas, amat..."

The summit temple, Degas had said. The answers were at the summit temple.

An image of a pink spire filled Metic Fallows's mind and fire raged in her blood. She squeezed air in and out of her lungs through gritted teeth, forced open heavy eyelids, and chanted.

When the first sliver of daylight crept down the blue-lit tunnels of *Actaeon*, she trembled, and this time not from lust.

"Get up," she croaked. When the other didn't stir, she kicked over a stool.

The *CLANG* knocked Doctor Plectrum off her perch. Lillian Chatterjee jerked upright so fast she banged her faceplate against the underside of the table.

"Thulliver?" the doctor asked, groggy.

Metic shook her head. "We'll find her. In the meantime, we've got someplace to go."

"Where?" Chatterjee sounded drained and distant.

"The summit." Metic had prepared her lie. "If I were trying to get above this stuff, and get comms reception, that's where I'd go. The highest point."

She would be the *one who knew*, she told herself. The *one who knew* had power. The one who had power would not be controlled.

She turned her back on the other two without looking at their faces.

The pink landscape mocked her, an army of wagging tongues.

Metic ignored the taunting and marched up. Like Xenophon, she thought grimly, slowly losing my troops.

The summit temple could only refer to one building, she guessed. It had been invisible from the lower slopes of the butte, and she had failed to notice it in the darkness the night before, but emerging from *Actaeon* it was unmistakable. On the highest spur of the butte, glowering down at them and ringed by outward-thrusting stone slivers, buttresses that buttressed nothing, was an enclosure made of arches, like an old Terra-Prime cloister from the medieval era, or like a huddle of massive pink-encrusted trilithons.

The burning had become an ache, as if a fist inside her was grabbing her most tender parts and twisting them into a knot. A hungry knot.

She could not ignore the feeling, so she marched. A trail rose up in zigzags from the pink-scabbed city, clambering the sides of the butte up towards the summit. Metic wondered if the man she had talked to last night might be watching from the peak. If he were armed, she was exposed on the trail, and he could easily pick her off, even with a weapon as primitive as a dropped rock.

She wondered what he looked like. Was he handsome? Tall? Did he have the ugly face of a warrior? The high forehead of a ship's captain? The gentle hands and whisper-like touch of a doctor, stroking, stroking?

Then she wondered if the man even existed at all.

"I don't feel good," Lillian Chatterjee muttered.

"Suck it up," Metic muttered back. *You little sapphic*, she wanted to mutter, but she was afraid if she voiced the reality of Lillian's obvious attraction to the sapient, even inside her own head, the aching lust of her own body would drive her to respond to the Lieutenant's feelings. She softened her voice. "We'll rest at the next switchback." The whisky-and-lust huskiness in her own words embarrassed her.

"Yes sir," Lillian mumbled. Then she threw up.

The sound of retching and the splash of vomit against the inside of the exosuit's visor burst loud over the comms unit. Lillian staggered backward, a yellowish-pink soup sloshing visibly around her face, and she crashed into Doctor Plectrum.

They fell down the slope together, tumbling like kittens, and when they struck a column in their path and stopped it was with a loud *CRACK*.

Lillian continued to vomit. Metic lurched down the hill with long steps, scuffing bare long patches of rock where her heel dug away the pink covering. She grabbed Lillian by the shoulder and jerked the comms engineer forward, trying to push her face down so she wouldn't swallow or inhale her own bile.

In the moment of turning Lillian Chatterjee over, Metic saw clearly the mass of the comms engineer's vomitus. It was a yellow slime, thick with wriggling pink worms.

She pushed Lillian down with a hand on the girl's shoulder. "Get it all out!" she barked, shaking the crewwoman of *Atalanta*. Even splashing around in vomit, the sight of Lillian's body writhing on the ground caught Metic's breath short. Her mind's eye flooded with obscene images, she was gripped by a raging desire to hurl herself upon the engineer and slosh about like a rutting pig in the frothy puddle of vomit.

She jerked her eyes away. Who's the little sapphic now? Metic felt sick, and still aroused.

Doctor Plectrum stepped closer, boots crunching on the ground. "Look." The doctor pointed at a spot beneath Lillian Chatterjee's arm.

A neat hole was punched through the exosuit, a neat hole with the cauterized crisp edges characteristic of a blaster bolt's work, exposing beneath it the skin over Lillian's ribs. Skin that should have been ivory-pale, warm, and supple.

Metic staggered back, shaking her hard and trying not to join Lillian in vomiting. Lillian Chatterjee's skin was crusty with interlocking pink rings, rings that burrowed into the skin, absorbed it, coated it, turned Lillian Chatterjee's body into a single massive scab. Lillian flailed on the ground, pounded at her exosuit helmet with both hands.

"It's my fault," Metic hissed, remembering what she thought had been a near miss the night before. "I almost shot her. But this..." This was worse.

"It was an accident," Doctor Plectrum said.

Metic looked at the doctor and hissed again, wordlessly. She now saw the source of the loud cracking sound—Plectrum must have struck her exosuit's visor against the rock when she landed, and it was now missing a chunk the size of a human thumb.

"Beware the wind." Metic made connections out loud. "Degas was trying to warn us. The seed is in the wind. The seed... it took *Actaeon.*"

Lillian ripped off her helmet and spat writhing worms all over the ground.

"We don't know what this is," Doctor Plectrum said, her voice shaking. "We don't know what happened to *Actaeon.*"

Lillian staggered to her feet, stumbling away from the other women. A wordless shriek of pain burst from her. Pain, Metic thought, or desire.

"It killed them." Metic knew it had to be true, though she couldn't explain how or why. "Whatever it did to them, it's doing now to... to her." She jerked a thumb at Lillian Chatterjee.

"What's the matter!?" Lillian howled. "What's wrong with me?" She staggered sideways and turned to face Metic. The skin of her face writhed with worms, puffed, blistered, split, oozed. "Why don't you want to *take* me?"

Metic bit the inside of her own cheek. Her body pulsed, her stomach churned, and she *did* want to ravish the scabby pink comms engineer. "Stand down, Lieutenant," she said calmly. She had the presence of mind to draw her blaster and point it at the ground between the two of them. She had never killed anyone, never even shot anyone... not *deliberately*, she thought, avoiding looking at the hole she had burned the night before in Lillian Chatterjee's exosuit.

"Stand down?!" Lillian hurled the words like a weapon. She threw back her shoulders, looking taller with each sentence she shouted. "I will not! *You* stand down!" She towered over the sapient and the doctor. What in Tesla's name? She *was* taller. "*Lie* down, and I will fill you with my seed!"

She leaped at Metic.

The attack was lightning-fast, and only the fact that Metic had already drawn her weapon saved the sapient's life. Lillian Chatterjee hit the ground in a smoking ruin, the scabrous disaster of her face forever charred clean by the blaster bolt, her neck reduced to a smoking stump. Pinks worms wriggled from the stump of her neck and dropped to the ground about her.

"Hooke," Doctor Plectrum muttered.

Metic trembled. "It's worse."

The doctor laughed, a single jagged sound like the bark of a Luathan sand-sloth. "How could it be worse?"

Metic kept her blaster in her hand. "Check your visor."

Doctor Plectrum ran her fingers over the plate until she found the hole. She poked a finger into it and her eyes widened. She stared wordlessly at Metic.

"There's no guarantee what happened to her will happen to you," Metic pointed out. She wobbled on legs that felt like water.

Plectrum exhaled slowly, unlatched her exosuit helmet, and pulled it off. She tossed the headgear aside and scratched her head vigorously, prying free iron-gray curls that had been plastered down by sweat. The gesture made Metic's own scalp itch with envy, and then a sympathetic itch ran down her entire body like an arpeggio played top to bottom on a harp.

"No," the doctor agreed. "But it's likely. Aboard *Atalanta* I'd have my diagnostic tools, pharma-synthesizers, cryostasis chambers. I'd stand a chance."

"Down here..." Metic didn't know how to finish her own sentence.

"Down here," the doctor did it for her, "when I go crazy, you shoot me."

Metic jammed her blaster into its holster and turned away. The slow, moist fire engulfing her frame hid her tears from her until she tasted their salt as they puddled in the corners of her mouth.

She stepped over the smoldering ruin that had been Lillian Chatterjee and continued the climb up to the summit.

The outward-lurching buttresses made a crown, Metic decided, as she trudged upward. A grand pink head, noble, virile, topped by an ancient crown. Indomitable, alluring, wise, invisible eyes keen with insight.

As she shuffled among the columns, though, the crown faded and was replaced by so many hostile fingers. Fingers... some memory stirred in her, throbbing and breathless, but she couldn't quite hold it. Instead Metic stepped closer and stared, letting the images sink in and exploring the nearest column with her gloved hands. The stone had at one point been scraped clean—she could see the marks of a blade—but it was furring again with the pink fungal worms, twitching in a breeze Metic couldn't feel.

The stone was covered in markings; Metic's heart throbbed dully within her, some delight at potential discovery making itself heard through the pounding drums of lust. Glyphs, pictures of the six-limbed creatures again, twisting, sinewy images some of which might have been stars, or plants, or body parts, or other unknown creatures. The glyphs were cut deep, weathered around the edges, and speckled in their depths with flakes of some clinging paint. She tried to imagine her baritone sun-worshiping lizards, ambling down their grand avenue at the solstice, and couldn't.

Scratched alongside the glyphs were more Latin characters.

Metic squinted, stared. Tried to force the characters into words, and here and there succeeded. *SEMEN* recurred over and over, usually near a stylized spiral image. *VERMES*, *worms*, sometimes near the same spiral and sometimes near clusters of short, wiggling lines. The word *SEX* threw her off until she realized it was the Latin number *six* and referred to the alien creatures whose images were so prominent on the columns.

She squinted harder and tried to force the words into sentences. And failed.

Degas had been here. A hot fist of jealousy clenched around her heart when she realized that he had somehow deciphered some of these glyphs, had learned to read a previously unknown language that belonged to an apparently dead sentient race. It was a feat she herself would pay almost any price to replicate, she thought.

Degas's own price had been madness and death.

And it looked like the madness had dragged down whatever he had learned with him into his solitary suicidal grave.

Madness. Lust.

The men burn.

"There's nothing here," Doctor Plectrum said.

"There's knowledge." Metic didn't look away from the column. "I thought you wanted knowledge."

Metic's head spun.

Madness. Lust. Knowledge.

The doctor panted. "About people. About *us*. What is this?" She joined Metic at the column. "Worms? Fungus?"

"Knowledge. Truth about the universe in which we live, and the fate of this planet."

"If I have anything to say in the matter," Plectrum said, "the fate of this planet will be to catch a series of *Atalanta's* nukes. Even if I'm standing in the blast myself. We should go back to *Actaeon*, try to get communication working. We need to get out of here."

A man's voice croaked from behind one of the columns. "We cannot allow that. We *will not* allow that."

Madness. Lust. Knowledge. Sex. Madness.

Metic knew the voice, and its dark timbre made her shiver.

"Who are you?" she called.

Slow scuffing footfalls scraped a robed and hooded figure into view. He was a tall man, Metic thought, and for a moment she imagined that the figure would throw down his robe and turn out to be a six-armed reptile, seven feet tall.

But that was ridiculous.

"We... I am Salazar Gupta." The voice rolled from the shadowed recesses of a baggy, all-concealing hood. "I am... I was a physicist. We are... something... else... entirely."

His voice held a lascivious curl to it, a flippant, ironic note of seduction. Metic's breathing came so shallow she wondered whether she was getting any oxygen at all. She felt light-headed, and then she knew.

She *knew*, but there was no triumph in it.

"You are telepaths," she said. "You've been harassing us in our sleep." And in our waking. Madness. Sex. Knowledge.

"We are *a telepath*," said the hooded figure calling itself Salazar Gupta, "or perhaps an empath, but neither term is really sufficient."

"You've invaded our dreams."

"I would have said your *loins*. Your lust does not reside in your dreams, Sapient Metic Fallows."

Doctor Plectrum stepped forward, shoulder to shoulder with Metic. Metic heard rasping breaths and couldn't be sure whether they came from *Atalanta's* medical doctor or *Actaeon's* physicist. Or both.

"What do you want from us?" the doctor asked.

A silence followed. A thin cloud of pink spores drifted over the summit; Metic wiped her visor clean with one hand and shuddered; Doctor Plectrum's face began to look pink-furred.

"We are the original inhabitant of this planet," Gupta said. "Eons before you warm-blooded bags of blood and mucus dragged yourselves from the juvenile primordia you once knew as Earth, we came here. We came here from the stars."

"Orion's belt," Doctor Plectrum quipped. "He wants to tell a story." She leaned forward slightly in her stance, as if the pink spores were heavy and dragged her down.

Gupta laughed. "*He*. Very good. He. That is what is at issue. You are an impatient race, a quivering horde of upstart flesh, and if you must cut to the chase, as you so quaintly and unintelligibly say, then that is what we want from you. To be *he*. And *she*."

"I like stories," Metic said. "Tell me what you mean."

Gupta nodded, a low bow that nearly bent him double and only served to emphasize again how immensely tall he was. The bow also brought him forward a step, and Metic struggled to keep her hand off her blaster. She felt dizzy. She wasn't quite sure how, but she had arrived at a dead end. And Gupta's rasping, gravelly voice struck a physical chord in her, a low note that continued to resonate long after the man's... the creature's... every word.

"You human beings were not yet alive in any sense in which you would recognize the word when the Sixlings came."

"The lizards," Metic hazarded.

"They had warm blood. And they fled an old world, a world on which their god had arisen to crush his worshipers, who in their age and their wisdom longed for the nothingness of the abyss. Those who escaped came here, took from us our world, and for a long time enslaved us with their cruel technologies."

"The green lichen," Doctor Plectrum hazarded. The sound of her voice snapped Metic out of a deep reverie—she had forgotten she was not alone.

"The green lichen. They made it, from life forms they had brought with them, and they sprayed it on us. It bound us to stone and locked us into a long and dreamless sleep." Gupta's voice drew Metic in. In its somber tones there were piping discordant notes, as if he had scarred his vocal cords with smoke and alcohol and then swallowed a whistle to boot.

"Something woke you." Plectrum scraped at her face and arms, wiping away the accumulating pink fuzz.

"The Sixlings brought with them their own death. Not all of their party were rebels against their god, and some of the worshipers saw in us a way to achieve the destruction they desired. They found us down in dark caves, out of reach of the lichen that was our nemesis, and they freed us into the air of this world."

"This is Schrodingered beyond belief," Doctor Plectrum snorted. "You're Salazar Gupta, and you were not living in a cave beneath this pink planet eons ago."

"*I* am Salazar Gupta," the still-faceless man agreed. "*We* are... nameless."

The word hung in the air a long time.

"You destroyed the civilization of the Sixlings." Metic felt a small tone of sadness amid the intense fascination as her mind flooded with images of peaceful six-armed creatures being encrusted, scabbed over, and devoured by the pink worms. The image cranked her arousal to an even higher pitch. She wanted to throw herself among the pink-flocked aliens of her imagination, naked, wild, and free, in an orgy of violent self-satisfaction and death.

"As they wished."

"As *some of them* wished," Doctor Plectrum corrected Gupta. "That's a serious difference. Still, you win. We're leaving now, and you can keep this useless rock."

"I cannot allow that. We *need* you." Gupta said the word need with fiery lust in his voice. "We *want* you."

"The lichen," Metic guessed. Her mind raced. "It hadn't gone anywhere, so once you devoured the Sixlings, you and your predator settled back into permanent stalemate. You're not dead, but you're pinned by the green stuff, you can't go anywhere. Except maybe the parts of you that are still deep underground."

Gupta exhaled, a dry, gritty cackle of satisfaction. "We have been waiting a long time for you, Sapient Fallows."

"Leibniz," Doctor Plectrum cursed. "Sexual reproduction. That's what this is all about. You can't get around the lichen and it can't get around you because you both reproduce asexually. All of your... spores... worms, whatever, are genetically identical, and so all of them are identically vulnerable to the lichen. You need something to break out of the stalemate."

Metic's heart twisted into a hard ball. "And that something is sex?"

She heard a whimper from a different direction, and though the sound was soft it nearly made her jump. She turned and saw *Atalanta's* rangers. Durmont and Thulliver both limped into her view, dragging bodies across the pink-furred stone that at first appeared to Metic to be horribly mutilated.

When she realized what she was really looking at, she nearly broke into tears.

Lust. Sex. Knowledge. Madness.

The women dragged themselves forward on all fours, laboriously because their bellies had swollen to vast proportions. Gone were Elsa Durmont's cat-like poise and the apple-torsoed solidity of Wyot Thulliver. The gross distortion of normal human dimensions threw Metic off for a moment, but when she had gotten over the general pallid frog-like appearance of the two rangers, who both seemed to be naked and encrusted from head to toe in patches of pink, she realized their true state.

Madness. Her mind revolted. Was this the end of knowledge?

Her body burned.

They were pregnant. Or at least, they were in some state that caricatured pregnancy, that bloated their bellies, slowed their movement and threw off their balance.

"Metic Fallows," Commander Thulliver said. Her lips flapped loosely over her words and slurred them. Her voice had gravel in it, and a high-pitched buzz. "What a pleasant surprise to see you here." Pink worms fell from Thulliver's mouth as she spoke.

Salazar Gupta scraped another step closer.

No," Metic whispered, but her heart said something different. Madness. There was no knowledge that did not end in madness. Sex. Lust. Madness.

Cold death the only alternative.

"No!" Doctor Plectrum barked, with considerably more conviction.

"This is so much better," Elsa Durmont muttered, thick, pink drool sliding down over her chin and onto her bare, bloated breasts. "I don't burn any-more."

Gupta straightened his back in a movement so swift it sent Metic and the Doctor both staggering back in surprise. The same movement whipped back his hood and tossed aside the folds of his robe, revealing a body that was as misshapen as it was tall. He curved through his spine, and his flesh bloated, scabbed and knobby around bones that had elongated and become thicker. Even his head, with worms dripping from its eye sockets, no longer looked quite human, though the festering eyes gleamed with a light that Metic recognized and desired. It was not the light of lust, much less love, but the light of knowledge. Madness. Knowledge.

Metic spun, weightless and disconnected. She didn't know which way was down.

Salazar Gupta the giant worm stroked his own pink, rugose flanks with long-fingered hands. "You may view this body as a curse," he whispered, a hoarse urgency in his voice. "But is not every body a curse?"

"No!" Doctor Plectrum snapped.

"Yes," Metic whispered. She burned, and sweat dripped down her skin inside the exosuit. Knowledge. Lust led to sex led to madness led to knowledge madness knowledge madness.

"And think what is to be gained." Gupta smiled, crooked, twisted, toothless. "Immortality. And knowledge."

"Yes," Metic whispered again.

"You will be Queens Consort. You will be *us*. You will live forever, and your children will be a new race of gods. With the gift of your loins, and the seed of the man Gupta and his comrades, we will escape the hold of this Sixling curse and retake our place as ruler of this world. Indeed, with your vessel *Atalanta*, we need not be limited to this world, or to any world."

More scraping footfalls among the pillars dragged more misshapen giant man-things into view. Metic looked upon them and wanted them, not for their flesh, but for the fleshlessness that union with them promised, the sensuous knowledge madness life and immortality that they could give her. They nodded heavy heads in her directions on long necks like flower stalks.

This was not madness. Knowledge was illusion. Madness was illusion. Sex was life was existence was knowledge madness knowledge madness.

Sex and life were all there was.

"Yes!" she cried.

"No!" A blaster bolt flashed past Metic, and Elsa Durmont exploded into charred flesh and a floating cloud of pink. To her horror, Metic could discern little creatures in the carnage, creatures that were not quite worms and not quite human fetuses either, but some horrid-fascinating thing between, something with a tail and arms and an eyeless face.

She staggered back and grabbed for her own weapon. The once-men-now-gods of Homship *Actaeon* reared back shrieking, and then pounced forward.

Doctor Plectrum fired again, and Commander Thulliver's howl of pain was cut short as her entire body above the bloated belly burst instantly into a cloud of ash. She toppled sideways in two pieces, and the pool of viscous red fluid that pooled around her body swarmed with more of the same little creatures.

The god-men of *Actaeon* sprang forward, nails extended like daggers.

Doctor Plectrum swung around to face Metic. Her face was scabbing around the eyes, nostrils, and mouth, and her expression twisted into something that might have been self-loathing, or fear, or hatred. She raised her blaster at Metic—

but the sapient pulled the trigger first, and the bright flash of energy ripped through Doctor Plectrum, tearing her in half.

The doctor hit the ground.

The god-men paused.

Metic felt tired. And uncertain. And afraid.

But she looked up about her at the former men of *Actaeon* and felt the desire of their collective flood into her. She dropped her blaster to the ground.

They sighed, a chittering, gurgling sound of relief.

Metic stepped over to the ruined bodies of her fellow crewwomen, bent, and scooped up two of the animalcules thrashing about in their conjoined gore. The things were perfect, godlike in their staggering inhumanness, something she might have seen on a Mesopotamian façade or in the oldest writings of Tibet, little devil-angels. Tentacles at their sides probed the fabric of her exosuit, thin but strong tails wrapped around her fingers, and long-tooth mouths mewed tiny, demanding cries for tribute.

"It is a hard birth, as births go," Metic Fallows, Queen Consort, said.

With one trembling hand she undid the clasps holding in place the helmet of her Exosuit. The air was thick and warm with love, and with the scent of scabrous, bleeding, love-loathsome, and lustful flesh of divine-demonic beings. The only true knowledge.

"But it is only the beginning."

Raising her bloody, screeching step-children to her lips, Metic kissed them both. Then she set them on the ground, and waited patiently to receive the seed of her many husbands, the seed of her self, the seed of her new *we* that would live forever and know the only thing there was to know.

FULL DARK

NATHAN SHUMATE

We weren't even through our post-transit checklists after the jump, and I still had that nauseated tang in the back of my throat, when Jimi sang out from his station. "Picking up refined metal ahead."

I pulled back from looking over Kessler's virtual shoulder. "Details."

Jimi gestured, and the contents of his heads-up display overlaid itself on the data already in front of my eyes. I foregrounded the new data as Jimi's gestures and eye movements focused us both in on what had triggered his telltales: a bead of metal gleaming against interstellar space, no different to the naked eye than the spray of stars in its background, but clearly identified via spectrography as a mass of mostly pure and thus likely refined metal, only a few kilometers ahead of us.

"Is it one of ours?" I asked.

"No ID beacon."

"Is it Faction?"

After a second Jimi shook his head, a movement which transmitted as a slight wiggle through his HUD. "Showing as entirely powerless, energy signatures invisible against background radiation."

"So one of the Dead Races," I said.

"That's how I'd bet my pudding."

I nodded and pushed his overlay off my HUD. "Relax a notch, then," I said. "After jump checks, we'll put together a roster for an ex-ex team. Tell Moise to start scoping for ID matches. She'll be tickled."

I was, too, a little bit. Adrenaline had spiked at Jimi's call-out from the possibility of either another Emergence vessel out in our survey path, or a Faction ship startled into a confrontation. But a Dead Race derelict was colorful, too—not technically rare or newsworthy in the grand scheme of things, but worth exploring before we turned to geosurveying the nearest star system. It was the first one I'd ever run across while sitting in the captain's chair. And if it was previously undiscovered—which it could easily be, as the whole point of this survey route was to tag rocky planets beyond current exploration—then it would be the first I'd seen unclaimed in two decades in space. Probably not enough salvage value to tow it through a jump, but a pleasant surprise nonetheless, and few surprises in space are pleasant.

"Captain!" Kessler almost bounced out of his seat. "Can I reserve a slot in that ex-ex team?"

With a gesture I pulled his work area into my HUD. Kessler was Transit officer; his role was to prepare the complex gravitonic calculations necessary for a successful transit jump, and protocol required that there always be a valid jump calculated from wherever we were, even if we had just gotten there. I could see that his work was barely begun, charting and quantifying the gravitational wells and rolls in space-time which transit jumps had to negotiate.

"You know the answer to that," I said. "Get gravitonics completely nailed down for here and now, and you might get a look. Until then, you're not going anywhere."

Kessler's face fell. I knew he was the biggest Dead Race theorist on board the *Anaximander*, and the very real possibility of not being on the initial external-exploration team aboard a freshly discovered vessel was probably souring his gut.

I said in a more conciliatory tone, "I'll tell Moise not to be in too much of a hurry to get over there, okay?"

Kessler tried to put on a brave face as I tugged off my HUD collar, automatically signaling to the ship that I was going off bridge duty and transferring command functions to Jimi; Jala, my command relief, was due on duty in only a few minutes. Then I wafted myself to and through the hatch from the command module.

I found Moise in the cramped "common area" of the survey crew section, consulting duty rosters for her ex-ex team. Moise was the official liaison between the *Anaximander's* crew, of which I was captain, and the geosurvey team that we were there to ferry between rocky planets and asteroid fields so they could assess exploitable resources for the Emergence.

"Captain," she acknowledged, her eyes still on the personnel lists as she rubbed her chin.

"Moise," I said in return. "Hey, I don't know if any of your guys are Dead Race theorists, but Kessler's big into all that stuff. If you're okay with waiting a bit until he gets the gravitonics nailed down on this side of the jump, he'd be a good member of the *Anaximander* crew to include in the ex-ex."

She nodded again, still scrolling through names. "He's already spoken to me. We've identified it as a Slugger ship, which means it's probably been drifting since our ancestors were trying to pull themselves onto dry land. I figure a few more hours won't hurt."

"A Slugger ship, huh?"

She finally minimized the list and looked at me. "Sluggers are fine by me. No solid bodies, so there's probably nothing left of them except some hydrocarbon stains on the bulkheads. A lot better than Crabbies." She shuddered. "I was on a first-in team on a Crabbie ship a decade ago. The pics and holos, they don't do those critters justice."

Crabbies were one of the five Dead Races—though by some tallies, there were only four and a half, and they counted as the half. Carapaced, multi-limbed lifeforms with a half-dozen regular subspecies in each of their semi-organic ships—which resembled transit-jumping interstellar anthills more than anything else—they had been a source of academic and cultural controversy. Some exobiologists insisted that they weren't an intelligent space-faring race as such, but instead a hive species which had evolved in and was perfectly adapted to life in space, and operated more like the terrestrial social insects they resembled than like us or, presumably, any of the other species which had gotten into space by intellect and technology.

I said, "If Kessler takes too long, don't put off the ex-ex. A Slugger ship is interesting, but they're all the same, and we've got real work to do. He'll just have to cry in his milk."

When I got into my quarters, back at the top of the crew section, I found Yvains waiting for me. When he was in the command module, as he had been with me during this last duty cycle as we made the jump, he was a quiet, almost shy junior officer, navigating our path through normal space. When he had me in private, though, he was a different person: confident and more than a little abrasive. Only I knew that Yvains was the Purity officer, whose duty it was to be sure that the activities of the *Anaximander* served the best interests of the Emergence when separated by distance from the mass of humanity. That gave him, from a certain point of view, an authority that could overrule a ship's captain, even though no one but the captain knew it. In the open, Yvains was a competent and deferential officer; in private, he was a condescending prick.

"Moise to lead the ex-ex," he said as soon as I had sealed the door. "Any particular reason?"

I had hoped that the discovery of the Slugger ship wouldn't prompt this visit; I had the residual headache that jumps have given me for the past few years. I pushed off from the door and guided myself into my bunk, making him wait until I was comfortable before responding. On a survey ship, the captain's palatial cabin was approximately half again the size of a normal two-bunk cabin, which meant that having Yvains in here overcrowded my personal space.

"The Slugger ship isn't really in the bailiwick of either the ship crew or the survey crew," I said. "Put Moise in charge and she'll assemble a team that bridges the two crews. If there's anything valuable—or if anyone thinks there's something valuable—no one'll have cause to complain that one crew or the other took it over."

"If there's something valuable," Yvains echoed, smiling that knowing half-smile that was the sign to me that he had his metaphoric Purity officer hat on. "So no other reason?"

"What other reason could there be?" I said, sounding more defensive than I had meant to. "You know that she hasn't been slipping into my cabin off-shift or anything."

He nodded, still half-smiling. I could tell that he was trying to look like he was debating whether to tell me something that he knew and I didn't, and even though I recognized his mind games for what they were, they still served to assert silent authority over me. As they were meant to.

"Moise," he said, pausing just slightly for the added dash of dramatic effect, "is an ESPer."

"What? No. I scanned her personnel record when the survey crew was assigned to the *Anaximander*. There's no way I would have missed that, and anyway an ESPer wouldn't be relegated to a geosurvey..."

I trailed off as I watched that damned half-smile, knowing too late that I had just revealed to Yvains that I didn't think as quickly as I spoke.

"If she's an ESPer and she's here," I said, "then the Emergence doesn't know."

He continued smiling and waited.

"She's Faction?"

He continued smiling, with no intention of elaborating on the secret he had so graciously let slip.

I couldn't help myself. "But how did *you* know?"

His smile didn't move, but he let go of the handhold he had been using to maintain his position and pushed off toward the door. "I just wanted you to be on your guard," he said as he drifted toward the hatch. "In case there is, as you say, something valuable on the Slugger ship. I assume that you feel confident in the state of your anti-incursion training?"

I nodded wordlessly. He would have known that, too; even if my own record hadn't been open to him, he'd know that I couldn't certify for active captaincy without a refresher within the last three years. All of us who don't test as psychically Inert are required to undergo incursion defense training; we're all one big happy family in the Emergence, but there could always be Faction subversives looking to worry at the edges of the Emergence. Such as aboard the *Anaximander*, apparently.

"Are you saying she should be off the ex-ex?" I asked. He stopped with his hand on the hatch.

"No, that might seems suspicious," he said. "Now that we both know about her, we'll keep her where we can see her."

He paused a moment—his back was to me, but I could imagine him smoothing that supercilious smirk from his face, preparing to enter the gangway wearing the proper expression of a junior officer leaving his commander's presence.

Once Yvains left, I found myself looking around my cabin, searching for... what? Some clue as to how I should feel? Finding a Faction rebel on my ship should prompt an emotional reaction, but what? What did I feel? Frustration? Betrayal? Neither seemed ready to assert itself.

According to Yvains, Moishe was an ESPer, the highest pinnacle of human evolution. So the Emergence said, and the Emergence would know. Once humanity had progressed from being a mass of individuals to being a single supra-organism, a self-organizing "emergent system" greater than the sum of its parts, the appearance of ESPers in the population was a natural part of the self-regulation of such an organism, as well as being the greatest evidence that the Emergence was, in fact, emergent. Did a supersystem need conflicting viewpoints and protected political opposition? Of course not, no more than a body needs to war with itself. Should any individual's rights impede the activities of the Emergence? Of course not, no more than a single cancerous cell should be allowed to put its misguided goals over that of the body as a whole. As with everything essential to the Emergence, ESPers were more than telepaths: they were axiomatic evidence that the Emergence was the destined face of humanity's expansion and progress forward into the future.

When I was young, before I understood the importance of ESPers as a sociopolitical symbol, I fantasized about the privilege of having those exceptional abilities; I think most children did. Then the standardized tests placed me at the apex of the bell curve, the poster child for the "Median" designation. Not even a Sensitive somewhere on the spectrum between Median and ESPer. Wholly unremarkable, as the great majority of people must be for the purposes of the Emergence. I had thought—or hoped or dreamed —that I was special, that I *had* to be special. Now I know now that even that desperate desire was the common lot of the masses.

So now an ESPer was on board the *Anaximander*: an undocumented ESPer, an adherent—according to Yvains—of the Faction, that splintered-off segment of humans who denied themselves a place in humanity's shared future by refusing to subsume themselves to the supra-organism. If ESPers were the highest expression of the Emergence, then faction ESPers must be its most brazen betrayal, keeping selfishly for themselves what the Emergence had meant to be a benefit for the whole.

I settled more comfortably against my bunk and began running through the anti-incursion mantras that every ship's officer learns early. They filled my forebrain with enough innocuous white noise that an ESPer wouldn't be able to read the thoughts on the surface of my mind without effort.

But while one part of me refamiliarized itself with the mental chant, another part looked inward at myself and wondered: What am I feeling about Moise, and what should I be feeling? Shock? Betrayal?

Envy?

Moise dithered on her ex-ex selection for almost four hours, until even Kessler knew that she was stalling for his sake. But no matter what he did, the gravitonic equations wouldn't resolve into the clear trajectories of warped spacetime that would allow a jump if needed. I returned to the command module and watched the frustration mount in creases on his forehead, his hands waving at the virtual objects in his HUD with sharper and sharper movements, until he slumped back.

"I feel like an apprentice cadet!" he barked. "I've accounted for every body in the solar system, dark matter density, wrinkles from our inbound jump... Everything's still coming out skewed. Tell Moise..." He grimaced. "Tell her to enjoy herself over there."

His seat was close enough that I could reach over and clap a hand on his shoulder. "Don't worry," I said, "I don't think she'll carve her initials into anything. We'll get you over there soon. Kuhl, all metrics still showing the vessel to be inert?"

"Yessir," Kuhl said. "The survey crew double-checked with their own equipment, too—no radiation signatures, heat sources, or other signs of anything active."

I poked the air where my HUD showed the available comm channel to the planetary lander that would be used for the ex-ex. "Captain Ingers to *Hesiod*. Moise, you're clear at this end."

"Roger, *Anaximander*," she replied. "Away we go."

The main display picked up the glow of the *Hesiod's* exhaust as it cleared the lander bay and subtly increased magnification as it moved away, so that everyone in the command module was treated to almost a lander's-eye view as it approached the Slugger ship.

Slugger ships found over the last century had varied from each other only slightly. Each was constructed with a long section, roughly cylindrical, which housed the living areas, though the lack of anything resembling either dormitories or private quarters just emphasized that we didn't know what "living" was for a Slugger, or even what they looked like. Discrete patches of organic residue had been found on interior bulkheads on most Slugger ship found so far, enough to know that they were organisms without hard body parts—thus the name "Slugger," which was used far more commonly than the official designation that no one could remember.

The other section of a typical Slugger ship was even more mysterious. Like a giant lollipop in space, the cylindrical trunk of the ship ended in a bulbous chamber, an enclosed empty space which gave no clue as to its function. The best guess was that it had something to do with propulsion, but that was supposition by process of elimination, as nothing else in a Slugger ship gave any clue as to how the thing moved. Alone among the five (and a half) known space-faring civilizations, counting ourselves, the Sluggers were the only one who didn't use transit jump technology in any form we could recognize.

The *Hesiod* slipped closer to the dull gray of the Slugger vessel. "Visual confirms what scans showed," Moise's voice said. "This is a remarkably intact specimen, considering how long it's been out here. I can see a couple of meteoroid punctures in the trunk, but nothing that compromises structural integrity."

I glanced over at Kessler, who was watching the main display with half his attention, one hand still twitching at data visible in his HUD as he kept worrying at the gravitonics problem.

The *Hesiod* settled gently and extended magnetic grapples against the Slugger hull at a point just back of the junction between trunk and bulb, near where something analogous to a control room had been present in previous ships. Moise left Atkins, a pilot from the survey crew, aboard the *Hesiod* while she and the other two members of the ex-ex, secure in snug EV suits, left the lander and entered a panel in the hull of the Slugger ship.

The display shifted from an exterior view from the *Hesiod* to a visual feed from Moise's helmet. The interior of the ship was lit for the first time in millions of years by the crisscrossing beams of the ex-ex members' lights, and Moise's helmet compensated for extremes of bright and dark to present a steady view of the surroundings. Unadorned bulkheads created tunnel-like corridors, scaled to match the inferred bulk of the Sluggers.

"Moise," I said, "is that writing up to your left?"

Moise turned and focused her attention on the bulkhead, and another of her team members brought his light to bear on the dark lines there. Philologists on Earth were still congratulating themselves on recognizing—or declaring—that the Slugger script *was* writing, despite the fact that it resembled nothing in human experience: a series of concentric circles, half-circles and arcs, joined by line segments radiating from the center. We still had no idea how to read them, of course; context aboard the Slugger ships never gave any clue to the import of any symbol, and no homeworld or planetary colony had ever been identified for the species. We couldn't even assume, as we would with any human script, that it was based on a spoken language—we had no idea if the Sluggers had used sound or some other medium to communicate with each other. Still, at least the Sluggers *had* writing; none of the other Dead Races had left behind any evidence of recorded language.

Moise made sure she had focused at least momentarily on every part of the Slugger script to record it for posterity, then she and her team turned and followed what they has pre-assumed, given the data she had assembled from previous discoveries, to be the way to the putative control room. Everyone who lives their life in space becomes adept in moving and propelling themselves in zero gravity, but the conduits in the Slugger ship were subtly different than our own connective passages, and the unaccustomed clumsiness with which Moise and her companions moved shows clearly in the images from her helmet.

"Feels cold," said Moise. I blinked.

"Moise," I said, "say again. Are you feeling the cold through your suit?"

"No. Negative. My suit is fine, I don't feel the cold, I just..." She laughed in embarrassment. "And it's not like it's colder in here than outside, right? It just feels different. Like the difference between a ski slope and a meat locker. The stillness. The..." She searched for the word, then her hand waved in her field of vision as she cut off the unfinished sentence. "Forget I said anything. Byrne, are you there?"

"Just crossed through the entryway," came the voice of one of her team members—I saw so little of any survey team before they started their planetary daytrips that I hadn't even learned half their names—and Moise and her companion drifted forward into a space filled with other geometric shapes that would have been consoles if engineered for humans. There were plenty of flat surfaces but no sharp corners; people smarter than I had surmised that rounded edges were more comfortable for the Sluggers' soft bodies to flow over.

The picture on the display began flickering persistently. "Moise," I said, "the live visual's not making it from deep inside. We're going to follow you on audio only for a while." I glanced at Kessler, who was sucking his teeth in frustration. "We'll have Kessler review your recordings as soon as you get back."

"Roger that," came Moise's voice. I flipped the display back to the exterior of the Slugger ship as seen from the *Anaximander*.

Moise and her companions kept verbal contact with each other and us as they drifted through the control room and toward the junction of the ship's trunk with the huge chamber. On every other Slugger ship, that junction had been ruptured, blown into the trunk section by what looked like tremendous force from inside the chamber. Some xenotechnologists had speculated that the ships had been scuttled, with the crucial and utterly alien propulsion technology removed in the face of danger, or as salvage. Others had noted that the same rupturing and emptiness was present whether the ships were empty of biological residue or thick with the carbonized discolorations on the bulkheads that showed where Slugger corpses had mouldered. Would the Sluggers abandon their ships, taking their fabled propulsion technology but leaving their own fellows? Or was it done by later salvage teams? Trying to second-guess a long-dead intelligent species which bore no resemblance to *homo sapiens* was a fool's game. But *homo sapiens* had always had a weak spot for fool's games, Emergence or no.

"Approaching the juncture with the chamber end," said Moise's voice. Then: "It's... intact. Not ruptured."

I looked at Kessler. He had the expression of a man who had popped a bit of bell pepper into his mouth, only to discover it was actually a habanero. "Say again?" he stammered.

"The juncture with the chamber end is intact," she said. "The bulkhead is undamaged."

"Jimi," I said, "are there any meteor punctures on the chamber end visible from the outside?"

"None," he answered. "Some light creases and dents that we didn't look to closely at, but no obvious signs of compromise."

I looked at the Slugger vessel on the display, waiting patiently in the barren space between the specks of starlight.

There was an unexpected sound on the audio link – unexpected, but not entirely unfamiliar. It took me a moment to realize that Moise was softly crying.

We held what Jimi jokingly referred to—once—as a "war council" in the command module once the ex-ex had returned, with Moise invited to join the ship's officers. An intact Slugger vessel was something definitely out of the survey crew's jurisdiction, which put it solidly into mine, but Moise had led the ex-ex and was needed in this discussion. I also wanted to do it in the command module so that Yvains's presence would be unquestioned; a meeting elsewhere would make the attendance of that particular junior officer unusual, and I didn't want to have to recount the details later to Yvains and his Purity smile privately.

I gave Moise the guest collar so she could have her own HUD. Kessler was already devouring the recordings of the ex-ex; Jimi was reviewing everything previously recorded from the outside to see if there was any overlooked flaw in the chamber section. Jala, normally in command when I wasn't, now had no station of his own and chose to anchor himself deferentially at my side.

"We should tell someone," was the first thing Moise said.

"Yes, well. We've got a few technical bugs still to be worked out," I said. "Kessler, any progress on the gravitonics front?"

He waved the flat of his hand to clear the images he was reviewing from his HUD and frowned at something only he could see. "I regret to state," he said formally, "that the gravitonic functions are not balancing as under normal parameters."

I shrugged apologetically at Moise. "He's been having some trouble lining up the transit mechanics." To Kessler I said, "Bellis is the transit tech backup. Have you had him maybe look at your work, see if he can flag something?"

Kessler snorted. "No offense, but Bellis's strength lies in situations that look just like the textbook. And this is *not* a textbook situation. Off the record, Bellis would lock in the equations the best he knew how even though they were off, and the next transit attempt would find the ship—and us—reconfigured as a baryonic filament."

Being out of communication with the Emergence was a normal state of affairs for any jump ship, which is why Purity officers were necessary. I didn't understand all the ins and outs of transit jump mechanics, but I did know that the ability to travel from one point in space to another non-contiguous point in space was contingent on the ambient gravitational spacetime texture, as well as the transiting body's trajectory, momentum and mass. The mass requirement meant that jump ships had a minimum size;

something as small as our landers could never make a jump, even if the tech material needed to make it happen could fit on board. That same mass requirement meant that all broadcast media, whether radio, tightbeam, or Feynmann frequencies, were limited to the functionally useless speed of light. To get a message back, we'd need to jump to where there was someone to receive it.

I said, "Well, you'll have to shuttle some of the grunt work off to him if the presence of the Slugger ship is going to distract you, and I know it will. So make it work." Then to Moise I said, "Without taking a poll, how do you think the survey crew would react to further delay here with the Slugger ship before we start surveying the system?"

She shrugged. "Surveying is how they earn their pay," she said. "I don't know a lot of them that well, but..."

Jimi said, "Well, first priority—I think I'm right in saying this, Captain—is to inform the Emergence about this ship. That means not only working on the gravitonics problem, but also having enough to tell them to make it worth the effort of jumping back."

I nodded. "Agreed. And since we've got a dozen idle surveyers on board, they might being well occupied with examining—noninvasively—that ship out there and finding out what they can about it, especially the chamber end, so that when we're finally able to punch a hole in the sky we'll have a valuable report to relay, instead of just a buck to pass. Any objections?"

There were none in evidence as I looked around the module. When my eyes fell upon Yvains, he let a half-smile curl his lip for an instant—just letting me know that he was there with both hats on.

When my gaze got back around to Moise, I noticed that her hands were clasped between her thighs. "Are you cold in here?"

Moise shook herself and blinked, and her hands disengaged and retreated to her sides. "No, I—no."

The only specimen of the Dead Races that I had seen personally was a Noid, and that was at Roanoke Station a decade ago, when a discovered vessel had been towed in and the captain of the discovering ship allowed some tours—for a slight honorarium, naturally—before the xenobiologists and xenotechnologists descended on the station and appropriated the vessel for the good of the Emergence.

The Noids had been the first Dead Race discovered, even before the Emergence had been formed—or rather, before the nascent Emergence had been recognized for what it was. The Japanese Colonial Corps found the vessel adrift, and reported excitedly that they had proven the existence of other spacefaring intelligence in the universe, even if the particular specimens they had encountered were all dead. After all, if there were dead ones out there, it shouldn't be hard to find the live ones too, right?

That was before a bevy of scientists had determined that the Noid ship had been derelict for twelve to fourteen thousand years, the same time frame into which Noid ships found later fit. Whatever had caused the extinction of the species—or at least forced it to become non-spacefaring, as no one had yet discovered either the Noid home world or any colonies to absolutely prove their extinction – it had struck suddenly, at least speaking on a cosmological time scale. Maybe on a biological scale, too; that two-thousand-year uncertainty was just because of the difficulty of measuring age of an object without being able to rely on radiocarbon results.

So the first Dead Race found was also the most recently dead. Then the Crabbies had been discovered, then the Sluggers, the Amorphs, and the Flats: the Noids being the youngest, the Sluggers the most ancient, and the other three (or two and a half) distributed chronologically between those two extremes of galactic prehistory. Aside from the Sluggers, all of them used some form of jump physics—filtered through a variety of technological paradigms—to get out amongst the stars; also aside from the Sluggers, none left behind anything which we could even broadly interpret as a written language. And aside from the Crabbies, whose traveling colonies arguably might have simply petered out, the other species seem to have met extinction with a sudden bang rather than a protracted whimper. Of course, the older the artifacts are, the harder it is to pinpoint the end of that particular civilization. Even the two-thousand-year uncertainty window for the Noids would have seemed like an eternity while living in it, to me or any other human and possibly to the aliens who experienced it.

Of them all, the Noids weren't just the first discovered, they were physically the most similar to us. In fact, their nickname came from that first press conference in which the discovery of the ancient ship was announced. The lead biologist—there wasn't such thing as a xenobiologist yet, of course —described the aliens' physical shape as being not unlike our own: bipedal, four limbs, bilaterally symmetrical, head at the top.

A clueless but exuberant journalist had blurted, "So they're humans?"

The biologist, flustered at the interruption, had replied, "Well, huma*noids*, at any rate..." and that emphasized syllable had become their name.

I know that there was still a dying thread of protest—more like resigned disapproval, really—that none of those common names showed much respect for these species that had skipped across the stars before humans even realized that those stars were more than pinpricks in a firmament. There were official designations, of course, as well as scientific conglomerations of Latin that tried to describe each species's main characteristics and credit its discovers in only two over-compounded words, but each race was almost exclusively known to the masses by its colloquial name. Sluggers. Noids. Crabbies and the rest. It was like referring to the statesman whose statue graced the town square by his boarding-school pet name. Disrespect for the dead, especially the dead whose existence hadn't directly resulted in our own, was another one of *homo sapiens's* weaknesses.

*＊＊

Under Moise's management as liaison, the survey team began repurposing their exploratory equipment (where doing such wouldn't render the tools unusable for their original purpose) to examine the Slugger ship minutely, via every metric available. Despite the popular conception of exoplanetary survey teams as the ultimate in interstellar blue-collar workers, these men and women were capable engineers, accustomed to quickly and expertly measuring the exploitable resources and drawbacks of every solid body put in front of them, largely from orbit. Now a dozen mechanical eyes were aimed at the empty vessel: radiographic, magnetic, spectrographic, baryonographic, and several other "-graphics" whose particulars I had never learned. Some could be used from onboard the *Anaximander*; others were loaded aboard the *Hesiod* and the other lander, the *Scylla*, and flown out as the survey team inventively experimented with the proper range for the equipment to peer at a target several orders of magnitude smaller than the targets for which it had been constructed. A few devices were planted on the Slugger ship's surface itself, looking like microscopes attached the hide of a rhinoceros to examine its bone structure.

An amazing amount of work was done in the next twelve hours and then the twelve after that, limited only by the number of people needed for each task and by the cargo and seat space on the landers. Kessler, still beating his forehead against his unresolvable gravitonic problem, watched the work being done on his beloved Slugger ship with a disappointment that grew more resigned each time he came up for air.

Every few hours, as a particular scan was finished, Moise reported directly to me. These reports quickly took on a frustrating pattern: Magnetometers showed that the volume of the chamber held no metallic substances beyond the shell of the chamber itself. Spectography couldn't tell anything more about the external composition of the hull than had been revealed in earlier recovered Slugger vessels, which hadn't revealed then and didn't reveal now the past or present contents or purpose of the chamber. Baryonography had trouble penetrating that hull, but as far as that machine's inscrutable squiggles and dots could be connected, there was simply no substance at all inside the chamber. Without rupturing a bulkhead ourselves and looking inside, we couldn't prove that anything was in there.

After every meeting with Moise, I had to turn around and relay all the salient details to Yvains, his smile radiant in its condescension. There was no way around it, he explained; with Moise a known agent of the Faction, her every move had to be observed, every word analyzed. Yvains wanted to have my meetings with Moise recorded without her knowledge, and I almost agreed until I realized that he also expected me to be present through the entire playback with him to answer questions. That time-consuming redundancy was where I drew the line.

"You know," Yvains commented as I finished up the summary of another negative report in the privacy of my cabin, "we need to call it something.

The Slugger ship, I mean. We can't simply keep calling it 'the Slugger ship.' It's ungainly."

"Well, the official name for the Sluggers is five words long," I said. "It's even more ungainly, and I'm not about to look it up every time."

"No, I mean we should give it a name," Yvains said. "Christen it. It's the first Slugger ship found with an intact chamber; it deserves the distinction of a name." He thought a moment, and his smile widened to both sides of his mouth. "The *Integrity*. In honor of that hull."

I thought about this name coming from the lips the Purity officer, whose most important duty to the Emergence was concealed from the entire crew save me, and who was meeting with me because another crewmember was likely a sleeper agent for a seditious body and we wanted to make sure we knew more about her than she knew about us. I swallowed the irony, hard, and nodded. "Sure."

When Yvains had left, I pulled up Moise's service record and reviewed it to see if their was some clue to her Faction affiliation that jumped out at me in hindsight. All reports showed her as competent but not exceptional, comfortable working by herself or in small groups. Prior to her posting here on the *Anaximander*, she had shipped out once each on three previous geosurvey missions, twice as liaison and once as survey team logistics officer. Before that, she had served two stints on pre-colonial resource teams on habitable planets. All of these assignments were in enterprises useful to the Emergence's growth and prosperity, but scarcely sensitive or mission-critical; this was not the resume of an insidious sleeper agent probing the weak spots in the Emergence's structure.

Just to double-check my suppositions, I searched the records for any publicly known Faction plots involving geosurvey ships. There were none, and that stood to reason; who is going to lash out at the monolithic Emergence by sneaking aboard a small ship heading out to catalog rocks?

I thought about where we were and how many transit jumps the average survey mission makes from what anyone would consider a populous arm of the Emergence. Perhaps Moise was an enemy of the Emergence for withholding her ESPer talents for the good of the whole, but did it necessarily follow that she was willfully and deliberately working against it, as the popular conception of the Faction demanded? More than anything else, it seemed she was simply trying to stay out of the Emergence's way and keep to herself.

And yes, I knew that even that was considered an individualistic, anti-emergent impulse. But I couldn't really stoke my sense of righteous indignation over someone wanting to be left alone.

***

At Moise's next check-in—I didn't even to pretend to understand what this specific repurposed geological scan did, but the results were predictably negative—I presented the idea of calling the Slugger ship *"Integrity"* as if it were my own idea. She responded without objection, but she looked tired enough not to have energy for anything less than a mission-critical argument. We who live in space usually overwrite the last remnants of our circadian rhythms within three or four years, but Moise's fatigue wasn't just from being up past her bedtime. Shadows hovered around her eyes, which blinked only half as often as they should and for twice as long, and her statements were pared down to save the effort of every extra syllable. Her arms were crossed in front of her, with her fingers wedged under her upper arms.

"Are you cold again?" I asked.

She shook her head minimally, her eyes aimed in my direction but definitely not focused on me. I suddenly realized myself just how the coffee I had been sucking down was yielding diminishing returns. It was a kinship of exhaustion.

I yawned, only slightly for effect. "All right, I've reached the end of my usefulness," I said. "And you don't look much better." She actually looked much worse than I presumed I did. "Your engineers are working in shifts, aren't they?" She nodded. "Well, I'm going to bunk down, which means you'll have no one you need to report to, which means you've no reason to stay on duty. Tell your teams to keep all the negative reports to themselves —they can wake you when they've got something positive to tell you."

She nodded again—I think she was too tired even to show relief—and moved to the hatch. She hesitated a moment before exiting, as if she wanted to say one more thing, then left.

I glanced out my porthole, the forty-centimeter perk that comes with being the captain. Thanks to the gentle spin of the *Anaximander* at rest, the Slugger ship—the *Integrity*—was rising into my field of vision, like a lollipop-shaped moon. It had integrity, all right; the damned thing had kept its secrets to itself since before terrestrial vertebrates had vertebrae, and wasn't about to roll over and give them up just because we finally had arrived late to the party.

The urgent beeping didn't mesh well with my dream of swimming through dark, organic tunnels, and eventually towed me out of sleep. At my hoarse response, Kessler popped through my cabin's hatch. His face showed fatigue, too—was everyone on the *Anaximander* operating solely on caffeine and obligation?—but relieved triumph shone through as if his skin were translucent.

"Sorry, Captain, but Jala said you'd want to know I figured out the gravitonics problem."

"Poor addition?" I rubbed my face with hands that felt like they had ballast attached to them.

"Nope." He smiled. "It's the Slugger ship."

"*Integrity.*"

"What?"

"We're going to call it *Integrity*. Make a general announcement, will you? I don't want to have to inform every crewmember personally."

"Okay," he said. "The *Integrity*, then. It's the center of enough gravitational warp that my equations were thrown out of whack."

I felt like my brain was playing catch-up, and poorly. "Not possible. There's no way that ship has enough mass for that."

"Impossible, but true," Kessler said.

"And anyway," I said, "every scan from the survey team shows that the chamber is empty. No metals. No radiation. Not even baryonography showed anything."

"That's right," he said. "It's got mass, but not metallic, not magnetic, not radioactive, and not even baryonic."

He paused, and I scowled. I wasn't playing catch-up so much as he was playing keep-away.

"Spit it out," I growled.

"It's dark matter," he said. "By definition, really."

"Non-baryonic mass, without charge..." I mumbled. There was a heated coffee dispenser built into my bulkhead—another perk of captaincy—and I hit it to release a hot bulb of coffee into my hand. I sucked it and felt it start to lubricate the gears in my head.

"You said you scanned for dark matter," I said.

"No, I said I had *accounted* for it. And I had, by normal parameters. Dark matter has a predictable pattern of dispersal through and around a galactic disc, and I had used those ascribed values in my calculations. There's really no way to scan for dark matter directly, since it doesn't interact with normal matter or energy except by its gravitational pull, and you can't actively scan for gravitation's warp in spacetime; you just observe its effects."

The coffee helped, but I still felt like Kessler was outracing me into the conceptual distance. "So the chamber of the *Integrity*, that all our normal scans show as being empty..."

"...Is full of enough dark matter to warp the local gravitonics," he finished. "Not just bend it, like a body of normal baryonic matter does to space-time; there's such a concentrated density that even if the overall gravitational effect is subtle enough for us not to notice it when we're standing right outside that pinpoint, that there are... well, for want of a better term, wrinkles and creases in the fabric. And that's why we can't reach gravitonic equilibrium anywhere around the Slugger ship, not for quite a distance."

"But still." I put on my shoes, feeling the hint of energy somewhere inside me; a course of action seemed like it might be on the horizon. "We move far enough away from the *Integrity*, and we can jump again?"

"I'll have to figure out exactly how far—"

"Do that. Or just take your safest guess and double it. I'll talk to Moise

NATHAN SHUMATE

and see how long it'll take to get all the crew and equipment back. Then we can finally make a jump and tell everyone what we've found."

He turned to leave as I snapped up my jacket.

"Hey, Kessler... what the hell's the dark matter for?"

"Not my department," he said cheerily. "But as a matter of curiosity, I have to tell you: I don't have a clue." He smiled as he said it. Maybe he'd missed the exploration of what turned out to be the first intact Slugger ship ever discovered, but he had found another facet to the mystery that tickled his little Dead-Races-loving heart.

Kessler opened the hatch and almost collided with Yvains reaching for the buzzer.

"Sorry," said Yvains, the picture of an apologetic junior officer. "Captain Ingers is awake?"

Kessler confirmed the fact and moved out into the gangway, letting Yvains propel himself through the door into the cabin. The knowing smile of the Purity officer sprang onto his face as soon as the latch clicked, as if that were a rehearsed signal.

"Make it quick," I said as I straightened my uniform. "I need to go wake up Moise."

"Moise is sedated under medical care."

That stopped me short. "Why?"

"Nightmares. Something more than normal nightmares, really. She woke screaming and flailing, and her bunkmate had to call for help to restrain her. We got her to the dispensary—quite a task, really—"

"'We?' How did you get involved in this?"

"Potentially dangerous behavior by anyone on board is automatically a matter for the ship's duty command, which was Jala, who delegated the matter to me."

Yvains had been awake for at least as long as Moise or I had. Didn't the eyes of the Emergence ever sleep?

Yvains continued, "As the nominal leader of the exploratory team is now both a Faction subversive and mentally unstable, you should realign the assignment. Because I've been briefed on all of Moise's reports from the beginning, I am the logical choice, so I will—"

"You will do nothing," I interrupted. "Not until I make the decision." I was taller than Yvains, but personal height is harder to assert in zero gravity. Still, planetborn instinct asserted itself and I drew myself up at an angle from which I could look down at him. "I'm still the captain."

"And you always have been," said Yvains, unperturbed. "But the import of this discovery extends beyond the politics of the *Anaximander*. As the Purity officer representing the Emergence, I—"

"—Will shut up until I tell you to speak," I said. "Until we make a jump, and you can bring your influence to bear with the Emergence, you are a junior officer who needs to learn his place. That place is in your quarters, awaiting further orders. Is that clear?"

I thought his half-smile would finally falter. Instead, it widened—not to the other side of his mouth, but further up the one half of his face until he looked like a fish with a hook firmly caught in its cheek. "Yes, sir," he said in the same unperturbed voice, and excused himself.

I needed to talk to Moise. Faction or not, when an ESPer wakes screaming, you need to find out why. But instead of double-timing to the dispensary, I found myself looking out my porthole at the alien ship framed there. The melodrama aboard the *Anaximander* was in danger of eclipsing the true mystery in front of us.

Dark matter. As humanity had become the Emergence and expanded through the galaxy in wave after transit-jumping wave, so many cosmic conundrums had fallen to the onslaught of human ingenuity. Dark matter, though, was one of those that retreated before the perimeter of our knowledge, like a rainbow that keeps its distance from its dogged pursuer. A particularly colorless rainbow.

Even the label "dark matter" had now become a misnomer; it was *unseen* matter. You couldn't put it under a microscope or excite it with radiation or fire neutrinos through it and watch their spin. It was something entirely other than what we thought of as matter, like a shadow twin from the womb of the Big Bang that had spawned us both, and that interacted with anything we could see or touch or feel only by the gravity of its insubstantial substance. And it was the more massive twin by far; the best cosmological estimates said that dark matter composed ninety to ninety-five percent of the universe, and the gravity of its invisible mass was essential to the formation of galaxies, stars... all of the radiant matter that ultimately had led to us. We couldn't detect it at all except by noting the gravitational lensing by which its mass warped the light of distant galaxies and quasars, and yet it was entirely essential to the existence of the universe we knew, the structures of particles and charge which were everything we were, but which were nothing more than the scraps floating on the surface of an immense dark ocean that we just couldn't see.

By every measure in the survey team's toolbag, the bulbous chamber at one end of the *Integrity*—the bow or the stern, we didn't even know that much—was nothing but solid mass without charge, without radiation, without any feature that was a characteristic of anything we would call "matter." Nothing except mass. Kessler had been right; this was dark matter, by definition—and whatever it was, it held more mass in that volume than the heaviest of known elements, enough that it could create enough local gravity to make jumps impossible. Normal matter is mostly empty space between subatomic particles whose repulsive electromagnetic charges kept them at a healthy distance; did dark matter have nothing like that, nothing preventing it from being forced into ultramassive concentrations? To hell with wondering what it was for; how could a Slugger ship even move that? But that assumes that dark matter mass has inertia analogous to normal matter; were all bets off, with absolutely no analogy to the properties of normal matter? And what was the inside of the chamber lined with, that could hold and contain a form of matter which didn't otherwise interact with any non-dark form of matter or energy? How—

The lazy spin of the *Anaximander* slowly turned the *Integrity* out of my field of vision. I looked instead at the sparks of starlight, which people had for so long seen as separated points of matter and fiery energy separated from one another by a void. There had always been more void than matter —but there was also more *to* the void than to the matter.

Moise was quiet when I entered the infirmary, though it didn't sound as if she had relaxed any; her breath was ragged and sibilant, and corded muscles stood out on her neck. Her bunkmate, a drained-looking geophysicist named Vestal, stood watch over her.

"How is she?" I asked stupidly.

Vestal gestured to the transparent medical waste compartment on the wall, where I could see four empty syringes. "It took four CCs of petrazine just to get her to stop screaming so hard she sprayed blood." Vestal's own voice was not much above a throaty whisper, like a radio set to its minimum audible volume.

Moise was strapped to a treatment rack with the attached straps, and then other makeshift restraints—bandage tape, power cords, someone's shirt—had been used to tie her more tightly at the knees and ankles, the elbows and wrists, and the neck. Moise's mouth hung open, lips quivering, and droplets of rosy spittle disengaged unheeded from her lips and floated lazily in the air.

We were a self-doctoring crew; no one with a chronic condition was shipped out as part of either a survey crew or a ship crew, and virtual guides could walk us through normal test, triage and treatment. I knew that two CCs of petrazine could tranquilize and anesthetize someone with three times my body mass. The fact that some part of Moise was still trying to assert itself through that industrial-strength sedative was possibly the most frightening thing I had ever seen.

The display from the bioreader attached to the side of her neck showed both raw data—elevated respiration and heart rate, low blood pressure, copious perspiration—and a helpful interpretive guide, which confidently informed us that the patient was well into circulatory shock.

"Did she say anything?" I asked. "When she was screaming?"

Vestal shook her head. "Not that I could make out."

I could see the bump of Moise's irises jumping back and forth as if they were trying to find an escape path from under her eyelids.

"I relieve you," I said to Vestal. "Go get some sleep."

Vestal nodded, pushed off for the hatch, and closed it behind her.

I queried the friendly display and yes, there was a stimulant which largely alleviated the effects of petrazine, and indeed, we had a stock of it. I withdrew a single CC of cleridimide, administered, and waited. The rasp in Moise's breathing speeded incrementally, but there were no other indications the drug was working. I tried to pull back an eyelid, but she thrashed her head so violently at my touch that she almost dislodged the bioreader.

After four minutes without any more reaction—which, the display volunteered, was the longest a live body would take to exhibit a reaction—I gave her another dose. She strained against her bonds, and the green of her irises was visible through the slits of her eyelids as they jumped back and forth.

"Moise," I said, trying to sound both gentle and authoritative. "Moise, this is Captain Ingers. Can you hear me?"

She twitched, but I didn't know if she was reacting to me or to the dueling pharmaceuticals in her veins.

"Moise," I said, and stepped closer. I could smell the tangy fear in her sweat. "Moise, I know you're an ESPer."

Her breath hitched. Had she heard me? What she listening?

"And," I said softly, "I know you're Faction."

Her eyelids flickered, and her dilated pupils focused on me, then spun crazily around the cramped dispensary, then back to me.

"I'm telling you this," I continued, "because I want you to understand that you don't need to keep secrets anymore or be worried about what you might say. I want to know what you saw. In your dreams. I need to know."

Her lungs convulsively filled with air as she got ready to scream again, but before it could come out, she clamped her teeth on her lip so hard that blood spurted. I moved out of the path of the blood droplets, perfect spheres moving in a straight line from her mouth until they spattered on a bulkhead.

"Moise," I said. "I need to know."

Her eyes came back to me, left, came back to me. The stimulant was fighting against the sedative, which fought against the traumatic shock. She shuddered, and her bloody lips trembled as she tried to form words.

"So... dark..."

"What is?" I prompted. "What's so dark, Moise?"

"The *dark*... is so..." Her head lolled against the restraints and drifted back and forth with its own inertia in the zero gravity. "It's so *full*," she whispered. Then she just started crying. No more screams, just full sobs that shook her from head down to pelvis and back again. Her tears drifted off lazily into the air and spun around the two of us.

"So full?" I repeated, trying to sound like a counselor. "What is, Moise? The chamber?"

She started to shake her head, then her neck seized up as if she wanted to nod at the same time. "Not just that," she said *sotto voce*. If I had just screamed my throat bloody, I'm probably whisper too. "They... they must have known. The Sluggers. They must have... How could they know?" She blinked and stared back and forth at my eyes, as if desperate for some answer there. "How could they stand to know?" She started crying again.

I started talking just to give her a rest from answering questions, and maybe to answer a few of her own. "Moise, Kessler's figured out that the chamber is full of dark matter. Maybe that's what all the chambers were filled with originally, on all the Slugger ships."

She nodded, her head drifting lazily on her neck again, her eyes unfocused.

"All over," she mumbled. "Everywhere. There's so much of it." She squeezed her eyes shut, launching tears again into the air. "Never get away from it." Silent sobs started trembling up her torso again.

She hadn't given me any answers; the fragments she had managed to say seemed like they were part of a bigger answer than any question I could put together. I decided that she had had enough of both wakefulness and dreams for now. The display brightly answered that sorumate AD, an anesthetic that we had aboard for impromptu surgeries and bone-setting, would put her into complete and dreamless unconsciousness, no matter the amount of adrenaline and cleridimide swelling her veins. I administered the shot and watched her as everything that wasn't autonomic relaxed and found peace.

The question of why none of the Dead Races had a system of writing, save debatably for the Sluggers, had added spice to the endless debates and speculations. Those who regarded the Crabbies as a non-sentient social species simply tallied that as one more evidence for their contention, until it was invariably pointed out that the Noids, Flats and Amorphs had undeniably been tool-using sapients, and they had left no more examples of a written language than had the Crabbies. And so the argument went around and around.

Of course, the Emergence had suggested a hypothesis which, while untestable, had the value of being flattering to itself. If the three (or four) other species, aside from the Sluggers, had all achieved their own analogs to the Emergence before venturing into space—if they had, in fact, become fully able to communicate mind-to-mind as component parts of a supra-organism before written language had become an integral part of their intellectual culture—then our puzzlement at lack of writing would be as ridiculous as wondering why there wasn't a buggy whip in the hand of a starship pilot.

Because the Emergence had only promulgated that hypothesis as possible but not incontrovertible, the debate still circled, but mostly among die-hard aficionados. When most people thought of the mysteries of the Dead Races, they really only thought of a single mystery: how each one had died out. The exploration of their lifestyle didn't seem nearly as important as their cause of death.

Something Moise had said—or hinted at, or maybe not said—had left an unsupportable suspicion in my mind, a dark fancy I could neither confirm nor dispel, that perhaps the two questions were not completely unrelated.

***

Jala saluted and vacated the command console when I entered the module. It was sparsely crewed; aside from Jala, only Jimi and Kreckell were at their stations. I snapped my HUD collar around my neck and saw the command functions spread in front of me.

"I thought Kessler was on-duty, Jala. Or did you give him the rest of the shift off after he found the answer to the gravitonic problem?"

Jala looked confused. "He—Captain, he's on the *Scylla* with Yvains, per... your orders."

"I ordered no such thing."

"But Yvains came and got him. He—the orders had your code on them." He wiped his finger across the air, "throwing" a digital document from his HUD to mine. There it was, plainly spelled out over my digital signature: Yvains and Kessler were to take the second lander, the *Scylla*, over to the Slugger ship—funny how *"Integrity"* had dropped out of use so soon—to assist with operations. It was flawlessly forged. Even compared to other Purity officers with whom I had shipped out, Yvains seemed to have an inflated sense of the scope of his duty to the Emergence. And what was there to restrain him? Who watches the watchers?

There was me, for one.

I immediately hailed the lander, which was just touching down on the hull of the Slugger ship. *"Anaximander* to *Scylla,* come in," I barked.

After a moment, we heard Kessler's voice, no video. *"Anaximander,* this is *Scylla."*

"Mr. Kessler," I said calmly, "can you explain back to me the scope of your current operation?"

I could almost feel his puzzlement in the pause before he answered. "I... You just wanted me to have a look around finally, sir. Correct? Am I mistaken?"

"Private channel to Yvains."

An icon floated in the air in front of me, showing that my HUD was also blocking sound from reaching beyond the virtual confines of my display to the rest of the command module.

"Yvains here, Captain."

"Please explain your actions to me, Mr. Yvains."

"I don't know what you mean, Captain," he said smoothly. "I am transporting Mr. Kessler to the *Integrity,* as per your orders."

"Stow it, Yvains. What's going on?"

I could hear his damned smile over the crystal-clear transmission. "I'm sorry, Captain, you're breaking up. There must be interference from the *Integrity."*

"Yvains!"

Another part of my HUD showed that the transmission was now coming from inside the Slugger ship. Yvains and Kessler were aboard.

"Damn it," I said, "what are you up to? What's Kessler doing in this?"

"Do not attempt to limit my latitude on this, Captain. Mr. Kessler is guiding me to the junction of the shaft to the chamber."

"Did Kessler tell you about the chamber? It's full of dark matter. We don't know its function or purpose—"

"I've read Kessler's report," Yvains interrupted. "And anyway, I know. It's full." Then he laughed. All the times I had seen his smile, and I didn't recall him ever laughing. "It's so... *full.*"

Ice water trickled down my vertebrae.

"Yvains! Damn you, turn around! Surrender yourself to Kessler and get back here!" From the looks Jala and Jimi tossed my way, I could tell my voice was leaking out past the privacy shield. "Yvains—how did you know Moise was an ESPer? How did you know?"

"I'm sorry, Captain, I can't listen to you anymore. It's calling me."

"How did you know?"

The channel went dead.

"Private channel to Kessler," I snapped.

An icon blinked red on my HUD.

"Kessler!" I called.

Jimi said, "Yvains has got master control over Kessler's comm, somehow. I don't know—"

"I do. He's the Purity officer," I said through gritted teeth. "And he's an ESPer. And I think he's insane."

Jala looked confused, just as he had ever since I entered the command module. "What's he doing? Is he after something?"

I ignored him and paged the lander bay. "Is the *Hesiod* prepped for flight?"

A voice came back, someone I didn't know from the survey crew. "Not really, Captain. We've got some equipment half-unloaded, and it's a quarter way through recharging and realigning—"

"I need it ready to fly! How soon?"

I know that an answer started to come back, but it got drowned out by

dark
full dark
from dark to dark
confined no released
rejoining the dark
the full dark
filling all the everything
becoming all the everything
except that crust of light
crust that had held it
stupid crust
free now
free to think with the everything

feel with the everything
be with the everything
am everything
am so much more than alone now
am everything
are everything
am/are I/we everything
filling everything
full dark

I stared at the display. I gasped for air like a drowning man. The *Integrity* looked just as it had before, floating lazily in interstellar space, but I knew it was different now. It was like all the other Slugger ships ever found. The chamber was now empty.

Jala slapped both hands over his mouth, but he threw up anyway. Vomit jetted between his fingers and spattered against far surfaces. The air scrubbers cycled on.

the dark

I shook my head. There were things in there, in my head, things I hadn't put there, things that had just come without any volition. I knew things that I had no means of knowing. One thing I knew was that Yvains was dead. He might have still been drawing breath, but there was no longer any bird in his birdcage. It hadn't been opened to let his bird free, no; Yvains had opened a different cage, and what burst out of it had flown like a solid wall of force through the birdcage of his mind, extruding the bird through the wire mesh on the far side before it had even had a chance to tweet in alarm. Tweet, tweet, tweet...

I gripped my supports and found out that I was laughing. I didn't mean to be. Laughing was better than tweeting, anyway. Jimi had curled into a fetal position, but he hadn't been strapped to his station, so he just drifted through the module's airspace, flecked with vomit as he nudged into the floating beads still coming up, with regularity but much less payload, from Jala's throat.

I knew also that Moise was dead, well and truly. Her mind had already been raw and bleeding, and now it had been stripped out of her, and with it her brain as well, her nervous system shredded as if it had been forced through steel wool by the force of the...

Of the...

dark

I tried to remember how to make my HUD function. It sat there, patiently waiting my input, and it was only with difficulty that I dug out second-nature habits now buried under hurricane flotsam in my mind. I accessed personnel records. Jimi bumped by, and I could smell that he had soiled himself.

There were seven identified Sensitives aboard the *Anaximander* in both of her crews, two Inerts—both geomagnetic analysts, what were the odds?—and everyone else was a Median, like me. The Emergence had determined that we were just ordinary folks, Emergent-speaking, no more sensible to psychica than anyone else, and yet my mind hung in strips and cross-sections, my mind was a dot of oil on a watery surface that had immediately expanded and lost any cohesion, any integrity—

Integrity. Whatever had spoken to my mind in passing and told me *things...* was that what had had Moise in tears aboard the *Integrity*, and what had later invaded her sleep and refused to let go of her wakeful mind? Of course it was. It was what had drawn Yvains to it, compelling him—or maybe just persuading him, enticing him—to breach the chamber and let it out. *It*. The dark fullness.

The dark inside that was now one with the dark outside.

As much dark matter as fit inside the chamber—however much that was, as its contained density was still unknown—was an intelligent, sensate consciousness, so violently inhospitable to the human psyche that its touch had blown out circuitbreakers in the brains of probably everyone on board.

And now that discrete body of dark matter had rejoined the substance which was ninety-five percent of the universe.

Which had welcomed it back.

I felt the warmth spread out as my bladder released, and my palsied hands grabbed my face, scratching, twisting, slapping, trying instinctively to use pain to distract synapses which could do nothing but try to wrap themselves around this new understanding, try and fail and try and fail and spread wider and try and fail until the enormity turned me inside out, like a garden snake trying to swallow a moon.

Because it was all alive.

All of it.

All. Of. The. Dark.

Our visible universe was the crust clinging to the edge of the *real* universe. It was that drop of oil, spread infinitesimally thin on the surface of a limitless and heedless ocean, an ocean which filled the post-Big Bang expansion, dwarfing galaxies and clusters and super-clusters and poor little Captain Ingers, quaking in his own piss.

And all of it was alive. All of it thought. All of it *knew*.

Who would ever discover how the Sluggers had managed to invent a way to trap a discrete portion of this conscious foundation of all reality, to force it to obey their will and transport them across the stars? If the Sluggers had been able to do that without cascading into insanity, they were more alien than we had imagined any biological entity could be. Because all of the other Dead Races—each connected by their own version of the Emergence, allowing them all to know the bottomless truth when one of their numbers found and pierced a Slugger ship's chamber—had immediately collapsed, individually and as a civilization, once that true picture of existence had forced itself from mind to mind...

I looked to Jala, whose hands had fallen from his face, his fingers still woven together and cemented by drying vomit, his face smeared and masked by fluids from his mouth, nose and eyes. His eyes were too bright, as if the pulse of conscious darkness had ignited some spark that was burning out his brain. Close enough to the truth.

How many of us were there with enough scraps of ego and motor control to pilot the *Anaximander* home? And once we got there, babbling and incoherent and wallowing in our own offal, the Emergence would immediately put its best and brightest ESPers on digging through the collapsed middens of our minds to discover what it was that had done this to us, tweet tweet tweet, and when they found it... when they *found* it... when they found *it*...

"This is the way the world ends," said a voice close at hand. "This is the way the worlds end." I was fascinated by the voice, especially because it sounded like it was coming from my own mouth. "This is the way *all* worlds end. Not with a bang... but with a gibber."

I was somehow proud of the fact that that had come from somewhere in my head disconnected from the part of me that admired just how clever it was. And how true. The Emergence would end, humanity would end, as all other post-Slugger spacefaring species had ended when we infected the collective consciousness with what we knew.

Unless we didn't infect them.

My hand was on my face again, clawing at my cheek and eye. Funny how I didn't feel it, I only knew it when blood started spotting the air in my view. I used my other hand to grab the workspace from Kessler's inactive HUD. There it was, in primary colors, twirling in the void: the graphic representation of the rough calculations he had been able to sketch in before he had made the conceptual leap about the dark matter. It was close to being right if you squinted, but "close" wasn't good enough when a transit jump based on faulty equations could spread your dissociated quarks in a two-dimensional ribbon three parsecs long.

I grabbed the incomplete equations and stuffed them into flight control. Jala was staring into space; I didn't know if he was watching my actions in his HUD, or if the last functional neurons in his head were firing randomly and distracting him with the pretty colors. Jimi had bounced softly off the bulkhead above me and to the left and bobbed slowly back the way he had come, like an abandoned bathtoy.

I keyed in the double- and triple-check codes that confirmed that, yes, these were exactly the transit equations I wanted to use. The engines cooled themselves, superconducting in pulses like great frigid birds anxious to fly into the void behind the darkness, tweet tweet tweet.

As the countdown passed the cutoff point after which nothing could stop the transit jump, I realized the effort with which I had mentally gripped the fragments of my mind still within my grasp, like wrapping my arms around a house of cards to keep it from falling down. That was an image from my childhood, way back when I hadn't given gravity a second thought. Here in space, a house of cards could never hold together. Out here, every direction was down. Down and dark, and tweet tweet tweet, here we were like a canary in a big black mine that was as dark black as all of creation.

Humanity would not learn the truth from us. And we would be spared from our unwanted understanding by the absolute destruction, right down to the protons and electrons, that would rescue us when the counter reached zero and we jumped past the dark.

FALL OF THE RUNEWROUGHT

Howard Tayler

"The problem with rune-tech, a problem exacerbated by our reluctance to acknowledge it as a problem, is that despite twenty-eight years of research, development, application, and deployment, it remains indistinguishable from magic." –Saadiq Sebastian DuChamps, RUNExpo Chicago, 2055

"Captain Tamrielle Surinam." I give my name to my medicine band, a shiny bracelet on my right wrist. "Sanity is nothing more than consensus of perception."

My passphrase. It's not strictly true, but I like it. Dad used to say that.

The band flashes green and scrolls my vitals. Looks like I'm going to have a good day. The medicine band monitors all kinds of things from its vantage point on my wrist, but every so often I'm required to talk to it directly. Presortie is one of those times—last-minute assurance that my head is on straight. My brush with insanity eighteen months ago notwithstanding, I'm still the best runecracker that Runewrought Ampersand Dynamics has.

Sometimes I wonder whether my value to R&D went up after I touched the crazy place. Not that it matters. They've invested ten years of education and training in me, not to mention whatever it cost them when they bought my commission from the army. And then there was the soulbone surgery. I'm an expensive asset.

"Tasty drugs today, ma'am?" Milholland shouts over the roaring engines. He's a big white guy with an easy smile.

"I'm too high to taste 'em," I shout back. "You'd better ask me how many fingers I'm holding up." And then I flip him off.

Laughter. We're not nervous. No more so than usual, anyway. The six of us—me, Milholland, White, Betts, Nguyen, and Groberg—are flying from Vegas to Delta, Utah, where a power station has gone dark. There was no 911 call, there were no calls at all, and now nobody picks up. Whatever happened, it was big, it was bad, and it was fast.

That probably means it swept in from another world and needs to be put down or put back. Or both. R&D dispatched us with two fire teams and three trucks of support to troubleshoot.

"This one's kind of spooky, Cap'n," says Nguyen over the group channel, his voice clear over the now-muted engine noise. "I think we may want the rest of the trucks to hang further back, just in case."

"I'm with Nguyen," says Milholland. "Those folks have families to go home to tonight. We need to be the canaries in the coal mine on this one."

"You do know that the canary-in-the-coal-mine thing only works if the miners can watch 'em die," says White, his pale, skinny hands pantomiming a fluttering bird suddenly dropping dead.

"Nice try," says Groberg with a frown that nicely complements his mustache. "They've got our telemetry. They can watch us die from Wales. I say keep 'em back."

"What do you think, Betts?" I ask. Me, I don't want to risk hauling forty-eight people into a death trap if six will accomplish the same senseless waste.

"They should stay the hell back," she says. "I want to be able to shoot indiscriminately."

Betts has a pig iron, just like Nguyen. People with magic bullets are allowed to shoot indiscriminately.

"Milholland, call dispatch," I say. "Keep 'em two klicks out, south side, between the plant and town."

We're AFTT. It's short for "Angels Fear to Tread," the name we selected over "Fools Rush In." Same difference. We go in first. We never know what we're in for, but we're the team that expects the unexpected and delivers the impossible. Maybe we're heroes. Maybe we're the canaries in the coal mine.

From above, the Intermountain Power station in Delta looks like giant stacks of white concrete boxes in the middle of a vast, verdant pasture marked with a pair of radiating streaks of brown. Our response truck circles above the facility, banking to give us a better view of the site. No smoke, which is a good sign for a power plant. Canaries haven't been used in coal mines in a hundred years, and coal hasn't been burnt for power in a decade. Intermountain Power is all rune-tech these days. It's efficient, clean, and reliable. Except right now, when it's not. At any rate, nothing is supposed to be burning here, and nothing is.

I don't see any structural damage, but there are some star-like dots...

"I make out four bodies in the quad," says Nguyen.

Yup. That's what those are. Damn.

"Confirmed," I say. "What else?"

"Are those brown swaths normal?" Milholland asks.

I look where he's pointing. The station is surrounded by rich pasture, but there are two dry, dead streaks running through it for maybe a thousand meters, with several smaller streaks branching off of them. The station itself has no green amid it.

"I don't know," I answer. "Driver, swing us over that."

The truck responds with a fresh whine atop the engine roar. It's unsettling. Most vehicles are silent, but we're not flying on rune power. If something has gone crooked with the rune-banks here in Delta, we're better off avoiding possible interference. We're aloft on jet fuel and Tesla turbines—conventional engines delivering ordinary, air-driven lift. Loud, smelly, and very unlikely to fail.

Or, at least, unlikely to fail here. I know of several rune combinations that could shut down internal combustion, weld moving metal into a solid block, suck a battery dry, or just swat us out of the sky. In fact, I can do all of that with my soulbone. But weapon-words like those don't belong in a power plant.

"I think the brown is new," says Nguyen. "The whole plant is brown like that. There should be some landscaping in the quad."

"Pulling it up now," says White, swiping his finger back and forth across his tablet. "Green, green green, yeah. Apple, Bing, Google, Glyphi, and NASA agree. The site should be green all the way to the concrete. Muddy on the driving path, but green everywhere else."

Five sources. White's thorough, if skittish. I like him. Not enough to date him, even if that were something that HR allowed, but he's solid.

I consider the brown streaks again. They're wide where they meet the facility, curving and tapering to crisp points out amid the green a kilometer away. The smaller intersecting streaks make it look almost like a rune of some—

"SHIT!" I hit the panic button on the left side of my goggles, and the left eyepiece goes black. So do five other left eyepieces—the panic buttons work for the whole team.

"What've you got, Captain?" asks Betts, her hand on my shoulder.

"Gimme a sec," I reply, shrugging her hand free. I take a moment to collect my thoughts, and to take inventory. Did I see anything besides the rune? Hallucinate any movement? I run through a mental checklist, assessing whether or not I'm still sane. Insanity is a real risk for us if we've got both eyes open, and I know this better than anybody in the truck.

Aside from the adrenaline rush, I'm thinking just like I did five minutes ago. Also, my bracelet's still green. Good to go.

"Okay, sorry for the scare. I didn't get any rune-hot effect, but the northern brown streak is a perfect lead stroke for any of the second series ductiles, the cross streaks look like they've got Fibonacci spacing, and the taper is pointing "—I double-check my HUD—"magnetic north, exactly."

"Damn, Captain," says Milholland. "That's rune enough for me, whether or not it's wiggling."

Our goggles are far better than the eye patches used by the pioneers of rune-tech. Wedded to a bit of rune-tech themselves, they can selectively block runes while still letting us see through both eyes. Unless, of course, the rune isn't in the library. And whether or not this pattern of brown is a rune, we only saw part of it at a time. And I'm not taking unnecessary chances.

"Left eyes black until I get this one added," I say. "It'll only take a minute.

We circle again for the full picture, and I get the rune—an integral-curved base stroke with six crosshatches and a circular spot just off center—into my glyphie.

To my generation, goggles and eye patches are what hazmat suits and lead aprons were to my mother's. I wish I knew why rune-tech drives people mad when they see enough of it with both eyes. Ah, the good old days, when people understood what they were defending themselves against.

But my world is a better place than my mother's—something she will remind us of any time she's reminiscing after Thanksgiving dinner, usually just before she looks down her nose at me for not having children or prospects yet. "Why, some people used to worry that ours was no world fit to bring a child into," she'd say. "You don't have that excuse, Tamrielle."

She's got a point. We have clean power sources and amazing direct-effect engines running alongside the best conventional technology the twenty-first century has to offer. The climate is under control, our cities are bright and shiny, and poverty is a bad memory. We've finally got the flying cars that Great-Grandma claims somebody promised her, except ours safely drive themselves, and the rune block under the hood will power the vehicle for weeks without fresh blood.

And there's plenty of food. Rune-tech works best with old stone and fresh blood, so the marriage of the meat-packing industries with the repurposed power plants was inevitable.

Just like the facility below us. Pastures, a stockyard, and a drive path feed cattle into the power plant, where they're hoisted up and their blood is spilled on stone altars amid hanging racks of engraved stone. The magical energy spins turbines to generate electricity. A few members of the herd are slaughtered on rune words spelled out for different effects—keeping the herd healthy, the air clean, and the pasture green here in the middle of what used to be a desert.

Until something goes wrong. As we circle again I can see that the brown stroke—visible to my right eye, but with edges blurred when I look with my left—is dead. All the way dead. The grass is withered and pale, and the few cattle that had been freely ranging in it are on their sides.

I've never seen this effect before. If one of the rune panes inside the generator dropped askew, it could have been catastrophic, but it should have been a kinetic catastrophe—thirty-ton inscribed tablets launching themselves through concrete containment, pulverizing anything in their path. This looks like the work of a direct-effect series, a set of runes spelled out for killing in broad, sweeping strokes. This doesn't look like a power plant accident. This looks deliberate.

I don't have children or prospects because I've wrapped my life around solving dangerous problems, and I'm wound pretty tight.

"Driver, put us down next to the northern swoop," I tell the truck.

"Affirmative," comes the pleasant, male voice of the truck. It banks and heads down with another change in engine pitch.

"What's the plan, Captain?" asks Milholland.

"Start at the outside and work our way in. Try to figure out how the cattle and the grass died. That might let us help survivors on the inside. Might even let us defend ourselves."

"My kind of plan," says White.

There are signals of assent from the other four.

"Attention," says the truck. "We will be landing eight meters north by northwest of the tip of the area of interest in three, two, one..."

The landing is as smooth as only an autopilot can deliver, the truck ceasing motion and settling onto the ground as gently and gracefully as a dancer's footfall. Cameras around the edges of the truck flash our perimeter to the HUDs in our goggles. Nothing shows up, but there are things that can't be seen by cameras. There are entire hierarchies of invisibility, in fact.

"Go!"

Groberg and Nguyen are the first out, weapons at the ready. White and Betts are next, sweeping in the other direction. Milholland and I wait until they've swept around the truck, and then we debark with our hands empty and our hips covered with instruments. We're not unarmed, though. We both wear shoulder holsters, and I can fire up my soulbone faster than any pistol.

The grass is low but lush. Great grazing for free-range cattle. We fan out and move toward the brown patch. The grass there is completely dry, but not high-summer dry. It's withered and twisted, like somebody put it in a dehydrator. The line between lush and desiccated is a little fuzzy up close. Death appears to have affected whole plants, not portions of them. I stoop in the lush grass, tear up a green handful, and toss it into the dead zone.

It does not wither, disintegrate, or burst into flame. It flutters and falls to the ground, where it lies in stark contrast, deep green on pale brown. Whatever killed the grass isn't still killing things.

"You don't trust your goggles, ma'am?" asks Milholland.

"The goggles are test number two." I touch my goggles with the ring on my left index finger. I feel a prick from my tap ring, and then my vision changes as the goggles charge up on a drop of my blood. I brush my thumb through the blood, and then hold it on the levee-pulsatile rune that attunes the goggles for life sight.

The living grass has a faint amber glow to it. My team members each glow brightly in red, as does the nearest living cow. Tiny sparks of yellow move through the green grass—insects, spiders, and roly-polies.

Inside the dead patch everything is grey. Whatever killed the grass and the cows also killed the bugs. And none of the living bugs have migrated into the dead area.

I slide my thumb over the marquee-pulsatile rune, looking for power sources, direct-effect rune magic, and anything else that might show up. The living cattle sparkle in blue-white, and each of my companions blazes like a star. Milholland has his air sampler out, and it twinkles yellow. Betts's and Nguyen's rune rifles and helmets shine with a steady red, as do the goggles everybody's wearing. Several glows emanate from various pouches and pockets and sheaths—miraculous first aid kits, supernaturally sharp knives, and good luck charms that actually work. The MP30s, the grenades, the sidearms, and the ammo bags don't shine at all.

Neither does the rune-shaped dead patch. Whatever energies were unleashed here, they're gone now.

"No field effect. No sign of no-see-ums either."

"No sign from here, either," says Nguyen.

"I can live with a milk run," says White.

I concur silently. Large bursts of rune magic can open breaches into the void, allowing some truly vicious things into our world. The most common of these are psychic parasites. Having an eight-kilo, transdimensional, invisible baboon-crab removed from its perch on your head is not pleasant. When it's survivable.

"The 'stat likes the air," says Milholland.

"We're breathing it, aren't we?" growls Groberg.

"And it's tasty. Normal mix of atmospheric gases, no airborne toxins, humidity is about where it should be, and pressure suggests they were planning to bring in some rain this evening."

"Let's go look at a dead cow, then." I signal the team, and then I step into the dead patch. The grass crunches and crumbles underfoot.

Despite all of our preparation, I feel a slight thrill. Something very deadly came this way, and we know so little. Angels fear to tread...

The cow did not go happily into the great pastures of the beyond. It is lying on its side, its neck and back are arched unnaturally, and its legs are contorted. Skeletal structure shows clearly under taut skin, like the cow starved to death and then was freeze-dried. I can't tell for sure how much of the positioning is the postmortem result of whatever rune magic sucked the beast dry, but something about the pose suggests that the cow's last act was to snap its own neck trying to scream at the sky.

Milholland tries to shove a probe into the cow's abdomen.

"Tough as leather," he says with a wink and then leans into it, grunting. There's a tearing noise, and the probe sinks clear to the haft. Milholland looks down at it and shakes his head.

"Dust dry, but cold." He taps on the probe's controls. "Not going to get time of death this way."

"Work the other direction," I suggest. "Assume this happened the moment the plant went dark."

"Oh, good thinking." He taps some more. "Okay, the cow cooled to about four degrees above freezing when the water was taken. There was probably dew here for a bit, but it burned off under the sun."

Betts speaks first. "If what happened to this cow happened to people, they're beyond any medical help, conventional or rune-powered."

"Time to stop poking the dried cow, then," I announce. "We need to move to the facility." I wave my hand over my head in a circle and point back to the truck. "Pile in and pull out!"

After consulting the schematics in my goggles, I direct the truck to fly us to the annex. Turning to the team, I explain: "Security is stationed there. Hopefully they'll have video of the event."

"That," says White, "is something I'll let you watch first."

I've got my goggles charged for the whole trip over the dead patch. Nothing's shining. The range on life detection should be just under four hundred meters, and I keep hoping that as we get closer something human will light up.

The lawn around the annex is withered like the fields were. Other than that the building looks normal. Groberg and White enter first, weapons up. They go straight in and then button-hook to the corners as Nguyen and Betts slide in just after them and fan across the room.

"Clear," says Nguyen. The word is barked out three more times, and then Milholland and I step inside.

There's a stale, musty odor, a little bit like dry rot. I see four bodies in here, each fully clothed, badly contorted, and completely withered. They're face down on the floor, and they look stiff.

"The console will be behind the counter," Milholland says. He steps around the security desk and pauses. "Oh, geez."

I follow him.

A fifth corpse is still "sitting" in its—no, her—chair. Her badge identifies her as Tynah Jones. The photo shows an attractive, thirtysomething black woman with a ready smile. In that picture she looks like someone I would have liked. Somebody with children, and prospects, whose triumphs and travails I could savor vicariously over beer and ribs at a July Fourth block party.

Her back and neck are arched so far that ligaments have certainly snapped, her mouth is locked open in a silent, skyward scream, and her hands are frozen clawing at the heavens. Supported by the chair in that pose, she tells us of her last moments. She died surprised, terrified, and in exquisite pain.

I look more closely. I've seen pictures of unwrapped mummies. Tynah died sometime this morning, but any coroner could be forgiven for guessing that her body was four thousand years old. Absent the current context, we would have to carbon-date her to determine the century of her demise.

"Oakley," says Milholland, pointing at her goggles. High-end consumer. Nice.

"Goggles on these, too," says White.

This close to this many runes, everybody would be wearing eye protection full-time. Nothing out of the ordinary here.

Milholland crouches next to the late Ms. Jones. "Her sidearm is holstered, snapped down tight."

"She's still in her chair, locked in a position of terrible agony. I think she was dead by the time she raised her arms, and was completely desiccated within seconds after that. No time to draw."

"I wonder if bullets would have helped."

The question Milholland doesn't ask, the one that nobody seems to ask anymore, is *How does that even happen?* Rune-tech appears to operate outside the purview of any physical law you care to name. Most people just assume anything's possible these days. If physics won't support it, some combination of runes certainly can. Rune researchers are pushing the frontiers back every day. Freeze-dry a human being in seconds? No problem.

"I'm getting motion," says Nguyen. He points down the corridor.

I look that direction and nothing registers. I charge my goggles with another drop of blood. There it is, faint, like it's extremely distant, right at the edge of our range. Big though. If it's four hundred meters away, that life sign is the size of an apartment bui—

"It's right on top of us!" Nguyen shouts, and then I see it too. We're not getting full range on our goggles. A no-see-um has turned the corner of the corridor and is bounding toward us, maybe twenty meters away.

The creature is about the size of a pit bull, but it looks more like a cockroach with squid tentacles. It is running, jumping, and flapping toward us. We've faced these before. This is a squidroach—our naming conventions for these things are aptly straightforward. Like most no-see-ums, squidroaches are nasty up close, but gunfire will take them down, easy. The trick, of course, is hitting them. Without rune goggles, these things are invisible. I slide my soulbone out of its sheath.

BOOM. The report of Nguyen's pig-iron rune rifle sounds far louder than usual. The squidroach doesn't slow. The magic bullet missed?

Groberg fires a three-round burst from his MP30, straight to the creature's center of mass. The squidroach stops cold and drops, shedding chunks of carapace on the way down.

"Groberg, White, cover that corridor with MP30s," I say. Then I turn to Nguyen. "What happened?"

"Misfire, maybe?" He ejects the magazine and peers into the breach; then he pops the tanglebone out of its slot in the etched ebony stock. The tanglebone is one-half of a sow femur, carved square and heavily inscribed. The rest of that bone was whittled and etched into fifty finely inscribed slivers, each of which sits inside a hollow-point round in one of Nguyen's magazines. He adjusts his goggles as he looks down at the magazine and the tanglebone. I'm wondering if he got a magazine matched to a different bone. Possible, but unlikely. He'd have to work hard to make that mistake.

"They match," he says. He slides a round from the top of the magazine. "Goggles show aura alignment, and the dyes are identical." He reattaches the magazine, chambers a round, steps up between Groberg and White, and aims at the dead squidroach.

"Emergency field test?"

"Do it," I say.

BOOM. Again, it's louder than it should be.

The pig iron, as it's affectionately called, should be silent, the weapon report muffled by rune magic, and the supersonic crack of the needle-cored 12 mm bullet completely absent, since the bullet teleports to its target.

It teleports, but it only materializes if the weapon is set to "instant." The pig iron lets you shoot first and ask questions later. Don't like the answer? The helmet, its ebony rune plate paired to the pig iron's stock, will hear you think the word *kill*, at which point the bullet appears inside the target and magically inflicts death.

It doesn't explode. It doesn't do bullet-things with hydrostatic shock. It just appears, and the target dies. Anything living, the pig iron can kill.

In this case, the bullet doesn't teleport. It spalls against the floor in front of the squidroach.

"Well, shit," says Nguyen. "If I'd known I wasn't firing magic bullets I would have taken an extra half-second to aim for the center of mass."

"I told you that thing made you sloppy," says Groberg.

"I don't remember you complaining when that vegan who jumped you suddenly dropped dead."

Having Nguyen on overwatch was a luxury.

"So, we've got an equipment problem?" asks White.

"More than one," I say. "Goggle range is too short. That no-see-um was on top of us before we saw it." Damn. What else might not be working?

"Betts, gimme a test fire."

"Yes, ma'am," she says, stepping forward.

BOOM.

Damn.

"Nguyen and Betts, switch to sidearms. Blood-mags."

"Yes, ma'am," says Nguyen. He's already got a magazine out and is running his tap ring along the groove. A little fresh blood in the tip of a hollow-point will let a conventional round injure several kinds of intangible things.

I start checking my gear. I'm getting auras from everything, including my soulbone. But Nguyen was getting auras from his ammo...

"I need to test this," I say, holding the soulbone in my right hand. It looks like a leather-wrapped, carved-ivory club, with a single stroke of rune exposed at the base of the haft. It's actually forty-six centimeters of densely inscribed human femur. My femur. The replacement in my left leg is a polyceramic composite with a titanium shaft.

Unlike most other rune-tech, I don't need to touch specific runes to get effects from the soulbone. It's tied to my soul. I just need to bleed into that single exposed stroke and then believe.

I charge it with a drop of blood and step to the security desk.

"Blade test, stand clear." I imagine a two-meter blade affixed to the end of the bone, and the air ripples as the blade appears. It weighs nothing, cuts anything, and is invisible to anybody without rune goggles.

I swing it down at the corner of the granite countertop. The blade embeds itself deeply. It's devastatingly sharp, but it should have gone all the way through with little or no effort on my part. I push down and complete the cut. The corner of the counter drops to the floor.

"Comm lieutenant's log," says Milholland formally. "Again, Captain Tamrielle Surinam is the first to inflict collateral damage."

"This is serious, and that hardly counts."

"It's probably a thousand-dollar countertop," he replies.

"At least your soulbone still works," says Betts, frowning down at her pistol.

"Not nearly as well as it should," I say, sheathing it and drawing my own pistol. "We've got some sort of dampening effect here, and we can't see far enough. This place could be crawling with void vermin or worse."

"Orders, ma'am?"

We are the canaries in the coal mine. We haven't really done our job until we've gone to the dark, gassy bottom of this pit. So to speak. And if there's an open breach here, we need to find it quickly.

"Call dispatch. Keep everybody out, and ring this place with a henge."

Milholland relays that to dispatch, who assures him that the rest of the teams were standing by for just such an order. The henge—rune-inscribed stone blocks around the perimeter, charged with blood—is going up before he signs off.

Time to move out.

We make our way through the security annex, Groberg taking point with his mundane, conventional, and 100-percent-effective MP30. There are more bodies. More instant mummification. Desiccated in agony, wearing clothing they'd not expected to die in and goggles that could not protect them, the corpses of Intermountain Power's Delta employees stare with empty eye sockets at walls, floors, empty space... and us. It's hard not to imagine them staring at us.

We exit the annex and fan out, making our way across the yard toward the power plant. The landscaping might have been nice once, but it's dead and brittle now—shrubs, trees, and grass all completely dried and crunchy. The larger trees dried so quickly and unnaturally that they've twisted and split, deep into the heartwood.

The drive path from the stockyard to the power plant is full of dead, magically freeze-dried cows. The rails alongside the path keep them propped upright, mostly, and they're all staring up at the sky, eternally lowing in terror.

"This is bad," says White from my left. "Forget what I said about milk runs. I'd rather have a new bastard breed of no-see-um on the loose. Something to shoot at."

"We got to shoot at something," says Groberg, further left. "Or at least I did."

"You know what I mean," says White, scanning and sweeping with his MP30 ready. "No way a squidroach or a crabboon did all this."

"So, the no-see-um is just an opportunist here?" asks Nguyen.

"That's my thinking," I say. "The energy released here opened a crack or two, and no-see-ums love the smell of living things."

"That bad boy had to be hungry," says Milholland. "Everything here is dead. No psychic energy at all. Nothing here to eat."

"Nothing but us," says White.

"Which explains why it was coming our way," says Groberg as we arrive at the east personnel entrance to plant B. He steps up to the large, metal door, charges his goggles, and stares.

"Bingo. Multiple signatures."

White is alongside him, also peering.

"Confirmed," he says. "I see six. If range is down to twenty meters, there might be a lot more in there."

"Where angels fear to tread," I begin, "does not mean we can't set up a proper killing field and let them come to us."

So we do. Eight meters back from the door we form a firing line. Nguyen would usually have overwatch with his pig iron, but that's useless, so he joins us on the line. Besides, no-see-ums, especially hungry ones, are too single-minded not to run straight at their food.

I'm the one getting the door. Hinges on the outside, it will swing outward. If things get tough, I can try to swing it shut again, but that shouldn't be a problem. I charge my soulbone and step to the far right of the firing line. The bone seems thirsty. Probably the dampening effect.

A little TK shouldn't tax it too much. I imagine my left hand on the doorknob. I can feel the doorknob in that imagined hand.

Turn and pull.

I release the imagined hand, consider firing up a protective effect from the soulbone, and decide against it.

"No protection, Cap'n?" asks Milholland.

"I don't trust it here. Not going to rely on it."

With my left hand I cross draw my pistol and thumb the hammer back.

The no-see-ums reach goggle range and begin bunching up as they converge on the door.

We've done this before, and we've drilled it hundreds of times with dozens of weapon combinations, with shielding and without. We open fire by the numbers: burst from Groberg, double tap from Milholland, burst from White, double taps from Nguyen and Betts. Back to the top of the order with another burst from Groberg.

I'm not in the rotation. I'm looking for strays, scanning our flanks, and getting ready to slam the door.

The no-see-ums are acting just like they usually do, like a mob of mindless alien menaces from a B-movie, rushing the door and shattering against the accurate hail of combustion-propelled metal.

Groberg ejects a magazine during Milholland's double tap. He slides a new one home during White's burst. By the time his turn comes up again he's ready to send another burst downrange, into that doorway. Next time around it's White reloading.

After thirty noisy seconds we run out of shimmering life signs. Plenty of ammo left.

Okay, we're good at this, but we're not going to gloat.

"Betts! Check it."

She steps wide of the line, clear of our killing field, and then advances. When she reaches the wall, she puts her face against it.

"Nothing."

Okay, so it's clear twenty meters in. That's a big building.

"Hold position," I say. "If there are more, they'll smell us soon, and this seems like a very nice place to meet them. If there aren't any more of them we lose a few minutes."

Ten minutes is twice as long as I've ever known a no-see-um to take under these sorts of circumstances. I plan to wait twenty.

Twelve minutes in, Milholland's comm sounds.

"AFT2 Lieutenant Milholland."

Silence while dispatch, or whomever dispatch has connected him to, speaks.

"You should have—" he responds, and then he stops, interrupted.

"Roger. I'll pass that along."

"What was that?" I ask

"NTSB is investigating a crash north of here. They want you there as soon as we're done here. Your new rune is on the ground at the crash site."

"I uploaded the rune already. Anybody can investigate."

"I was about to explain that to them, Captain. Apparently the NTSB is very agitated."

"Patch me through. If they're that agitated, they get to talk to your boss."

"MOVEMENT!" Betts shouts, backpedaling from the wall. "Big, kind of fast, moving like it can—"

Like it can run through walls. Some of the creatures from the void can do exactly that. Some can only do it in the void, like no-see-ums. Some are selectively tangible in our world, like the four-meter-tall hexatroll that passes through the wall where White was standing just a moment ago.

The wall shakes as the monster passes through it, and some of the siding pulls loose. That's not how it usually works, but there isn't time to puzzle over that.

"FALL BACK!" I shout.

A pig iron would be really nice right about now. One shot, one kill, guaranteed. Our hexatroll has six muscular limbs, each twice as wide as a man. It is covered in ragged, warty tumors and has a low-slung head that looks baboonish, with a dash of hippopotamus. If it's like other hexatrolls, conventional bullets won't connect, but its fists will surely connect with us. Selective tangibility—it only touches the living. People have theorized that the reason these things can stand on the ground is because on some level the Earth is alive. Maybe running a hexatroll off a cliff would work.

The blood-mags can touch it, but those are very small bullets. There is another option. My soulbone can also touch it, and I know the blade works here.

The team is falling back, but I'm charging. With a thought, the voidblade springs to shimmering life at the end of my precious femur, and the hexatroll stops in its tracks.

So this one's smart enough to know that I can hurt it.

I prefer dumb, but I'll settle for scared. I can easily hobble and slaughter this monster if it decides to turn and run.

It rears up on two limbs and draws the other four back, each of the four ending in a clenched fist the size of a refrigerator. So it's not scared enough to panic and run. It's the smart kind of scared.

That's exactly the kind of scared I am right now.

I can't afford to depend on my soulbone to deflect punches like wrecking balls. It's just me, my voidblade, and good shoes. I run forward, lean a little to my left, and then dart hard to the right as a pair of fists slam into the ground where the monster thought I'd be. I immediately jump back toward one of the fists, plant a foot on it, and take a running leap straight up.

The second pair of fists comes down next to the first, and now the hexa-troll's head is within reach. I swing, and the voidblade connects with the back of the skull and sticks.

I didn't swing hard enough.

The hexatroll howls in pain, but I don't think it's the mortal kind.

I dismiss the voidblade with a thought, freeing myself to drop to the—

—waiting, three-digit hand of the hexatroll. The hand closes around me with crushing force and—

BOOM

—flinches open—

BANG BANG

—and drops me.

An agonized howl comes from an enormous throat, and I hit the ground and try to roll clear.

BOOM

Something hits me, hard.

"Few of us consider the marginalization and disenfranchisement of moral vegetarians. Think about this, though: anyone who conscientiously objects to rune-tech will find it astoundingly difficult to live by their principles. Rune-tech is not only indistinguishable from magic, it is ubiquitous. It touches everything." –Saadiq Sebastian DuChamps, RUNExpo Chicago, 2055

I can hear the roar of the truck as we take off. I'm lying down, comfortable, and I feel great. Not a good sign.

My wrist buzzes. The medicine band wants me to talk to it.

"Captain Tamrielle Surinam, sanity is nothing more than consensus of perception, and I'm happy to be alive."

The band flashes green, and my vital signs scroll by. I check the time. It's been twenty-five minutes since that thing came through the wall at us.

"Happy to have you back, Captain." It's Milholland. "Tasty drugs today?"

I flip him off.

"Didn't you two have this conversation earlier?" asks Betts. She sounds concerned.

"Milholland is wondering how much I remember," I say, sitting up. I look out the armored window.

We're zipping over the magically verdant landscape of midwestern Utah. Are we being pulled out?

"I asked him to count my fingers," I continue, "and a hexatroll has six legs. I assume it landed on me?"

"Do you have any idea how hard it is to lift something that size when levers go right through it?"

"How'd you drop it on me in the first place?"

"That was me," says Betts. "I figured the pig iron might still have lethal effect. I was right." She smiles. "The teleportation word wasn't working at all, just like in the annex, but the kill word must have had a little juice. Either that or hexatrolls are severely allergic to slivers of bone moving at Mach 2."

"Well, thank you," I say. "How badly hurt was I?"

"Hey!" says Milholland. "You're skipping ahead, past the part where I bled myself onto a breaker bar so we'd have a lever that worked."

"Quick thinking, hero," I say with a wink. "Now, how crushed did I get before you figured that out?"

Milholland looks away.

"Pretty crushed," says Betts. "Groberg called the truck while everybody lifted, and we raced you to the perimeter, outside the dampening."

"You flatlined," says Millholland. "Thank God for magic medicine. They poured two units of bona fide human blood across that slab of petrified wood in the hospital truck before they got your heart started again."

That's just about dead. Not quite. Not far enough gone to be irretrievable, but far enough that everybody gets to wonder whether it's me who comes back or something void-born opting to move into an empty house.

Some people say that this is what happens when people see active runes with both eyes wide open, but I don't believe them. I don't recall having anything else living in my head eighteen months ago, but obviously nobody's going to take my word for it.

Hence the medicine band test. I've been required to wear this ever since my incident eighteen months ago. I don't mind it, even if Milholland sometimes harasses me about it.

"Well, do I check out?"

"I sure hope so. The three of us are on loan to the NTSB go team, and they'll be extra upset if our star rune-cracker turns out to be doppel-damned." Milholland hands me a set of goggles. "Yours broke. New briefing's in the HUD."

"Wait, how'd things wrap in Delta?"

"Haven't wrapped yet. Groberg took command. He brought in Bravo and Whiskey teams, and they're doing a visual sweep from the outside in, taking the shorter goggle range into account. Once it's clear to the walls of the plants, Groberg will take White, Nguyen, and a couple of Whiskey scabs in for a sweep of plants A and B. When they're done, we all compare notes. It looks like these events are related."

Groberg's plan sounds fine, and even if it didn't, I'm not in charge anymore. And if I were still in charge, he's the man on the ground, and I know better than to play rear echelon.

I put the goggles on and run a dry finger over the runes in the strip of bone around the rim. Standard issue. I toggle the HUD up. Also standard issue.

"Start with the telemetry, Captain," says Betts. "Don't start with the video from the cabin."

Milholland snorts. "Or get it over with."

I start with the telemetry. It's just numbers—airspeed, ground speed, altitude, coordinates, and assorted engine data—except someone has entered some helpful notes in the margins. Flight 4830 was under rune power at 12,100 meters directly above Delta, Utah, when the blood atop the rune block flashed into steam, the cabin pressure dropped explosively, and the craft began losing altitude. Emergency systems—conventional engines and batteries—kicked in automatically, spinning up turbines on the craft's stubby wings. The driver got no input from the human flight crew and began an emergency descent toward Nephi, Utah. Three minutes and twenty seconds later the telemetry ended. The note in the margin directs me to the page detailing the crash site.

The crash site is a debris field six kilometers long and two kilometers wide in the forest that used to be called the Little Sahara Recreation Area. Ironic for them to rename it, since the big Sahara is also forested these days.

Nothing larger than two meters square hit the ground, and the trees hide most of it from aerial views. Families camping reported the debris falling. Nobody on the ground was injured. But based on what we saw back in Delta, that's a lot more miraculous than it sounds.

The rune block, a standard one-point-two-meter cube of carved granite, landed intact, right in the center of a patch of dead forest. The patch, roughly 150 meters in diameter, with spurs running north and south, is completely dead. When seen from the air, it is shaped exactly like the dead patch surrounding Intermountain Power. Thankfully it's less than a tenth the size. If anybody had been within that rune when the block landed, we'd have some gruesome, instant-mummy casualties.

I think. I'm treating this like physics. It's magic. Something completely different might have happened.

Still, based on everything I know, a vehicle rune block shouldn't be able to throw off a killing effect, especially not if it's dry and cut loose from its housing.

Lots of questions. I move on to the cabin video.

It looks like the interior of any modern aircraft. It's streamlined, but it's not cramped, not like the airplanes of yore. Large seats, wide aisles, people sitting and reading, talking, eating. The flight has more older people in it than usual, but this flight is going from Vegas to—

I blink, and I miss it. One second everything's normal. The next second the cabin is a ragged mess, the back of the craft open to the cold, high-altitude sky. It happened as fast as a gunshot. I scroll back and frame advance it from the beginning of the event.

It takes place in two frames.

In the first frame the forward third of the cabin is a visual smear, everything blurred by motion, appearing to streak to the back of the craft. In the second frame the cabin is empty of people, and most of the other contents are gone. Fittings for the seats jut from the floor, bolts shorn off. The seats are nowhere to be seen.

There is no blood, no gore, no clothing—no indication at all that anyone was here just a sixtieth of a second ago.

The rest of the frames show nothing but the ragged insides of an empty runecraft as it tumbles and then recovers. Emergency masks deploy from the ceiling and whip around in the wind for a hundred seconds or so. I keep waiting for somebody to appear in the frame and grab a mask, but there's no one.

The video ends twenty-six seconds before the telemetry does, probably because that was the end of the last thirty-second burst uploaded by the flight data recovery system before the craft exploded.

I don't know why these things aren't just always transmitting in real time. Then again, I don't know why it took us a hundred years to get black boxes to scream everything they knew while their damaged vehicle was still in the air. I guess implementation always runs way behind technology.

There's more video. An exterior camera shows the back of the craft exploding in a cloud of steam and debris. I assume the steam is what remains of the passengers and crew.

"Sobering, isn't it?" asks Milholland. "One moment you're skipping through the top of the troposphere taking your gambling winnings with you to Canada. The next, you're vapor."

The engine changes pitch, and I realize we're on the ground. If we'd been on rune power I probably wouldn't have noticed.

"We have arrived at picnic ground Lebanon, the field HQ for the NTSB go team, 420 meters northeast of the target debris," says the driver.

Milholland slides the door open.

"Weapons ready," I say.

"Weapons ready," Milholland and Betts reply in unison.

Time for an on-your-toes talk.

"A rune block fell from the sky in these woods and somehow painted a previously unknown rune out of desiccation and death. The last time we saw something like this, our equipment malfunctioned and I almost got killed by an eleven-ton invader from another plane of existence."

"Yes, you did, ma'am," says Milholland. "We're not the first ones here, though. The NTSB—"

"Doesn't know Jill-damned-Jack shit about securing a site. Maybe they've got SWAT here. Maybe not. Weapons ready."

"Weapons ready, ma'am," Milholland and Betts reply in unison.

We debark, sweep the truck's perimeter, and then advance on the go team's tent. I draw my soulbone and hit it with my tap ring, hard. Power flows around and through me. I'm done messing around: weapons hot, shields up, eyes wide open. My soulbone and I are hot-blooded. There is a faint ache in my chest, sympathy pains as my living blood is transduced. Another reason I don't just swing this thing around all the time.

"That femoral bazooka is making the locals twitchy, Captain," says Milholland.

"Power like this should make people twitchy."

The NTSB in their neon-green vests and old-school eye patches are wide-one-eyed, staring out from under their hard hats. Juiced up like this, I can taste a mixture of fear, amazement, and respect wafting off of them. They can see the power emanating from me and the soulbone. Also, my team and I are surrounded by a shimmering dome. The NTSB hard hats will protect against a dropped hammer. My dome will protect against a meteor strike.

"Captain Surinam?" asks a hard-hatted black man in a vest. He steps toward us but stops well clear of our shield. "Barry Jensen, NTSB go team lead. Is, umm... is there a problem?"

With soulbone-enhanced sight I scan the NTSB crew. Nobody has no-see-ums affixed to their heads. There is rune magic present, but it's the usual prepackaged stuff, locked away in no-user-serviceable-parts-inside housings. Nothing "naked" like the things my team carries. With a thought I expand the dome to cover the entire HQ. Someone gasps in surprise.

"Not in here there's not," I say with a smile. "Sorry for the rude approach. Rough morning."

Barry steps forward and offers me a handshake, but then realizes my right hand has a magical weapon in it. He withdraws his hand.

"Err... Thank you for coming."

Barry sounds nervous and genuinely gracious. I'm going to assume that the NTSB official who pulled strings to reassign us midsortie was somebody else. Probably somebody in an office, wearing a necktie. Somebody rear echelon.

"Happy to help. Now, have you done a sweep?"

"Drones are doing passes with high-res radar right now. About 60 percent of the debris is accounted for." He points in the direction of the dead trees. "Four of my guys walked into the woods, checked the block, and threw a cover over it. We'd already figured out something was weird with the dead trees, so we backed off and waited for help."

"Very good. I'm taking command of this operation now, unless you have a very convincing objection."

"Um, sure."

"Thank you. Keep your people back until I say otherwise, and keep telemetry up with your home office. Their finger on your pulse at all times."

"Will do, ma'am."

I turn to Milholland and White. "Charge your goggles up hot. Life, magic, EM—scan for everything."

"On it already, Captain," says Milholland. I'm pleased with his initiative.

"Captain, did something at the power plant cause this crash?" Jensen asks.

"Maybe." I shrug. "Could something in that craft have caused what happened at the power plant?"

He looks surprised at the question.

"Seriously?"

"Mister Jensen, I've never seen anything like this, but I play with unnatural, inexplicable magic every day. Just because I've never seen a thing doesn't mean it can't happen."

"Okay," he says, "but the rune blocks in Delta are huge, use a slaughterhouse full of blood, and deliver power all over the southwestern United States. The block that landed in the woods uses less than a liter a month."

He's got a point.

"You're right. In terms of raw potential for magical power, the banks in Delta win. A team of runewrights will be examining them shortly. If those banks were altered or damaged in a way that caused this crash, we'll know about it."

He points down at the soulbone in my right hand.

"I haven't ever seen one of those in person. Aren't they superrestricted?"

"They are." I shrug. "They're still the best tool for some kinds of jobs."

"Do you worry that somebody else might get ahold of it, and, you know..."

"Do what, exactly? Only I can use it. Also, I wear a pistol against that sort of contingency." I nod in the direction of Betts and Milholland and lower my voice. "Of course, my team would probably mangle the offender before my weapon cleared the holster."

Betts steps closer to me and flashes Jensen a smile. Then she turns to me.

"These woods are gorgeous, Captain. Also, they're clean all the way to the dead parts. We'll need to get closer to see more."

"Let's move out." I pull an earbud from my pocket and hand it to Jensen. "You and your people stay here. If something happens here, call for us. If something happens to us out there in the woods, you'll hear about it. Run. If we tell you not to run, we might be lying. Run anyway."

He holds the earbud as if it were a live scorpion.

"It goes in your ear."

"Right." And it does. Good man.

Betts, Milholland, and I move southwest, with Betts on point. I reconfigure the soulbone's protection for three individuals, top it off from the tap ring, and add a tap to my goggles for redundantly enhanced sight.

The tree line at the edge of the picnic area is healthy enough, but we don't have to go very far in before we start seeing brittle yellow where lush greens should be.

"I'm getting life signs from the far side," says Milholland. "Ordinary forest stuff. Bugs, birds, bunnies. Nothing showing up inside the dead patch."

"Confirmed," says Betts. "No void signs. We're clear."

"Confirmed," I add. "Stay sharp."

We advance until we reach the edge of the dead patch. The aspens look like the maples in Delta did—the bark has blistered and split, and cracks are visible deep into the heartwood. The leaves are yellow and dead but have not dropped.

Betts pauses at the edge.

"In?" she asks.

"In."

As she steps into the dead patch I feel a heavy strain on the shield around Betts. It drops before I've got my mouth open to warn her.

Betts stops and looks around.

"Did you do that, Captain?"

"No, but I felt it happen. Get back out here."

Betts steps back out of the dead zone.

"The way it felt, I thought you were under attack. Rune magic is definitely dampened inside the dead patch," I say.

"Yup," says Milholland. "That's why we trucked your crush-mangled body to the perimeter in Delta, instead of bringing an ambulance in."

"Dampened, and if the effect being dampened is energetic enough, it just doesn't work. Like the teleportation in the pig irons. Smaller stuff seems to work okay. My voidblade worked in Delta, but not as well as it usually does."

I point into the dead patch.

"This rune is smaller, a lot smaller."

"No such thing as crop circles, Captain," says Milholland. "We don't know that the dead patch is the source of the effect."

"Humor me. My shield is a pretty big effect, and it went down fast, but not instantaneously. I could test my voidblade in there and see if it's sharper here than in Delta."

"The engine block is a lot smaller than the rune plates in Delta. You're closer to it. Too many variables to prove anything."

Milholland is right, but I'm still going to take a swing at a tree.

We walk in, and again there is a split second of strain before the shield drops. The life signs on the other side of the patch vanish as our goggle range is reduced. The dead aspens are eerie. The deep splits and twisting make the trees look agonized. Time to add insult to injury.

I select a small tree and imagine the blade. No problem summoning it. I swing at the tree.

The blade sticks three-quarters of the way through. I don't know the relative densities of desiccated aspen and granite countertops, and there are so many other variables at play here it wouldn't matter if I did.

We try, we really do try, to treat rune magic like science, but it's not. I dismiss the blade.

"On to the rune block, then."

The engine block is covered in a blue tarp, edges staked to the ground. I pull half of the stakes out and throw the tarp back.

Until now I haven't really looked at any rune-tech today. I work everything by touch. But now? Even unpowered, outside the housing of control runes and swabs, this engine block looks powerful. Long words are formed in multiple directions by pulsatiles, ductiles, and motiles, with a scattering of rhotiles and lesser sigils. To someone not versed in rune-tech, the best metaphor is a completed crossword puzzle, in which the words not only interlock but also sound out a poem. And the little black squares create larger letters, larger words, which also interlock. And as cool as that crossword puzzle would be, a rune block is cooler.

This engine block is art, and as both a practitioner and an aficionado I find it difficult to look away.

Very difficult. The runes seem to shimmer, as if from heat. At first I wonder whether the block could be getting enough sunlight for that to happen, but the longer I look at the block the more the runes move. Dancing. Writhing. I haven't seen an effect like this since—

"SHIT!" I hit the panic button on my goggles and my left eyepiece goes... cloudy. The dancing and writhing doesn't quite disappear.

"Oh, goddammit, is that what I—" Milholland begins.

I cut him off by shoving him into Betts, throwing all 130 pounds of myself into the task of taking their heads to the ground.

"Stupid stupid stupid!" I've been stupid.

The goggle function that obscures runes from the left eye is powered by a tiny battery driving power to a tiny processor that happens to be mounted on a tiny sliver of rune-inscribed petrified wood: high-speed optical processing married to a little bit of rune magic.

Rune magic which is being dampened. Dampened just enough that I didn't notice. I'm so angry with myself right now I could kill something.

My cognitive training, all that therapy, it kicks in hard and suggests that the desire to kill is not a good sign and should be dialed back.

"I can still see them!" says Betts. "WITH MY EYES CLOSED!"

So can I. Just like last time, except last time I had also been shot in the face by militant vegans on a weather-control platform in the Gulf of Mexico. I guess this time around I'll have more time to think about the fact that I can't get these out of my head.

My wristband buzzes. It senses something wrong and wants me to check in.

"Captain Tamrielle Surinam. Sanity is fuck all. Hit me with drugs before I kill somebody."

The bracelet flashes red and buzzes. Scrolling text appears.

HEMISPHERE BREACH DETECTED. ADMINISTERING TREATMENT.

It's always administering treatment to me to some degree. Now it's flooding my system with some very individually tailored antipsychotics. My mouth begins to taste like garlic and gunpowder, and my desire to open my wrists for making that stupid rookie mistake becomes more of a distant longing to bang my head against the wall until I'm smarter.

Betts and Milholland have never been exposed to runes the way I have. They've never had arcane energies writing permanent damage across their brains. They don't wear med bracelets. Not yet. Once we get out of this, I can rib Milholland about tasty drugs instead of the other way around.

I don't have the tools or the training to fine-tune their neurochemistry. I'm going to need to hit them with a broad-spectrum before we end up at each other's throats. I slip the hypo out of the med kit at my belt.

Milholland sounds worse than Betts does. I press the hypo against his neck with a pop and a hiss.

"Ohhhh...," he says.

That's the noise he's supposed to make. It's the sound of relief, when depression, anguish, fear, and paranoia are washed away on a tide of chemical bliss. It was probably a bigger dose of bliss than he needed, though. The runes we're sitting next to aren't currently powered, and this dead patch we're in should be dampening them, too.

Shouldn't it? Regardless, we need medication. And eventually therapy.

I recharge my hypo and turn to Betts. She's already on her knees, head arched back. Well, that exposes her throat. I reach forward to—

She grabs my wrist.

"Not yet. Captain, look *up*."

Her eyes are wide, staring into the sky. A vein throbs at her temple. I don't know what she thinks she sees up there, and I'm not sure I should—

"LOOK UP," she says, tears welling up in her eyes. "I need to know if you see it too. Before the drugs kick in."

I look up.

When this happened last time, I was indoors, surrounded by rack-mounted tablets of engraved granite. Everywhere I looked there were runes, and I hallucinated all kinds of movement, sigils slipping their stony bonds and spinning long, powerful sentences around the room. I didn't see anything beyond that generator room, but within it I was awash in mirage and overwhelmed by alternating waves of panic, depression, euphoria, and paranoia.

This exposure is tame by comparison, and I'm already medicated. I'm not experiencing raw, irrational emotion. I'm afraid, but it's justified.

So what I'm seeing in the sky is not a hallucination.

There is a ring of runes high, high up to the southwest. How high are clouds? Higher than that. Too high for human depth perception to place, but it feels to me like these are at least a hundred kilometers above the ground, above a patch of ground half again that far away. And it feels like they're moving, sliding southwest across the sky. Feels? Maybe I *am* hallucinating. Still, if I've got the distance right, that ring is twenty kilometers in diameter, ringed in runes five to ten kilometers high.

The rune ring is a ductile series in transit modality with location information I've never seen before. If I'm reading it correctly, it is a city-sized doorway to somewhere humans have never traveled.

AFTT deploys with extreme prejudice for breaches less than a thousandth that size...

"Do you see it?" Betts asks.

"Doorway in the sky. Big. Persistent. Unknown destination."

"Not that. What's reaching through it."

I shiver. I don't see anything coming through it. Do I? Maybe a glimmer? I concentrate. Nothing.

"What do you see, Betts?"

"It keeps shifting, like it doesn't want me to see it. And..." She gasps and lowers his eyes. "And I *don't* want to see it."

I'm staring at the sky and can't see what she saw. I look down and meet her gaze.

"Describe something."

She closes her eyes.

"It hurts to think about."

She still has a grip on my right hand. I drop the hypo into my left hand.

"No pain, no gain," I say, hoping to appeal to that brass-uterus streak she and I share. "You do difficult, painful things all the time."

She shudders and sobs.

With my left hand I jab the hypo against the back of her hand. Her eyes fly open, glaring at my empty right hand. Gotcha.

"Take another breath and try again," I say. "But let go of me. I need to pull the tarp back over the block." She puts her head in her hands and sobs some more.

I stand and face the rune block. I'm not scared of you. I put my hand over my left eyepiece and use my other hand to pull the tarp back over the block.

"Long and tapering. Carapace covered, segmented, like an earwig without the legs. Maybe rounder than that. And at the end it looked more like the business end of a star-nosed mole. Except huge. The size of a football stadium."

"That's pretty good, Betts."

"It's gone now."

"So either it's a hallucination or there's something in the antipsychotics that prevents us from seeing it."

"Grohhh," moans Milholland, still face down.

"What?"

"Groberg. His goggles... he's in the plant in Delta."

Oh no.

Groberg, White, and Nguyen are walking into the same trap we did, their goggles working just well enough to fool them into thinking they're safe.

"Up! We're moving out!" I slap Betts on the bum and tug on Milholland's shoulder. They're both lethargic, swimming in a much heavier cocktail than I am.

"LET'S GO!" I bark. They both stagger to their feet. I tap my earpiece.

"Dispatch, this is Captain Tamrielle Surinam, AFTT. Betts, Milholland, and I have been exposed, hemisphere breach."

"Understood. Telemetry places you three hundred meters from your truck. We are detaching a medical team from Delta base."

"Negative, dispatch. Get to Groberg. The goggles aren't working right. If teams are already in the plant there in Delta, they'll need your help more than we do."

"Affirmative. Captain, your driver will bring you back to Delta. Hang in there."

"Got it."

I wonder how much of this Jensen heard.

"Jensen, are you there?" I ask.

"Not anymore, ma'am."

Well, good. He heard the whole thing, and he can follow instructions.

"Outstanding. We've covered the rune block and swept the area. My team is leaving, but we are dangerously unstable. Keep your distance until we're gone."

"Umm, yeah. No problem." His voice is cracking a bit. "What should we do once you've left?"

"There's a rune-dampening effect surrounding the block. Wear patches, and don't depend on runic tools until you've gotten the block out of that dead zone. After that point I think your usual recovery practices will work fine."

"Thanks." Pause. "You actually sound pretty stable, Captain Surinam."

I could tell him this was a very mild exposure, that I came into it premedicated, and I've got months of cognitive behavioral therapy and a custom drug package keeping me sane. I could tell him that I feel pretty stable, with absolutely no urges to paint the landscape with human blood.

I could, in short, lower his guard.

"STAY AWAY FROM US, JENSEN."

Milholland and Betts are stumbling as we head back to the truck. At least they're moving under their own power. I had to be carried off that weather-control platform strapped to a gurney, paralyzed by drugs, and staring up into space. Beyond space, even. It seemed deeper then.

I check the sky. The runes are still there, but I can't see anything protruding through them. Which is good, because if something big enough to require that door is actually dangling through our airspace...

If something invisible and selectively tangible was in the path of an aircraft...

The cabin video makes sudden and terrible sense. Everything flesh and blood slams into a wall, while everything else keeps moving at what, two or three hundred meters per second? A mass of flesh, blood, bone, and hair hits the back of the craft like a giant, sodden bullet, blasting through it explosively.

We arrive at the truck, and I help Milholland and Betts buckle in before harnessing myself. I imagine my body suddenly tearing through the straps and blowing out the back of the truck in a cloud of pulp.

"Captain, I have medical override orders to return you and Lieutenants Betts and Milholland to Delta."

"Understood, driver." I toggle my earpiece. "Hey, Jensen, are you still there?"

"Yup. Just waiting for you to get further away."

"Have you found any trace of the human remains?"

"No, but that's probably because they're impossible to distinguish from the ground, not from the altitude the drones are at now. And if that video is any indication, none of the individual remains are going to be very large."

"Humor me for a moment. If a human body slammed into a wall at aircraft speed, how much of it would stick?"

"That depends on the materials of the wall. Of course, most hydrophobic materials ablate or denature under those sorts of conditions, so no matter what your hypothetical wall is made of, there should be quite a bit of adhesion."

"So, a lot of it would stick."

"Captain, are you suggesting that there might be some sort of giant, invisible void wall hanging in our flight lanes?"

"A selectively tangible obstacle would explain the cabin video."

"But not the subsequent crash. The driver had the craft under control on emergency systems." A pause, and then a sigh. "But if your obstacle is a temperamental monster that holds grudges, it might have chased the craft afterward and swatted it to the ground." Another pause. "Captain, I'm going to have the drones start sweeping the sky for remains. The adhesion layer is going to be thin and might not have much of a radar signature at all, but if the passengers hit something up there, we'll find them."

Good man. Great man, now that he's back in his element.

"Let me know what the drones find, Jensen." Oh, hang on. I'm on a medical suspension at the moment. How did *that* slip me? "And tell your superiors, too. And the FAA. Anybody who will listen."

Anybody who still has authority to do something about it.

"Will do, Captain Surinam. I hope you feel better."

"Thanks. Surinam out."

Out is probably a good plan. My driver neither needs nor will accept instructions from me, so I might as well relax the rest of the way into these drugs and enjoy a nap.

"Rune-tech studies are similar to other disciplines in at least one way: those with the greatest investment of time in the subject matter are the most likely to let extreme subjectivity color their studies. The difference is that when rune-tech is deeply understood, this extreme subjectivity tends to manifest as psychosis rather than obstinacy, and the phrase 'color their studies' becomes rather unfortunately apt." –Saadiq Sebastian DuChamps, RUNExpo Chicago, 2055

"Captain Surinam, please wake up."

That sounds like my driver. Am I still in the truck? I could open my eyes, but it feels very good to keep them closed. Seen too much already today. The memory of that rune block shimmers in my dream sight, as if it's still right in front of me.

"Captain Surinam?"

I'll concentrate on what I'm hearing. Engines are idling, so we must be on the ground. I wonder where we are. I have this uneasy feeling that I'm waiting for medical, and they're going to be here any moment to slap restraints on me and—

"Captain Surinam, this is an emergency. Wake up."

Of course it's an emergency. The three of us need medical attention.

I smell smoke. It's kind of pleasant, really. Not the oily plastic stench of an industrial fire. It's like a campfire, only—

I smell *smoke*. There should not be smoke. I snap awake and look around.

Betts and Milholland are strapped in and asleep. The truck has landed, and a door has been popped ajar. The driver is more clever than I give him credit for, letting some of that smoke in.

Looking through the armored glass, I can see lots of smoke, blowing low, streaming past us as if originating from low flames. Grass fire.

That makes sense. If the dead patch was creating a rune-dampening effect, a fire should disrupt the patch. We would have had to do this to bring the power plant back online, but until that project begins, it'll be helpful just to have all our gear working up to spec.

Except I'm not going to be working. I close my eyes again, and the rune block is there waiting for me behind my eyelids. Only instead of engine runes, it's got a ring of transit-series ductiles on it, with a gateway to distant stars in the center of the ring.

I'm going to need therapy again. And I'm not going to get any more sleep in here.

"I'm awake now, driver."

"Connecting you with dispatch, Captain."

Dispatch? What is going on?

"Captain Surinam, are you fit for duty?"

"Are you kidding me? I'm drugged, I just woke up, and when I close my eyes I see runes! Live ones, wriggling across my eyelids."

"Captain Surinam, you were right. Groberg, Nguyen, and White were exposed, along with members of Whiskey and Bravo teams. Medical deployed to assist, and then we lost contact with them, and with everyone else."

"Everyone?" I slide the door open and step out of the truck. The grass here is still lush, but I can see a fire line a hundred meters or so away. "What happ—"

"Captain, stay in your vehicle!"

There's a body in the grass. Female. A henge tech. Not desiccated. Her eyes are wide open and sightless. She looks like she is about to say something to me. Forever about to say something, but never, forever-never, actually speaking. There are no obvious wounds on her body, and she looks almost relaxed.

A pig iron kills this way.

"Captain!"

The truck is between me and the power plant. Screening me. Keeping me hidden and saving my life while my brain tries to catch up.

I dive back into the truck.

"I'm back in the truck," I growl. "If you suspect that Nguyen has gone psychotic and has murdered fifty people with his pig iron, you should have considered telling me that first."

"Captain, you have new orders. Neutralize the breached personnel in that facility. Use of lethal force is authorized."

I feel a rush of anger, a hot flash behind my eyes, a tingling in my fingers. But am I angry at dispatch, or at my teammates? Or have the drugs worn off a bit, allowing me a taste of that sweet, murderous rage?

Does it matter? I try to keep the anger out of my voice.

"I'm leaving Milholland and Betts strapped in. They're unfit. And unconscious."

"The closest qualified support is forty-four minutes out. Can you do this by yourself?"

"I'm not doing it by myself." I slide my soulbone out of its sheath, give it a drip from the tap ring, and then cast my sight as far as fresh, hot blood will let me reach. There are three human auras inside plant A, and the plant itself is radiating. They've gotten it running again, though I can't imagine why they'd bother. Still, I know where they are, and now that I know how to look for it, I can tell that the dampening effect is gone.

Only three auras, though. Not a good sign.

"What's your plan, Captain?"

Another flash of hot anger. I indulge myself and lash out a bit.

"Dispatch, you just gave me orders to neutralize—and authorization to kill—my friends. The first thing I'm going to do is stop talking to you in case they're listening in. Surinam out."

White and his flickering fingers are hot shit with comm tech, but I don't know where his limits are, so I'm not taking any chances. Nguyen is murder incarnate with a pig iron, and there's a corpse outside the truck telling me that whatever his limits might be, I'm now within them.

"Driver, has dispatch lifted the medical override?" I ask as I recline Milholland's seat and check his harness.

"Override has been lifted, Captain. Orders?"

"Gimme a standard combat insertion, setting down in the courtyard in front of plant A." I recline Betts and make sure she, too, is secure.

"Captain, you do not have a full fire team. A modified—"

"Driver, the enemy does not know I do not have a full fire team. Standard combat insertion on rune power." I prepare a countdown timer in my HUD. "Begin run in thirty seconds. Fly like you really, really mean business. Now open the door for me, because you are the diversion."

Tap ring to the soulbone for more blood. I imagine myself, seen from a distance. Then I imagine myself unseen, and I fix that picture in my mind. I can feel myself vanish. This isn't the invisibility of a no-see-um. This is deliberate, rune-powered, I-don't-want-you-to-see-me invisibility. My friends with their goggles won't see me coming.

The timer on my HUD counts the last ten seconds away, and I roll out of the truck.

With just a whisper of displaced air, the driver takes the truck up three meters and then zips off. He's flying like he was meant to, blood on stone making three tons of vehicle dance against the sky like three grams of hummingbird.

I take a deep breath and imagine the path I will take, a path with lots more "up" in it. I'm going ballistic, like an artillery round, like John Carter of Mars, or maybe the original Spiegel brothers' Superman. A single bound, and I don't even have to jump.

The ground drops away below me as I shoot skyward, launched in excess of a thousand meters per second, an invisible bubble of magic preventing my instant death from acceleration. I feel no wind, no push, and God help me, I feel no fear. Just anger, now tinged with chest pain, as more of my blood dies to fuel hot magic. If it didn't feel like the onset of a heart attack and terrify everyone around me, I'd travel like this all the time.

Okay, that's not true. I don't care who I scare, but these chest pains, they're really goddamn annoying.

I approach apogee. Gravity finally consumes the last of my upward velocity and begins to draw me back down to Earth, but there is no physical sensation. That would be exhilarating, but not feeling it is a small price to pay for not being instantly crushed on this trip.

My HUD says that the driver is taking small-arms fire. Groberg is doing a fine job spalling conventional rounds against the armored hull of the truck. Just like he's supposed to. Keep the fire team in that truck heads-down. I reach deep for vision and track the rounds back to an aura on the lower-most roof of plant A. It's a good position. Groberg has a building behind him, an open field of fire in front of him, and a door through which he can fall back.

He does not have cover from above.

My HUD says I'm a thousand meters above him, descending at sixty-two meters per second, terminal velocity for a magically shielded human. Thirty-two seconds until touchdown.

I need to be close for this to work. Tom Petty had it right; the waiting is the hardest part. I know Groberg can't see me if he looks up, but I still worry about him looking up and drawing a bead on me. I'm not careless enough to actually envision that, to trace a rune word in my mind's eye that might empower him to see me, but I do consid—

Groberg looks up, right at me, and swings his MP4 up, drawing that bead.

How in the hell did he—

A pulse in my soulbone tells me that at least one round has slammed into my shield. I've seen Groberg take down faster targets from a greater distance. He is a wizard with that MP4. His weapon doesn't actually pose a threat, but Groberg will be calling in my position to Nguyen.

I land on the roof with a silent slam, eighty gees of deceleration signaled by no more noise than a falling leaf. I'm not crouching to absorb impact. I'm crouching because I want to keep my head down.

Groberg falls back into that doorway, but he's not getting away. I leap after him and envision a very special hook at the end of my soulbone. His aura resolves into sharp detail, its twists and folds revealing his vitals to me as clearly as if he wore a med bracelet and let me read it. But it is more than just visible to me. It is tangible.

My leap takes me past him faster than he can react, and the shimmering hook at the end of my soulbone passes through his clothing and flesh with no effect.

His soul, however, is snagged and ripped free from his body.

Yeah, this thing I can do scares people a lot more than the voidblade does. Hack 'em to bits and you make the newsfeeds. Painlessly slide their souls from their bodies and Congress starts passing laws.

He drops. He's clinically dead right now, but I can bring him back. If I want to. I'm not sure I do. That mustache makes him look like a real asshole sometimes. Whatever. I've got a couple of minutes to decide. I look for the other auras. Maybe I can finish this up with three souls on a stick, cuff the corpses, stuff their quintessentials back inside, and be home in time for that one show with the sexy mummies.

I see them, two and a half stories below me, deep inside the plant. They're out of reach, but I can see that one of them is fading.

Somebody is dying.

I check my rune shield. It's still up, and so is my cloak. I don't know how Groberg saw me, but hopefully—

There is a pulse of magic, and then something is inside my chest. It startles me, and I release my grip on my shield, my strength, and my soul hook all at once. I feel Groberg slip away from me.

Okay, now he's really dead. Glad I didn't have to decide.

Now, this thing inside my chest... no, not inside. Inside out. There, and not there. Without my soulbone I doubt I'd be able to feel it at all, but there is something affixed to me, connected to me but not yet fully material.

Well, damn.

"Surprise, Captain." Nguyen's voice comes over a loudspeaker system. "You didn't think I could see you? Captain, I can see everything now. *Everything.*"

The pig-iron bullet has its own aura. I can feel the runes on the sliver of bone that has not yet materialized in my chest. They are a killing word, a word that will be "spoken" by my own blood spilling into that rune the moment the round materializes.

I am a dead woman walking.

Except Nguyen hasn't killed me yet. Maybe I can talk my way out of this. Sweet-talk him, sane-talk him, do that negotiator thing, except Groberg was our guy for that. But I've got to give it a shot, so I turn on my headset and try for friendly.

"Fuck, Nguyen. You shot me. What'd you do that for?"

Pretty good, pretty good.

"Come down here. Bring Groberg."

"Groberg's dead. Sorry."

"He knew he was going to die. We all are, unless we can bring it back, so you bring him to me, because I need his blood. We all need it. Blood to power!"

Ngyuen has lost it, clearly. One common symptom of hemisphere breach is a passion for messy murder. Killing and spilling. I'm feeling a little bit of that myself, but at least I've got it in check.

"I'm on my way."

"Don't you swing that magic sword at me. If I fall, even if I just fall asleep, you will die instantly."

I carry Groberg across a catwalk and down a flight of metal stairs into the belly of the power plant. Heavy steel frames support vertical slabs of inscribed stone, their rows arranged like magnetic field lines, a cardioid pattern whose sweeping strokes are themselves a ductile rune, a rune which draws my eye from the distant bank of turbines to a central altar. There is a blur to all the runes, because only my right eye can see them completely.

My goggles are working correctly now, protecting my brain from the power ripping through this room.

Nguyen stands next to that altar, his naked face distorted by raw emotion.

Naked face. He's not wearing his goggles. He's drinking this all in, then.

Lieutenant White hangs upside down over the altar, his boots tied together and strung over a hook typically used for hanging cattle. His pale arms hang down, spread wide, wrists slit in a pair of long strokes that run clear up to his elbows. He is bleeding to death onto a rune-bank usually powered by common cattle.

The bank is running very hot, all the turbines are spinning, and the direct-effect runes are pouring their magic into the earth and the sky. The fire out there might sweep across the fields, but this power could restore the grass by nightfall. Human blood is far more potent than animal blood, but even so, the blood of one man shouldn't be enough to turn all these turbines like

—

There is a pile of corpses next to the altar. I can see the insignia for Whiskey and Bravo teams on a few shoulders. Nguyen has been busy.

"God, Nguyen, what are you doing?"

"Restoring power. Trying to bring it back. We have to bring it back, Captain."

"Lieutenant, this is not how we are supposed to—"

"Seal the breach? Oh yes we are! And what a breach! A few lambs for the sake of the flock, lambs to the slaughter, little lambs eat ivy! We have to bring it back! And you, you and your bloody bone must be here, here where it started. Here where the power runs hot!"

I can still feel that sliver of instant death waiting to manifest in my heart, tied to my aura. It pulses as if alive, with an aura of its own, drawing life into itself along a faint tendril, a magical umbilical connecting it to the ebony plate in Nguyen's helmet that's pressed against the skin of his forehead.

That aura is spun from twisting runes, runes I can read as I follow the connection from Nguyen's soul to mine. He's right. If I break that link, break the rune plate in his helmet, do anything to sever his connection to the bullet bound to my soul, it will finish its interplanar journey and end me.

But he hasn't killed me yet. Why not? I'm standing next to his pile of corpses... did they all wait like this?

I killed Groberg. Dammit, that was me who did that. He was my friend. I could have clubbed him, could have swept his feet...

I have to stop this. Too much killing.

"White is dying, Nguyen. The truck is right outside. We can still save him, but you have to let me go."

"Save? SAVE? Nothing is saved without every drop! And everything is lost without you!"

"Then why do you have a bullet in my chest, Nguyen?"

"You're fast. Too fast. Had to explain. Had to make you see. Captain, look up and see!"

I glance up. The ceiling is three stories above me, and quite opaque.

A call buzzes in my ear. Oh, that's right. I reactivated my comm. I answer the call while still obediently staring at the girders and struts of the ceiling.

"Surinam."

"Captain Surinam! It's Barry Jensen, NTSB! We scrambled more drones and found that patch of remains. It's thin, but it's there, right where you said it might be—twelve thousand meters up, moving south-southwest, and making good time. It's not over Utah anymore."

"Do you see it, Captain?" asks Nguyen insistently.

"No, and I'm taking a call. This is important!" Dammit, this is why I have a communications officer. If Milholland were here I wouldn't be trying to have two conversations at—

My head snaps back as Nguyen rips my helmet and goggles from my head.

There's no time to close my eyes. By the time that thought crosses my mind, there's no point. It's too late. The sweeping lines suggested by the rune plates here in plant A are now flowing with writhing runes, sigils sliding over and under one another, shifting meaning as the shifting script cycles through the syntax of sucking power from human blood. And I can read it all.

I'm dizzy, overcome by vertigo, and it feels like my feet are a thousand feet away. I remember this sensation, remember the sundering of all barriers in my mind. The doors, the windows, and some of the walls of the house in my head have been thrown open or torn down, and all four seasons are ripping through at once. I can taste autumn, smell spring, touch winter, and hear summer.

I look up. Up and south.

The ceiling is still there, but I can see through it. I can see through everything, once I set my mind to seeing. The walls vanish from before me. That ring of runes we saw from the crash site is lower in the sky and more distant, closer to the horizon. Hanging from it I see a long, tapering tentacle, segmented like a centipede, terminating in a mass of writhing appendages, and studded along its entire length with waving filaments.

The scale of this... the appendages at the tip are bigger than entire city blocks, and those "filaments" are wider than the largest of the old freeways. This thing is twenty kilometers wide and ninety-five kilometers long, and the entire length is inscribed with shimmering runes. I can only read a few of the larger ones from here so I can't possibly divine the full meaning of the inscriptions, but I'm catching a sense of them. A desperate hunger washes over me.

"NOW do you see it?"

"Oh, God."

"Then you know what I'm doing! We have to bring it back!"

I do know what he's doing. Nguyen is using the energy from this plant as bait. It makes sense, all this death and blood on stone, and for just a moment I wish I'd been here to help because there's something really tasty in the look and the touch and the smell of—

My wrist stings under my bracelet, and as a cool feeling rushes up my arm, I realize just how far gone I've been. How much medication can this bracelet dispense? I suppose if it's concentrated, instead of in solution, and —hang on, that's not the issue here! The issue is that Nguyen's well-meaning, murder-fueled plan has a problem.

That sense I got from the monster.

"Nguyen, this isn't going to work. Have you felt it? The intent? The ravenous, all-consuming hunger?"

"It hungers for power, not flesh! POWER! I've severed the relays so the turbines are just spinning power back in on themselves, banking blood magic. We stand in the hottest spot on the planet right now! When that thing comes back, when it returns to drink this in, you take your soulbone, and you fight it!"

I dispensed with feigned humility a long time ago. I can open a number-ten can of whupass when my soulbone drinks my blood, but I know my limitations.

"Nguyen, I don't think you understand. This bone, it's mine, but it's outside my body, and it's only forty-six centimeters of inscription. That thing in the sky has a hundred kilometers of inscriptions, carved right into its own carapace. Anything I can do, it can do better. I may have the sharpest knife in the world, but I'd still be bringing a knife to a gunfight. Besides," I point at the distant monster, "it's still going south. Your bait just isn't tempting enough."

"More wood on the fire!" Nguyen hauls Groberg's body to the altar and heaves our dead friend into place under White's dangling arms. He draws his service knife, a razor-sharp, never-dulled blade with an ebony grip. With three strokes he cuts Groberg's armor free, and with three more he opens the man wide, letting gravity do what Groberg's unbeating heart can't. Killing and spilling. Blood and entrails rush onto the altar, mingling with the last of White's blood, which has now stopped flowing. My head spins from the massive pulse of power, all sound and color and tasty touch with stench and all the letters of every alphabet.

I'm completely immersed in this power, but it's not enough. The monster grows more distant, and I can see why. Las Vegas teems with humanity. Nguyen has spilled a lot of blood into this generator, but the inscribed monster can bathe in a thousand times that much blood, activating a million times as many runes up and down its segmented length. I don't know the physics of it, but I'm suddenly quite sure that's how this thing has planned its next repast. It doesn't hunger for flesh, but the meal it does hunger for has flesh in the recipe.

Why did it start here? Perhaps the power generated in Delta was brighter, more readily seen from across the void? And maybe once the hungry monster arrived, only then could it make out the fainter glow of stored potential in our cities.

Then again, it could just be really pissed off about that crash, so after it smote the crippled craft into the forest, it traced the runecraft's path of origin and headed for Vegas in search of a grisly revenge.

Or fuck, maybe this is the beginning of the rapture, and the noodly appendage of God is here to draw the faithful into the sky. Obviously it's starting in Sin City to warm up, lifting a light set of Vegas's remaining righteous before heading north to draw up the mob of self-proclaimed saints surrounding the Great Salt Lake.

I laugh aloud. Nguyen turns toward me. He has taken his armor off and is stripping out of his uniform.

"Together! Keep it together!" He points at me as he shouts.

"Rapture of the Noodly Appendage!" I shout back, tasting a moment's delight in the absurdity of the concept and the delectable roll of the concatenated syllables. They have color, too, and a sweet smell. I laugh again, and it feels so good, my head spinning, my diaphragm spasming, my heart—

The aura of the pig-iron bullet in my heart vanishes. Nguyen has willed it away.

"Tams! It has to be you! Only you!" He has cut the last of his clothing away and stands atop the altar, stark naked except for his knife, his rope bracelet, and a determined grimace. His Vietnamese heritage has teamed up with our rigorous PT regimen to present a deliciously fit, smooth-skinned model of a man. He'd be attractive, really attractive, except for that look on his face.

He stands on Groberg's body, one bare foot in the empty abdomen, and reaches up to cut White's bootlaces free. White's limp body drops to the altar and then rolls clear. Nguyen slips the cattle hook between his own wrist and the rope bracelet and pulls down, cinching it in place. Then he reaches down with the knife in his other hand and with a single stroke opens his left inner thigh, his femoral artery suddenly spurting blood on the altar.

Through it all he doesn't scream, doesn't groan, doesn't even acknowledge the ruin he's made of his flesh. He just grimaces, like he's in ecstasy, or perhaps on it. He looks at me, and I can see the life quickly ebbing from behind his eyes, as if through sheer force of personality he can pour himself out in mere seconds. His legs go limp, and he hangs above the altar from that bracelet, the bound hand outstretched and completely white.

"It has to come back," he says weakly. "Or you have to go. But it has to be you, you brain-breached, soulboned badass."

Doesn't he see that it's impossible? Knife to a gunfight is the wrong metaphor. I'm facing a column of armored cavalry, and I'm hoping to win by inflicting a paper cut.

Is that what I tell a dying man?

Is that how I face the death of a city?

"Fine. I'm going. But if I see you on the other side, I'm going to fuck you up for this."

He doesn't respond. His eyes are already glassy, his whole body hanging limp from his upstretched arm.

The room throbs with energy, power sufficient to carry the entire building across the stars if the right runes were written on this altar and the surrounding planes—all of it wasted if the beast doesn't return. I'm swimming in it, but I can't store it. I can draw it through my soulbone and burn it for whatever purpose I choose, but I can't do that from a distance.

Unless there's a connection. Something attached to my soul, with an anchor here.

I bleed on my bone and leap out to the truck.

Milholland and Betts are still asleep. I grab Betts, sling her over my shoulder, and haul her into the belly of the power plant. With a telekinetic sweep I clear the altar and the space around it, ripping Nguyen free of the hook and throwing him, Groberg, and White into a heap with the poor sods from Whiskey and Bravo.

Gently I lay Betts down on the altar and pull her goggles off over her helmet. Then I crack a stim pack open and stab Betts in the neck.

Her eyes shoot wide open and she howls.

She's going to need to soak this in for a bit. I've been soaking it in, my bracelet keeping the worst of the crazy at bay, and I still feel like screaming with Betts, creating a harmony whose scent might chase away the smoldering sweetness of Groberg's entrails.

Her scream warbles, and in my enhanced sight I can see, actually *see*, the power in this room course through her brain, carving new, high-speed neural paths like a low-bid mass-transit contractor with unlimited eminent domain. "Hemisphere breach" is what the doctors call it, but it's far more complicated, and ever so much more wonderful, than that. Betts's senses are expanded, her understanding infinitely enlarged, and her sanity... well, sanity is just consensus of perception. If she and I perceive the same things, then we are, by definition, both sane.

Like me and Nguyen, and we got along *great* just now.

She stops screaming and sucks in a deep breath, which she then holds. She looks around, the writhing runes no doubt reading themselves to her the way they are for me. Then she looks south, and a little up. Her mouth opens and then snaps shut.

"Oh god god god there it is again—it's REAL!" she says through clenched teeth. She puts her hands over her eyes and sobs. "It's not going away!" She pulls her hands down from her face and looks at me. "Tams, what have you done?"

"Nguyen started it."

Betts frowns at me, glaring through tears, and I realize that sounds more like an excuse than I wanted it to.

"Betts, you see the monster again, right?"

"I see it. I can't not see it."

Consensus of perception. We are sane together, having some nice, rational clusterfuck.

"It's headed for Las Vegas. I need more power if I'm going to fight it."

She stares.

"You can feel the power in here, can't you? Nguyen killed everyone, killed them all right on this altar. The turbines are wound up, banking that blood and power, raw and ready, but I can't take it with me. It's useless to me unless I can tap it somehow."

Betts draws in a ragged breath, her eyes darting left and right. Then she locks her gaze on me, and I feel a thrill of power surging behind those eyes.

"Tap it? WE ARE FUCKING DROWNING IN IT, YOU STUPID BITCH!"

I bite back an angry response. I very much need Lieutenant Betts to *not* be murderously angry at me right now, and if I get angry at her I'll just gut her and cut her and shut her up, and that's not the plan. I need to get a grip. Oh, wait... I almost forgot the second part of this.

I jab Betts in the leg with another hypo. She's got stimulants; now she needs to be able to ride out the crazy without hurting anybody. Her pupils go wide and then draw back to pinpricks. I think that means it's working.

"Ohhhh... thank you."

Definitely working.

"Betts," I say softly, "I want you to shoot me with your pig iron."

Her jaw drops, and then she snaps her mouth shut. She looks around the room and then back at me.

"That could actually work," she says. "You'd have to fly fast, though. And I'll need some blood. Your blood."

"Really?"

"Smeared between my helmet plate and my head, a tiny blood sandwich. It'll make for a longer, stronger connection. So much stronger—you have no idea. It's not very useful in the field, 'cause by the time I've got a blood sample from the target, the team doesn't need me to put more bullets in it."

"Right. That makes sense."

"The team..."

"It's just you, me, and Milholland. He's sleeping."

"Get my gun. I... I need a moment."

I bound back out to the truck, checking on Milholland while I'm there. He's still out cold. I grab Betts's ruck and her weapon and race back inside.

She has her helmet sitting upside down in her lap and is staring into it.

"It's... it's like I never knew what this actually meant," she says.

"What what meant?"

"The chip my pig iron uses." She looks up at me. "I mean, I always knew what the rune did, and how to make it work. I could carve a new one pretty easily. But now? Now I can read it like I really speak the language." She shakes her head. "This is not a very nice word."

"The bad word needs to take its medicine now." I tap a drop of my blood onto the small chip of inscribed ebony, spilling just a little onto the foam it's glued to. Betts dons the helmet and straps it down.

"Oh, dear. Oh, Tams, oh dear oh god oh god I can taste you, Tams. The bullet is hungry for you. All my bullets are hungry for you."

"Is this safe?"

She whips her pig iron up to her shoulder and fires it from a foot away, straight into my chest. There is no report, but I can sense the aura of that sliver of inscribed, entangled bone poised to write "die" straight through the muscles of my heart and into my soul.

"Go fast, Tams. I hate you, and it tastes like salt and sounds like sunshine and I want to kill you so much. But I'm going to swallow that and you're going to drink it and GO."

"It used to be that when you plugged in a toaster you knew where the electricity came from. Now you only think you know. You plug in the toaster, and the electricity is coming from runes. But what are the runes plugged into? More importantly, what if there's a power company out there watching our meter spin? Will we know how to pay the bill when it arrives?"
–Saadiq Sebastian DuChamps, RUNExpo Chicago, 2055

The forest-green and rock-red contours of southern Utah race by beneath the truck as the driver takes me toward Vegas at Mach what-the-fuck. Three, maybe? I honestly don't know. I removed Nguyen's spleen before exiting the plant, and I wrung it out onto driver's rune block, at which point driver revised our estimated travel time from sixty-two minutes to eight.

Nobody says so in polite company, but you haven't really drained a body until you've wrung out the spleen. Killing and spilling and filling—it's thrilling. I thought about grabbing a second one, but then Betts gave me this look and I decided against it.

My connection to Betts feels taut, but it continues to stretch, thousands of times farther than any pig-iron shot she's ever taken. I suspect she's bleeding onto the tanglebone in the stock of her weapon to power this connection. It's what I'd do, but I'm not going to ask. Limiting my communication with her seems prudent since we've both ridden way past the ragged edge of crazy, consensus notwithfuckingstanding. If I say the wrong thing and push her over whatever the next edge is, she'll turn this lifeline into my silent death.

A buckle snaps open behind me, the sound a mixture of metallic overtones and the flat slapping of plastic on plastic. My heightened senses and runewrought brain deconstruct the sound and map it across my awareness. The plastic sounds brown, like the letter *T*, only warmer and not as salty. The metal sounds like starlight, a string of sixes in cold, sweet pins and needles. Full-bore, sixth-sense synesthesia. It's really goddamn distracting. I hope I can dial it back somehow before I face the beast. Or maybe not. It might be interesting to find out what sounds, smells, colors, flavors, and letters of the alphabet are associated with the pains of death.

Distracting. The buckle unsnapping means Milholland is awake. I spin my seat to face him. He has raised his seat back and is staring out the window.

"Captain, where are we going?"

"Las Vegas, but not in a straight line. We need to kill a monster."

He looks out the rest of the windows, squinting and blinking as he turns his head.

"What monster?"

"The one Betts saw. I see it now, too."

It hangs like a stalactite from a glowing ring in the distant sky. I've been trying hard not to look at it.

"Can driver see it?"

"No, but the NTSB drones have painted a small, visible patch for him.

It's the spot where Flight 4830 hit, and it's covered in pulverized remains."

"Okay, I've got the summary, sir. Fill me in?"

He sounds surprisingly cogent. I guess I shouldn't be surprised. He had a diluted exposure to a cold rune block, got a heavy dose of antipsychotics, took a nice nap, and has his goggles on. Compared to me he's the very model of sanity, and there's not much consensus of perception here. But really, I've got other things on my broken mind.

I relate the story quickly: how dispatch ordered me to take down my own team after they got breached and wiped out the entire response force, how Nguyen shot me and made me kill Groberg, how I couldn't save White, and then how Nguyen killed himself as part of his crazy scheme to lure the monster away from Vegas and back to Delta.

Milholland shifts in his seat as I talk. He pretends to stretch.

I explain my modified version of the scheme, how I wrecked Betts's brain and then made her shoot me so I could tap the power in Delta and wind it around the weapon-words on my soulbone. Milholland unbuckles the rest of his straps and shifts around some more.

Yes, Lieutenant, you're trapped in a hypersonic magic truck with a madwoman. It's okay to be nervous, to prepare yourself to jump to the back of the vehicle where your ruck and weapons are. I'd do the same thing. I don't say any of this while I'm telling him about Nguyen's plan, but I'm thinking about it when I tell him about Nguyen's spleen.

He's going to call me on it. He thinks I've hallucinated half of this and am inventing the other half to cover up a dung heap full of freshly sprouted psychoses.

"Understood, Captain," he says. "Have you coordinated this plan with dispatch?"

Oh. That's not what I expected him to say, but it makes perfect sense. I should have thought to do that.

"No, Lieutenant. Thank you for identifying my lapse." I stare at my soulbone, which hasn't been back in its sheath since I woke up in Delta. The runes shimmer like spearmint, right through the grip, and the shaft is quite warm in my hand, that not-quite-uncomfortable temperature of a men's choir humming a tall, major ninth. I can hear that humming in the heat of bone against my hand, and it smells like prime numbers.

"When was the last time you heard from them, sir?"

I shut out the humming, the spearmint, and the spinning numbers. Distraction. When did I last hear from dispatch? And then another distraction as the truck starts to slow and driver interrupts us.

"Captain Surinam, we are twenty kilometers east-southeast of Henderson, Nevada, and thirty kilometers from the small radar signature indicated by the NTSB. I now require additional guidance."

I look out the window. I've flown past Mount Rainier before. That view is grand and stunningly impressive. Mount Rainier dominates the horizon from a distance and is majestic when you're flying a couple dozen kilometers away from it. The beast is bigger than that. I think we're about fifteen kilometers away from the near side of the thing, and it fills half my field of view. From five klicks out, it will be so wide that the edges will be approaching my peripheral vision. It's as tall as the sky, and its anemone blossom of tendrils trails the ground.

Driver can't see the whole beast, just that one patch of sticky human remains ten thousand meters above us. The patch is on the southwest side of the monster, and since we're on the east side, if driver tries a direct path we'll end up crashing just like Flight 4830 did.

"Swing to the southwest of the city, climbing to twelve thousand meters, but stay at least thirty klicks from the geographic center of the city." That should keep us well clear of collision and out of range of those tendrils, too.

"Captain," says Milholland, tapping his ear. "I can't raise dispatch. When was the last time you heard from them?"

Uh-oh.

"Delta. I cut them off because I thought White might be listening in. It's been at least half an hour."

"Well, I've got no carrier now. No signal at all."

That's because dispatch is outside of Las Vegas, at the airport, which has a rune-covered tarmac designed to shove vessels through the void and onto other worlds. If this thing eats rune magic, that tarmac is a standout buffet in a town full of great buffets.

"I think dispatch is dead, Milholland. The creature's tendrils dragged straight across that airport."

"That can't be right." He flips open his comm and starts tapping.

"I don't think they'd have been able to offer much advice. Nobody down there was crazy enough to see this thing."

He's not paying attention to me. He's gone pale, and his face has fallen so far I can't remember what his easy smile used to look like.

"Static. Lots of static. We need to reach up the chain, but everything's chaos and noise right now. No clean frequencies. Even the rune band is dark."

"Right now we are the chain."

"Fine." He thumps his chest. "I'm only a little bit crazy. Crazy enough to take your word on that monster for now, but I'm still the sanest one in the truck."

"Okay."

"So tell me your attack plan, and I'll advise."

This will be like the blind leading the blind. No, wait. Blind and sane advising crazy and sees-too-much? That might actually work, now that I think about it. Of course, if I concentrate really hard I can taste breath fresheners in the textures of my soulbone's grip, so me thinking something's a good idea is probably not a good—oh, fuck all, I'm circling the drain here.

"Driver will position us using the one spot he can actually see. I'll read the runes on the carapace, and figure out how to attack. If I can't figure it out, I'll just bleed half to death on my soulbone, draw as much power from plant A as I can, and then stab until there's nothing left to stab."

"Well, okay. Start reading." He looks out the window, his eyes focusing in the deep distance. What does it looks like if he can't see the monster there? I can't see anything past the monster.

I focus on the inscribed carapace and try to concentrate.

The runes rush past as we circle and climb. I should only be able to read the largest of them from this distance, but now that I'm closer, now that I'm embracing the breaches in my brain, the runes on it seem to want to be read. They reach out to me, speaking to all of my senses at once.

These words are beautiful. Agonizingly beautiful, inducing lust, and heartbreakingly beautiful, inciting a righteous longing. There is the beauty of a sunset, and the beauty of autumn. The beauty of supple flesh, and the beauty of fountaining blood. The beauty of a steaming crater, and the beauty of a sea of bones.

Oh.

If the word in Betts's helmet was not very nice, these words are even less nice. They're beautiful illusions laid over murderous intent. They are shields and traps and weapons and bait. But above all, they are power, and lots of it. If they could be spoken aloud, no ear could withstand them, and the tongue that uttered them would flay itself to ribbons in the speaking.

The words want me to read and feel, not read and understand. They are a layered steganogram, a tone poem of longing, pain, and hunger hiding a silent, secret instruction set, except unlike a hidden message in a handwritten letter, reading the letter might ruin my mind and prevent me from ever being able to comprehend the buried syntax.

There might be an answer for that.

"Captain Tamrielle Surinam. Sanity is nothing more than consensus of perception."

The thick, shiny bracelet on my wrist flashes at me. The indicator has been pulsing red ever since our incident at the crash site. Now it flashes a single blue light, faintly, and a message scrolls across the band.

TREATMENT IN PROGRESS. ADJUST?

"You okay, Captain?" asks Milholland.

"Adjust. Double dose of broad-spectrum mood suppressor with stimulants. No sedatives, no antipsychotics. Just flatten my mood."

TEAMMATE CONFIRMATION REQUIRED.

I turn to Milholland and hold out the band for him to read. He reads it and then looks up at me and nods.

"Lieutenant Andrew Milholland, confirming adjustment. Captain Surinam needs these drugs."

I barely have time to read *"TREATMENT ADJUSTED"* before a rush of neurochemistry sets my skin tingling and tunnels my vision. My heart starts to pound, and my head clears. There's a metallic taste in my mouth, but it's not associated with a sound or a color, and not even one of the letters of the alphabet. Pain, longing, pleasure, joy, and a swarm of other feelings drain away, and how could I ever have been so foolish as to weep or laugh or grimace, because I am a machine.

A killing machine.

"Thank you, Lieutenant." I turn back to the window.

The hidden message is clearer now, patterns of rhotiles and transitiles themselves drawn in nested patterns of ductiles and pulsatiles. If Flight 4830's engine block was a clever crossword puzzle, this is a crossword puzzle in four dimensions. The words still are not very nice, but that doesn't faze me because I can see them for what they are. Some provide material strength, which makes sense since nothing this big could support its own weight and still move. Others grant invisibility, and even though I'm heavily medicated, I'm not taking enough antipsychotics to chase out the crazy that lets me see through that.

This is actually hopeful, and I feel a moment's surprise as hope manages to crack through the drugs. I must be feeling a lot of it.

Well, yes. Despite thousands of runes protecting the creature against detection, I can see it. I have defeated them. The second line of defense, the runes meant to destroy any who can see, and who attempt to read further? I have defeated those, too. So... what's next?

Ah. Armor. A mixture of selective tangibility and hardening. Most things can't touch it and will go right through. Those that can touch it won't be able to do much damage. After all, what can mere flesh do against a magically impervious carapace capable of supporting incalculable mass?

My voidblade is not mere flesh.

"Okay, Milholland, I have a plan."

"Let's hear it."

"I'm going to draw power from plant A and spawn a voidblade a hundred times bigger than anything I could create myself, and then I'm going to cut this thing to ribbons."

Milholland is sitting close to me, knee to knee here in the truck. He meets my gaze.

"Where will the pieces land?"

I think about that for a moment.

"Below us. But if I injure this thing, maybe it will retreat, it will flee back through its gate. And I can stab instead of slicing."

"So... you stab and stab and nothing happens. Then what? Keep stabbing? If it doesn't leave soon enough, you'll maim it, huge pieces will fall, and if they're selectively tangible they'll fall straight through buildings. There will be nowhere to hide. Even small pieces will crush people, just like that hexatroll crushed you. Tens of thousands, maybe hundreds of thousands, will die."

"Life ends eventually."

"You did not just say that, Captain."

"I did. Life ends, but if we don't do this, all life ends at once."

"You don't know that."

"You haven't read it. You can't even see it. You are the one who doesn't know things. This creature wants to eat the world. If I could somehow stop it by destroying Vegas myself, that would be a small price to pay. What is Earth worth? A city? Ten cities?"

I feel a tug at my right hand, and suddenly my soulbone is gone. Milholland holds it and has jumped to the back of the truck.

"You've lost it, Captain. I can't let you do this. Whatever's happening, we'll figure something else out."

Milholland has my soulbone, has ripped some of the grip clear, and is rubbing his thumb over the runes at the end. I want to tackle him and take it back, but I can't. I can't even move.

I open my mouth to speak, but my mouth is already open, and nothing is coming out. Not sound, not air. I try to breathe, but I can't even do that. My grip on the power plant begins to slip. That power is flowing into Milholland now, even though Betts's bullet is in my chest. The soulbone is so named for a reason.

"When you breached in the Gulf, the company added a few words to your soulbone. They had to write really small. We all learned how to use it in an emergency." He shrugs sadly. "That medicine band isn't protection enough from what you're capable of becoming if you lose your mind."

I am empty. Just as hope cracked through the medicated haze a moment ago, despair cracks it now. The trust I thought I had from my team, my friends, my comrades in arms, was a charade, and the power I had bound up in the soulbone is gone from me. It all flows into Milholland, and though he can use that kill switch, he doesn't have the true connection required to maintain any of the effects I had up. The power from plant A continues to flow to me along my connection to Betts, but "me" is the soulbone, and now that precious energy, our only weapon against this monstrous god of the void, it all radiates wastefully from Milholland like heat from a furnace.

"Is this what it feels like for you?" he asks in a half-whisper.

I can't answer.

I am more than empty. Milholland is letting the raw power flow through him, in and straight back out, and he is drinking my own power in as he does. He is consuming me. I can feel my soul stretched taut between my flesh and my soulbone, pulled tight and pinched to a taper, the taper strung out to a hair, and the hair turning to dust.

If souls can live independently of the flesh, and my limited experience suggests that they can, what Milholland is doing to me is worse than murder. He is ending me forever, and doing so as wastefully as possible, like a vintner pouring wine across his hand and onto the ground instead of into a glass.

I remember a photo on a corporate identification badge. The face of Tynah Jones, a beautiful black woman, smiles out of that photo. The photo is pinned to the chest of a corpse that was sucked dry, a corpse that looked as if the process was not quite instantaneous. There was time for pain and fear and the dawning awareness that life does continue after death, just not for her.

What is happening to me feels like that, muted only slightly by drugs that have themselves despaired in the face of what rushes out of me. But it's happening much more slowly, because Milholland doesn't even know he's doing it, and he couldn't control it if he did. He shines with lost power, radiating uncontrolled energy like a forest fire, spewing it forth like a volcano.

Or maybe like a giant star, burning too fast to live long.

My sight is dim, tunneling from asphyxiation, but I can see Milholland

and his fountain of power. I wonder if anybody else can see him.

Or any *thing*.

Milholland abruptly seizes, his back arched, his hands outstretched. In that movement he throws my soulbone clear, and my connection to him is lost. I suck in a long, deep breath; at the same time, something unseen sucks Milholland to an ice-cold husk.

It takes about two seconds, from seizure to the final, shriveling end, but it seems much longer than that. Milholland's skin blackens, and his flesh withers and shrinks beneath it. There is no scream, no sound, save a final splintering as his bones freeze and split and whatever is drinking him finishes with the desiccation of deep marrow.

I am free, though. I dive from my seat, praying that the invisible, selectively tangible thing that took Milholland can't see me for my emptiness. I grab my soulbone and do more than pray. I will myself unseen.

It's not working.

I can't feel Betts's bullet in my chest anymore. Mercy on her part, maybe? Or maybe we just took too long. It doesn't matter. The only power left to me is what I can bleed out of myself, and that's not going to be enough to carve much off of this monster. In fact, without the hot fuel of plant A behind my blade, I'm not going to carve anything. I've read those armor runes. All my voidblade can do is scrape the surface clean.

Clean. Perhaps I can paint something.

I bleed onto my bone and find power sufficient to disappear. I am unseen, and then bubbled in armor.

"Driver, open the door; then fly to R&D HQ in Los Angeles. Get clear of this radio cloud as quickly as possible, and then broadcast flight data info and mission logs. If I fail, maybe somebody smarter, stronger, and crazier than me can save the world."

"Yes, Captain." The doors open, and I leap from the truck.

There is a clap of thunder behind me as driver follows my orders under acceleration he can only use when nobody's aboard.

The beast moved a lot closer to us in order to reach out and kill Milholland. I can see it again, and it shines with furious power. Fresh power. With one of its side-sprouted tendrils it drank Milholland dry, and ten kilometers below me, its knot of appendages sucks the life out of hundreds, maybe thousands, of people in Las Vegas. Their essence is consumed directly, their souls gone. Their vital fluids are drawn up into the monster and pushed out into rune paths, strengthening the beast.

That patch of passenger remains is only about fifteen hundred meters away. I bleed hard into my soulbone and fly. My chest burns as I pour power into the direct effects of speed and lift. In that burn I can tell that my medication is gone, my bracelet spent, and the drugs themselves purged from my bloodstream like impurities from smelted ore.

A tendril swings toward me, thick as a skyscraper but tapering to a tip so fine it seems to vanish into its own point. So it can see me after all. I stop spending precious blood on being invisible and spend it on a proper voidblade.

It feels like a heart attack as I tap still more blood and will two hundred meters of preternatural, interplanar sharpness into existence. There is a fist clenched in my chest, knuckles so tense they're ready to split, a twin to the grip I have on my soulbone.

I fly, and flick. Dodging that tendril and sweeping with the blade is exhilarating. The armor on the creature's carapace does not extend to the appendages, and the end of this tendril, a piece roughly the size and shape of that old tower in Dubai, the Burj Khalifa, drops away, falling just as surely as that run-down skyscraper did, if quite a bit further.

Out of reach of the nearest tendrils, I now have the patch of shattered, pulverized travelers directly before me. It is about five meters in diameter, and only vaguely pink.

I give more blood to the bone, but the ache in my hand says my tap ring may be tapped out, my body finally fighting back and shutting off flow to that finger. Still, I've strength enough to stay aloft, to reach out telekinetically, and to finger paint.

The rune drawn in the fields of Delta and again in the forested crash site, it seemed to dampen rune magic. I paint that rune now, or rather I unpaint it, shaping it in the clean space, the void created by wiping the pasty, flaking remains off of the carapace. That was why the crop circle actually worked—it wasn't a rune inscribed with crushed cornstalks; it was a rune of dead space surrounded by living material.

With the final stroke I feel the effect, but it is faint.

Fuck.

I hoped that this creature could somehow be robbed of all its power, but the rune in Delta only dampened rune-tech, and it was thousands of times the size of what I've drawn. My void painting is small, this drying people-paste lacks sufficient essence, and the carapace against which it is plastered is simply too ancient and too alive to suffer more than a shallow weakening.

Ancient and alive. And weak at the surface?

I need more blood. I draw my utility blade and with a quick stroke open the veins of my wrist. Blood rushes out and over my hand and my soulbone, killing and spilling and filling, God willing. But I don't have much time, because this ache spreading down my left arm is saying that my heart may have stopped.

My voidblade is now a grinding tool, whirling with cutting power. I go back over the rune I smeared clean in the paste, etching it now in the carapace of the beast, obliterating the creature's own runes as I do. My vision begins to tunnel, but I'll be able to finish. I think.

Just one more stroke.

I carve the last cross-stroked serif, and this time the final stroke has a real effect, beginning with the restarting of my tired heart.

And this time I understand. The rune is not for dampening magic. That's just a side effect. This rune is for drinking it.

I am drinking from the fire hose, awash in a hundred times more power than I felt in plant A, and I must burn it, shed it, slough it, because if I try to contain it I will end up as ash.

With a thought I streak away from the monster's flank on a gout of blue-white flame. With a silent curse I blast that flame up and into the creature, my shaped, blinding roar playing like six senses of torch with power sufficient to melt mountains. It carves deep gouges in the magically toughened carapace and cuts another tendril free. With a flick of my wrist I turn that tumbling column of doom into expanding vapor. It might have landed on somebody, but not on my watch.

The power flowing into me tastes like pain, fear, and surprise, except with an otherworldly accent.

So, I have your attention now.

You think that was surprising? Chew on this, world eater. I streak further away, power flowing into me, through me, and back out in a flaming scythe, with which I begin to again sculpt the rune of drinking in strokes a thousand meters long.

The power flowing into me tastes like terror, the desperation of the doomed, but I will not let you flee. Killing and spilling and thrilling and filling, and whether or not God is willing, there will be no retreat for you. I will drink you dry, and then race through the sky and drink everything in your ancient house down to dust.

With the last stroke I am awash in, blinded by, and deafened with power. I can feel it in my teeth, in my spine, in my soulbone—

My soulbone explodes, taking my hand and empty wristband with it. In a flash of silence and darkness, the power is gone. No flight, no sight, and nothing with which to fight.

Empty again.

My vision returns in spots as I blink away the blackness. My right arm now ends in a ragged stump somewhere south of my elbow, and there isn't much blood.

Empty forever.

I begin to fall, and the sensation of weightlessness is quickly drowned out in the rushing of wind.

The creature hangs before me, its bulk obscuring half of the world. I am falling, but the creature in front of me is not moving.

No, that's not right. It is moving *with* me. I look up, and the ring of runes is gone. The doorway to wherever this came from is now shut, and I am falling alongside ninety kilometers of severed monster. It is not hidden from mortal sight, nor is it armored against physical attack.

It is fully material, completely tangible, and suddenly subject to physical laws.

Oh, shit.

I am falling onto Las Vegas alongside a million, billion megatons of armored meat.

CONTRIBUTORS

D.J. Butler (Dave) is a lawyer by training and a consultant in his day job, and he's been writing speculative fiction for all audiences since 2010. He's working on getting published by the traditional route; in the meantime, he entertains readers with adventure tales.

Rock Band Fights Evil follows the escapades of a ragged dive bar band of damned men, struggling against the powers of Hell to get back their souls and keep their freedom. *Rock Band* comes out in e-book form, and then is collected into paperback omnibuses. *Rock Band* #1 is *Hellhound on My Trail*. *Rock Band Fights Evil Volume One* contains *Hellhound on My Trail*, *Snake Handlin' Man*, and *Crow Jane*. As of this publication, seven installments of Rock Band are available.

City of the Saints is a four-part gonzo action steampunk adventure set in the Rocky Mountains. U.S. Army agent Sam Clemens rolls west aboard his amphibious steam-truck, the *Jim Smiley*, with a mission: to ensure that the Kingdom of Deseret, with its air-ships and rumored phlogiston guns, brain children of the Madman Orson Pratt, enters the looming civil war on the side of the United States. Can he outrace and outmaneuver his competitors, Captain Richard Burton and the secret agent Edgar Allan Poe? Will Deseret's own defenders, Orrin Porter Rockwell and Eliza R. Snow, thwart him? Or will he be caught up in the coup d'etat of the mysterious Danites? Part the first of *City of the Saints* is *Liahona*; the entire tale is also available in a single paperback volume.

The Buza System is a dark science fiction saga set in a world of brutal manipulation, cynical lies, and blood rites. Young Dyan discovers that in order to become a full-fledged member of the System, an Urbane, she is expected to murder an innocent young man. Her response puts her entire world on the line in the first book: *Crecheling*.

Read about D.J. Butler's writing projects at *http://davidjohnbutler.com*.

Michael R. Collings is a Professor Emeritus at Seaver College, Pepperdine University, where he directed the Creative Writing Program for over two decades.

He has published over 100 volumes of poetry, novels, short fiction, and scholarly studies of such contemporary writers as Stephen King, Orson Scott Card, Dean R. Koontz, and Piers Anthony. Recent works include *Writing*

Darkness (2012), a collection of essays on prose narrative; *The Art and Craft of Poetry* (1996, 2009); *Toward Other Worlds: Perspectives on John Milton, C. S. Lewis, Stephen King, Orson Scott Card, and Others* (2010); *In Endless Morn of Light: Moral Agency in Milton's Universe* (2010); *In the Void: Poems of Science Fiction, Myth and Fantasy, and Horror* (2009); *Matrix: Growing Up West—Autobiographical Poems* (2010); *BlueRose and Other Chapbooks* (2012); *A Verse to Horrors—An Abecedary of Monsters and the Monstrous; HAI-(And Assorted Other)-KU* (2012); *Deep Music: A Collection of L.D.S. Musical Readings* (2012); and a Book of Mormon epic, *The Nephiad* (1996, 2010).

His fiction, also published through Wildside, includes: *The House Beyond the Hill: A Novel of Fear* (2007); *Wordsmith, Volume One: The Thousand Eyes of Flame* (2009) and *Wordsmith, Volume Two: The Veil of Heaven* (2009); *Singer of Lies: A Science-Fantasy Novel* (2009); *Wer Means Man, and Other Tales of Wonder and Terror* (2010); *Three Tales of Omne: A Companion to* Wordsmith (2010); *Devil's Plague: A Mystery Novel* (2011); *Serpent's Tooth* (2011); *Static!: A Novel of Horror* (2011); *Shadow Valley* (2011); and *The Slab* (2010), the story of a haunted tract house in Southern California... that consumes people.

With his wife Judith, he has also published a unique cookbook, *Whole Wheat for Food Storage: Recipes for Unground Wheat*, a revision and expansions of their first joint project, *Whole Wheat Harvest* (1980).

He is now retired and lives in his native state of Idaho.

Michaelbrent Collings is a #1 bestselling novelist and produced screenwriter. He is a member of the Writers Guild of America, Horror Writers of America, and International Thriller Writers, and is one of Amazon's Most Popular Horror Writers. His bestsellers include *The Colony Saga, Strangers, Darkbound, Apparition, The Haunted, The Loon*, and the YA fantasy series *The Billy Saga*. He hopes someday to develop superpowers, and maybe get a cool robot arm so as to punish evildoers (like people who text during movies). Michaelbrent has a Facebook page at *http://www.facebook.com/ MichaelbrentCollings* and can be followed on Twitter through his username @mbcollings. Follow him for awesome news, updates, and advance notice of sales. You will also be kept safe when the Glorious Revolution begins!

Larry Correia is the New York Times bestselling author of the *Monster Hunter International* series, the award winning Grimnoir Chronicles trilogy (*Hard Magic, Spellbound*, and *Warbound*), and the military thrillers *Dead Six* and *Swords of Exodus*, all available from Baen Books. He has also written novellas and the novel *Into the Storm* for Privateer Press set in their Warmachine universe, and published over a dozen short stories in various anthologies. Larry was a Campbell finalist for best new writer in 2011, a

Verlanger finalist for best novel in France, and has won two Audie Awards for best audiobook.

A former accountant, machinegun dealer, firearms instructor, and military contractor, Larry is now a full time writer, and lives in the mountains of northern Utah with his very patient wife and children.

Robert J Defendi has worked on many projects. He is a former *Writers of the Future* winner and the writer of the popular podcast audiobook *Death by Cliché*. His fiction appears in many RPG supplements and smaller venues.

Robert was born in Dubuque, IA to parents who, frankly, should have known better. After a bleak early period, punctuated by too much bad science fiction produced by Walt Disney, he began to read such greats as Tolkien, Niven, Clark, Asimov and Clavell. He's been influenced by dozens of writers, from Tom Clancy to Barbara Hambly. He studies bad fiction as well as good in every medium but poetry (with which he is abysmal). He feels that writing is a constant process, continuing through every aspect of one's life, and that the time spent at the keyboard is only a small part of the process.

Steven Diamond has been involved with the book industry for years now. It was while managing a bookstore in 2006 that he realized getting published would be way better than just reading novels. After all, how hard could it be? He has published several short stories, and has several more pieces of short fiction forthcoming through Skull Island eXpeditions in the Warmachine universe. Steve also runs Elitist Book Reviews (*http://elitistbookreviews.blogspot.com*), which was nominated for the 2013 Hugo Award for Best Fanzine.

Steve currently lives in Utah with his wife and two children. An accountant by day, writing is one of his major escapes. When not writing he is either spending time chasing his kids, managing Elitist Book Reviews, or watching sports (Geaux Saints!).

Steven L. Peck is an evolutionary biologist and writer living in Pleasant Grove, Utah. His novel *The Scholar of Moab* (Torrey House Press) was named the AML best novel of 2011, and was a Finalist for the Montaigne Medal. His existential horror novel *A Short Stay in Hell* (Strange Violin Editions) and middle grade novel the *Rifts of Rime* (Cedar Fort Press) were published in 2012. His poetry has been nominated for the Association of Science Fiction Poetry's Rhysling Award. A book of his poetry called *Incorrect Astronomy* was published by Aldrich Press this year. His speculative work has appeared in *Abyss & Apex, Daily Science Fiction, H.M.S. Beagle, Encounter Magazine, Irreantum, Jabberwocky Magazine, Lissette's Tales of the*

Imagination, Pedestal Magazine, Quantum Realities, Silver Blade, Silver Thought Press, Tales of the Talisman, Journal of Unlikely Entomology, Warp and Weave and other places. He has received a number of awards for his fiction. More about his work can be found at *http://www.stevenlpeck.com*.

Nathan Shumate is the instigator of the *Space Eldritch* anthologies, but in his own defense, it's not like the rest of these guys needed much encouragement.

For a dozen years, he wasted every available moment watching B-movies old and new, and reviewing them at length at *www.coldfusionvideo.com*. A selection of those reviews form the basis of his book *The Golden Age of Crap*.

Nathan's fiction has appeared in such venues as *Amazing Stories* and the recent anthologies *Monsters & Mormons* and *Finding Home: Community in Apocalyptic Worlds*. He also edits the *ARCANE* series of anthologies, also available from Cold Fusion Media. He blogs at *NathanShumate.com*.

Eric James Stone is a Nebula Award winner, Hugo Award nominee, and winner in the Writers of the Future Contest, and has had stories published in *Year's Best SF 15, Analog, Nature*, and Kevin J. Anderson's *Blood Lite* anthologies of humorous horror, among other venues. Over two dozen of his tales can be found in his collection *Rejiggering the Thingamajig and Other Stories*. In addition to his day job as a website programmer, Eric is an assistant editor for *Intergalactic Medicine Show*. He lives in Utah with his wife, Darci. His website is *http://www.ericjamesstone.com*.

Howard Tayler is the writer and illustrator behind *Schlock Mercenary*, the Hugo-nominated science fiction comic strip. His novelette, "Flight of the Runewright," appears in the first *Space Eldritch* anthology, and he writes fantasy tie-in fiction for Privateer Press under their Skull Island X imprint. His artwork is featured in *XDM X-Treme Dungeon Mastery*, a role-playing supplement by Tracy and Curtis Hickman, as well as in the board game "Schlock Mercenary: Capital Offensive" by Kevin Nunn, published by Living World Games.

Howard co-hosts the Hugo and Parsec award-winning "Writing Excuses" podcast, a weekly 'cast for genre-fiction writers, with Mary Robinette Kowal, Brandon Sanderson, and Dan Wells.

His most recent printed work is *Schlock Mercenary: The Body Politic*, which was on the 2009 Hugo ballot. New readers may find *Schlock Mercenary: Random Access Memorabilia* to be a delightful introduction to the work for which he is best known.

He lives in Orem, Utah with his wife Sandra, their four children, and one ungrateful, archetypally imperious cat.

David J. West can't remember a time he wasn't writing. From the primordial splash of a drowning Atlantis to a pair of vigilantes' six-guns blasting raw justice in the Old West, from obsidian-tipped arrows raining down on Cumorah's slopes to crusaders' broadswords sweeping over shadowy terrors, and on to the cold vacuum of space and the birth of a new star, David is there, recording it all for your edification and amusement. Check out his first novel *Heroes of the Fallen* and his other short story collections and anthologies at *http://david-j-west.blogspot.com*.

If you enjoyed this book, check out some of the other publications from Cold Fusion Media:

SPACE ELDRITCH

Science fiction goes occult in *Space Eldritch*, a volume of seven original novelettes and novellas of Lovecraftian pulp space opera. Featuring work by Brad R. Torgersen (Hugo/Nebula/Campbell nominee), Howard Tayler (multiple Hugo nominee), and Michael R. Collings (author of over 100 books), plus a foreword by New York Times bestselling author Larry Correia, *Space Eldritch* inhabits the intersection between the eternal adventure of the final frontier and the inhuman darkness between the stars.

ARCANE SAMPLER
Edited by Nathan Shumate

A bite-sized collection featuring twelve unsettling original stories, *Arcane Sampler* demonstrates the kind of macabre storytelling that characterizes the *Arcane* series of anthologies — for only 99 cents! Included:
- The performers in a traveling carnival suddenly find themselves in mortal danger from their latest exhibit...
- A Bible salesman discovers a reclusive family who worships something older... and closer...
- A good Samaritan stopping to give roadside assistance encounters something far more dangerous than a flat tire...

ARCANE
Edited by Nathan Shumate

The first full-length anthology of this series features thirty stories by some of the freshest blood in the horror, dark fantasy and weird fiction fields! Included:
- An office worker returns from bereavement leave to find his workplace changing before his eyes...
- A priest excites his village to the greatest show of devotion to their god ever seen...
- A mortician sees all of his immaculate handiwork destroyed when his clients start rising...

ARCANE II
Edited by Nathan Shumate

This second volume of the *Arcane* anthology series presents twenty-one more stories of dark imagination. Included:

- A landlord finds something left behind by a former tenant, something with a will of its own...
- A bride explores her new husband's manor house, seeking the mystery that overshadows his life...
- A survivor of the apocalypse sees an insidious change infecting the few remaining humans...

THE GOLDEN AGE OF CRAP
by Nathan Shumate

Just because you can't respect a movie doesn't mean you can't enjoy it. *The Golden Age of Crap* serves up a sampling of junk-food flicks that gained their audiences on videocassette rental shelves during the '80s and '90s, a time when one couldn't visit the video rental store without being tempted by Italian post-apocalyptic adventures, ninja revenge yarns, and zombie-filled "camcorder epics." The movies covered here run from sleeper hits (*Phantasm II*) to cult favorites (*The Dead Next Door*), from unknown stinkers (*Plutonium Baby*) to undiscovered gems (*America's Deadliest Home Video*), all examined with a critical but fun-loving eye.

Cold Fusion Media
http://www.coldfusionmedia.us

COLD FUSION
MEDIA

www.ingramcontent.com/pod-product-compliance
Lightning Source LLC
Chambersburg PA
CBHW020232260626
47156CB00002B/649